SURVIVAL

SIXTUS BECKMESSER

Matador
9 Priory Business Park,
Wistow Road, Kibworth Beauchamp,
Leicestershire. LE8 0RX
Tel: 0116 279 2299
Email: books@troubador.co.uk
Web: www.troubador.co.uk/matador
Twitter: @matadorbooks

ISBN 97 81800462 366

British Library Cataloguing in Publication Data.
A catalogue record for this book is available from the British Library.

Printed and bound in Great Britain by 4edge Limited
Typeset in 12pt Adobe Garamond Pro by Troubador Publishing Ltd, Leicester, UK

Matador is an imprint of Troubador Publishing Ltd

To the people of Europe, my friends, in gratitude.

PART ONE

WALPURGIS NIGHT

1
BEFORE THE DELUGE

Thy sports are fled, and all thy charms withdrawn;
Amidst thy bowers the tyrant's hand is seen,
And desolation saddens all thy green;

GOLDSMITH: THE DESERTED VILLAGE

She really enjoyed it. She could swivel and turn controlling the ball and keep her small nine-year-old body twisting between the ball and the frustrated defender. Even the boys grudgingly admitted that she wasn't bad 'for a girl'.

The foreign ministry butted onto the diplomatic quarter with its large old German houses with their rich red and gold gables. They had miraculously survived the wars and the occupations. Between the embassies and the ministry with its residence, was a grassed square where they played. The Italian ambassador had twin sons the same age as Tamara. They persuaded the ground superintendent to put up two goal posts. With them the football became more serious. The two Italians fought over whether they were Juventus or Roma and demonstrated their precocious, if not always productive, ball skills that they had seen from their seniors. They also, less admirably, practised diving dramatically in the penalty area, before deciding that the thin grass was too hard and, anyway, there was no referee to fool. Gradually French, Russian, Dutch and German children joined in. They were short of players and two Dutch girls were brought in to help to make up the numbers. When Mara was spotted with her cheeks pressed to the iron railings she, also, was recruited. From the lowly role of defender, she worked her way up by sheer ability until she became the second striker for the blues. It wasn't clear whether the blues were *les bleus* or *gli azzurri* depending on whether one listened to the French or Italian contingent. When she tried to argue that she should have the black and red of Moltravia, the Italian boys vetoed it, arguing that that would make her a *Milanista* which was, she was given to understand, a fate worse than death. It did however result in her nick-name, *la Milanistina,* which stuck with her while the games lasted. It was many years before she saw the real Milan play in the Champions League in Königshof under very different circumstances.

On one misty autumn morning with the veiled sun trying to penetrate from the frosty bay, France (or Italy) was playing Holland (or Poland) Mara filtered through the large but clumsy Dutch (or Russian) defenders and scored. A few minutes later she received a short pass from Charles, a neat older French boy, confronted a different defender, feinted, turned and shot low into the right corner of the goal. After apple juice, she danced and weaved through the defence, beat the rattled keeper and scored again. The Russian – he was Russian – goalkeeper was mortified. To be at the receiving end of a hat trick was bad enough but when it had been scored by *a girl,* the shame was insupportable. Mara was tactfully modest, and, over more post-match apple juice, attributed her good fortune to the poor visibility. Inwardly, however, her small frame felt ten feet tall and it was the proudest moment of her childhood, which she knew that she would remember forever.

When she was eleven the diplomatic corps, possibly as a result of the increasing political tension, underwent a lot of changes. There were now few children and the football came to an end. Nicklaus Oblov realised that his only, rather isolated, daughter missed it. After discussion with Gisela, his wife, he suggested that she took up dancing. Mara was reluctant but eventually was won over when her father pointed out that the body skills of ballet were very similar to those of football.

For all that, it never worked, and although she continued, Mara's progress was modest and her enthusiasm less. She also reacted against football. The game the boys at school drooled over, with its pin men running about a miniature stadium on television seemed overblown and trivial. To her, it had nothing to do with the game that she had briefly loved in the wind and mist on those happy, distant Baltic days. She never mentioned that she had played and kept the precious hat trick to herself. If she had mentioned playing, she knew that the boys would have just laughed. Anyway, it would be like revealing a secret treasure trove.

She knew that she was growing up but felt uncertain of its meaning. She knew her parents adored her but she also realised that they were fraught with worry and somehow they became distant. One day her father took her for a walk along the beach from their seaside chalet and tried to explain what was happening and why the grownups were so worried. He explained that the present government in which he served as Foreign Minister, believed in people being allowed to do what they liked, as long as they did no harm to other people. However, the country was isolated and alone and it didn't have much money. There was hope that a big organisation called the European Union would help them but unfortunately the nearest member of the Union was Germany and because of the terrible things that Germans had done in the past, it was difficult to ask Germany for help. Increasingly some people blamed the government for the lack of money. An unpleasant group of people had formed a sort of private army and were putting it about that they would manage things much better 'like in the old days'. Nicklaus knew, of course, that she didn't remember back that far but he assured her that it hadn't been better in 'the old days' at all. Nobody had been allowed to think for himself or herself and if anybody criticised the Russian overlords, they just disappeared and, in many cases, were never heard of again.

On other days she would walk with her mother out along the shore beyond the town, wrapped against the cold in kapok and high necked

5

leather coats. They might take a picnic or sometimes just a flask of coffee in winter or a bottle of apple juice as summer came and the days were getting warmer. It was a low isolated coastline running north and a little east of Königshof. The shore was flat – punctuated by the occasional group of fishing huts or sometimes just a boat or two with nets or long lines drawn up on the shore. But the sea was different, it had a thousand faces, sometimes sparkling grey, sometimes leaden, sometimes reflecting the blue of the sky, sometimes the path of the eastern dawn or the westering sunset miraculously appeared. Sometimes it was just misty and mysterious. She grew to love it. She thought that she could share her soul, her fantasies and her lonely hopes with it. After a while she took to going down to the sea by herself. Her parents disapproved and scolded her when they found out but much of the time they were too preoccupied with the deteriorating political situation to notice. She had just celebrated her fourteenth birthday, which her parents had tried to make as happy a celebration as possible. The cloud hanging, ever more threateningly, over the family and the country had made it, in truth, a sad affair of false jollity unsuccessfully covering deep angst. As soon as she could, Mara had slipped off to gaze at her beloved sea, now wondering about its long history, now about her own fate. She was aware that she was chief amongst her parents' personal anxieties. Trying to save the country from totalitarian collapse was bad enough but having an adolescent daughter to worry about made it far worse. Originally Mara was to have stayed at her day school in Königshof, which had high educational standards and a very happy atmosphere. One day, however, Gisela, her mother, had said to her that they had something important to tell her and after *abendbrot,* both her parents had sat her down and explained that they thought it best that she leave her present school and go as a boarder to the Sacred Heart Convent in the country just outside Königshof at Ziatov. She knew about the Sacred Heart and its fame, but was very miserable at the prospect of leaving her day school and her friends.

She complained and argued bitterly until, at last, her father said quietly, 'It is for your safety, Mara, we live in bad times and nobody knows what will happen. You will be safer at the Sacred Heart and it will take a great load off our minds.'

6

She realised then how serious he was and went quiet. After a long pause, she said miserably,

'OK, but will I be able to come home at weekends?'

'Yes, three times a term.'

It was on one of these leave weekends that she had now returned to her sea and was gazing across its darkening surface in the bitter cold.

Suddenly she was aware of somebody behind her. She turned quickly, instantly scared recalling the stories of kidnap and mugging which were rife in these unsettled days. Relieved, she saw the figure of a girl, not much more than her own age, swaddled like her against the cold. The other smiled and said simply,

'It's wonderful, isn't it?'

Mara nodded and recognised her companion.

She had known the prime minister's daughter, Andrea Hoffman, for as long as she could remember. Andrea was nearly a year older than Mara and they had usually only met at the children's version of government and diplomatic events. Königshof, although the capital, was a small city and the politicians and foreign envoys could easily become friends. Both ministers and diplomats were encouraged to be, as far as possible, relaxed and informal. Mara had found Andrea, with her seniority, rather stuck up, irritatingly superior and a bit intimidating. She decided that she didn't like her and they were anything but close. They both now went to the same school, the Sacred Heart Convent, but Andrea was a second year with all the superiority that that implied whereas Mara was in her first year only settling in after a term and a few weeks.

On this occasion they exchanged a few friendly words about the sea and its ever-changing romance then Andrea said, 'I must get back, my parents are terrible worriers.'

'Mine too,' said Mara.

'See you at school,' and without pausing the other girl started walking fast towards the canal bridge and the city. In a few minutes Mara followed her. When they returned to school they still only saw each other occasionally. It was a big school and being in different years and different houses, they had different friends and activities. When they passed in the corridors, however, Andrea smiled warmly and Mara, slightly flattered by the acknowledgement by the older girl, changed her mind about Andrea's high horse.

Their friendship came about almost by chance. During the summer holiday, a replica of a cob, the famous trading vessel of the Hanseatic League, which had been built in Lübeck was doing a leisurely tour round the Baltic visiting, where possible, other cities with a Hanseatic past. The ship was enthusiastically received at Königshof and it was arranged that a group of youngsters could sail with the ship to Visby in Gotland, thus experiencing a complete replica Hanseatic voyage. As soon as Mara heard about it she pestered her parents to be allowed to go. Gisela had great doubts. It was bad enough facing the horrible uncertainties of the political crisis without having the added worry of their only daughter, not yet fifteen, on the high seas in an uncertain medieval craft. Nicklaus, however, reasoned that, at least at sea, Mara would be safe from injury or kidnap. The deciding factor was when they discovered that Andrea Hoffman was going. There was comfort in that the prime minister felt it was safe for his daughter to go and also in the provision of a slightly older companion for Mara. The girls shared a cabin and immediately recognised again each other's interest in the sea. Both had read avidly all the books about the sea that they could find. It didn't matter whether they were historical, factual or fictional as long as they featured the sea and the people who sailed on it, both girls would gobble it up. Nobody else, perhaps because they were pre-occupied by the rising instability, seemed interested in the trip. At a time when most of their girl friends were becoming swamped in rock music, make up and, increasingly, boys, they were delighted to share their unusual enthusiasm with each other. On the four days that they were at sea in the cob, they talked together at every moment when they were not learning about the ship, her history and her working, from the enthusiastic German sailors. They learnt that according to Hanseatic and old German custom the skipper was called the *Schiffer* and that the term *Kapitän* for a merchant skipper only came in the nineteenth century. In the old days there was a saying *Schiffer nächst Gott* – the skipper is next only to God.

'I wish,' the *Schiffer* said laughing, 'that was before red tape and health and safety.' But for all the grumbles, he was obviously passionate about his ship and the history that she represented.

Before they arrived at Visby, the *Schiffer* told them with a smile that if they ever needed a replacement *Schiffer* and *Maat* he knew where to find them. He didn't think the Hanse ever had a *Schifferin* but they could always set a precedent. The girls laughed and from then on Mara always called Andrea *Frau Schifferin*. They were flattered but they sensed that the admiration was genuine. It meant a lot coming from a man who had spent his life at sea and most of it under sail. It was said that he was a great teacher but had no time for fools of any age or sex. One of the crew, who apart from the captain and mate consisted of four enthusiastic amateurs, told them a bit more about him on the last night watch before they arrived at Visby. Apparently the *Schiffer* belonged to a famous family of Hamburg sailors. His great-grandfather and grandfather had commanded some of the great sailing ships out of Hamburg in the days of the mythical Laeisz Flying P line, the last firm in the world to build ocean-going commercial sailing ships. His own father had been lost in the wreck of the *Pamir* during a hurricane in the nineteen-fifties. It was particularly tragic as he had survived U boat service in the Second World War before going back to sail, when *Pamir* was bought back from her Finnish owners and again became German as a training ship. The girls listened enthralled and wide-eyed to this and more stories of the traditions of the great Hanse ports. They were very sad to say goodbye to their beautiful cob and its crew and the flight back to Königshof and its troubles was a terrible anticlimax.

However, they did find a chance to go back to sea but in a very different way. Looking wistfully out into the bay they began to watch the cloud of dinghies round the *Standbild* rock and come flying back to cross the line of the yacht club.

'I think that we should do that.' Andrea said quietly in her 'anything is possible' voice. There were more arguments with parents but at last it was agreed that the girls were less likely to be drowned than kidnapped in the present climate of unrest.

Hoffman called the commodore of the Königshof Sailing Club. Immediately lessons were arranged with Kurt, a postgraduate student at the university, who had competed in 470s in the Olympics and won a bronze medal in the World Championships. He took each of them out separately and taught them the mysteries of the helmsman and the acrobatics needed by the crew on the trapeze so that both became expert in each role. They learnt quickly and, after a few lessons, they had learnt a lot and their instructor was full of praise. After two or three weeks he announced that he thought that they were good enough to race in the Junior 470s at the weekend regatta. They spent the rest of the week dealing with start tactics, rounding marks and race rules and etiquette. There was a lot to remember but at last the great day came. Although Kurt had mentioned that perhaps they would be a bit faster with Mara at the helm and Andrea with a bit more weight and longer legs on the trapeze, however, for this, the first race, it was agreed that the senior girl would skipper and the nimble, if small, Mara crew on the trapeze. After all they were not in the Olympics, 'yet,' added Kurt with a grin and could afford to sacrifice a little extra leverage. Andrea made a pretty good start and found herself about the middle of the fleet of some thirty boats. The first leg was close hauled on the port tack. The boat started to plane and was going like a train, the feeling of speed exhilarating, and best of all, they actually passed two other boats. The world or at least a patch of the Baltic seemed all theirs. Andrea went about deftly round the marker buoy and Mara goose-winged the jib for the run and busied herself setting the spinnaker. It wasn't lightening quick but she felt quite satisfied as she crouched off the trapeze with the wind astern. Andrea squinted tensely trying to keep the boat balanced running free. To their chagrin they were passed by one of the boats they had overtaken on the wind but they still had a very reasonable position for a first race as they came to the second mark outside the clubhouse to jibe onto a broad reach completing the first circuit. It all happened very quickly. The wind had freshened in the last few minutes and Andrea was taken unawares and didn't control the jibe. They lost balance. The capsize was very sudden, although it seemed to take an age as both girls tried, unavailingly, to regain control. A few minutes later two mortified young women in their life jackets were making a closer acquaintance with the waters of the Baltic prior to a silent dripping journey back to the Club hard in the rescue launch with their borrowed Club 470 in tow.

Kurt was very sympathetic, 'We have all done it.'

'Yes, but I've practised jibing hundreds of times and it has never happened before.'

'It's always different when you're racing. You've a lot more things to think about – all the other competitors for a start. Forget it, there's another regatta next week at Seesovils.'

There was and, although the water was unfamiliar, they had an excellent day and finished ninth in the junior class of twenty five. Kurt was ecstatic and amazed them by stating that he had never known a couple of youngsters learn so quickly. It was the beginning of the long summer holiday and every day they were down at the yacht club at dawn changing into their wet suits, getting their sails then off into the gulf. Sometimes Kurt, as enthusiastic as they were, would come out in an inflatable and coach them in tactics. The big thrill was the moment that he brought his own crew, Stefan, another student from the university and took out his own shining new 470 alongside them. Neither of them could quite believe that they were sailing leg for leg and tack for tack alongside an Olympic helmsman.

It was an exhilarating day and as they brought the boats out of the water, Kurt called across, 'That was really well done. You had me round the second mark. I'm going to give up coaching you. I can't stand the competition.'

They knew that he was being kind but they still flushed with pride. The best, though, came as they went into the Clubhouse. A friend of Kurt's, Alex, came up from the car park and button holed him.

'Kurt, you don't know anyone who wants to buy my 470. I'm going to the USA on business for a couple of years and I don't think I can keep her until I come back. She's a really good boat but you know that.'

'I'll say I do. You've given me a good run around in her.' Suddenly he stopped and looked at the girls. Mara's mouth dropped open but Andrea was immediately businesslike.

'We might try, but how much?'

'I would like her to go to someone young here,' he said. 'How does 3,500 thalers sound?'

'It sounds wonderful but we still have to square *unsere Eltern.*'

Die Eltern were duly squared, both fathers agreeing quietly between themselves that a first class 470 was probably better value for their teenage daughters than endless designer clothes. By the end of the week MTV39 was duly registered and insured as the joint property of Frau Andrea Hoffmann and Frau Tamara Oblova. It was the first time that Mara had seen herself referred to as 'Frau Oblova' and that gave her an extra flash of excitement.

They missed the next regatta to practice in their new acquisition and re-set her up for them as her proud new owners. Once, with a lot of help from Kurt, they had her right, they both noticed the step up from the club boat. In their first regatta, Mara took the helm and although, because of Andrea's greater height and weight, this was theoretically a better combination, Mara, with less experience, missed the start and they finished down the field. Tactfully Andrea insisted on Mara being helmsman in the next race and this time they did much better finishing eighth. After that they changed round again and came second by half a length – by far their best performance. They were walking on air and talking enthusiastically about next season, oblivious to the gloom and doom surrounding them ashore.

2
NIGHT

The clouds cast moving shadows on the land
Are you prepared for what the night will bring?

PHILIP LARKIN: THE NORTH SHIP

She turned over in bed and prayed. In this land of uncertainties God might help her – although in her fifteen-year-old heart, she doubted it. She fell into a fitful sleep, in her dream she saw a figure of strength and security, part from the fairy stories that her mother had read her as a tiny child, part more real, more modern. A sort of medieval knight and yet with her in her present need. There was something different, which she grasped only as she awoke. The great bell of the *Frauenkirche* started to strike, familiar and reassuring then at the third stroke there came a tortured shriek of fractured metal. It was a terrifying sound, the bell, her old familiar friend, in dreadful agony. Only later did she realise that a stray fascist shell had, incredibly, pierced the stone tracery without damaging it to shatter the fourteenth-century bell to shrapnel fragments. Downstairs were her parents – or were they? Earlier in the night she had heard the crash at the door followed by her father's angry voice. Then there was her mother in shrill despair then nothing. She was too terrified to go down and find out.

Suddenly a loudspeaker echoed round the street outside:

'Keep calm – nothing will happen to you. We have taken over the government to prevent a blitzkrieg from the Bosh, the Germans, united and powerful are about to overrun the country as they did sixty–five years ago. Hoffman was selling you to the enemy. We have mounted a patriotic revolution to stop them and survive. It was the only way.'

She searched the house. It was empty. Panicking she looked for her father and mother. Nobody – not a sound. She rang Andrea on her mobile phone. To her amazement, she answered immediately.

'Where are you?'

'Hiding in the wood store, I made myself a hide here in case I needed it. They took my father and mother last night. Klaus is away and I don't know how to contact him. How about you?'

'The house is empty. I can't find Mutti or Vati. I think that they must have been taken. They would have told me if they had gone willingly. What do we do, Andrea, what can we do?'

There was desperation in her voice. A long pause.

'We take the boat and sail to Gotland.' Andrea's voice was flat as if she was aware of the madness and danger of her proposition. To sail across the Baltic in a racing dinghy was crazy at any time but in the middle of the night during a revolution, it was insane and yet… and yet… What would happen if they stayed where they were?

Following Mara's thoughts, Andrea said quietly, 'If all goes well we can phone from Visby and fly back. If our parents have really been arrested they will want us too and at least we will be safe if we reach Sweden or are picked up by a sympathetic boat.'

They collected their sails and changed quietly into wet suits and life jackets behind a cruiser hauled up on the slipway. The dark shapes of the beached yachts and motor cruisers loomed high and slightly ghostlike and sinister above them. There was nobody about now and all around a flat, paling night signified the breathless pre-dawn calm. They extracted their 470 from the boat park. The trailer clattered on the dark hard as they freed it. They paused holding their breath but there was no reaction from the darkened buildings and, after a moment, they slipped her cover off and ran her quietly down the slipway. Andrea collected a pair of paddles carelessly left beside an inflatable as they went towards the water, lapping quietly on the slip. From the centre of the town there were sporadic shots and one fairly large explosion.

'We'll return the paddles later but we might need them,' Andrea muttered with half a chuckle.

As it turned out, they were necessary because there was still not a breath of wind and they had to paddle quietly out from the old port, with the commercial docks against the *Zehnheligenweg* away to port. It wasn't all bad. The 470 creeping along in the flat calm was a lot less conspicuous than she would have been under full sail but it was slow, painfully slow. At last, as they cleared the last starboard hand buoy of the bay, the first cat's-paw of the dawn breeze ruffled across the mirror sea. Andrea nodded and, well practised, they hoisted the main and the jib, sheeting them in close-hauled on the port tack. The exhilaration was still there as they gathered speed. Mara had a feeling of unreality, apart from the unearthly time of day, it was all so normal. The lightening sky to the east over the land and in the distance – Riga, Tallinn, St Petersburg and Helsinki were up there but she wasn't quite sure which was where. The still dark north hid Stockholm and Marienhamn and, halfway there, Gotland, with the dunes of Ljugarn, their ambitious destination. The wind was becoming consistent and strengthening slightly westerly. She hoped that it would settle at about twelve to fifteen knots. That would be fine as long as it did stay that way. There was enough now for the trapeze and she swung out, feeling the spray on her wet suit as they began to plane. The light came quickly followed by the sun, sensed by Mara rather than seen, hidden behind the mainsail. From time to time Andrea glanced at her wrist compass and grunted with satisfaction. Apart from her aching arms and legs, Mara felt as if she was in a dream world, mesmerised by the phosphoric sea sluicing out from the dinghy's bows.

An hour passed then a second, Mara fought with her body, which was getting very tired, out on the trapeze planing on the endless broad reach. This was much longer than any racing leg but there was no doubt that they were reeling off the miles and the breeze was right – enough but not too much.

The plume of spray appeared to come from the north. At first it could hardly be made out, possibly just a shimmer on the late summer horizon. Then it was definite, a fast big inflatable coming directly towards them. The boat had no markings but Mara's first thought was that relief for her aching arms and legs was at hand.

Andrea muttered hopefully, 'They must be Swedes,' and hailed them in Swedish. To her relief the reply came in Swedish.

'Where are you from?' There was no point in trying to deceive them as, after all, they had a large red MTV39 on their sail.

The next moment they were looking down the barrel of a machine pistol.

'We need to know who you are and what the hell you are doing sailing out of Königshof at night at a time like this.'

They were not given time to answer and a moment later rough arms pulled them into the inflatable. The powerful twin engines fired up and they were off, crashing southward through the sea. Mara's first and, she realised later, completely irrelevant feeling, was distress that their beloved 470 was left forlorn, abandoned with her sails, flapping in the middle of the vastness of the morning Baltic, intermittently reflecting the rising sun in their bright whiteness. Clearly no seaman would have abandoned a racing dinghy at sea as a hazard to shipping and possible evidence to others of the fate of its occupants. Only the helmsman in the inflatable seemed to be any sort of seaman and he stuck strictly to his task of driving the boat back towards Königshof. Irrationally, it struck Mara with a sense of wonder, just how far they had sailed. Sadly, she realised, the eastern coast had followed them so that they were never far from the Moltravian land. Had their passage been out into the open sea towards Gotland, they might, just might, have made it unnoticed.

'Aren't you going to bring our boat?' she blurted out.

'You won't need it where you're going,' came the sinister answer from the pistol bearer. He was clearly in charge, but wore no sort of uniform or other clues to his identity. He was probably in his mid forties with a slick of dark hair, already thinning. He had an aquiline nose and pale blue eyes. The whole was eerie but the only individually striking thing

16

about him was his right eyelid, which drooped lower than the left. She looked into those eyes for a moment and then recoiled from them with a shock of hidden horror that she didn't understand. It seemed to go far deeper than the superficial brutality of the machine pistol and anyway his expression was bland, almost bored. But suddenly it seemed that her childhood world, secure and loving, had dropped out of sight into a bottomless hellish abyss.

She turned away perturbed and uncomprehending to look at the others. There was an enduring anonymity about the crew. Two were young, late teens or early twenties, both with cropped hair and faces bearing a studiedly mean expression copied, thought Mara, from American soap opera cops. There the similarity ended. One was already paunchy but spoke only in monosyllables taken from current TV German slang. He suggested, thought Mara, a preference for beer over conversation but apart from his theatrically tough expression, his only activity was endlessly chewing gum. The other darted about the boat, lean and hyperactive, uttering, almost to himself, a series of observations and instructions in *platdeutsch*. The helmsman had an ochre face and grey, grizzled hair. He seemed faintly familiar but she dismissed the thought. He was a type who could be found in a fishing boat in any Baltic port. Andrea sat with her head in her hands saying nothing. It occurred to Mara that she might be trying to avoid recognition. Rather strangely, however, there was no evidence that any of the quartet had recognised either of them. From Mara's point of view that wasn't entirely surprising. As the young daughter of the foreign minister, she had not yet been exposed to much press hassle, but Andrea, a little older and the prime minister's daughter, was probably a bit better known and her photo had certainly appeared from time to time in family holiday pictures as part of a group with her father. Mara wondered what would happen to them when they got to the shore.

They were slowing and apparently heading for a part of the port near the western end of the *Zehnheligenweg* where it curved round to meet the sea. They drew in to a battered breakwater with an old concrete pill box on it. Abandoned from a war, possibly German, more likely Russian thought Mara.

A man wearing a bottle green armband was on the Quay. He didn't seem pleased to see them.

'What are you doing here?' he asked, crossly, of the crew 'You must keep up the watch at sea. A lot of interesting people are trying to escape.'

'We found these two in a racing dinghy heading north.' He indicated the girls, 'I thought that we should bring them in.'

The man on the quay exploded. 'We are trying to run the country and you go fishing up *zwei jungen Schnepfen . Du bist hirnrissig!*[1] Give them to me and get back out there. We have captured the proper patrol boats and they will take over by this evening.'

As Mara and Andrea were pushed unceremoniously up the rusting iron ladder fixed to the quay, the thin youth muttered behind them '*Schade,* I thought we had made a good catch for later.'

Mara shuddered. Once on the quay surface, the man in the armband pulled out a *Handy* and punched in a number. Somebody answered and armband said, '*Herr Mäne, ich bin Sintov, National Agentur Sicherheit,* I have two young girls here found in a boat trying to get to Sweden. Shall I question them or will you?'

There was an answer then armband said, 'OK, *Herr Mäne,* I will send them as soon as I have transport.'

He rang off and indicated the girls to go into the pillbox. Once in, the door was shut and padlocked. It was damp, dark and suddenly cold.

'I don't think this can be bugged,' said Andrea, being practical, 'it's too primitive and provisional. Look, you know who they are?'

'No.'

'They are the NAS. The Fascist strong arm men. They have unpleasant habits. Look I am going to be Anna Hotter and you are Teresa Ostmann. We must try and keep our real identities secret. It is probably not going to work but we will try. We are not Moltravian. Our parents are German and were in Moltravia on a trade mission. Something to do with chemicals we think but we're not really interested

---

1   Two young sluts. You must be crazy

18

in that sort of thing. We are not sure who they were seeing. We lost touch with them in the disturbances but we thought that they had gone to Sweden with all our papers so we tried to join them. We were very frightened in the street fighting.'

Mara nodded. For some minutes there was silence. Mara looked unseeing at the grimy rubbish on the floor, preoccupied by their peril and their isolation. She looked up. Andrea was slumped in her corner of the damp malodorous wall, her head on one side, fast asleep. She realised how tired she was and in a moment her head also slumped and she fell into the cramped but deep sleep of the exhausted.

She woke with the door being unlocked and crashing open. Two men came in and peered at first one then the other by the light of a torch. After a close inspection of them both one man said, '*Diese,*' pointing at Andrea and the other grabbed her by the arm and dragged her out.

The door slammed shut, the padlock clicked and Mara was alone. Only now she realised how much she had been comforted by Andrea and how much she had relied on her. She had never thought that they might be separated and the desolation was terrible. Hour after hour passed. The glimmer of light through the high pill box slits faded. It must be dark again. The autumn days were beginning to get short. She slept again; it was a restless dream-ridden sleep. She woke looking for Andrea in the corner and then realised with misery that there was no Andrea. She wondered if she had been forgotten entirely and would be left for all eternity in that damp dreary hole to starve to death. She worried about what was happening to Andrea and tried to comfort herself, unconvincingly, that they would be together again soon. Fortunately she did not know that she would never see her friend alive again.

At last she dropped into an exhausted sleep once more. She was woken by the noise of the padlock and glanced at her yacht racing watch to find it was eleven o'clock. The door swung back revealing a woman in a parka with a bottle-green arm band like the one worn by the man who had locked them in.

'You want the WC?' she enquired, and Mara, surprised, realised she did and nodded. The woman pulled out a pistol and motioned Mara

19

to walk in front of her. The wind had got up and a whole gale was now gusting across the quay under grey racing clouds. Mara wondered inconsequentially whether they would have reached Gotland by this time and if not whether her strength would have held out. Irrelevant now. The lavatory was in a sort of dock office across the road from the pillbox. The woman stood with one hand holding the door open while Mara relieved herself. It was very public but fortunately nobody else seemed to be in that part of the building. As she still only had her wet suit to wear, dressing and undressing took a bit of time but there seemed to be no hurry. When she had dressed, her guard lead her into the outer room, which was some sort of office. Two men sat behind tables reading computer print-outs. From a distance Mara thought that they were some sort of lists.

'Etwas zu essen?'[2] Even this staccato question revealed a coarse local accent.

Mara nodded. The woman went over to the vending machine and obtained a plastic cup of coffee and a cellophane wrapped rye bun. It tasted like the cement dust that she had once inhaled while watching the builders on her uncle's farm but she was too hungry to care. The drink and bun apparently brought her captors' hospitality to an end but it did not seem that she was to be returned to the pillbox. As the feeble autumn light struggled towards midday, the two women stood and waited while the seated men made occasional marks on their print-outs.

It was about ten to twelve when a rumbling behind the office announced the arrival of some sort of, as yet unseen, vehicle. Mara who was expecting a black prison van with high barred windows was a bit taken aback when a small local bus, already crowded with people pulled round the building into view. Her guard pushed Mara on board and, leaving her to stand, sat down with two other guards in the front seats which faced backwards into the body of the bus. All three had unsheathed pistols on their laps. Mara, who had steeled herself for the third degree, looked round at her fellow passengers and felt rather foolish. There was an elderly woman with a shopping bag, two men who

---

2   Something to eat?

might have come from a building site or the adjacent docks, a man in a suit who could have worked in an insurance office, two young women and a quartet of schoolboys. These, together with some indeterminate others who were not clearly visible in the crush, were the passengers – or prisoners – she wasn't sure which. What they must have thought of her, still incongruously dressed in a wet suit, she had no idea. Most of them seemed too occupied with their own thoughts and fears to talk. After about a kilometre, twisting and turning round the dock roads, a fatherly looking man in a woollen Königshof FC supporters' hat and a grey parka that had seen better days looked up at Mara from his seat.

'Been swimming then, *mein junge Ding*?' He asked smiling up at her.

'Just didn't have time to change.'

'Same for all of us. Don't suppose it matters where we are going, it'll be the Winterburg, the old barracks and the whisper is that they don't care much what you're wearing when you get there, they soon soften you up all the same.'

Mara shuddered. She had always found the Winterburg, lowering over the old centre of the town intimidating. As a youngster, she had realised that she had had nothing really to be frightened about. The old fortress was simply a straightforward barracks for the small Moltravian army. The appearance of the place was scary and the gossip told of its history, which she was gradually able to piece together. Originally it had been built by an old order called the Knights of the Sword to control the local tribesmen then it had passed to various owners. During the Hanseatic period it has been used to defend the town against the Danes, then various armies and tyrants had used it as a police headquarters and prison. Almost nothing except the underground dungeons were left from the original buildings and indeed so much had been added and altered that the whole walled complex was now a hideous towering mess. Any foreign conqueror or domestic dictator, and there had been plenty of both, had always found his prison and torture chambers needing only a modicum of updating to be conveniently ready for use. Most recently first the Nazis and then the Soviets had employed it to the full and many of the older people had suffered or had friends and relatives who had suffered within its walls. Now it appeared that the Winterburg had already been taken over and the whisper was that, in only a few days, the country's new masters had fortified the building and were using it for interrogations. With a lump in her mouth, Mara's fertile imagination could almost hear the screams of the present prisoners joining those echoing down the centuries.

As they drove through the darkening winter streets, she was too frightened to think clearly. She had now no family, no friends and apparently was being taken to a fiendish fortress where anything might happen. Her heart thumped, her brain whirled and she was too dry and scared for tears.

She was so far away in her terror that at first she didn't realise the bus had stopped. She came to with one of the guards shouting at her and pointing to the open door of the stationary bus. They had stopped, not in the Winterburg, but at a large old suburban house, unremarkable except for a hastily erected barbed wire fence round it. Outside the open gate was a man with the obligatory green arm band and the equally obligatory machine pistol. Mara was joined by two boys of about her age, also from the bus, and ushered inside the long entrance hall. The house appeared to date from the German period with high ceilings with mouldings and generous rooms, which were now shabby but had clearly once been elegant. Perplexed, she felt that her new life had begun, but what was that new life to be?

3
AWAKENING

Alas! The love of women! it is known
To be a lovely and a fearful thing.

BYRON: DON JUAN

The next days passed almost in a dream of unreality. Mara had prepared herself for the third degree, possibly torture and certainly a prison cell. Instead she found herself in a comfortable, if dilapidated, suburban villa under the care of a certain Frau Ilse. Frau Ilse, apart from her bottle green armband, could have been a boarding house landlady or a pillar of the local women's guild. She had looked askance at Mara's unconventional attire and had found, from somewhere, jeans, sweaters, pyjamas and spare underclothes. None were in their first youth but clean and a great improvement on a wet suit. Best of all was a nearly new padded winter tracksuit, which became Mara's favourite, as the weather, inexorably, got colder.

It appeared that they were indeed being detained but more to keep them out of the way rather than for any sort of punishment or interrogation. The main problem was boredom, as apart from a few household chores; there was virtually nothing to do. The TV put out endless propaganda for the new, 'greater' Moltravia punctuated by quiz shows of increasing idiocy. The question masters humiliated stupid contestants lured onto the show by the combination of superficial televisual fame and the possibility of a few extra thalers. Mara, who had always been a rapid and voracious reader, soon exhausted the small collection of ancient books in the house.

There were four other residents. The only other girl was a willowy eighteen-year-old called Johanna who was superior and unapproachable. Mara had to share a room with her but in spite of this intimacy soon discovered that friendship and even basic conversation was impossible. When Mara tried to talk about their predicament, Johanna searchingly gazed round the walls of their room like a frightened rabbit and then hissed, 'You see I cannot talk. There will be bugs and I am Dutch.'

Mara was left to puzzle the implications of this, her roommate's only contribution to their relationship. Bugs there might be but she could not figure out the significance of Johanna's claimed Dutch citizenship. At times Mara wondered whether the stress of recent events had unhinged her companion who seemed more and more wild-eyed as the days passed. Her conversation, if you could call it that, degenerated into monosyllables and the odd inconsequential phrase. Certainly there was no question of mutual support or understanding.

From the start, she fared rather better with the boys. Yuri and Andrei were light-hearted seventeen-year-old twins who enjoyed putting on an act for the benefit of the others. Sometimes their jokes at meal times about the new 'glorious' regime were sufficiently sharp to make the others search anxiously round the dining room for Johanna's bugs.

To Mara, though, by far the most interesting was the youngest, Stefan, only a couple of years or so older than her but who seemed mature beyond his age. He had actually arrived at the house the day after she had. He had come in a closed car and had been pushed through the front door onto his face in the hall. He did not talk much but when he did speak, it was usually to say something understanding or kind. He was so different from the teenage boys that Mara had known and despised with their brashness, vulgar stupidity and chaotic testosterone. He was the first boy of her own generation who talked to her as if she was an intelligent human being and not someone to be either ignored or alternatively treated as a target for the demonstration of insecure sexual prowess. As soon as she had reached puberty, Mara had known that as a pretty, petite, natural blond she was always going to be noticed by boys and men. She had come to realise that she was, however, more often than not, regarded as a superficial sex object, a sort of baby doll, which she found hugely insulting and came to hate. This boy, she felt, was different. In addition, to his sensitivity, he was unusually good looking with his raven hair and the deepest black eyes that she had ever seen, and to add to that there was a twitching crooked smile.

One slate-grey early winter afternoon, Mara had finished her stint of washing up and had gone to sit in the downstairs common room, the old drawing room of the house. She looked for a book to read but found she had little choice between the classics which she had already read and old Russian manuals dealing with such entrancing subjects as 'Hydroelectric Installations in the New Five Year Plan' by A.D. Rasputin. After a moment's amusement at the name (or nom de plume?) of the author, she pulled out an ancient coffee-table book with a torn dust jacket, which, because of its size, was lying flat under the other books at the top of the bookshelf. The title was 'The Golden Chalice of Zablovsk and other lost Livonian Treasures' and as she leafed through the pages she became ever more enchanted by what she saw. Wonderful things – silver, armour, pictures, books, jewels and all of them bearing names of places that she knew – mundane familiar places that she had been to and had played in as a child. It was astonishing to see these marvellous objects associated with drab real life locations, staggering from years of Nazi war, civic unrest and Soviet vandalism. But it was sad, too, how much had her unhappy country lost? How much was it still losing or going to lose? She felt a terrible sense of powerlessness. She wanted to do something but what could she do – a sixteen-year-old girl under guard and separated from her family?

She leafed through the pages again now no longer enthralled by their beauty but filled with frustration and anger. She stopped at the picture of the Chalice of Zablovsk – small, plain but hugely moving as the symbol of the once, now lost, country.

As she gazed, a quiet voice behind her said, 'It's so sad and beautiful… and moving.'

She turned and there was Stefan standing close behind her chair, gazing past her at the book open on the table. She must have looked surprised but with the anger she had been feeling still showing in her face.

'I'm sorry. I shouldn't have disturbed you; it was very rude of me.'

She blushed, 'No, It's just… it's just…'

She stopped, blushed deeply and couldn't find the right words, which made her more frustrated. She now felt humiliated and realised with a shock that she valued his good opinion. But why? She asked herself. This lad was nothing to her. She was not interested in boys; in fact she hated their arrogance and their ignorance. She ought to be concerned to keep her purity with God and her peace with her family. Who was this lad? They had been thrown together and hadn't even chosen each other's company but…

As he bent forward to turn the page of the book his arm brushed her tee shirt and the warm scent of his body enveloped her. In spite of herself, she felt a shiver which she knew was not part of virginity or convent life. He smiled at her again and those deep black eyes searched her for a moment. Then, suddenly, he turned and left.

'Fräulein Oblova,' she said to herself very formally and seriously 'You are in a very serious situation and it is not going to be helped by falling stupidly in love.' But falling 'stupidly' in love she certainly was.

She saw little of Stefan for the next fortnight and never alone. She was a jumble of emotions, half yearning for his company and fearing that he might be taken away from the house, half fearing the feelings that he had aroused in her. When it happened it was almost as if it had been stage managed. The twins were with guards fetching wood for the large boiler, which was the house's only defence against the fierce northern winter. Frau Ilse and another guard had taken Johanna to the dental clinic with toothache. Two more guards were stationed, as always, at the gate, front and back. The house was silent and Mara took the opportunity of going to her room to work at her Russian. She had had no schooling since the autumn coup and there appeared to be no chance of getting any. She wasn't a particularly conscientious student but she knew that her parents, wherever they might be, would be concerned that she had already missed virtually a whole term's work. In a way she felt that she owed it to her mother and father to do something that would please them and Russian was the only thing that she had available to study.

There was a soft knock at the door and Stefan was standing, blushing in the entrance wearing his ancient Walkman.

'Just listen to that, *Tamarushka*,' said Stefan passing his ear pieces across to her. The chorus through the little insert swelled into:

> *Va, pensiero, sull'ali dorate;*
> *va', ti posa sui clivi, sui colli,*
> *ove olezzano tepide e molli*
> *l'aure dolci del suolo natal!*
> *Del Giordano le rive saluta,*
> *di Sionne le torri atterrate.*[3]

'I don't understand a word of it but it's beautiful. You could march and fight for that,' she said with tears in her eyes.

'I recorded it from the radio last night; I thought that you might like to hear it. This is very old fashioned but it has an internal radio that you can record from direct. I heard the introduction on German radio. It's a slaves' chorus. They are longing for freedom and their homeland.'

He smiled at her and those deep dark eyes sparkled.

Impulsively she kissed him. Afterwards she was not sure entirely sure

---

3   Go, thought, on wings of gold;
    go settle upon the slopes and the hills,
    where, soft and mild, the sweet airs
    of our native land smell fragrant!

    Greet the banks of the Jordan
    and Zion's toppled towers.

27

how what had happened next, occurred. She felt him grip her tightly and together they rolled onto her bed tripping the clothes off each other until, naked, they were entwined hungrily kissing and exploring. Mara had heard something about first love and expected it to hurt – it did a bit but she was so carried away by her sensations that she hardly noticed. Eventually they relaxed and lay together.

Stefan whispered, 'Tamara, I'm so sorry I didn't realise you were… were…'

'A virgin?' she said giggling in a way that she certainly hadn't been taught at the convent. 'Well I'm not now. I'm a proper woman and thank you, thank you and please call me *Tamarushka*, I like it.'

It was the first of many. Mara loved him, loved love and didn't care. He seemed caring and responsible and even remarkably found a supply of condoms left in a drawer by a previous occupant of the house.

Winter gripped with its Baltic rigor. Snow fell deeply and at least they all got some exercise clearing the yard and the path to the wood store and to the guarded front gate. Anonymous NAS thugs who swore and stamped and leered at the girls replaced the soldiers. Somehow it didn't frighten Mara, as it would have done previously. She felt that her new status as a 'proper woman' gave her strength in the face of this vulgarity. She was careful, however, not to show herself to the guards too often. Sometimes she did reproach herself. She had been brought up as a good Catholic girl and she wondered if her new feelings would send her to burn in hellfire.

*

Frau Ilse announced that the Government had abolished Christmas and replaced it with a 'National Day' celebrating the achievements of the regime to be held on the 25th September, the day of the coup that brought them to power. There was, however, to be a sort of low key Winter Festival. Mara didn't see how you could abolish Christmas but thought it was better to keep quiet rather than argue the point. She had a suspicion that Frau Ilse wasn't entirely in sympathy with some of her colleagues' and masters' pronouncements but that she also felt it was safer not to argue.

As the Winter Festival approached, Mara, amused, noted that barley sausages and a pig's snout appeared from somewhere and there was even no comment when the boys came back with a railway sleeper to form a traditional Yule Log.

The winter meant their lives were even more restricted. The boys still went, on rota, to their wood chopping and fetching. The girls and indeed all women in the land, Frau Ilse explained, were expected by the regime to stick to 'appropriate' domestic tasks. They should look after their household and family. With very few exceptions, they could only do approved outside work like cleaning and cooking in schools, offices and barracks. The NAS had to employ women but apart from that emancipation was a dirty word and a thing of the past.

The cleaning, cooking and clearing up in the detention house only occupied a portion of the time and for the rest the boredom was crushing. Mara found an anthology of English poetry, torn and coverless, amongst the pile of discarded books in the attic and tried to make sense of it with her primitive school English. At least it was something to do and the 'bitter chill' opening of *The Eve of St Agnes* resonated with her present situation. But she was stumped by the 'woolly fold' and wondered, dictionary-less, what a Beadsman was.

The monotony was broken, albeit shockingly, by a new arrival. Mara was clearing the breakfast bowls in the early morning when a black windowless van drove up and stopped outside the house. Two men in full NAS uniform leapt out, spoke rapidly to the duty guards and went behind the van. The back door was swung open and a young boy dragged out. He appeared weak and gasped for breath as the two thugs pulled him upright and marched him up the path to the locked front door. They banged impatiently and aggressively until a flustered Frau Ilse rushed down and unlocked the door. With hardly a word they pushed the boy inside and left him slumped against the hall wall with his head lolling to one side. Mara even wondered whether he was still alive. Then the men shouted something at Frau Ilse, turned on their heels, got back in the van and drove off. Frau Ilse called to Mara to get some bedding and put it on the floor of the boys' room as all the beds were occupied. Between them they helped the young man up the stairs and into the bedroom. He seemed utterly weak and exhausted.

'He must rest,' Frau Ilse murmured.

'But what on earth has happened to him?'

'Winterburg,' she answered through pursed lips as if that one word explained everything.

As they undressed the boy, Mara got a chance to have a closer look at him. He had two black eyes and a bruised cheek but the main damage consisted of open welts and massive bruising stretching over his chest, belly, back and buttocks. Clearly he had been subjected to the most appalling beatings. But that wasn't all, on his mouth, fingers and genitals were scorch marks that Mara thought must be due to burning or electric shock.

'You'd better stay with him and look after him.' Frau Ilse showed her usual combination of rough care and brusqueness.

Mara's only medical knowledge was a short first aid and care of the sick course given to the ten-year-olds at her first school by the *Thérèsienbund* sisters but she was delighted to have something to do, and something useful at that. Frau Ilse provided an out-of-date field dressing pack and a bottle of liquid soap and Mara busied herself with bowl and water bathing her charge then attempting to dress his wounds. He said nothing but screwed his face up when she got too close to the raw areas. The winter northern light was failing rapidly, although it was still early afternoon and, in order to be more careful around the wounds, Mara got up and brought a table lamp over and placed it close to the boy's chest. She was horrified when he let out a blood curdling scream and writhed about for some minutes. She didn't understand what had happened to frighten him but managed to calm him, talking quietly. Stefan came into the room with a load of logs for the fire. Mara turned from her work to smile at him and was amused to see a flash of jealousy cross his face at seeing her tenderly caring for the newcomer. She stood up and put her arms round Stefan and kissed him.

'He's terribly injured,' she said, 'how could anybody do that to another human being?'

Stefan looked momentarily ashamed and then muttered, 'Winterburg,' and then to her, 'Do your best, *Schatz!* Give him my bed. He needs it more than I do.'

Between them they gently raised him off the floor onto Stefan's bed. Mara noticed how careful Stefan was with the tortured boy. None the less he moaned as they moved him and then lay shivering on the bed. When they had finished, Stefan seized her in his arms and kissed her again then turned picked up the empty log rack and left. For a moment Mara stood looking out of the window at the bare trees and the dirty, tramped snow in the yard. She tried to come to terms with the turmoil of her young life. Captivity, benign but boring, had now given her the thrill of love, as the jealous glance and the thrilling *'Schatz'* had just shown. But underneath were dark thoughts. She lived in limbo, her beloved home and dear parents had disappeared or she had disappeared from them. She didn't know which. Her mobile phone had been confiscated as soon as she had been captured. Several times she had asked to contact her home or her mother or father but Frau Ilse had greeted this request with her stony NAS face and just said, 'That would not be possible.'

When Mara had done her best with the dressings, she began to make her patient comfortable with blankets from Stefan to add to the couple that Frau Ilse had left.

As she tucked in the blankets he moaned, 'My hands, my hands.' – his first intelligible words.

'How can I help?' she whispered but he was already in an exhausted, restless and pain-wracked sleep. She tiptoed out.

After three days he was talking disjointed sentences. Mara asked him for his name. He smiled and said in a whisper, 'Call me Lukas.'

Mara had a feeling that it wasn't his real name. It was probably a code name used to protect others. His other mutterings were words like *Bund, Karl, Solandu* mixed with distressed cries and long periods of silence just staring at the ceiling. However, each day the newcomer said a bit more and little by little told her something about himself. He was called Lukas and the son of a blacksmith from *Litovsk* on the Russian border. He had just started his apprenticeship with his father at the time of the coup.

'What happened then?' Mara asked innocently.

He suddenly seemed very agitated, 'You mustn't know,' he said. 'It would be very dangerous – much better you don't know.'

Mara realised that he was very distressed and left the subject. The following day, Stefan came again with the logs just as Mara had finished her nursing duties. She waited outside the door to speak to Stefan. It was one of the few opportunities they got. To her surprise instead of coming straight out Stefan remained inside for a long time. Mara could hear low voices through the door. Eventually Stefan appeared with a very grave face and Mara looked enquiringly at him.

'What was all that about?' she asked.

'He has told me – shared with me – a lot and I think that I know now what he was doing and what happened at the Winterburg.'

Mara felt angry and hurt.

'Why on earth didn't he share it with me? After all that I've had to do for him. All the intimate things. Why couldn't he talk to me?'

'Isn't it obvious? He admires you – is beginning to love you perhaps, jealous I may be but I can't blame him for that, but what he knows is dangerous. If he had told you they might have taken you to the Winterburg and treated you as they had treated him. And besides you are very young and a girl and he wanted to protect you – old-fashioned chivalry, if you like. But he felt that he should share what he knew with somebody and I was the only other person available. I respect his reasons for not involving you, so I shan't tell you either.'

'But that's ridiculous, I should… I could…' The words trailed away into a whispered, 'Perhaps you are both right, I won't press you.'

Stefan looked relieved and kissed her. They stood silently both deep in thought.

She realised now more than she had when she had awoken alone and frightened and run to the harbour hearing shots behind her. She realised more than she had on the boat with Andrea, more than she had when locked in the dreadful pill box. At last she realised just how really serious things were. She now knew how the peaceful little country of her childhood had been changed once more into a brutalised bear pit where human life counted for nothing. The NAS stalked the land and used torture and execution to smooth their path.

The lights went out suddenly. Power cuts were quite frequent and gave them their best chance of stealing a few moments privacy. Mara pulled Stefan into the girls' bedroom. Johanna, much to Mara's relief, had been taken away to help on 'government business'. Mara wished Johanna no harm, but this absence did not seem like a Winterburg interrogation, and she was glad to see the back of her icy room-mate – at least temporarily. They undressed quickly and clasped each other eagerly. They explored their nooks and crannies with cries and giggles of pleasure. Both were now more confident in their loving and, when they came together it was with a new vigour and ardour. The lights went on suddenly as they lay as one. Frau Ilse stood in the doorway at her most severe but that was not all, behind her stood a man in NAS captain's uniform his face cold with cruelty.

Mara heard Frau Ilse turn to her companion and whispered, 'You were right,' and out aloud, 'What are we to do with them?'

'Lock him in the cellar and her in the bathroom up here. Take their clothes and bedding away and tell the others they must use the WC downstairs. Perhaps a night naked in the cold will damp their ardour.'

He laughed an unpleasant grating laugh.

'We will decide what to do with them tomorrow. The Winterburg will probably want to find out what he knows. Apparently, he has a troublesome record. They may want to discover what he has told her too. That should be fun. I will send for a van in the morning. Naked and locked in they should be safe enough tonight. I'll warn the guards at the gate.'

So saying he seized Stefan's arm and, twisting it painfully behind him, he pushed him out of the door. Frau Ilse bundled up their clothes and bedding and followed them. She then returned and grabbed Mara by her hair and pushed her into the bathroom, locking the door. Weeping and shivering she sat on the icy edge of the bath. It was the longest night that she had ever known. She knew that she was in real danger from the cold. She knew that she must do something. She looked frantically for a towel or a bath mat to put round herself – nothing. She must exercise to keep warm, she thought. She tried to remember school PE. She started press-ups, running on the spot and anything else she could think of. It was exhausting and still extremely cold but somehow she managed to pass what seemed like an age. Eventually, however, she fell asleep with exhaustion on the floor. She didn't know how long she slept for. It probably wasn't long, as she knew when she woke that a long sleep would have been her last. Shouting outside and the rattling of the bolt on the outside of the door awoke her. She tried to get up but was so stiff and cold that she remained on the floor.

Frau Ilse was at the door with her face contorted in a mixture of fear and fury. 'Do you know what we should do about this, *du kleine grazni Hutte*? Tell me or I'll send you down the road for a good thrashing.'

Like many Moltravians, she tended to mix Russian and German when excited or anxious. Mara tried to sound calm, 'We are in love, Frau Ilse, I don't know why there is something so terrible in that.'

'I'm not talking about you fucking, *blöde Hure*, he's escaped, he's gone and God knows what he has taken with him.'

She was oblivious to the abuse thrown at her as she tried to make sense of it all. Her head whirled. Had Stefan, stark naked, really escaped in a Baltic winter from a locked and guarded cellar? At that moment two NAS men appeared. One was a sergeant and the other the usual standard young thug. The sergeant took no notice of the nude shivering blue Mara but the young thug leered lecherously at her.

'A cupboard has been broken open. What was in the cupboard in the cellar?'

Frau Ilse blanched, '*Mein Gott!* Nothing, nothing much – really.'

Her face belied her and the NAS sergeant was unimpressed.

'Really, that was why a toolbox was on the floor with its contents scattered, I suppose? You're in enough trouble already. I want the whole truth and quickly otherwise it's only ten minutes to the Winterburg and you know we will find out there.'

Frau Ilse shrunk with her bulky frame collapsing like a pricked balloon. She spoke very quietly, 'The working clothes and tools of the maintenance man were kept there – it was always locked.'

'So well locked,' he shouted, 'that a boy with an old poker, which nobody had noticed or removed, could force it then use the conveniently stored hacksaw to cut through the grating. You will fry for this, you criminal bitch. You'd better come down and tell us what's missing then we'll take you off.'

He turned to the thug, 'Guard the house with the others and no monkey business with the girl, we may want her – whole!'

Mara shivered and shuddered. She didn't know whether to be reassured by this warning or horrified by the final menace. It seemed to have its effect, however, for with only a quick backward gawp at her naked body, he went down the stairs. They were so preoccupied that nobody had locked her in. Gratefully, she was able to stagger across the landing, collecting her clothes and bedclothes still piled in a jumble on the floor and go into the girls' room and begin to dress. The feeling of security of her clothes was irrational but still hugely comforting. Warming up, however, was much more painful. He fingers and toes burnt horribly as they warmed up. She tried to convince herself that it was good sign showing that she had no permanent frost damage but the pain was excruciating. She noticed Stefan's beloved Walkman still left on the ledge over the bed where their lovemaking had been so cruelly interrupted. In spite of the pain in her feet, she leapt up and quickly hid the little box under her mattress.

She covered herself with blankets and lay back and listened. Not a sound. She thought over the events of the last twenty-four hours. Above all there was Stefan. At first she rejoiced that he had escaped and comforted herself with warm thoughts of a reunion when she could return his precious Walkman. Then she cursed herself for being juvenile and stupid. Stefan was alone with few or no clothes in the Baltic snow being chased by a vicious and ruthless mob. He probably would not get far and, gloomily, the best that she could hope for was that he would not be recaptured but would have a quick and painless death. The alternatives did not bear thinking about. Then there was her own situation. The NAS sergeant had hinted that she would be interviewed and questioned. They obviously thought that somehow, perhaps from the two boys, she might have obtained important information. She realised that she might be savagely interrogated and knew that if that happened it would be at the Winterburg. It did not need a vivid imagination to contemplate its horrors. Frau Ilse had several times threatened to have one or other of them sent down the road *zu einen Tracht Prügel bekommen* – for a good thrashing. Frau Ilse's bark was worse than her bite and Mara realised, with some distress, that she was probably at this moment facing the treatment that she had threatened. Nobody had been sent to be flogged but, after seeing Lukas, Mara had no illusions that such things did in fact go on now in the grim, ugly fortress. Gloomily, Mara wondered how much pain she could stand and whether she would cope with such treatment. She had been brought up in a gentle loving family and been to civilised, caring schools. She had never been punished, certainly not physically, by her carers. She knew that she must protect Stefan but she knew so little that her interrogators might think that she was lying. If that happened torture would follow. A series of lurid images flashed through her mind. She knew it might not only be the lash. Lukas had been tortured with electric shocks and then there were the thuggish guards. Were they controlled or were they allowed to rape at will?

With a shudder she decided that it might be better to know something. If she remained completely ignorant would she ever be believed? On an impulse she went to see Lukas. He had struggled back from the brink with her help. As she came in he was sitting up and smiled at her.

'What on earth is going on?' he said, talking clearly for almost the first time, 'I've heard all the shouting and noises but don't know what it all means.'

'They found Stefan and me together and thought we were part of a plot. They separated us and locked us both up. Stefan escaped from the cellar. God knows where he is. They think that I know something about it and say they will take me 'down the road' for interrogation. They won't believe that I know nothing.'

'Oh, my God! That is exactly what we tried to prevent. That bitch, it was her doing.'

'They've taken her too. Said she hadn't secured the place and that's why Stefan escaped.'

For a moment Lukas looked puzzled then urgently he said, 'No not Ilse, I don't mean her. I'm talking about the pseudo Dutch bitch Johanna. I think that she is a *Spitzel*, a stool pigeon, working for them. What's more she recognized me from the *bund*. I'm sure of it. She's probably denounced us all to her minder. They knew all that they could find out from me anyway. They stopped because I was unconscious and dying. I think they expected me to die, which is why they let me out. I probably would have died if it hadn't been for you. But you and Stefan were different. They bugged your room and thought that you might give something away – pillow talk you know. When she couldn't find anything, she told her minder and they decided to set you up and interrogate you both separately. She conveniently went away so they could set a trap to catch you and Stefan.'

'They nearly overdid it. How long can you live naked below freezing – at least it seemed so?'

'God, that was terrible and stupid as well. What was the point of doing all that if they had frozen you to death. They are like that. Sometimes their sheer sadism hinders them but if you are brutal enough you usually find what you need eventually. Don't worry too much about Stefan. He has a chance. We talked about it but you must not know. To protect you under interrogation – you understand.'

'But will it? If I say that I know nothing they simply won't believe me and torture me more.'

He thought for some minutes.

'Unfortunately you may be right,' he said at last. 'You had better say that you heard us say that there was a revolt near *Solandu* and *Solanova* but that we would not tell you anything else as we thought that you were a girl and too young.'

He suddenly smiled gently and Mara realised that he must have been, must be, a very attractive young man.

'I'm sorry to be sexist but it will play to their ghastly prejudices.'

'Don't worry. I can put up with a bit more sexism if it will help.'

The next days passed in ominous quiet. Johanna never returned. Mara thought that presumably she was employed spying on some other brave people. Frau Ilse was replaced by a vacuous woman with a flat country accent. She seldom spoke but managed the daily responsibility of the house. The guards stood as before, front and back of the house and, as before, looked as if they were dying of boredom. Everyday Mara expected the arrival of the black prison van to take her to the Winterburg for interrogation. Everyday she imagined different scenarios and tried to work out how she would react. Every time a car or van drew up, she looked terrified out of the window but a week went by and nothing happened. There was no news, good or bad, of Stefan but she didn't really expect it. She had just begun to think that they had really forgotten about her when, at ten one bright frosty morning, a large official car did arrive.

Mara waited trembling in her room. She heard voices on the stairs and then, unbelievably, a knock at her door. She was startled. Police taking suspects for interrogation do not knock at bedroom doors. After a pause she croaked, '*Herienkommen!*' and waited.

The door was opened by the nameless substitute Ilse, 'Kolonel Karkov, to see you Fräulein Oblova.'

Behind the woman was a smiling rubicund man, wearing, not the terrifying green of the NAS but a normal army colonel's uniform.

'*Guten Tag,* Fräulein Tamara, I have come to take you back to your school, back to the Sacred Heart. Please get your things together and then we will go.'

It took little enough time to pack the few things she had been able to obtain in the house. There was one thing she had to take. She slid Stefan's Walkman from under the mattress which was concealing it and then, concealing it from view again in front of her, she tucked it away at the bottom of the plastic carrier under her coarse pyjamas. Then, in a dream, she walked down the stairs, out of the door, down the front path past the guards who snapped to attention and into the chauffeur driven car.

4
THE WINTERBURG

At Pandemonium, the high Capital
Of Satan and his Peers: their summons call'd
From every Band and squared Regiment
By place or choice the worthiest;

MILTON: PARADISE LOST

He slivered along the snow. The rags tied round his feet gave him some grip. He was half convinced he was fortunate. The plan had been put together in a rush and it could so easily have gone wrong. The bar to open the locker had been easy to find. Even then there might have been nothing inside. The whole elaborate masquerade could have failed completely, but it was cold comfort and it was getting colder. A boiler suit is no protection against a Baltic winter. He wasn't sure where he was going. It was roughly the right direction but that wasn't enough. It had been convincing so far. He shuddered – a damn sight too convincing and it wasn't over yet. He turned a corner, instinctively avoiding a pile of dog muck staining the snow dark brown fading into streaks of yellow ochre right across the pavement. It must have thawed a bit recently, he noted subconsciously. It certainly wasn't thawing now. He looked down the mean street of towering, lowering apartments, twenty-six, twenty-eight, thirty, thirty-two. This must be it. The basement had a separate entrance. His hands were too cold to knock. He picked up a dust bin lid and thundered it against the peeling door. The noise was far too loud and he looked around guiltily but nobody stirred. To his huge relief he heard the bolts being drawn back. An old woman with folds of skin sagging from her emaciated face peered suspiciously through the gap between the door and the frame. The door was still secured by a rusty iron chain. The old woman showed recognition but no welcome,

'Stay where you are,' she snapped, then closed the door.

He heard the chain being slid back through its channel and then it was opened just wide enough.

'Well then, come in. Don't just stand there'

He pushed through the half-open door and found himself in a sort of kitchen. It wasn't exactly warm but compared with the outside it was heaven. He crept nearer the old iron stove.

'You took your time,' growled the old woman.

He suddenly felt angry.

'You expected me to bring this off with split second timing, I suppose.'

She scowled but didn't answer.

'Is there anything to eat?'

'There's some soup on the stove. Help yourself.'

He found a mug encrusted with food in the sink and a spoon amongst the filthy crocks. She made no attempt to help him as he washed the mug in the freezing water from the tap. He crossed to the stove, uncovered the caldron and dipped the mug into the amorphous, glutinous mass revealed inside. He caught a lump of what he hoped was potato and two thirds filled the mug. There was nothing to wipe the side on so he was compelled to lick it quickly to stop it dripping. He was reminded of the last time his father took him out before he was killed in a mining accident. They went to the beach and his father bought him a small cone from the ice cream stall. It was an unusually hot day and he had to lick all round the cone quickly to stop it dripping. This was the same.

'Got any bread?'

Reluctantly she went to a crock on a back shelf and pulled out a stump of black rye. She cut off a small lump and held it out to him.

'I don't get paid for feeding you, you know.'

'Never mind,' he said sarcastically, still feeling angry, 'the NAS will give you your pieces of silver to-morrow. It should be enough to pay for a loaf.'

'Don't take that tone with me. After all, you are the Judas here and anyway Travsky has abolished God.'

She went to the only cupboard and took out a pair of moth-eaten blankets and threw them across to him.

'Isn't there a bed?'

She cackled a mirthless laugh.

'Or at least a mattress?'

'I suppose that Sir expected the Hotel Bristol, well it isn't. Make do with what you've got, you miserable little grass. I'm going to bed.'

She went through a door and Stefan caught sight of an unmade bed before the door slammed and he heard the sound of it being bolted on the inside.

With a sigh he rolled himself in the blankets, got as close as he could to the stove and tried to sleep. He couldn't. He was dog tired but the old woman's last gibe about 'a miserable little grass' went round and round in his head. He should have been triumphant. It had been difficult and he had brought it off, but instead he was miserable and muddled. He almost envied the broken, tortured lad who he had left the day before. Stefan was sure that he had convinced Lukas that he, Stefan, was going to join the rebels. He was almost sure that, during the last long conversation that they had had, Lukas had told him everything he knew. Lukas was no more use to Travsky now. He would almost certainly be executed when he recovered but he would die a hero at peace with his soul and his conscience. Stefan had to live with himself and what is more he had to live with the image of a beautiful diminutive creature who loved him and who he had betrayed.

He realised as he tossed on the draughty stone floor that the worst part of all was that he had loved her too. Why was I born in this bloody country? He thought bitterly of his childhood. His mother, dying as she gave birth to his dead sister. He didn't remember it. He had only been a year old. All he had of her was a photograph of a pretty school girl. She was only twenty-one when she died – not much older than him. As a child he never knew what it was to be wanted, let alone loved.

At first he had been at home with his father and his grandmother, his father's mother, who he remembered only dimly but was gentle and kind. Then she suddenly got ill. He remembered her wasting to nothing and dying in hospital where he never had a chance to say goodbye to her. He was just five. His father knew that he could not work and look after his young son so he had sent him from the mining village near *Litovsk* to live with his father's aunt in Königshof. He remembered the silent train journey and his miserable farewell in the austere gloom of his great-aunt's front room – cold and dark on that winter's day. The grate was lifeless. Nobody had bothered to light a fire 'as they wouldn't be in there for long'. They weren't. His father had been bundled out with hardly time for a goodbye this time. Stefan had been miserable, friendless and lonely but that was not all. He was still wetting the bed. His grandmother had treated this kindly and sympathetically. Now it was different. His great aunt-flew into a rage on the first occasion calling him '*ein schmutzig Bengelein*'.[4] She pulled his wet pyjamas over his head covering his face but not before he had glimpsed his 'uncle' undoing his studded belt. It was the first beating of many. The bruises on his thighs and buttocks hardly had time to fade before he was 'taught another lesson'.

However, his screams and sobs must have been heard by some neighbour. One day there was a knock at the door and Stefan, from the top of the stairs, glimpsed a man and a woman standing in the porch showing a pass. Oddly, he heard them asking to see him; he couldn't understand it – nobody wanted to see him. He heard his great-aunt, lying, saying that he was out. Taking his courage in both hands, he had run noisily down the stairs to the door and, enquiringly, faced the two unknown visitors. His great-aunt, her lie exposed, spluttered helplessly. The two visitors had then announced that they wished to see Stefan

---

4   A filthy urchin

alone. A short time later, bruises revealed, he was being lead by the hand by the woman into the waiting car.

His new home was run by Holy Fathers of St Andrew's Monastery. He was no longer lonely, in fact, in one sense there were too many other boys around him. Aged ten, he was one of the youngest and was frightened by the older teenagers. He discovered from conversations that the home was part orphanage and part reformatory for teenagers convicted of crimes. There was no distinction between the two types of residents and the older boys, many of whom had pretty unsavoury records, rejoiced in terrifying the younger ones.

However, it was not all bad. His bed-wetting almost stopped and, when it did happen, the two matrons, who assisted the monks, quietly provided a plastic sheet and didn't make a fuss. Stefan realised that he was a nice looking boy and soon this gave rise, inevitably, to difficulties. The problem did not lie with the monks, who, whatever their inclinations, were well enough disciplined, but with the older boys. One night five figures dressed up in sheets and black rubber masks appeared, howling like wolves at the foot of his bed in the junior dormitory. Terrified and screaming for help they dragged him out of bed by his feet, across the rough splintered floor and onto the freezing tiles of the adjacent bathroom. There they gang raped him. The biggest thug, whose mask was embellished with artificial but realistic bloodstained fangs, threatened to slit his throat if he said a word. He provided him with a black rubbish bag to lie on so the bleeding wouldn't show then left him sobbing, terrified and in agony. His tormentor said ominously, he would be back. He was. This time he took the bloody rubbish bag. He left Stefan with a plastic carrier full of shredded newspaper and instructed him to put it in his pants in the morning to hide any bleeding 'or else'.

The other youngsters in the junior dormitory knew exactly what was going on, in fact many of them had had the same treatment, but they were only too glad that it wasn't their turn and, burying their heads under the blankets, kept quiet.

The following morning Stefan was teased by the other juniors with 'what a pretty girl!' and similar knowing taunts. He hated his body and wanted so much to die. The worst part, though, was the awful fear at lights out each night. After the horror of the first weeks, a very senior boy, not one of the worst, approached Stefan and offered him protection in exchange for his favours. Stefan had no alternative but to agree and from then on the others left him in peace. Kurt was relatively gentle with him and unpleasant as it was, it was a huge improvement on the brutal gang rape. The worst part was being known to the other juniors as 'Kurt's tart'.

For more than three years he suffered. He was treated like dirt and thought that he was dirt. Then suddenly it all changed. One morning in April, the Father Superior announced, disapprovingly, that there was to be a talk by a visitor about a new movement. Stefan was old enough now to know from the TV and radio that there was political unrest in Moltravia. The government of the Democrat Party under Hoffman had been cobbled together after the fall of communism. It had never been strong and had failed to deliver the unreal prosperity expected by the people. It was now coming under increasing pressure from the right wing National Party of Anton Travsky who promised work, discipline and punishment for 'the criminals who had brought the country to its knees'. The NP was not yet in government and was opposed by liberal elements in the country appalled at its fascist neo-Nazi approach. Nonetheless it was too important to be ignored and growing more powerful every day. Attached to the NP was a paramilitary branch, the NAS (*National Agentur Sicherheit*), a title which claimed a spurious official status. The NAS also ran a youth branch entitled the *National Kommando*. The NK was vigorously recruiting and considered the Königshof orphanages fertile ground. That morning, the visitor appeared in front of the boys, splendid in his immaculate green NAS uniform. He was all smiles and jokes. He talked to the boys as adults. They were captivated and none more so than Stefan who felt, with a surge of pride, that for the first time in his life, he was being treated with respect as a fellow human being. He volunteered.

A large number of other orphanage boys joined the NK and a sizeable group attended the parade meetings twice a week. The organisers went out of their way to make the whole thing fun. There was little obvious indoctrination and, as summer came on, plenty of field days, barbecues and trips out. Stefan was captivated. He worked hard at learning the NK manual and attended every possible activity. Several of the others were quite keen but nobody else showed his intense commitment. This was noticed and he was made Group Senior and then Unit Leader. Nobody now teased him or bullied him. He was top dog, worthy of respect and even a little fear. He had status and he loved it.

He arrived for the parade one evening in late summer and on entering the section hut as usual by the boys' back door, he found a different atmosphere. There was a feeling of bustle and anticipation. He knew the local captain well, by this time, almost as a friend, 'What is going on?'

'Great things, Stefan, and you will have your part to play. I have been told to send you to Central Office to see Oberst Ziehert in person. Of course, you know who he is?'

Stefan did know. Ziehert was deputy head of The NAS and a personal friend of Travsky. He was effectively head of operations of the NAS and had a terrifying nationwide reputation.

'There is a personal car waiting for you outside.'

The captain ushered him to the front door, normally reserved for officers and VIPs. There was the car, black and polished. The driver, in smart green NAS uniform, snapped to attention and saluted. It was, of course, the normal thing to do when an officer appeared, but Stefan had the strange feeling that the salute, which both he and the captain returned, had been addressed to him.

Sitting in state in the back on the leather seats of the car, he had a sense of unreality but also huge enjoyment. The car drove from the suburbs into the centre of Königshof. He was silent, listening and wondering. The Central Office of the NAS filled the second and third floor of an anonymous office building several blocks behind the towering mass of the Winterburg Fortress which dominated one of the two main squares of the city. The car stopped outside the glass swing doors: the driver had jumped out and opened the door for Stefan.

At reception the driver spoke conspiratorially to the girl in NAS uniform, 'Herr Moser for Herr Oberst Ziehert. He is expecting him.'

Stefan's jaw dropped. He had never been referred to as 'Herr' before.

He felt in a different world as he entered the lift. His driver, still escorting him, knocked discretely. Stefan felt his heart pounding. There was a loud, fierce *'Herein!'* from within.

Ziehert was scowling over some papers on his desk. He looked up and the scowl dissolved as he stood up.

The driver saluted. 'Herr Moser, Herr Oberst.'

'Welcome. Glad to see you. I've heard a lot of good things about you.' Then to the driver curtly, 'You can go.'

'Sit down, Stefan, I may call you Stefan, *darf ich?*'

Stefan blushed. 'Natürlich, Herr Oberst,' he stammered.

'You need to know several important things. Soon, very soon indeed, we are going to move. Nothing can save the dreadful apology for a government which we have got to eliminate, together with many of its members. We will restore this country to its proper size and greatness. With discipline and firm measures it will happen but we still have opponents and we must prevent them from harming our great enterprise. Tomorrow the city will be in turmoil as we act but the resistance will not last long. The traitors will get what is coming to them. You understand that?'

Stefan had nodded wondering what was coming next.

'But we have need of you for a very special role. There will be a number of young people – spawn of the communist trash who have been wrecking the country. They are not themselves very important but they have lived in houses and amongst groups of people where treachery is rife. We are going to set aside a house for some of the most important of these as we get hold of them. You will be introduced into the house as a fellow traitor. You will be given a full and convincing cover story. You must then report anything of importance to us. You will be given the equipment – it's safe but very simple. When we have stabilised the country, you will be extracted from the house without busting your cover. The Party will reward you. Do you think that you can do this?'

He had no doubts.

'I will be honoured to serve, Herr Oberst.'

'Good, I knew that you would not let us down. This is your commission as a Leutnant NAS. Now I have arranged for you to be briefed by my staff. The only piece of equipment that you need is a Walkman.'

Stefan looked puzzled. Ziehert smiled.

'Not an ordinary Walkman – at least it is but it's more than that. They will explain everything. Just one more thing, we don't know at present who most of your housemates will be, but there is one who will certainly be there, she will be known to you as Johanna or Johanna Adriana. She is an extremely skilled and trained South African agent but says she is Dutch. She was sentenced to death for subversion under the apartheid regime for sedition. She is a member of the Party and was living with a senior colleague of ours and officially works for us but we have discovered a bit of her hidden history. We think that she was planted or turned by our enemies abroad, possibly in Germany or the Netherlands, to act for them as a double agent in the event of our revolution being successful. We will allow her a certain amount of rope, before we put it round her neck, (He laughed) but watch her carefully. She is skilled and dangerous if misguided.'

He stood up and shook Stefan by the hand, 'Good Luck! The next time we meet my office will be in the Winterburg.'

*

She was kicking him with the toe of her boot on the back of his legs. 'Get up you idle oaf. They've come for you.'

Realising that after his long night tossing and turning he must have fallen into a deep sleep, he blearily shook himself awake and shivered with the cold. He groped for his boiler suit and pulled it on; he had nothing else to put on. He felt in the pocket for the Walkman/transmitter and realised it wasn't there. He then realised that he had been naked when taken to the cellar. He must have left it in Mara's room. Well, he supposed it was safe enough as the security code which opened the micro technology and converted it from an ordinary Walkman to transmitter receiver was well hidden; anyway, he could hardly get it back now. Running his hand through his hair he staggered to the front door. It was cold inside but nothing to the blast of icy wind that greeted him on the doorstep. The van had *Koch Sohne Installateurarbeit* on the side. The driver in a white boiler suit handed Stefan a bag of tools and told him to put them in the back. Stefan assumed this was part of the cover and played his part as a plumber's mate. They drove to a large suburban house hidden behind a line of pines, presumably there was no further need for secrecy as there was a guard in uniform on the gate who waved them through. The driver preceded Stefan up the wide white steps.

'I have brought *Leutnant Moser* for you.'

The girl on the desk in green NAS uniform with a Lieutenant's single star said pleasantly but brusquely, 'Ah yes, Herr Leutnant, we are expecting you.'

She rang a bell. A young man in fatigues appeared.

'Take *Herr Leutnant Moser* to the guest room. It is all prepared for you. Breakfast will be sent up and your uniform has been laid out. We had to guess the size but your Kommando Hauptmann was very helpful and now I see you I think that we got it about right.'

Stefan nodded and smiled but there was no answering smile. Flirting was clearly not part of the job description of female NAS officers.

'You have plenty of time to relax then at twelve-thirty a car will come for you to take you to the Winterburg for lunch with Oberst Ziehert. If you need anything else just ring.'

The young man deferentially led Stefan up to the first floor. There was no lift; only a wide semi-circular staircase which once no doubt had been very elegant. His escort opened a door and indicated the massive bedroom with adjoining bathroom. A uniform was laid out on the bed. For an instant Stefan thought that he had been shown to the wrong room but then he realised that the uniform with its single star was for him.

'I'll bring your breakfast at once, Sir. Would you like tea or coffee?'

'Tea, please.'

Stefan was ravenous and made short work of ham, cheese and fresh rolls. He then ran a deep bath and scrubbed the accumulated grim off. It should have been bliss but somehow he was troubled. He had not been happy in his undercover role ever since he had met Mara. She had told him nothing significant and to his great relief, he had not actually betrayed her. Nonetheless, she would have been horrified to know that he had reported consistently on all the other residents and was even now going to a debriefing which would seal their death sentences.

He dried himself in the unaccustomed warmth of the central heating and started to dress in his uniform. A month or so ago this would have been the proudest moment of his life. He was an officer in the NAS which had been his ambition ever since he had joined the *Kommando* but the pride and glamour had gone. Not even the ribbon of the so-called *Einlösungrevolution* thoughtfully, though prematurely, sewn on his jacket could abolish the image of a small pale face looking up at him, in his imagination, with hate and reproach in her eyes. He sighed, adjusted his tie, combed his hair and put on the beautifully-fitting jacket and cap and went downstairs.

The town was still strangely, eerily quiet. They swung into the massive security gates of the Winterburg pausing only to allow the NAS guard to look at the driver's pass. The great courtyard was surrounded by half-finished extensions in concrete to the old buildings. Here at least there was some activity; cranes carried blocks into place and concrete mixers rumbled. Round the edges of the new buildings, snow, grey and soiled, was piled in irregular lumps. None of this held Stefano's attention; his gaze was fixed on a platform in the middle of the square. About three metres above the platform was a long railing, over the railing dangled six ropes and on the end of the ropes were six bodies, their sex indeterminate, hung with their heads lolling and their faces purple. Most disturbing of all was the body at the end of the line which was clearly a child's – no more than ten or eleven years old.

Restraining his urge to vomit, Stefan got out of the car and just managed in time to return the salute of the sentry. The office was much larger than before but still plain. Oberst Ziehert was apparently, rather incongruously, watching television. He saw Stefan's surprised expression.

He got up and shook hands smiling at Stefan. Then he indicated the TV screen.

'This is a DVD about the *Chef*'s new policy for cleaning up the population. The government have taken over an old mental hospital. There will be a new centre in the grounds where well-bred girls from loyal families will volunteer to have the first generation of elite Moltravians, who will be totally educated in and committed to the cause. They will be mated with good quality soldiers. Because they don't need to know about the father of their child, they are blindfolded during "the introduction" so they cannot recognise, or be recognised by their partners later. It all seems rather complicated and some of us would prefer artificial insemination but the medicos say there are technical problems. After the baby is born, it will be taken away and reared and educated by the state in the proper manner.'

Stefan's jaw dropped.

'That's the happy side,' he went on, 'now for the more serious bit.'

What was happy about being blindfolded and 'volunteering' to be raped by an anonymous soldier? Stefan thought. What has this to do with the love that he had felt for his *Tamarushka*?

'There is a more serious bit. We want to rid the state of damaged blood lines. A second part of the new clinic will be devoted to cleaning up Moltravia. Physical, mental and moral defectives will be taken there and sterilised so that they cannot breed more of their kind. Traitors and grave offenders are of course executed like those that you saw coming in. But there are others as well as the defectives that the president has indicated are unfit for parentage. The men and boys will be castrated and the women and girls spayed.'

Stefan tied to hide his horror. He hoped he had misunderstood. He had only heard these terms applied to animals. Surely nobody could authorise this treatment of humans because they were handicapped or because of what they thought or said? Ziehert hadn't finished.

'No problem with the males –a simple elastic ligature does the job. The females are more complicated and at present will have their ovaries removed to give students practice. It's a bit clumsy; later there may be a more efficient method.'

He turned, smiling, to face the ashen Stefan.

'You look tired,' he said, 'understandable, I suppose, undercover jobs are never easy. You have done well but just fill in a few details for me.'

He asked some questions about enemy leaders and placements then said, with evident satisfaction, 'We have reduced the opposition in the south east to a few pockets of resistance and they won't last long. I think that we have got all that we are going to out of your fellow residents. We might get the boy back and have the double agent girl in here to squeeze the pips a bit harder to see if there is any more juice but I suspect we won't get much more. After that they will take part in the decoration of the courtyard here like that lot.'

He jerked his thumb towards the window overlooking the corpses hanging in the *Hof*.

'We change them every two days – a bit like fresh flowers on the altar. The newcomers pass them as they are brought in – it helps to soften them up before they are interrogated. We have a good supply of replacements. At the last count there were two hundred here waiting execution and plenty more outside. Let's have lunch.'

There was hardly a pause between the discussion of torture and execution and the suggestion of food. Oberst Ziehert led Stefan down to the mess. Fortunately, it was a cold table and Stefan managed to push food round his plate muttering that he had only just had breakfast. After some more discussion of the success of the revolution and plans for stabilising the country, Oberst Ziehert changed the subject:

'I am concerned about your future,' he said. 'I think that you've done enough undercover work – it's a great strain.'

There was apparent concern in his voice.

'I would like you to go to the south east and be second in command to Hauptmann Zhukov who is in charge of mopping up and civilian control. Take some leave first; you probably need a few days. But not in Königshof, I'd rather you weren't seen here at least for the time being. Have you family in the country?'

'I have no family at all, Sir, and I think that I would rather get on with the job.'

After his experiences of the last few hours, the last thing that he wanted was time to think about his life and the ghastliness around him.

'Very well, as you wish. You are entitled to a car to take you the whole way but we are short today and it may not be possible. Anyway, I will arrange a car to take you to the station. Collect a travel warrant on your way out from the office. Do you have any other questions?'

Stefan hesitated, just long enough to show his concern, 'What

51

about the other girl at the house, Sir?' He tried, unsuccessfully to sound nonchalant.

For the first time, Ziehert smiled:

'Ah, your *inamorata, die junge Oblova,* a very pretty child – I suppose that she couldn't help her parents. Was she a good lay?'

Stefan was in a trice of punching him but just controlled himself and said nothing.

'A piece of advice, Stefan, always beware of sleeping with the enemy. However, your intelligence that she had no contacts or knowledge of any value, although I suspect not entirely unbiased, accords with what we know from other sources. For the moment at least, she will be returned to her convent school unharmed. Her father is still here under house arrest and we need him to help with some tricky international matters. He may be more prepared to give us a hand if we mention that the comfort and well-being of his daughter may depend on it.'

That was all. He shook hands with Ziehert and wondered what he was doing. He went down to the transport office by the front gate. The *Wachmeister* in charge looked unimpressed by his uniform and saluted casually.

'I can give you a car back to your lodgings and then to the station but we are short and I can't spare a car to go down to *Solanova.* You'll have to go by train and it's only one class.'

Stefan felt angry. He was entitled to a car and it hadn't been a particularly diplomatic refusal. On the other hand, the anonymity of a train would give him some much needed calm and a chance to collect his thoughts. Reluctantly he muttered.

'OK.'

The same driver collected him and whisked him back past the dangling corpses and through the steel gates. There was no change in the dreary aspect of Königshof, as he drove back to the plush suburban house. He exchanged salutes with the female lieutenant on the desk. He asked the driver to come back tomorrow at 7am, and brushed aside his offers of help. There was raucous noise from a room at the back of the mansion which he imagined was a bar. Not pausing, he went straight up to his room and, although it was only just after 6pm, he miserably

52

went to bed. He didn't sleep in spite of his numbing tiredness. The things that he had seen and heard that day churned over in his head. He knew he could not go on as he was. He could not join in the torture and execution of people who only wanted peace and a decent life. Over it all was the image of Mara, angry and reproachful, calling him a treacherous coward. Mara, who he loved and whom he believed loved him, but who he knew would never, could never, forgive him. Briefly, he had had the most precious thing in his life, the only precious thing in his fearful life. But it had been based on a lie, his lie. He lay there for hours then sometime after the *Hof* clock struck five, he went to sleep. He was wakened, startled and sweaty by the night porter giving him his early call. It was still pitch dark. He shaved and showered quickly, put on his uniform, collected his bags and returned to the front hall to await the car.

'The *Hauptbahnhof*,' he said tersely to the saluting driver.

5
FIGHTING FOR FREEDOM?

Humanitarian liberals, deeply outraged by cruelty, injustice and
inefficiency, discover that the only sound method of preventing these
evils…but (is) by eliminating the motives for the pursuit of these
perilous ends.

ISAIAH BERLIN: POLITICAL IDEAS IN THE 20TH CENTURY

As the train crept stutteringly, through the flat grey, late winter
countryside of lifeless fields, punctuated by pine woods, he felt hopeless.
He wondered if it might have been better to have insisted on having
a car down to *Solanova* and the insurgent enclave. He turned over his
predicament. The joy and pride that he had felt in the NAS had turned to
a bitter loathing. But he was a serving officer. To desert was unthinkable
and anyway, where would he desert to? No, he would have to go
through with it. He looked out gloomily at the sparse, impoverished
villages. These people's highest aspiration was a life that much of the
western world took for granted, instead they were being starved and
worse, enslaved and tortured and for what? For the greed and power

lust of an unscrupulous few. He had had enough contact with the older generation to know that they had been humiliated and suffered under communism, but what had they got in exchange? The Winterburg with its interrogation chambers and gallows.

The train began to stop at primitive country platforms. The snow was still there at first but became thinner and gradually completely disappeared except for dirty piles by the roadside. Stefan didn't belief that spring would ever come to that benighted landscape. Occasionally a country woman would get on to the train with a sack or a basket. He wondered where they were going. Once he spotted a large country house by a lake in the distance. He asked the young woman, sitting opposite him where it was.

'Schloss Krenek,' came the reply. 'It used to belong to a count, then the party had it under the Reds. The good God knows what will happen to it next.'

She smiled. She could have been pretty if she had not looked so tired and worn.

'Is life very difficult for you?' Stefan asked.

The girl looked frightened and glanced down at his uniform before answering. Then she said, 'Oh no! Everything is much better since the revolution.'

The lie was obvious. She had signalled her terror. One word of criticism of the regime or the state of the country to a NAS man and it might mean a bullet – if you were lucky. If you weren't so lucky who knew... Stefan understood. He was beginning to appreciate a lot about the new Moltravia but he didn't like what he was learning. He left her alone realising her fear and feeling helpless that he could do nothing to comfort her. He had noticed the rosary hung round her waist. At least she wasn't too frightened still to wear that, even though Travsky had abolished God. Stefan, though a lifelong atheist, hoped that she might get some comfort from it.

Outside the junction town of Zoritz, where the line went off for Litovsk and Russia, following the upper reaches of the Fojn river, they stopped at a signal. Stefan's coach was stopped right over the river. He looked down from the bridge. The water, dark as pitch but much more lively, heaved in quick cream capped ripples flowing restlessly on to the Oder and the Baltic.

What is it all about? he said to himself hopelessly. He wanted to dive into that river, wash everything away and start again.

At last they drew into *Solanova*. There was a car waiting and the driver saluted.

'The *Hauptmann* is expecting you, Herr Leutnant,' he said holding the door open. The drive was short and bumpy. *Solanova* seemed like a ghost town. It had been a medium sized market town, active as a centre for the surrounding agriculture and forestry. Now it was still and eerie. Not a soul moved between the buildings. Some were gradually falling into disrepair because of normal dilapidation but some had obviously been damaged in the recent fighting.

The headquarters was a farmhouse on the outskirts of town. What had once been the farmyard was full of jeeps and lorries. All had the black and red Moltravian flag on their sides with NATIONAL AGENTUR SICHERHEIT underneath in black capitals. Hauptmann Zukov was in his office. Stefan noticed an empty schnapps glass on the desk. Zukov was large rubicund and overflowing with bonhomie. A few weeks ago, Stefan thought to himself, he would have found this attractive, even endearing, but now he was suspicious.

'Job's nearly done. Only a bit of tidying up left. You've arrived at the right time. We will have a bit of a party when we shoot the last bastard. Second thoughts – we might hang the last few – makes more of a show and the Chief likes hanging the stupid pricks who thought that they could best him.'

There was a knock at the door.

'*Herein!* Ah, this is Wachmeister Murch,' Zukov introduced them. 'I am going to put you in command of his patrol and he can show you the ropes.'

Murch was almost a double of his CO. He was tall but paunchy with small sunken eyes and a habit of darting glances around as if to see if he was being spied upon. He obviously had a good understanding with his CO but Stefan didn't find this reassuring. From the first he was pretty sure that both men had been told to keep a careful eye on Stefan. He guessed that vodka played a big part in both their lives. He was soon to confirm this. He was dog tired but had to survive a beer and vodka drinking session before he was allowed to go to bed.

In the morning Stefan woke with a parched throat and thumping headache to hear Murch loudly mustering the patrol in the farmyard. He got up and walked to the window. Below the troops fell out then started to spread straw up against the fence separating the yard from the road. Stefan wondered idly what they were doing but dismissed it from his mind and went down to have breakfast. Zukov, the only other officer, was not yet down so he breakfasted alone. He turned on the TV in the mess and was greeted by a smiling Travsky, apparently interrupted in weeding his garden. It appeared that, even in late winter Travsky's garden was immune from the snow that covered the rest of Königshof and the north. The president was benign and smiling and told the invisible audience that they 'must all fight for the freedom that they now enjoyed'. Stefan stood gloomily looking at the screen as *Travsky's* picture was faded out to the sound of tawdry brass band music. So that was what they were supposed to be doing in *Solanova*, fighting for freedom. Somehow the freedom seemed a bit illusory.

He had nearly finished breakfast when Murch appeared, entering uninvited after a perfunctory knock, '*Morgen, Herr Leutnant!*'

Stefan noted that obviously informality reigned here. He didn't much mind that; it was the rest which disturbed him.

'We have two jobs scheduled for today. First there's an execution.'

His matter of fact manner suggested that this was routine like opening orders or morning parade.

'Then we need to go out on patrol. There's not much left but one woodland area still has bandits in it. We are not sure how many.'

Suddenly breakfast seemed less inviting to Stefan. He made himself finish his coffee then dragged himself out into the feeble morning sunshine in the farmyard. He was just in time to see five young men who had been captured the day before brought out from the locked cellar. There had obviously been no trial, not even a sham drumhead one. Blinking in the sunlight they all seemed younger than him. One was weeping openly: the others were ashen automatons. The men from the platoon bound each man by the hands and ankles to the fence. There were no blindfolds.

The firing squad, for that was only too obviously what it was, finished tying the prisoners to the fence and returned to their barn. After a minute or two the squad reappeared out of the barrack hut, this time carrying sub-machine guns.

Murch came over to face Stefan.

'You give the order to fire, Herr Leutnant, and then you take your pistol and shoot each one in the back of the neck as the *coup de grâce*. Waste of bullets really, they can't still be alive after a good peppering from an HK53, but that's the rule so we must follow it.'

He laughed. The firing squad took up their positions and stood waiting.

Murch ordered, *'Vorbereiten!'*. They raised their weapons.

'Go on, Herr Leutnant!'

Stefan choked. Nothing came from his throat. There was a pause that seemed like hours.

Suddenly Murch shouted,

'Schiessen!', The guns cracked and the prisoners slumped spurting blood onto the straw. Horrified, Stefan realised the purpose of the straw; it was to stop the blood contaminating the mud of the farmyard. Murch, without asking, drew Stefan's pistol out of its holster, walked over to the prisoners and shot each in the back of the neck.

'Had a sudden choking fit then, Herr Leutnant?' Murch asked sarcastically as he returned the pistol. Stefan, frozen mentally and physically, said nothing. Murch turned to his junior NCO, 'Take the bodies to the pit then hose the truck down.'

Then to Stefan, 'We'll have coffee.'

It was more like an order than a suggestion or an invitation.

Murch went into the mess as if he owned it and poured two cups of coffee from the pot on the heater. Stefan played with his coffee, fighting nausea. Murch gulped his noisily. There was a long silence broken only by the noise of the returning truck.

'That really wasn't very good, was it, Herr Leutnant?' Murch said at last, with heavy sarcasm.

'Never mind I got you out of trouble and perhaps you will remember that you owe me a favour. Let's go.'

There was no doubt who was now the boss and Stefan recognised it. He felt powerless and hopeless.

They set off in a jeep with a truck with the rest of the patrol behind. Murch seemed equally at home with a revolver or the vodka bottle, which he pulled out from under the bench. He took a long swig and passed it to Stefan who shook his head.

'Perhaps you should – a bit of bottled courage, you know,' sneered Murch.

They drove along a lane past one of the few farms that still seemed to be working. By the farm gate there was a tabby cat washing itself on a high wall. Without a word Murch pulled out his revolver and shot the cat. It had for a moment a look of pained surprise on its face until it rolled off the wall – dead. Murch burst out laughing. Stefan, who loved animals and had found them more reliable than humans during his difficult life, was appalled.

'What did you do that for?' he croaked, overcome by fury and pain

'Oh, fun and target practice,' Murch shrugged.

At that moment Stefan made up his mind what he had to do but he didn't know how it could be done.

They stopped at the edge of a wood where a number of NAS trucks were parked. A *Wachtmeister* from another unit came up and saluted. He explained the situation. A group of rebels were surrounded on a knoll in the middle of the wood. Apparently they had dug themselves in thoroughly and fought very fiercely. The NAS hadn't been able to reduce the position and now it had been surrounded for several days. Stefan's unit now had the task of taking over and finishing the job.

They donned body armour and with Murch and the patrol in tow, set out to make a tour of the emplacements round the wood where the other unit had erected primitive trenches and earthworks. This was a bit more like real soldiering and Stefan at last felt more in charge. The firing squad incident seemed, at least temporarily, off the agenda. Their minds were concentrated even more when a high velocity bullet whistled between them. Clearly the rebels might be encircled but they could still fight.

'Must be getting short of ammunition by now,' muttered Murch. He was rapidly given the lie by another whining bullet. Stefan consulted with Murch the correct dispositions of the relieving troops. When they were reasonably satisfied that their force was safe and adequately placed to maintain the containment, he left *Murch* in charge and returned towards their makeshift headquarters.

The headquarters was another abandoned farmhouse. The troops messed in a barn, when out of the line. Zukov and Stefan occupied the first floor of the house itself with the NCOs quarters and the officers' mess, such as it was, on the ground floor. Stefan had been allotted the bedroom hastily abandoned by the last NAS lieutenant. He had not had time to unload from the car the night before. He now fetched the rest of his kit and dumped it on the floor. He then tried to clear up some of the mess left by his predecessor. He collected a load of empty bottles and abandoned food tins and took them down to the rubbish bin. It was full to overflowing and two huge black rats scuttled out of the bin as soon as he opened the lid. They looked very well fed but hadn't done much to reduce the volume of the rubbish.

The next few days passed in an expectant calm. Stefan took two men and went on a reconnaissance trip back to the line and into the wood. They had crawled a good way towards the centre when Stefan pushed a bush to one side. Not twenty metres in front of him was a very large World War II pillbox. From a slit came a burst of machine gun fire, they threw themselves to the ground and crawled back rapidly. The burst was very short and miraculously no one was hurt. Apparently through sloth or more likely cowardice, none of the NAS had previously got near enough to the centre of the wood to discover the pillbox. Stefan was quietly pleased as, at a stroke he had discovered the reason for the strength of the rebel position. He had restored his reputation with the men who recognised that he might be appalled by executions but that he was no coward. Even Murch treated him with a bit more respect.

They were, however, no nearer the objective of capturing the enemy position. Stefan was inclined to agree with Murch that after so much fighting the insurgents must be short of ammunition. For the next couple of days they used decoys of various sorts to draw the insurgents' fire. Stefan noted that although there were rifle shots, at no time was there any fire from the machine gun. This seemed to confirm their hypothesis. The rifle fire was more and more sporadic. They had been in position for a week and Stefan thought that it was time to act. He announced to Murch that he was going to lead an assault on the pillbox at first light the following day. He called the troops together and asked for volunteers, explaining that the rest of the unit would be required to make a diversion on the far side of the copse. To his surprise, three quarters of the men volunteered, which were more than he needed. He was almost sure that this was a tribute to his example. For the first time in months his self-esteem had moved off rock bottom.

It was a clear very cold night. They took up their positions silently, helped by a pale moon which appeared for the first time since they had been deployed. Stefan told the men this was a good omen. Privately he thought he was talking rubbish. Murch, grumbling, was in charge of the diversion. Stefan was delighted to be rid of him at this critical moment. He appointed a young corporal, not the brightest of men, but seemingly reliable, as his second in command on the main assault. He instructed him to take over if he, Stefan, was killed or unable to continue.

The diversion started noisily like clockwork. Murch might be an arrogant sadist but at a certain level he was competent. Stefan moved quietly forward at the head of his column. They got to the clearing that they had reached on reconnaissance. He was then taken completely by surprise. Before a shot had been fired a column of ragged figures, about twenty in all, emerged from the pillbox carrying a white sheet attached to a roughly hewn branch of a tree. Stefan stood up, realising that it might be a ruse and his last moment. He didn't care. It would be a good way to go and solve his dilemma.

A man in his early twenties appeared to be the insurgent's leader.

'We wish to surrender. We are out of ammunition. I suppose that you will shoot us.'

'I accept your surrender,' shouted back Stefan, 'and although I can make no promises, I will try my best to see that you are treated humanely as prisoners of war with full rights under the Geneva Convention.'

The young man laughed sardonically.

'What – humanity from the NAS? If you really believe that, what are you doing wearing that uniform?'

Stefan didn't reply but the question hit home and he himself wondered, not for the first time, what he was doing wearing that uniform.

Leaving the prisoners under guard, Stefan took two men and crouched through the narrow tunnel into the pillbox, the stench of old, damp concrete mixed with unwashed humanity rushed at them in the gloom. They collected a couple of dozen old rifles and two obsolete machine pistols. The only sign of ammunition was spent cartridge cases littering the floor. The few pathetic filthy pieces of clothing and the occasional sadder personal item, they left. Stefan muttered, 'They were brave,' – not caring who heard him.

They staggered out into the chilly but unaccustomed sunshine. It was still bitterly cold but it was the first day since Stefan had arrived at *Solanova* that they had had even a hint of spring. Murch was standing in front of the prisoners smiling broadly.

'*Erstklassig*, Herr Leutnant, well done, Mein Herr! I have phoned the *Hauptmann* and he's coming straight down to arrange things.'

Stefan, at first amused by Murch's effusive congratulations, noticed the vague 'coming down to arrange things' which sounded very ominous. Stefan had given a promise to these prisoners and he was going to do his damnedest to see it was kept although, in truth, he wasn't very hopeful. He said nothing to Murch – better to keep his powder dry until his senior officer arrived.

'I will load the prisoners into a truck while we're waiting.'

Stefan nodded and turned back to look at the still frosty woodland. The sun was not warm enough to melt the frost but it flicked brightly sparkling on the needles. There was still snow in the shaded patches. It could have been beautiful under different circumstances. Stefan had a fantasy of the white snow sprinkled with the blood he had seen spurting, beyond the straw, from young bodies a few days before.

They got the prisoners back to the HQ at *Solanova* in time for the evening meal and more important for Murch and Zukov, the evening drinking session. With a large vodka in front of him, Zukov pulled out his mobile and phoned Colonel Ziehert to give him the good news. The conversation was quite short and mainly consisted of Zukov giving the details of the days' events. He was full of praise for Stefan but speaking on the phone with him present, Stefan was realistic enough to know it meant nothing. In truth he was past the point where Zukov, Ziehert or even Travsky's good opinion of him meant anything. His only remaining concern was to find a solution. He knew what he must do, but how?

When he came off the telephone, Zukov, with the vodka coursing through him, was even more cheerful.

'He's delighted. He said it was particularly good that it was all done so neatly. He's going to phone the *Chef* and will send a team of interrogators down here to get what they can out of the prisoners. You know the sort of thing, collaborators, parents, siblings, wives and girl friends – that sort of thing. The law holds them responsible for the actions of their kin – old established principle *Sippenhaft*, it's called – everybody does it. Amazing what a few well placed shocks will turn up. The *Chef* is particularly keen that relatives of terrorists are properly controlled. It is important to keep subversive elements out of the new Moltravia and he has some interesting methods in place to do it.'

Stefan knew nothing about this horrible legal concept. Zukov might well be right that it was widespread but it smelled of Nazi law. How was it possible to justify the punishment of the ignorant and the innocent? Protest at this moment would be pointless.

Zukov laughed uproariously at what he saw as his own joke and toasted their success, tipping back another tumbler of vodka. Stefan felt that he had now been horrified to the point of numbness. He had found that the only way to deal with these evenings was to insist that he stuck to beer. He raised his glass mechanically, silently asking the good God, faithlessly, to open up the earth and swallow this dreadful tribe of which he was horrifyingly a part.

'We have really tidied this up. These were the last lot of terrorists with any strength. There may be the odd straggler but otherwise the job is done.'

They had just started to eat when Zukov's phone went off again.

63

From his deferential attitude, it was clearly Ziehert ringing back. This time the talking was at the other end, Zukov just listened interjecting 'wonderful, of course, good idea,' from time to time.

When the call ended Zukov produced a broad smile.

'He's been onto the *Chef* who is very pleased and wants a bit of a splash made of this one as it's the last. They are to be hanged, not shot, and so it has maximum impact to teach the locals a lesson, he wants it done in the *Rathausplatz* at *Solanova*. The interrogation teams will get the prisoners' nearest and dearest there to watch before they are taken elsewhere.'

Stefan was past shock and his brain was in overdrive. This latest horror might, just might, provide the answer that he was desperately seeking. He worked out many different plans trying to envisage every eventuality. At the end, he had to admit that he would be extremely lucky if any of his plans worked. He tried to think clearly and shut out the screams and groans of the prisoners who were taken one by one from their guarded barn to the old farm dairy which the specialist NAS team had deemed suitable for 'interrogation' which, he was under no illusion, in fact meant torture.

The executions were fixed for midday on the following Sunday. 'More people around then,' Zukov had remarked laconically. A party of prisoners had been taken into town on the Wednesday to erect their own scaffolds. To the great surprise of Murch and Zukov, Stefan had volunteered to be in charge of the guards of this gruesome party. Privately, he wanted to have a good look at the road into *Solanova*. An exact knowledge of the layout was vital to his plans.

On the trip into town he would have dearly liked to let at least one of the prisoners into his plan and get a second pair of hands to help carry it out. However, it was impossible. There were too many listening ears and always the possibility that a prisoner would try and buy his own life by betraying others. No, it had to remain his and his alone until the Sunday. Although Zukov and Murch were callous brutes, fortunately neither of them seemed highly intelligent and the vodka certainly helped to dull their wits. Not before time, the NAS interrogation squad left on the Friday afternoon. Zukov and Murch settled into a continuous drinking session and readily accepted Stefan's suggestion that he should arrange the transport for the executions. Citing a security risk from the local population, he chose three armoured trucks. The design of these separated the armoured drivers cab from the soldiers' space behind. Communication was only by means of an intercom. Normally the rear and side armoured doors could be opened from inside or out but as the trucks were also used to transport prisoners and civilian suspects, it was possible to disable the inside opening switches.

Stefan often went for a run in the morning, citing the necessity of clearing away the previous night's drink. Zukov and Murch protested that it was very dangerous to go out alone in this hostile zone. When he said he didn't go far and never saw anybody they shrugged, they would then say that it was his funeral and opened another bottle of vodka. Nobody on guard therefore thought it odd when Stefan appeared in running gear on the Sunday morning early. As he returned from a short run, he inspected the three waiting armoured trucks and quickly flicked the door indicators of the back two to 'external only'.

As they mustered to drive into *Solanova,* he held his breath in case somebody else should check the switches thoroughly and find the back truck was switched to external. One of the corporals casually looked at the indicator on the prisoner's truck and duly, and correctly, reported the reading as 'external' as he did so. He then asked Stefan if he should check the others although it didn't seem important.

'No, I've already done it,' replied Stefan as calmly as he could in confirmation.

'OK. Let's go.'

The forward escort truck had Stefan and a driver in front and half the guard escort in the back. The second truck had a driver, one armed soldier in front and the prisoners locked in the back. The third truck had the other half of the escort in the back with Murch driving and Zukov alongside in the passenger seat. This arrangement had been agreed in the mess the night before. After the huge quantity of vodka consumed, Zukov and Murch had forgotten the arrangements by the following morning. When Stefan reminded them, they defensively pretended that they remembered it all anyway. Stefan held his breath in case they tried to change anything at the last moment but, fortunately, everything went ahead as planned.

As they started off, Stefan casually drew his revolver and held it across his lap.

'Reasonable precaution – escorting dangerous prisoners,' he had murmured and the driver agreed.

He knew exactly where the critical bit must happen. There was one point where the road, after a long straight bit, bent sharply to the right where a little used minor road, almost a track, went off to the right again. Beyond the junction the ditch lining the road started again. Stefan had explored this road on his morning runs and knew that it had one priceless asset.

His heart thumping wildly, they approached the bend. As they reached the last part of the straight, Stefan shouted excitedly to the driver pointing, 'Look out. There are men in those trees, it's an ambush. Put your foot down!'

'*Jawohl*, Herr Leutnant!'

They speeded away. Stefan strained to look in the wing mirror. Sure enough there was a sizeable gap developing between them and the prisoners' truck with the second escort further behind.

'Slow down again now,' he ordered 'we must make sure the others are OK.'

The driver obeyed.

'I can't see them. Slow right down!'

At that moment Stefan hit the driver hard over the head with the butt of his revolver, pulled the wheel over so the truck slewed across the road. The cab finished up in the ditch. Rapidly Stefan opened his door and shot the right front tyre twice. It gave a satisfying hiss and collapsed. He opened the intercom to the back and said calmly.

'Sorry, men, burst tyre. We will transfer you to the other escort. I don't think it's an ambush but have your arms ready as you get out.'

He then telephoned the general call number and told the others his version of events. As he got down he noticed with satisfaction that their slewed truck had blocked the road just past the junction – perfect!

The prisoners' truck slowed and stopped with the third truck behind. Stefan went over to Zukov and Murch and said calmly, 'Bloody nuisance but I think that we can be pulled clear by Steinitz's truck without disturbing the prisoners. We mustn't lose any time or else the VIPs from Könighof will be getting anxious. I'll transfer my men to your truck and as soon as you both can get past, you can go on.'

They seemed happy enough for him to organise things. This was a mark of his increased status in the unit, he thought. Meanwhile the men from his truck were filing into the third vehicle.

He then quickly went to Steinitz, the driver of the second truck and explained the plan.

'Behind the cab in the front of the third truck there is a chest with a chain and hook recovery kit. I want you two to go and get that gear and then we can clear the road by pulling my truck out of the ditch in reverse. Look sharp, we are short of time.'

They quickly got down and went round behind the third truck and, following the last of the escort, climbed into the back to look for the (non-existent) recovery kit.

The moment had arrived. All the men except Murch and Zukov were in the third truck. Stefan quickly moved round and slammed the door. Escort securely locked away.

Murch had climbed down and followed Stefan round.

'What are you doing?' he asked, puzzled, as Stefan shot him. Stefan inspected him and for good measure shot him again. Zukov, hearing the shots, started to climb unsteadily down from the cab, his revolver waving in the air as Stefan shot him. He collapsed muttering, then was silent. Stefan hurried to the prisoners' truck and climbed into the cab and switched on the intercom.

'I am Leutenant Moser who took your surrender. I am sorry for what has happened to you since but there was nothing I could do then. Now, however, I am going to set you free. The guards are all locked away but we haven't got long. I want to talk to the tall patriot who I believe is your leader. Could he get down while the rest of you stay where you are because you are going to use the truck to escape?'

There was a rumble of surprise then assent. Stefan went round behind the truck and operated the door switch. Good as his word the tall man jumped down.

'Andreas Weber.'

'Stefan Moser.'

They shook hands.

'Look, Andreas, if you drive down this side track you get to the Ukrainian frontier in three kilometres. They are a funny lot but they have accepted your groups before so they will probably accept you. I would get everybody out of the truck before you actually try to cross. One more thing, can I come with you? I shall understand if you say no but after this I don't think I have future here. They will probably shoot me on sight in this uniform.'

'You can take it off in the truck,' said Andreas.

'Sure,' said Stefan, 'better alive in your long johns than dead in uniform.'

They both laughed. Then Andreas shouted, 'Look out!'

Stefan turned and the shot got him deep in the right chest. He collapsed coughing blood. Andreas knelt and seized Stefan's revolver from his hand. He shot Zukov twice rapidly and expertly. The second shot passed through his skull. This time he was really dead.

'That shouldn't have happened. What the hell can I do?'

Andreas, distraught, put the gun back on Stefan's lap.

'Nothing. Better take the gun. More use to you,' gasped Stefan. 'I had had enough of this hellish country and fiendish world anyway. The bastard's finished me, thank you for finishing him. Leave me here, go quickly and save the others.'

'Thank you from the bottom of all our hearts.'

Andreas turned to get into the driver's seat.

'Just one thing you might be able to do,' whispered Stefan.

Andreas stopped with a foot on the step.

'If you can ever get a message to Tamara Nickolaevna Oblova, currently, I think, a student at the Sacred Heart Convent outside Königshof, please tell her that, whatever she has heard about me, I died decently trying to save you and,' he added, 'try to protect her, if you are able to and give her this.'

He dragged a small green fabric First Aid Kit tightly bound in tape from his flack jacket pocket. He tried to throw it to Andreas but, with his strength gone, it fell on the road.

'I swear,' he just heard Andreas say as he picked it up. There was more but the cough and pain sharpened and the mist thickened.

6

THE SACRED HEART

Es pocht eine Sehnsucht an der Welt
an der wir sterben müssen

ELSE LASKER-SCHÜLER: WELTENDE[5]

The gates of the Sacred Heart had been equipped with an electronic lock. Whether this was to keep intruders out or the students, sisters and staff in, Mara did not know for certain. At all events a peremptory hoot from the NAS driver succeeded in getting the gate opened. Inside the gates nothing had changed. The brick and stone buildings still seemed gentle if cold and sad.

A young sister who was new to her greeted her in the front hall. The nun looked frightened and anxious.

'You are Tamara, aren't you? We were told to expect you. Reverend Mother would like to see you. Have you any luggage?'

Mara shook her head, then thinking that was rude added, 'You see, I haven't come from home.'

---

5   There is a longing for the world
    Where we have to die

'Yes, I know. I'll take you up.'

They climbed the silent carpeted staircase. A discrete knock and the firm but kindly invitation to enter.

'Thank you, Sister Lucia, you needn't wait. Sit down Tamara.'

Mother Katerina, the Mother Superior looked her over. She was smiling, but much more tired and old looking than Mara remembered. She looked an old woman, wrinkled behind her veil which, in defiance of the modern dress code, the Order still wore. The dynamic scholarly woman who had inspired generations of girls had faded.

'You have grown up, Tamara, but I am sure that it hasn't been easy. You know that you will be staying with us in the future – boarding – there are no day pupils now. Security, you know. Have you heard anything from your mother and father?'

'Nothing from my mother. My father is still in the city, I think. I had a message from him to say he was all right – nothing more. I think it was genuine but I can't be sure.'

'It's hard to be sure of anything, these days except the Good Lord. We are being sorely tried. So far we have been allowed to remain here and keep the school open but many have closed and the Church is not popular with our masters so we have to be very careful. I would warn you not to talk about anything; how shall I put it? Anything, that is or even might seem, at all controversial?'

She looked significantly all round the room and Mara was pretty sure that she was miming that even her room was bugged.

'Excuse me, Reverend Mother, but has Andrea Hoffman returned to the school?'

The Mother Superior looked very distressed but just said a bald, 'No and neither has Olga, your former study mate,' and then after a moment, 'now, we must get you some clothes and sort you out a study. Term started last week and many pupils stayed over Christmas so many study bedrooms are already allocated but we will fit you in somewhere and perhaps when we are more settled we can rearrange it, if you should wish. You will be able to complete your tenth year and continue with German, Russian, English, psychology and social studies although particularly in the last two you may find the curriculum a bit different.'

She said this with a dead pan face but Mara understood her without further explanation.

'You have missed most of last term and will have to work hard to catch up, particularly in English which was your weakest subject. We have a native English – or rather I should say Irish – student teacher this year who might be able to help you but she won't have much time, at least to begin with, as she will be working with the last year for their *Abitur.*'

Then a wan smile, 'Welcome back, Tamara, come and see me, if I can be of any help.'

She pressed the bell on her desk and her secretary appeared discretely.

'Please ask Sister Lucia to help Tamara find some clothes and sort out a study for her.'

A couple of hours later, bathed and dressed in jeans and sweater from the Sacred Heart store of emergency clothes, she looked round her new study/bedroom and the space allotted to her. She had met her new study mate briefly during the lunch break. She knew Brigitte Ehler to be a quiet girl who had been in the same year ever since they had both come to The Sacred Heart but they had never been friends, at least not close friends. This suited Mara very well as, in her present situation, she preferred being able to keep a polite distance between them. It would have been more difficult to avoid subjects, which she did not wish to discuss under any circumstances, if she had shared a room with an intimate friend.

She threw herself into her work and was surprised to find that she could concentrate quite well. Everybody, sisters, lay teachers and the other girls were extra kind. At first she thought that they were just being kind to her because she was known to have had a bad time. Slowly it dawned on her that many of them had had a bad time too and that they no longer had the heart for the veneer of brash, self-confident behaviour which had been the norm amongst the girls before. Moltravia was no longer a place where you could grow up confident and outspoken, aping the fashions of France, Germany or Britain let alone the USA.

It went deeper than that. Many of the girls knew nothing of the whereabouts or fate of their families. In addition, there was a cloud over the school, a menacing fear that nobody put into words but everybody knew was threatening their own future. Work was a relief and Mara found that she was making some progress even with her dreaded English. It was the times when there was no work which were the problem. She hated the free time, the meals with their required chatter and most of all she hated going to bed when she endlessly reviewed her situation and endlessly realised that there was no solution.

She was desperately lonely. Her mother had disappeared; she knew not where or how. It was only a lot later that her death was confirmed. Her father was, apparently, now not allowed to contact her and any attempt she made to contact him hit a brick wall. Her best friend and companion had also disappeared. Although nothing had been said, the expression on Reverend Mother's face when she had enquired after Andrea's whereabouts was not, to say the least, encouraging. She suspected that the Mother Superior knew more than she was letting on. Mara imagined that this was for reasons of security and also presumably because she did not want to alarm her young charges.

Worst of all, she had lost her boyfriend and lover. She regretted nothing about her tempestuous love affair; it had been a marvellous star in a grey world. She was proud of herself and remembered the sweet moments when he had murmured to her how much he loved her and her body had responded to him in an explosion of joy and fusion. Yes, she really was a real woman and he was certainly a real man. They were made for each other but it had all now ended. She told herself that, absent as he was, she loved him passionately. Very occasionally as she reminisced silently, the gloom lifted momentarily and she smiled quietly to herself. She realised that here she was in a convent, in a convent at the age of seventeen, recalling experiences and feelings that, at least presumably, most of the women, young and old, around her had never felt. The pleasure was transient, the reality was gloom laden. There was the puzzle about what had actually happened after they had been discovered *in flagrante*. He had simply disappeared and she found the whispered version that he had broken out of the cellar naked and run off down the road scarcely believable. In her worst moments, she imagined him getting a swift bullet in the back of the neck and the invention of

73

a cock and bull story to stop her, and the rest of the house, panicking. She just didn't know.

One of the advantages of sharing a study with Brigitte was that she was out most evenings. Almost every night she spent at least two hours in the music school practising her violin. She was a very talented violinist and came from a musical family. She had told Mara that her father and grandfather were both professional violinists and her mother played the oboe. Her brother played the cello and her cousin the viola. 'We are practically a family string orchestra,' she joked, '– apart from Mum of course.' Before the upheavals, father and grandfather had played in the Königshof orchestra and she had hoped to do the same. Like so many others, her family were now dispersed and she ached for news of them.

Mara, alone as usual, stared gloomily from her study at the late winter northern blackness through her uncurtained window. From the other side of the house she would have seen the distant lights of Königshof, but her window on this side showed only the flat countryside. Beyond the walls of the Sacred Heart she could see the odd dimly-lighted window in the misty blackness. She knew that beyond that the total darkness covered the salt flats and then the main coastal plain sweeping inland from the invisible Baltic, punctuated by the occasional village and farm. Many of these were now abandoned as the inhabitants were either in prison or the army. Many had simply fled. She knew that the government, unlike their admired Nazi role models, had failed to stimulate industry or the economy. In all of this, there might have been hope for change had it not been for the flourishing gun-running industry and the sale of supplies of enriched uranium. She was a bit vague as to the exact details of all this but apparently it had given Travsky enough money to pursue his revolution. He had promised prosperity but this had certainly not been delivered. For several minutes she just stared hopelessly into the darkness. She didn't know what was going to happen to them all. At this moment she felt too exhausted mentally to care.

Her thoughts turned to Stefan's Walkman. It was the only physical link that she had to him and had acquired a sacred significance since they had parted. She had not dared to use it. It had lain at the bottom of her tiny rucksack which was all that she had brought with her from

74

the house. She got it out and pressed Play – nothing happened. Not surprising, she thought, there was no tape in it. She had a large collection but they were all at her home and inaccessible.

Brigitte had a CD Walkman and a recording Minidisk player which she used for her violin work. She wasn't around and it wouldn't help anyway. Mara had no intention of discussing this intimate subject with a roommate that she hardly knew.

Absentmindedly, she turned the little recorder over in her hands. She knew that there was an internal radio, after all Stefan had said that he had been able to record the Slaves' Chorus direct from the radio. She looked again at the switches. She found the radio controls easily enough and switched it on – still nothing. She scanned the tuning up and down and turned to the medium wave all to no avail. Perhaps it had been left on and the batteries had run down or perhaps even got wet although she couldn't see how. She tried to open the battery compartment. It was stuck. She picked up her nail file and gently inserted it into the grove. Something clicked inside but the compartment still didn't open. Suddenly and for no apparent reason, the little machine burst into life – a man was speaking. She stared rigid, thunder struck as delight turned to horror and the sad smile faded as she stared into the pit of her personal hell. It was his voice not the cheap pop music or the mindless disc jockey that she had been expecting. But she instantly knew his voice and what he said left her in no doubt. He was reporting in full the conversation that he had had with Lukas and then added information that he had gained from Johanna. There could be no other explanation. The light of her life, her hero, her lover was a NAS spy planted in the house to winkle information out of them all. She wondered bitterly what he had said about her. Perhaps that she had been a virgin but he had corrected that, she thought with fierce hatred in her heart. She didn't see that she could have told him anything important but perhaps she had been spied on in order to get her to betray her father. Thank God that she hadn't. That was small comfort now. The tiny spark of light in her terrible world had been snuffed out and snuffed out in the cruellest way possible.

Brigitte burst in looking pleased with herself. Her latest examination piece was obviously coming along.

'Hello, I thought you'd be in bed. What on earth is the matter, you look as if you have seen a ghost?'

'Heard one.'

She wished she hadn't said it. Brigitte looked puzzled and waited for more. Except for the tears in her room mate's eyes, nothing came and she had the tact not to pursue it. She poured water into the wash stand and started cleaning her teeth. Mara stripped off her clothes into a heap, mechanically put on her pyjamas and the extra sweater needed to keep out the bitter night cold, pulled her *Federbett* over her and rolling into a foetal ball turned her face to the wall.

Brigitte was a deep sleeper and wasn't disturbed by the quiet sobs coming from her companion intermittently during the night. She was, though, aware of the black rings under Mara's red eyes when they struggled out of bed to face another uncertain day.

Brigitte was deeply worried and wondered whether she ought to talk to the sisters in order to get Mara some help. On the one hand she knew that something was desperately amiss with the normally resilient girl but on the other she hesitated to interfere. She was also mature enough to realise that not everything in a young woman's life could he shared or helped by nuns, however kind and sympathetic. However, she was puzzled. Mara had had no letters nor, so far as Brigitte knew, any other communication with the outside world. She decided to watch and wait hoping that in time Mara would talk to her.

Mara, in turn, realised that it would be nigh on impossible to hide her distress from everybody. She was determined that, although in the end killing herself might be the best way out, for the moment she would work hard to conceal her feelings as much as she could. She even prepared a speech about having a bad period to forestall any enquiries from the sisters. Normally lying was not part of her makeup but this was different. She had to use her story once when Sister Lucia, a sympathetic intelligent youngster in charge of their house, did indeed ask what was wrong. The sister accepted her explanation, asked matron to provide some tablets and to Mara's intense relief nothing more was said.

Endlessly ruminating in her sleepless bed, she thought of other answers that she might have given, 'Well, Sister, I don't feel very well because I have just discovered that my husband before God is a fascist spy and consorts with people who are torturing my friends.' She wondered if any nun, however well intentioned, would be able to cope with that.

Week dragged into week. She tried to work and had some success. The English romantics seemed remote, but the agonies of *Anna Karenina* and Goethe's *Werther* rang true and to a degree comforted her. She wondered if a religious life could provide the answer and if she should talk to Mother Superior about it. She drew back. She knew that if she admitted to a hint of a vocation, she would find it hard to retreat. Deep down, she knew that desperate as her present state was, relinquishing the world was really no answer.

Slowly but inexorably her feelings changed to deep anger. Where was the all loving God who presided over her life? Her loss of parents, friend, home and lover? She had made no extreme demands. She had just wanted to grow up normally and yet everything that she had valued had been shattered. She had read of the classical gods who treated the fate of humans as playthings. That was more like it – a cruel god who was amusing himself by baiting her – showing her the simple comforts that she wanted then snatching them away or worse, showing them to be treacherous and false. She had survived her separation from Stefan but she felt unable to survive his treachery. She was locked in a kindly religious house yet religion gave her no solace.

With Brigitte in the music school, she was alone as usual, staring again into the darkness of the winter afternoon through her icy window. After ruminating miserably in the growing cold, she shivered and stood up to turn the radiator up. She picked up the English book that she had to study. It was *King Lear*, with parallel German. She had found it boring. This miserable old man with his awful daughters, complicated speeches in a language she struggled to understand. She sighed and started to read:

As flies to wanton boys are we to th'gods:
They kill us for their sport.

That was it, exactly it. She read the whole scene, flicking to the German when the English defeated her. It was a short scene yet time and again a phrase struck home:

> *The lowest and most dejected thing of fortune,*
> *Stands still in esperance, lives not in fear*
> *The lamentable change is from the best,*
> *The worst returns to laughter*

At last she realised why people bothered about Shakespeare. In that short scene, which she read over and over again to try and get the most meaning out of the ancient foreign words, was her whole state. And yet, and yet, there was more than her state. The suggestion was there that the wheel of fortune rolled. At the top it turned down and at the bottom it might rise. She shrugged. It was fascinating but how could her personal wheel rise? Still the idea of the wheel gripped her imagination.

She had been given a book on the background to Shakespeare's plays by her English teacher. It had seemed rather hard going but now she picked it up and looked up *das Schicksal.*[6] A passage on the Renaissance belief in Lady Fortune and her capricious wheel, was all there. She read two more lines quoted from somebody called Boethius who apparently had influenced Shakespeare. These described exactly the way that she felt that she had been treated by fate. Fascinated she went to the library, looked up the author and *The Consolation of Philosophy* and found that the original had been written by an ancient Roman awaiting execution. The original Latin was there followed by a German and an English translation. She read the rather clumsy German of the whole passage. She then glanced at the English version underneath which, to her surprise she found easier to understand than the Shakespeare:

> *Her ruthless will has just deposed once fearful kings*
> *While trustless still, from low she lifts a conquered head;*
> *No cries of misery she hears, no tears she heeds,*

---

6   Destiny

But steely hearted laughs at groans her deeds have wrung.
Such is a game she plays, and so she tests her strength;
Of mighty power she makes parade when one short hour.
Sees happiness from utter desolation grow.

Again there was that hint that things change and sometimes for the better. She still could not believe that could happen to her. She was too low, out of reach of fortunes wheel, buried underneath it. Strangely, though far from convinced by the hint of change, she was comforted that others had shared her predicament. She smiled to herself and wondered that she found the companionship of a Renaissance English playwright and a Roman civil servant comforting. But she did.

She went back to her study and found Brigitte had returned. To the latter's surprise, Mara suggested coffee and sat down to chat. This had not happened for a long while.

Mara asked, 'Have you heard from home?'

'It's strange that you should ask. Reverend Mother asked to see me today and said that my father had come and asked whether I could play in the family quartet for a concert in the *Mariakirche*. She was delighted and agreed. He then asked if they could come here to rehearse a couple of days before so that I didn't miss too much school. Reverend Mother said that of course we could use the music school or the chapel between the offices so it's all fixed for next week. We will need some help to arrange the lighting in the chapel and in the cathedral. My cousin, Jan, the violist, suggested that you might be able to help. I think that he remembered me saying that you were very pretty and he's always had an eye for the girls.' She giggled.

Mara laughed, ignoring the innuendo. 'Of course, I'd love to. It would be good to go out and there isn't much opportunity now with all the security checks.'

At lunch break they asked to go to the chapel with Gregor, the odd job man, and, after a few false starts, they got lights for the music desks and the general lighting in position.

'That's fine,' Mara said dubiously, 'but will it be the same in the Cathedral?'

'Should be, Fräulein, if they've got a trunk lead and I think they must have because there have been concerts there before.'

Mara missed the chapel rehearsal which clashed with a German lesson but boarded the minibus with Brigitte and her family of players in the late afternoon for the final rehearsal in the cathedral and the concert. They had to pass security checks to get out of the convent and into the cathedral but much to Mara's relief there was no major problem. While the quartet began to rehearse in the sacristy, with Gregor's help, she found the provost's clerk who unearthed the trunk lead. After that it was fairly straightforward to set up the lights, which, to Mara's pleasure, worked adequately. Brigitte's father thanked her saying that they would employ her as a concert manager. Jan enthusiastically agreed.

The musicians settled down to rehearse. They were to play the Haydn Opus 20 no 2 Quartet and the first Rasumovsky of Beethoven. They only rehearsed snatches in the final position in front of the high altar to test the acoustics. Mara was privileged to be allowed to stay 'in case the lights needed adjusting'. It was all unfamiliar to her. She had never listened to classical music but she found the power of just four instruments and the emotion of hearing it made live by her friend and family, to her surprise, interesting.

Satisfied, they finished rehearsing and retired to the sacristy signalling Mara to join them for a hot drink, which was more than welcome on a bitter cold evening. In spite of the official atheist stance, the authorities had authorised the concert, stating that places such as churches needed to be used 'usefully for proper secular events'. Neither they, nor the cathedral authorities had run to providing heating, however, and Mara wondered how the musicians were able to play with frozen hands. The Sacristan, however, had provided a large thermos of hot coffee. The sacristy was large and lined irregularly with vestment cupboards.

Before the concert itself, to her surprise she felt excited and expectant. A Monsignor that she never remembered seeing before, introduced the quartet pointing out that the second violin was played but a talented pupil at The Sacred Heart Convent and that all were musicians from the same family. The cathedral was now quite full, despite official disapproval and the bitter winter weather. It was all new to Mara and she was surprised to find it so easy to listen to. The Haydn seemed so ordered and civilised, contrasting with the dreadfully violent world that surrounded them. She was particularly entranced by the gentle rhythms of the slow movement and the minuet. The Beethoven was a contrast, lively and, she thought, great fun but she wasn't sure that you were allowed to think that about classical music. All too soon it was over.

The Monsignor got to his feet and suggested that the musicians perhaps would like to join the audience for a closing prayer. In the dim light Mara was hardly aware of Brigitte's cousin the violist sliding into the pew behind her. As it has no clear view of the platform, it had been left empty by the audience during the concert itself. She suddenly realised that he was whispering to her. After Brigitte's joke about him, at first she thought he was taking the opportunity to chat her up, such things had happened in church before. But no, it sounded more urgent and serious than that.

'Tamara,' he whispered, 'don't say anything and don't turn round. I have an important message to give you. My colleague's brother has a friend who was a partisan at *Solanova*. His life and that of many others were saved by a very brave NAS officer who lost his own life helping them to escape. He asked particularly that if anyone was able to contact you, you should be told how he died and that he died loving you. I am happy that this concert has given me the chance to carry out his wish. He was a very brave man and you obviously meant everything to him. I am going to give you something he left for you. I am going to push it behind your back. Get hold of it and hide it quickly without turning round.'

Mara's heart leapt in her chest with contrasting feelings. It was terrible that Stefan was dead and she was sure deep grief would follow. For the moment though, she had her love restored and she was deeply moved. She was sad that she couldn't thank the courageous people who had risked a lot to get this message to her.

It was the following day before she had a moment to herself when Brigitte, as usual, had gone to the music school. It was a little green fabric first aid kit sealed with sticky tape. With her fingers trembling she tore off the sticky tape and unzipped the little bag. Inside a plastic bag, was a bandage wrapped round something hard. There were no other contents. Whatever else the kit had once contained had been removed.

Inside the bandage was a layer of cotton wool. It had all been carefully packed. Mara removed the cotton wool, uncovering an audiotape in a case further wrapped round with a sheet of paper. She recognised the writing on the paper immediately:

Meine Liebe Tamarushka,

Only one person ever called her Tamarushka everybody else called her Mara.

The tape tells my life story and how I came to join the murderers and torturers.

By the time you read this I may well be dead. By now you may have heard some horrible things about me. I have been involved in dreadful actions and have become more and more guilty at being part of the regime. I am now determined to do what I can to help and save the brave people who have been fighting against the devilry. I shall go on working until this land comes out of its nightmare or until I am killed. Sadly, it will almost certainly be the second as I can't yet see the possibility of the first. However, I want to die hating myself a bit less. More than anything I want you to know that I love you, truly love you and have always loved you. I hope that the way that I have chosen to risk my life will give me back your love.

Adieu, mein einzig Schatz.

Before she burst into tears, she realised that he hadn't signed it – he didn't need to.

At that moment Brigitte came back, she looked excited and couldn't make out her studymate's tearful, shell shocked expression. After a pause she said, 'Mara, again you look as if you have seen a ghost.'

She got the strangest response. Mara looked at her for a moment, then smiled, 'I think that I probably have,' she said, still smiling wistfully.

There was a long pause as Mara struggled with her tangled emotions. Brigitte, wisely realised that Mara was again grappling with something very private. This time, however, there was triumph as well as sadness in her roommate's eyes. She knew Mara was a strange girl with a history but she also knew that she would talk when and if she was ready.

7
A VISIT

Howl, howl, howl, howl! O, you are men of stones:
Had I your tongues and eyes, I would use them so
That heaven's vault should crack. She's gone for ever!

KING LEAR ACT V SC III

It was late afternoon the following day before Mara realised that Brigitte had not come back from the music school. When she still did not appear at supper time Mara was concerned enough to seek out Sister Lucia and tell her of Brigitte's absence.

The young sister looked uncomfortable

'She is in the sanatorium unwell.'

No other explanation was forthcoming and at least Mara was reassured that her friend was being looked after. All the same it was odd. At breakfast that morning Brigitte had been bubbling over with excitement at the success of the previous evening's concert with not a sign of illness. Oh well, thought Mara, some bugs do come on quickly. She went back to preparing her psychology revision on conditioning, untroubled. She found it hard to concentrate. So much had happened in the last couple of days. At last she gave up and reread Stefan's letter and listened to his tape again before going to bed. She woke in a sweat taking a moment to realise that she was alone in the study. In her nightmare, Stefan was there, trying to get away. He kept asking her what she had done with his tape. He must have it and hide it as it would incriminate him if it was found. She couldn't find the tape and was frantically looking for it. Then she woke up. She lay wide awake thinking about the nightmare and again worried as to exactly what had happened to Brigitte. Sadly, she thought, the tape couldn't harm Stefan. Then, with a start, she thought, but it can harm me. It was her most treasured possession but dangerous. A convent school study does not have secure hiding places. She could only think of one solution. She did not usually attend 6am matins, which was strictly voluntary for the students. In any case her feelings about religion in general had been less than lukewarm of late. This morning, however, she leapt out of bed, blinking as she switched on the light, dressed quickly and headed for chapel. She knew that confessions were arranged for the Sisters and for any student hardy enough to turn up after matins. Often Monsignor Karolenko himself was there for confessions but Mara on her rather infrequent visits had gone to Father Peter, a young priest attached to the local parish. Guiltily, she was grateful that she had confessed her fornication and been absolved to a locum priest when she had first come back to the Sacred Heart. After the service Mara noted gratefully that the confessional light was on. Father Peter was in attendance. She went through the normal ritual of the sacrament, struggling to find anything more serious than a few impure thoughts which merited a mild penance. She then broached the real reason for being there.

'Father, I have something in my possession very precious to me but dangerous for my safety. It is not improper in any way and, although critical of the regime, the person who sent it to me is now dead so represents no threat. It is his last letter and tape recorded before he died. He was very close to me and I am very anxious that this letter and tape can be kept for me safely. Is it possible that the Church could help me?'

'In these days, my daughter, nowhere and nothing is entirely secure but we do have secret places which will remain safe unless the regime decides to suppress the Holy Church entirely which is, thank God, some

84

way off. Give it to me, my daughter, and I will do my best. I hope and trust that the time will come when I can return it safely to you.'

With a huge weight off her mind Mara went to breakfast. There was still no Brigitte.

In the evening, she was back. She was lying on her bed rolled into a ball when Mara found her. It reminded Mara of how she had felt after she had discovered Stefan's deception. Her head was buried in the pillow sobbing silently. Mara sat down quietly beside her. After a long pause, Mara slipped into her own bed and dozed fitfully. She was wakened by Brigitte screaming, sitting bolt upright and staring. Mara slipped out of bed not sure if her companion was dreaming or awake.

'Tell me,' she whispered and turned on her bedside lamp.

Brigitte stared, pale in the shadows.

'They took me between them in this car, through gates, past horrible things. Bodies hanging and people shrieking in the background. Then they unlocked gates and took me into this room and sat me on a bench between them. We sat there. They seemed to be waiting for something. There was nothing in the room except a very thick wooden table all scored like a butchers block. One of them looked at me and said, "We will show you first how we punish traitors then it's your turn." I didn't know what he meant,' she paused trying to collect herself.

'After a long wait, two men in uniform brought in a young lad – our age or a bit younger. As a sort of explanation, one of my guards said "This boy fetched food for traitors". Then they told him to roll his sleeve up. Terrified, he obeyed. They strapped his wrist to the block. One of the unarmed guards took off his jacket and put on a plastic apron. He went to a cupboard and took out a butcher's chopper. Then he calmly walked over to the lad, swung the chopper and cut clean through his fingers. They splattered onto the floor. I fainted and fell on the floor. I woke up drenched in cold water with my right hand strapped to the bloody block. "Now it's your turn. That hand won't pick up any more traitor's messages." I could see my fingers splashing on the floor like the boy's. I thought of my violin. I closed my eyes not wanting to see what they were going to do to me. Then the strangest thing happened. The door burst open and another man came in shouting, "You idiots. You crazy, incompetent fools. You've got the wrong one. What the hell do you think you're up to. I'll have your hides for this." At first I thought that he was shouting at me, then I realised that he was shouting at the guards.'

"Take her back, come back here and don't do anything else until you are ordered. Attend the colonel in the morning."

'Then the guards took me back to the car and back here. I was so ill that the sisters took me to the sanatorium. In the evening they asked me if I would like to go back to my own room and I said yes.'

Mara could say nothing, she took her room-mates hand and stared into the deep space of hopelessness.

She lay awake most of the night. If Brigitte was the wrong one there was only one possible explanation. She had been seen collecting the package in the cathedral and, although mistaken for her study mate at first, she herself must be the 'right' one. She looked down at her fingers. Were they soon to be chopped off in the butcher's cell in the Winterburg? It didn't bear thinking about but she had no alternative, no escape, no way out. To escape was impossible. Her only slender protection was the reputation and honesty of the sisters. They would do their best to protect her she knew but she also knew that their best wouldn't be good enough.

*

The room was old fashioned but had once been warm and welcoming. The family furnishings were not luxurious but interesting and once had been full of life but now looked forlorn. Books, untouched, lined the walls. CDs, jazz and classical from all periods stood unplayed in their tiers against the wall. The central heating rumbled, as indeed in that bitter late winter it needed to but the grate was cold with ashes from last week, last month, last year? The fires that had once blazed were long forgotten. Outside the night blackened over the Baltic, blackened deeply over the countryside but most of all blackened hellishly over the grim, grimy fearful city and the souls within it.

Nicklaus Oblov sat staring into the cold grate as he had done for so many evenings. He could no longer read the books that he had loved or listen to the music that he adored. It had all turned to ashes like the cold remnants of the long-ago fire. Outside his gate he knew there were guards, not obtrusive but there all the same. He had been told clearly that he was under house arrest and knew that any attempt to leave would be doomed. He lived now as a prisoner without his beloved wife and knowing that his daughter was held as a hostage in the hands of his enemies. He knew that his house arrest was more than just the guards outside the gates.

He went off to sleep in his chair. He had slept badly, usually disturbed by nightmares. That night, as he dropped off, again he dreamed of the inhuman brutalities that were all around him. As he sunk in despair, he saw through the gloom a tall stranger riding towards him shouting with a foreign voice, 'Stand firm, have faith, you will win', then he realised that the tall horseman was a woman, young, handsome with auburn hair streaming behind her. It was a strange inexplicable dream. He awoke as there was a peremptory knock at the door.

Still drugged with sleep he shouted, '*Herein!*' The front door opened then the drawing room door. Instead of the uniformed guard that he expected to see, in front of him stood a man of less than medium height with very small strikingly blue eyes too close together for his disproportionately large head. He was balding with grey hair brushed neatly back over his temples. The fur-lined black leather coat that he wore was hanging open, revealing an impeccably neat, old fashioned grey suit. Under his jacket was a leather waistcoat covering a startlingly white shirt finished with a rather incongruous purple woollen tie. His black leather boots were polished to a mirror shine and he crushed a Russian style fur hat in his left hand. Nicklaus sensed a nightmare, worse than anything that he had experienced in his dreams. This was a man feared more than any throughout the land; a man whose obsession was power and whose passion was cruelty. Smiling in front of him was, Konradin, President Travsky's right hand and feared more than the president himself.

Nicklaus pulled himself together.

'To what do I owe this honour?' he asked. 'I have very few visitors and certainly didn't expect to be visited by Your Excellency.'

Konradin's little piggy eyes smiled again and seemed oddly detached from the hard lines of his mouth.

'I have some good news for you and I thought that I would bring it to you in person.'

His ingratiating smile was draped over the menace lurking behind it like an inadequate dust sheet. Nicklaus looked at him with quizzical unbelief.

'I have just saved your daughter from having an accident.'

In spite of himself Nicklaus flinched, then cursed himself inwardly for showing weakness. He said nothing.

Konradin looked disappointed but decided to continue with his story despite the minimal response.

'Some of our more enthusiastic NAS men wanted to chop the fingers off her right hand.'

Nicklaus flinched again and cursed himself once more.

'However, I stopped them, for the moment, and came to ask you for some help.'

'How?'

'You have contacts in the Pentagon from the previous regime. We need spares for several weapon systems. We might bargain help with weapons spares for Tamara's fingers.'

So that was the trade. Nicklaus was hoisted. Either he betrayed the future of the nation or he permitted his daughter to be tortured and maimed. He knew that he was effectively one of only two people left after the purges who could rally the forces of revolt with any hope of success against this appalling regime. The other was Ulrich Zahnsdorf, the former head of the air force. Nicklaus wasn't sure that he was still alive although when he had last had news from outside he had been told that Zahnsdorf had survived. He was also somebody that the regime might need. There was another similarity. He also had an only daughter. Liese was a few years older than Tamara but presumably was equally available as a pawn and a lever. He would dearly have liked to talk to Ulrich although he knew that this was out of the question. Currently he was under house arrest, helpless and Mara was a hostage. He was not even sure where she was but he was sure that his enemies had her at their disposal. Behind it all was the thought that renewed contact with the USA might be a route to escape but it still left Mara in Moltravia. At last he said, 'I might be able to help but I would need facilities. Secure email, fax, reliable couriers, etc. It might be impossible unless I went to the States myself.'

'That's asking a great deal but with Tamara closely watched... She's an interesting young lady. Although she is small she has a good body and the right racial characteristics. She might be suitable for the *Chef's* pure race breeding scheme.'

'But she's still at school! She's still a child!' Nicklaus broke in, in spite of himself.

'Oh, that doesn't matter. As long as they are past puberty, ovulating regularly, we take them as young as twelve. Inexperienced youngsters provide fewer problems. They don't make so much fuss. Many of them are teenagers and, how do you put it, inexperienced. This, by the way, certainly doesn't apply to Fräulein, or I should say Frau Tamara.'

'What do you mean by that?' asked Nicklaus angrily.

'Only that one of our agents has, or rather had, first hand evidence that your daughter is no longer a virgin.'

'You mean that she has been raped?'

'I didn't necessarily mean that. Anyway it's irrelevant. We couldn't take a girl with your and the Frau Doktor Gisela's genes into our programme. Quite the wrong breeding and the *Chef* believes that breeding had a lot to do with moral as well as physical purity. However, he added thoughtfully, 'that might be overcome. We might make an exception in her case.'

'You are disgusting, but tell me, at least, what has happened to my wife?'

He shrugged his shoulders.

'It's time I left. I will send someone round to co-operate with you in getting the *materiel* that we need. Meanwhile, never fear, we will keep an eye on Tamara for you.'

He smiled again with his smiling mouth detached from his tiny chilly eyes. 'Don't worry I'll show myself out. I know the way; in fact I feel quite at home, I have a key.'

Nicklaus sat in the dark reflecting late into the night. He was tied up, not literally but effectively. The threat to Tamara prevented him doing anything. She was all he had left although he hadn't seen her in ages. What did Konradin's cryptic remark about her sexual experience imply? The obvious, ghastly, explanation was that she had been raped by some NAS thug but somehow it didn't seem quite right. Konradin had refused to confirm his suggestion and the triumph in his voice was unusually muted when he talked about the offending officer in the past tense. What had really happened? It was yet another gloomy mystery that he could not unravel.

Late in the frozen night he suddenly realised something both terrible and yet liberating. The only possible outcome of co-operation with the regime was that he would do what they required and then, when they had no more use for him, he would be killed like so many others and Tamara would follow him, guilty by association, to a high profile execution. No amount of collaborating would save them. Therefore neither of them would be worse off if he took this half chance to escape from the country and to organise the seeds of revolt. There was even the possibility that his absence abroad might keep Tamara alive rather than the reverse. In spite of this, he realised that she might be tortured or even, as Konradin had hinted, forced into the ghastly form of state prostitution which Travsky had copied from the Nazis. It did not bear thinking about.

Nevertheless, as the cold late dawn came, he had made up his mind. If it were possible, he would go. He owed it to the country and the tradition that he loved. He thought of his Hanseatic forebears. Although only a loose association of trading cities they had challenged the might of the Danish king and they had won. Faced with the challenge, he could try to do no less.

*

She kept gazing at the fingers of her right hand. She assumed that it would be her right hand. She was right handed and it wouldn't be in character for them to subject her to the lesser mutilation of her subordinate hand. Day after day she expected the visit but no one came. Not yet reassured or freed from the nightmare anticipation, she was puzzled as to what had happened. Not that she had come to terms with it. How can you come to terms with your hand agonisingly being made useless? But realistically she expected it.

8
THE FARM

Preach the word; be instant in season, out of season;
Reprove, rebuke, exhort with all longsuffering and doctrine

2 TIMOTHY 4:2

As the pre-Lenten break approached at the Sacred Heart there was a
notable lack of the normal enthusiasm. Although the excesses of carnival
had never been a feature of life at The Sacred Heart, nevertheless it
had always been a season of colour and festivity. In former years the
entire community had arranged plays, concerts, parties and had always
thoroughly enjoyed themselves. This time it was very different. For a
start, many students were either not allowed or unable to return home
for any holiday. A few features did enliven the pervasive gloom. There
was to be a dancing display in which Mara, never hugely talented and
now with a great lack of enthusiasm, was to take part. Some of the other
events seemed dull and singularly irrelevant.

Still edgy and expecting daily to be taken by the NAS, Mara was
irritated by the prospect of this Irish student teacher from a posh British
university talking about 'Ireland Past and Present', while their own
country was losing the struggle for its decency and its life. Nevertheless

attendance at the event was expected and she went, yawning and angry, to hear it. Mara had seen the lecturer in the halls and corridors of the Sacred Heart but, not studying advanced English or music, had only once or twice been taught by her. She settled herself into her hard chair miserable, critical and bored. Sister Annunziata, the head of the history department, introduced the speaker as Bernadette O'Neill, a former pupil of their sister house near Athy, Ireland. She was now studying Russian and German at Oxford University in England and would talk to them about 'Ireland – Yesterday and Today'. Mara noticed the Reverend Mother sitting quietly at the back. Perhaps her presence was simply a compliment to the young teacher but she wondered if there could be another reason. Was she keeping an eye on her colleagues and charges in this uncertain time?

Frau O'Neill was dressed in jeans and a thick sweater. As far as her clothes went she could have been one of the students. In other respects she was striking. She was very tall. Mara reckoned about one metre eighty probably more. Even in a thick winter sweater, she was obviously well built but without any hint of excess fat. Her broad shoulders and muscular thighs encased in their tight jeans suggested an athlete and a formidable one at that. In the autumn before Mara had come back, it was said that this young woman had raced over eight hundred metres against the best athletes in the school and won as Mara's informant put it 'in a canter'. Yet she was enviably beautiful in features, figure and posture. Her most striking feature was her long red-gold hair, shining and clearly her own, with little or no aids to nature. Elaborate hair dos were discouraged at the Sacred Heart in staff and students alike. In any case under the present regime such luxuries were simply not available – no – Bernadette O'Neill's crowning glory was as nature intended, without artifice. Mara was jealous. Her own fair mop rapidly became straggly and unmanageable without expert help. She reflected sadly that the only person she might have wanted to impress was no longer around.

The speaker's formidable assets were beginning to irritate her if not actually to make her jealous. Stuck up cow, she thought angrily. At that moment Sister Annunziata finished her introduction. Mara's mind had wandered and she only caught something about singing in the sister's concluding remarks. The speaker, standing up, burst into a broad grin from ear to ear.

'*Danke,* Sister Annunziata,' and in a very passable imitation of the local Königshof *platdeutsch* accent added, 'I've got a nerve. I am twenty-one years old and, like many of you, have spent most of those twenty-one years at a convent school.'

There was a look of disapproval from Sister Annunziata but the girls laughed. Perhaps it wasn't going to be so boring after all. The speaker, gradually became more serious as she slid away from her cabaret mimicry into excellent high German.

'My convent education taught me many things and I am really grateful to it. I think, however, that my former headmistress would be the first to agree that it doesn't really qualify me as an expert on Ireland. But if you can't have the best, you have to make do with the rest, so here goes!'

The presentation was racy, informative and both romantic and funny. They had the *Fianna*, the little people waiting Ireland's call under the Hill of Allen, the High Kings with the harp music of *Tara*, the *Children of Lir* spending nine hundred years as swans, St Patrick coming from Scotland and casting out the snakes.

'But the one you really need to fear, girls, was St Kevin of Glendalough. He hated women and when one made advances to him he pushed her into a bed of nettles. Misogynists in Ireland are known as Kevins to this day. But we have our female saints too, particularly St Brigid who had good female common sense and founded Kildare Abbey near where I was born. And it may interest you to know that she was in charge of men as well as women.

'But my forebears weren't all saints, Brian Boru, the great warrior deposed my ancestors from the High Kingship, defeated the Danes and then got killed himself...'

And so it went on, racy informative and enthralling. The eight-hundred-year battle with the criminal English then Cromwell destroying the land and the people who he was supposed to protect.

'Hard to believe today,' she paused for the irony to sink in. 'Then the gallant rising of 1798, the defence of Wexford and the executions and floggings that followed.'

Like many others, Mara, by this time was on the edge of her seat. What is this girl doing? she thought. There will be spies in the hall; some of the girls belong to Travskyite families. Staff may be in the pay of the NAS. Yet the parallel between her description of old Ireland and present day Moltravia couldn't be missed. She didn't seem to care and went on regardless. Is she asking to be arrested or worse? Mara was worldly wise enough to know that, with the prevailing xenophobia, possession of an Irish European Union passport was no protection, in fact probably a liability.

But Frau O'Neill hadn't finished. She went on to describe the callous indifference of the landlords to the ghastly famine then the rising at Easter 1916 when the patriotic leaders were shot. One, Patrick Pearse, was so injured from the battle that he had to be shot in a chair. The dreadful war with England had dreadful cruelties. But the civil war that followed with Irishmen against other Irishmen, was worse. Mara wondered if there was a lesson for Moltravia in this too.

'And women were involved too. Women were a large part of all these events including the most recent struggle in the north of Ireland. Remember this, ladies, women can fight for freedom and justice as well as, perhaps better than, men.'

Is she really trying to get herself killed? thought Mara. There was a ripple of applause in the hall started by a few brave girls, It grew and grew until it seemed the whole hall was applauding and cheering. Perhaps there was safety in numbers but in corners names were being noted and miniature videos were running. The sisters knew this would be so and were pale and aghast. What was this woman up to?

She went on to describe how peace had followed the civil war and how after half a century of struggle the country had begun to bloom in tranquillity, prosperity and, most importantly, freedom.

'So that now my little homeland is one of the best run countries in Europe. Ladies, it can be done! I would like to finish by singing you a very popular Irsh folksong. It comes from the time of the dreadful famine.'

She picked up a mandolin that she had brought with her into the hall and began: *The Fields Of Athenry.*

Mara sat spellbound by the pure flowing voice and the soft English words. She didn't believe that she had ever heard anything more beautiful. For the moment she forgot her own misery and the enormity of the message before. As Frau O'Neill finished singing there was more applause, this time muted.

The nuns were pale and silent as they prepared to leave and the girls knew that they had just heard something outrageous, foolhardy and yet splendid. A defenceless young woman had given a clarion call for freedom and justice right at the heart of a brutal and oppressive totalitarian regime. Nothing would ever be the same again.

But the danger was present and terrible, and nobody knew it better than Reverend Mother Katerina. The abbess of the Sacred Heart was a woman of determination, decision, education and intelligence but the complexities of the present situation left her in an agony of indecision. Bernadette O'Neill had perhaps brought matters to a head but the problems had been evident even before the young Irish girl's inflammatory address. Nonetheless she was extremely angry with Frau O'Neill. To have given that sort of lecture without any attempt to clear it with the senior staff was irresponsible and insubordinate. The abbess smiled and said to herself, 'but I think she knew that and I think she knew that there was no chance of her being allowed to go ahead if she had sought prior clearance – no – and there might well have been another more worthy reason. Under the circumstances Bernadette could assume total responsibility for what she had said – nobody else had been involved or actually compromised. That, Mother Katerina had to admit, was courageous, if true.'

All these thoughts didn't help her come to a decision. Should she sack the girl immediately? She knew that the Sacred Heart was living on borrowed time. All the other monastic and convent schools had been suppressed and their staff and pupils disposed of according to their loyalties and in the case of the children their family's loyalties. Children and staff who were known to support Travsky had rapidly been found alternative posts and schools.

The clerics and those from families of dubious allegiance had been drafted into the army, the youth cadet corps or sent to re-education labour camps. Many of these camps had sprung up catering for various ages and sexes. The regimes varied in severity but the main objectives seemed to be to use the young people's labour while educating or brain washing them to accept the regime. There were some very ugly stories about the worst institutions and the Reverend Mother had little doubt that they were true. Travsky would not tolerate, and saw no reason to tolerate, any opposition.

The Sacred Heart had so far been spared because it was the most revered and eminent girls' school in the country and its suppression would involve some delicate decisions about disposal of pupils. But Mother Katerina knew that Travsky was only waiting his moment probably until he had cleared the decks of some of his other problems. Frau O'Neill might have settled the timing but their fate had been sealed beforehand. Her duty was to protect her children, her lay staff and her community, but how? What could she possibly do?

She needed to talk to somebody and there was only one option but a good one. Monsignor Karolenko, amongst his other posts, was chaplain to the Sacred Heart. He took his duties seriously and in addition to officiating at many Masses, he confessed the sisters and students. Every Thursday evening, he would attend Mother Katerina to discuss any problems she might have with individuals or the general running of the convent and school.

It happened that a Thursday visit was scheduled for the day after Frau O'Neill's lecture. For a long time, for these meetings, they had strolled together on the lawn of the convent cloister, summer and winter unless extreme weather prevented it. Mother Katerina thought that it was easier to discuss things in this informal setting and it was sheltered from the winter wind, although extremely warm clothing was still required. The greatest advantage, however, which had become apparent after the revolution was that they were out of range of the ubiquitous bugs.

Mother Katerina recounted to the Monsignor the events of the day before.

'What an extraordinary girl,' he said when she had finished, 'and you think that she knew what she was doing? It wasn't just stupidity?'

'I don't believe so.'

'But if not that – what?'

'Strange as it may sound, I think that she is genuinely driven to fight injustice and inhumanity. She told me how shocked she had been by the NAS treatment of some children in a neighbouring village just after she arrived. Mind you it did sound pretty brutal but perhaps we are just getting inured to it.'

'Not that, never that,'

'But what do I do with her? I must do something and I have asked her to see me tomorrow morning. Do I sack her? I am not inclined to as it would seem cowardly – on the other hand it might be the only way to save her. I think Travsky may well execute her as an example – you know how he deals with dissent. And I don't think her Irish passport will save her, he has shown himself only too ready to mock the impotence of the EU.'

Mother Katerina looked at him desperately. He thought for some minutes, 'Of course there is no easy answer and it's probably going to end badly whatever you decide. I would favour asking for her resignation but allowing her to continue to work until the end of term. I don't think that we will get to the end of term; it's a long way off but there is just a chance we might get her back to Ireland intact,' but he added grimly, 'in fact, I doubt if we will get to the end of the week.'

The following day, Mother Katerina interviewed Bernadette O'Neill and suggested that, for her own safety, she should return to Ireland or Oxford during the next holiday. On the lawn away from the walls she added, as they walked back to the refrectory, 'Bernadette, you have shown great courage, even if not wisely. To try and protect the rest of the community from the authorities, I shall portray your early leaving as a disciplinary measure. But you will know my real opinion. I look forward to your concert but I think it would be wise to stick to a conventional repertory. Whatever happens, God go with you.'

'I understand, Reverend Mother. May God go with you and your beleaguered country!'

*

Mara woke with the noise below of the doors being forced open. She had known that it would come and, sure enough, the NAS were there early, two hours before the dawn, when they knew that they would catch their quarries asleep, vulnerable and unprepared. Though why these brutal thugs had to employ these tactics against a crew of nuns, teachers and schoolgirls, she could not imagine. In her heart, she despised their stupidity almost as much as she feared their savagery. She was indeed terrified but at the same time relieved that at last it had happened. No longer would she have to look round corners for eaves droppers, search for hidden microphones and wonder which of her friends would inform against her.

There were new fears. She knew that her relative immunity to date had been due to Travsky's desire to recruit her father into his regime. She had learnt fast, listening and calculating for the last two years. She realised that Nicklaus Oblov with his network of international contacts would be invaluable in endorsing abroad Travsky's regime of terror. Equally, she knew that in the end he would not co-operate and indeed she would hate him, her own father, if he did. Her inevitable and dreadful conclusion was that her father was hesitating only because of the danger to her and perhaps to her mother, if she was still alive. Sooner or later he would have to show his true colours and stand up for freedom and decency against the pervading evil even if it meant sacrificing her. Gloomily she just hoped for a quick decent death but she knew even that was unlikely and the alternatives, too horrible to think about rationally, still kept flashing through her mind.

She grabbed a tracksuit from her locker and got the trousers on before her study door burst open and a green uniformed woman pulled her into the corridor. Most of her companions were standing in night clothes in a daze not moving or doing anything. She recognised two NAS men and a woman as they moved up the corridor looking under beds and tearing open wardrobes. Finally satisfied that there were no more students hiding, they started herding everybody through the corridor, down the wide iron railings of the stairs and into the courtyard below. The courtyard was a seething crowd of police, NAS, staff and students At one end by the gate arch two lorries had been brought in each topped by a wire cage. Eventually some sort of order supervened. Nuns and staff were told to line up at one side of the courtyard and the students the other. A senior NAS man with gold braid on his green hat ordered the nuns to fetch a trestle table and told the mother superior to get the staff and students record files. He then walked up and down the line.

Mara could hear each pupil being asked their name, their parents' or guardian's names and occupation. Based on this information, with occasional reference to a file, some were told they could go back to their dormitories whilst most were taken with the nuns and the lay teachers to the games hall changing room 'to await trial'. It was bitterly cold and almost all of them were inadequately dressed and shivering. Mara debated whether to try and hide her identity as she had tried once before. She knew, however, that the NAS would have access to her record and also that some of her fellow students would certainly inform against her. It was useless. When the scowling chief arrived she looked him in the face and said as proudly as she could, 'Tamara Nikolaevna Oblova, my Father is Nicklaus, Foreign Minister of Moltravia, my mother is Gisela, Junior Minister of Justice of Moltravia.'

The scowling face broke into a dreadful smile, '*Endlich die Oblova Luderlein,*[7] we knew you were here.' And then to a subordinate, 'Take her straight to the cage, she's definitely for the Farm and doesn't need a trial. By the way, you can come off *deinem hohen Ross,*[8] your father is the ex foreign minister of this country and your mother, depending on how your father behaves, will probably soon be or already is, ex-everything.'

He laughed as she was half pulled towards the metal cage. She stifled a sob trying hard not to allow him to see the distress that he had caused. In fact his brutal remark only cruelly confirmed what deep in her heart she already knew. The cage already contained several teachers and a few, mainly senior, students who were obviously regarded as the hard core criminals although it was difficult to imagine what they could have done to warrant this elevated status.

After a while the drumhead trials had obviously got under way and a procession of bedraggled students were added to those already in the cages. Eventually Mara's cage was full and an armoured army bus drove into the courtyard. The gates of the cage were opened and between lines

---

7   At last the little Oblova slut

8   Your high horse

of NAS with machine pistols the inmates were transferred into it. The seats in the coach were close packed benches made for troop movements. To her surprise Mara found herself pushed up against a teacher who she immediately recognised as the tall Irish student teacher who had stunned them all with her lecture and her wonderful voice before. This time the tall girl seemed very young and not surprisingly, very confused but nonetheless she somehow radiated a sense of resilience and strength which Mara found to be reassuring. Don't be ridiculous she said to herself, snatching another sidelong glance at her striking, if unkempt, companion, she's in the same boat and just as terrified as I am. At that moment, the girl chanced to look down straight into Mara's enquiring eyes and said, 'You're Tamara, aren't you?'

PART TWO

THE LAST STAR RISING

Daphni, quid antiquos signorum suspicis ortus?[9]

VIRGIL: ECLOGUE IX

---

9   "Why, Daphnis, gazing upward, do you mark
    The ancient risings of the Signs?"

1
COCYTUS

Quindi Cocito tutto s'aggelava[10]

DANTE: INFERNO 34 V 52

Cold menaced. It brooded like a sluggish viscous plague laying siege in every nook and cranny. Even the centrally heated buildings never really held it at bay. It seeped in everywhere and, in the face of the encroaching ice, all life seemed fragile. It penetrated the nose, the lungs, the fingers, the voice. Its doom-laden persistence crushed the natural good humour of the people and lay heavy on every aspect of existence. Above the ironbound earth the frozen fog, marinated with industrial filth, lay motionless in great impenetrable patches.

Detty had felt cold in Ireland and England but even in her wet and often cold Kildare, a winter morning could still suddenly sparkle with frost giving a beauty to the land. If the cold driving rain chilled, it was always somehow incidental, something to be viewed from a warm room or a heated car. Here it invaded the whole body and threatened to destroy the tough but vulnerable men and women who had to lead their

---

10   To lock Cocytus eternally in ice

lives in it. Here the cold penetrated the soul until it seemed that finding warmth was the only thing that mattered in the whole world.

The previous day, she had decided to take a trip to have a look at the capital, Königshof. It only took an hour by bus in spite of the bad state of the roads. She went down to the stop and hesitantly caught a bus into the city. She wasn't quite sure what she was going to do but was sure it would be different and interesting. Capital cities were places where you saw sights, shopped and had fun, weren't they? She had always gone to Dublin or London to have a good time, to see the bright lights, the stores, the markets, the shows, the pubs, the concerts, street musicians and many other things. Somehow, here though she wasn't sure, the ominous gloom that had penetrated even the convent made the prospect of bright lights and pleasure seem less likely. She got off the bus near the centre of the city. It wasn't what she expected and she wandered aimlessly. On her left were high walls. She asked a passer-by in Russian what the building was. A haunted look came into the old woman's eyes and she looked at Detty incredulously and then fixed her eyes on the ground and walked away. There seemed to be nothing in the centre of the city except high slab-sided blocks with a ghastly uniformity. One building only, opposite the high-walled fortress that she had asked about, seemed dignified and different. It was old and elegant but neglected and ruined. Over what once had been the main gate was a single shield with three fish on it. They reminded Detty of the herrings in the market at Howth, but surely nobody put herrings on a coat of arms? Somehow, however, there seemed a mystery and a history in that building that fascinated her. After the singular lack of success which had attended her first attempt to ask the locals about the city, she hesitated to ask again. Finally, she felt too depressed to stay in the centre and walked aimlessly back along her bus route into the suburbs. Eventually she would catch the bus back to the convent but in the meanwhile she wondered if she could find out more about Königshof away from the dreary, featureless and seemingly fearful, centre.

After walking about two kilometres she found herself in a squalid run-down suburb. The light was failing and she wondered if she had ever seen a drearier place. What had once been a shopping street led away at right angles from the main road. Most of the shops were abandoned with broken or boarded-up fronts and casual piles of unopened mail accumulating behind the doors, but a few were still open. She found herself wondering what sort of business they did as the shelves were empty and the customers were almost non-existent. Occasionally a woman would walk down the street looking cautiously at each shop in turn before finally diving into one, which seemed as bare as the others. Sometimes the shopper emerged with a small brown paper-wrapped parcel, which she tried to hide in her clothes, sometimes there were only shouted words and the would-be shopper came out with nothing.

The worst part was the children. Unlike the adults they seemed everywhere. Most were undersized and dressed in tatters. A few of the older ones were in some sort of uniform and appeared to lord it over the youngsters around them. Detty watched until the bully boys went away and then approached the saddest of the groups of urchins. None could have been more than twelve years old and the youngest were no more than six or seven. Conscious of her Christian duty to give to the poor, she turned out the pockets of her jeans finding seven thalers and a few groschen, keeping back only her return bus ticket. She offered these to the children but was amazed when, instead of accepting them gratefully, they scattered away like frightened rabbits. Some just disappeared, others, after reaching a corner building, turned to stare with wide hungry eyes at the strange, tall woman who was clearly a government agent out to trick them into betraying themselves. A perplexed unhappy Detty finally gave up the attempt to offer them help and hurried to the next bus stop to return to the relative familiarity of the convent.

At breakfast the following day she had asked one of the sisters about the building with tall walls that she had seen in the centre of Königshof.

'You really don't know what that is?' came the startled reply.

'No.' confessed Detty feeling stupid.

The nun lowered her voice. 'It's the Winterburg. Once there was a Crusader fortress on the site but now it's the headquarters of the NAS. They are the secret police but we mustn't call them that. Nobody knows

107

what goes on in there but not many that go in come out alive. In fact come to think of it I don't know of anyone who has.'

Detty had echoed the nun's involuntary shudder.

Now she looked out of the stone carved mullioned classroom windows in the convent and wondered whether it was the climate or the inhuman yolk crushing the suffering land, which was worse. Did they just fit together as two parts of a gruesome whole, which seemed to symbolise the history of these lands with their frozen armies, frozen prisoners and even frozen children? Now in this awful winter a tyranny was growing again and already showing evil on a scale that even its forbears might have envied. She pulled her lined parka round herself as her teenage class streamed in for their English lesson. Somehow Pope and the Age of Reason on the banks of the Thames at Twickenham seemed very remote. She brightened as she remembered the choir trip out to a local village arranged for that afternoon.

The dank conifer woods with their lifeless forest floor seemed to portend evil even from the relative insulation of the public bus. The villages along the road were empty and the country farms deserted in amongst the siege trenches of frozen muddy ruts. She wondered how the country managed to produce food at all amidst this ironbound chill.

She was not a gloomy person but she defied anybody not to feel gloomy looking out on that symphony of morbid icy grey. She made an effort to cast her mind away from the present and think back to the past for comfort. She began to mull over the startling change that had taken place in her life. The moment that she boarded the plane to fly to London events began to take over.

She thought back to the idyll of last summer and remembered its pleasures one by one in an attempt to forget the cold in the freezing, ice-draughty bus. The Commemoration Ball stuck in her mind as the high-point of pleasure. Perhaps even better was the day after the Ball when she had woken at about midday to June sunshine and a feeling of great contentment. The Ball had ended at five in the morning and after various late night carousings and a punt along the summer river with Steve, she had got to bed about an hour later. It was the end of a perfect year at university and she remembered the warm satisfaction, which had spread over her, as she woke in bed with the summer sunshine already at its height scintillating across the quad outside her window.

She reviewed for a moment the good things about university – getting in in the first place after the grind and restrictions of her own convent years, which had been enlivened only by music. Fortunately she found languages easy and her high grades in Russian, German and music made her scholarship never really in doubt. The first year she had done well with good results and by the second she had felt able to spread her wings a bit. She had represented the university at 800 metres, captained the college tennis team and won the university singing prize – almost too much. I sound like a proper little teacher's pet; she thought to herself and chuckled. What was it about Cinderella and the pumpkin? But there had been no midnight chimes at that ball. Heads had been turned it was true as she arrived at the reception with Steve, who wasn't exactly Prince Charming, but he was good enough. There was nothing special between them but she knew that several of her girl riends would have loved him to invite them. Although he danced enthusiastically with all of the gang, she had been his partner and she had thoroughly enjoyed it.

Her mother had written to say that the silver-olive Indian silk with black trimmings sounded desperately expensive and far too old for a twenty-year-old. She was a bit worried beforehand but she had had a generous cheque from her uncle in Kilkenny and couldn't think of a better way to spend it. As for being too old for her, she knew that her strong good looks, tall mature figure and long red-chestnut hair needed something striking, not just pretty, and she knew that she had looked stunning. She had known it, everyone had said it and the photographs had proved it as her mother had reluctantly conceded. Even the group's comic, Ben Charles' mouth had dropped open when he saw her.

'That's a bit different from jeans and a tee shirt, Detty,' he had said, and after a pause, 'I'll even forgive a colleen wearing British racing green.'

'If an Irish girl can't wear green,' she had retorted with a theatrical pout, 'I don't know who can, and anyway it's not British racing it's darker.'

'OK' he said. 'I'll shut up on condition you dance with me.'

So it was settled.

She would wear the dress again at the New Year ball at the Curragh, she thought as the cold penetrated even deeper through the bus.

The afternoon after the Commemoration Ball she had packed for the evening flight to Dublin. She was excited about going home. There had been so much to tell and so much to plan.

For some reason, that she didn't entirely understand, from early on she had always been determined to learn German and Russian. The German had presented no difficulties, as there was an excellent teacher from Stuttgart attached to the Convent of St Conleth where she had boarded during her sixth-form years. The Russian was another problem. Fortunately the sisters and Mother Bridged were sensitive enough to realise that they had an exceptional linguist in their charge and after some negotiation Detty was allowed to visit an eminent native Russian speaker to prepare for her leaving exams.

As soon as these issues were settled another had appeared. Detty had sung in a desultory fashion and had had piano lessons at home ever since she was tiny. As soon as she started at the convent at eleven she had joined the choir and sung at services and concerts. In her later teens two events occurred almost simultaneously. Her serious interest in music, particularly the high Romantics, became intense and slowly her voice began to develop in such a way that the other girls in the choir began to ask why she couldn't sing more softly. Detty promised she would try with her usual crooked smile and they stopped teasing her. She began to realise, however, that her voice was somehow different – much more powerful and even, she dared to think, more beautiful than the rest of the choir. She was often chosen to sing solos at the regular concerts and thoroughly enjoyed it. Most of all though she enjoyed wandering off with her borrowed scores into the Kildare fields, far from home and the convent buildings to sing Schubert, Brahms and Strauss, interpreted in her own way, and well out of earshot of her fellow pupils. She read all the music books she could lay her hands on and eventually persuaded her reluctant father to buy her a banjo and allow her to play Irish music with the locals during the holidays.

In time the music teacher, Mrs Lynch, persuaded the Superior that this lanky young doctor's daughter had the makings of a talent. To

Detty's delight she was allowed to enrol for lessons with Adele O'Mara, who had had a successful professional career as a mezzo soprano in London and Germany, before retiring to her native Dublin to teach. Detty was entranced with the thought of studying with a teacher who had sung Cherubino and Octavian in London but felt extremely nervous. Soon, however, they got to know and like each other and Detty sat entranced, at the end of her lessons, with Adele's stories of singers and other musicians in the great opera houses and concert halls. One day Adele entered Detty for the Brennan Cup at the Feis Ceoil for under eighteen-year-olds. To Detty's mortification she finished third. Adele told her that it was good for her and would damp her overwhelming ambition.

Detty, however, took the result as a personal insult and worked so hard at her music that she almost missed the top honours in languages that were hers for the taking. In the end all worked out well and she secured a scholarship to her English university. She was delighted but not so some of the less academic nuns who thought that she must be 'selling her soul to the divil and why did she need to go to heathen places when there were better Christian universities in Ireland?' During the first year she had worked hard at university and done well in her exams confirming her scholarship. She relaxed a bit after that and decided to enjoy the good things around her. More music, dancing, sport and men entered her life and she had enjoyed every minute of it.

After the ball her father had met her at Dublin airport and they drove back through warm evening sunshine. She remembered the fields had been still wet enough after recent rain to retain the intense green of home. In the old white house with her father's branch surgery attached she had been content to relax for once, changing out of the overdrive which had characterised her recent life. She helped her mother as much as possible, went for the odd ride and played the piano and sang in a desultory fashion. Peggy, her mother, was quite worried that her firebrand twenty-year-old was uncharacteristically prepared to relax but wisely said nothing. She contented herself with persuading her sixteen-year-old Nuala, that trips into Dublin almost every night to hear the latest rock group would do nothing for her scholastic career. She wondered, wickedly as she thought, why the good God couldn't have divided the talents more equally between her children. The dynamic elder daughter was as much of a problem as the lazy younger one. Anyway, Detty was growing up much too quickly and learning a lot of dubious English habits, but she rejoiced that they were both healthy and decided it was better not to interfere. She exercised what she called self-discipline, although it might have been cowardice, and didn't mention the offending green silk evening sheath.

After only a few lazy days, riding and seeing friends, Detty began to long to get going again and one morning she telephoned Adele and arranged to go to Dublin to fix up more singing lessons during the summer. She took her mother's car and drove to the quiet house, which she had come to know so well, in the leafy south Dublin quarter of Ballsbridge. Adele greeted her with a warm kiss.

'How was university? Congratulations on the prize – thanks for your lovely card but you didn't tell me the programme.'

Detty smiled, 'I didn't dare. I thought that you wouldn't approve,' she said, and then went on. 'There is a compulsory programme chosen from a list of Schubert, Butterworth and Mendelssohn this year. Then the four finalists choose their own programme for the final audition. I sang Dowland's *'Come again. Sweet love doth now invite,' 'Mein Auge'* and...' she paused *'The Abscheulicher.'*

The expected explosion came.

'You sang what? I don't believe I am hearing this. What on earth made you choose that – you are mad – at your age?'

Detty was suddenly serious and confiding, 'I know it wasn't wise and I shouldn't have sung it at my age but you have always said that my voice is exceptionally mature. Besides,' she now spoke very quietly, 'it is very important to me.'

'What do you mean exactly?' said Adele, intrigued.

'It is the hymn of decency against bestiality and hatred. It is not a sacred piece and yet for me it stands for everything – for faith. Adele, if I ever stood at the edge of death or at the gate of hell that music would resound through my head giving me hope and strength – but I'm sounding pompous...'

She trailed off weakly, embarrassed that she had declared so much of her inner self. She looked at Adele with her head shyly on one side and there was a long silence.

The latter thought for a long time and finally said seriously, 'I could agree with all that... but it's still fiendishly difficult and at your age... I once sang Leonore on tour with the WNO in the days when we got asked to do everything. It lay too high for me and I struggled – it wasn't my outstanding part but I was flattered that they asked me and once you have sung it you never forget it.'

Detty nodded, 'Well, I did win, anyway,' she said grinning again.

'Sure... incredible!' Adele laughed. ' The judges must have been very broad-minded but you must have had some coaching too. Who did you go to?'

'Haydn Roberts – he is living and teaching in North Oxford. I got an introduction to him through one of the college organ scholars. We hit it off at once. He encouraged me in all my bad habits, Wagner, Strauss, etc. and finally he put me up to doing the *Abscheulicher*. In his forceful Welsh way he said, "Detty, go for it. Don't worry what they think. You've got the voice even at your age. Slay them." So I did.'

'Arrogant minx,' Adele said laughing. 'But that sounds like Haydn – never conventional. Still you were very lucky – he was a wonderful baritone – a real musician and I hear that he's an excellent teacher. Give him my love when you get back. Tell him not to corrupt you too much. Oh and by the way, tell him I still remember the Wurzburg "*Forza*".'

Detty looked at her quizzically but clearly no more information was to be forthcoming about the mystery of the Wurzburg '*Forza*' as Adele went on briskly,

'Now to business – show me what you can do. Don't start with the *Abscheulicher*.'

Adele sat at the Bosendorfer grand and nodded as her pupil sang several scales. She then suggested Schubert's '*Nacht und traume*' and still Adele just listened and nodded. At the end she said smiling, 'What about this Wagner and Strauss then?'

Detty had fetched a score of *Ariadne auf Naxos* from the bookcase and said, "*Es gibt ein Reich?*" enquiringly to Adele who opened the score onto the piano.

Detty was determined to show her long-time teacher how her voice had matured. She put all the phrasing, clarity and emotion that she could muster into the scena. She felt good about it and after she closed she put her head on one side again awaiting her teacher's verdict.

Finally Adele had said quietly, 'Yes – that is now a voice that could encompass even the *Abscheulicher*. Well done, Detty. You have done well – so has Haydn – your voice has reached maturity very early the head register is now fully there without strain – and other things too – your intonation is much more sensitive and the attack is more certain. Of course your diction is excellent – one advantage of being a linguist and really understanding what you are singing. It's a very different voice from two years ago but that was to be hoped. At about your age a woman's voice should grow steadily in range and power if it has the capacity and is well treated. Yours is one of the rare ones that become ready really early. This is partly because you have the physique to do it and partly because you are a musician who learns very quickly. I think that you can sing these big pieces but don't start forcing it and above all don't sing too much. You are a great enthusiast and a bit of a show-off. Resist the temptation to sing Brunnhilde's Immolation Scene at every convent reunion. However, I would like you to give your competition programme in Dublin before you go back to university in the autumn – *Abscheulicher* included. Would it be possible?'

'Of course, I'd love to,' Detty replied without hesitation.

'OK, I'll try and arrange it with the Philharmonic Society Orchestra at the NCH. If we can get a spare evening.'

Adele went on. 'Possibly all Beethoven and Strauss, say the Egmont Overture to start with then *Ein Heldenleben*. Then you for the whole second part with three Strauss songs and the *Abscheulicher*. We will get you some press notices – no problem at the NCH. When would suit you? When do you have to be back in England?'

'It would have to be before mid-September as I go to Europe then until the summer – I shan't be going back to England until after that. It's the language year away from university.'

'That should be OK – where are you off to first?'

'Moltravia.'

'Moltravia! That's a bit primitive, isn't it?'

'Probably but it suits me – there are not too many places that speak Russian and German and there is a sister convent to St Conleth's that I went to here.'

'Your choice, but I think I would rather go to Germany or settle for six months each in St Petersburg and Berlin, Munich or Vienna. However, we should be able to do the concert in the first week of September before you go. I am off on holiday next week but we could have several rehearsals when I get back if you like.'

'Fine,' said Detty and set off for home with a feeling of exhilaration.

For the next few weeks she divided her time between daily practice, riding through the Kildare countryside whenever the rain stopped, reading her German and Russian texts and gossiping with her Aunt Deidre over home-made barmbrack and the best coffee in Ireland outside Bewley's. Aunt Deidre was her father's younger sister and they had always had a lot in common. Detty was like her aunt in both looks and character. They were both tall, athletic women with handsome chiselled features and sharp intelligence spiced with a mad humour. Deidre had spent much of her life abroad and was supposed to have unmasked a New York Mafia racket assisted only by her ready wit and her Irish setter. The latter was also reputed to have disarmed and emasculated the Capo in front of his Mafioso family. She still kept red Setters although not the original mythical American one. There was also a rumour that she had won a sheep shearing competition in Australia without revealing her true gender.

She had lost her wanderlust and returned home to Ballyinch where she was now happily married to a moderately successful racehorse breeder and trainer called Christy Lorne. She had twin nine-year-olds called Eileen and Connor who showed every sign of taking after their mother. She had always been close to Detty and they had become very good friends and chattered together endlessly about Ireland, men, travel, books and sport. The only thing Deidre didn't share with her niece was music. She had no interest in this and maintained that her brother had made Detty waste a lot of time practising when she could have done something more useful. Gradually, however, she realised that her niece had an unusual talent and furthermore genuinely loved music. Thereafter she stopped being critical and even occasionally came to listen to Detty sing or play. She was now anxious to hear everything about university and the projected trip to Moltravia. Several of the more anxious family and friends had expressed concern over the unstable political scene in Moltravia but Detty was scornful. 'If I don't go to any country that is politically unacceptable I shan't have many left to choose from and anyway I am hardly likely to be abducted from a convent,' she had snapped back when doubt was expressed.

She was more concerned about the concert and as the day approached she practised ever more seriously at the battered upright which she had played ever since she was a little girl. Her mother, who was no musician, remarked rather absentmindedly that her voice sounded wonderful and somehow different. Apart from that her only audience was her father's young registrar, Roger Flynn, who made any excuse to loiter in the hall after the end of his branch surgery to listen to her with a sick calf expression on his face. Fortunately Nuala, who teased him unmercifully, was away staying with friends in France for the summer holidays but the whole family were aware of Roger's unconcealed admiration for his boss's beautiful elder daughter. It made Detty cross and embarrassed, as she was a kind-hearted girl and genuinely liked Roger. She didn't want to hurt him, but high romance followed by a life as a country GP's wife was definitely not on her present agenda. University, Moltravia and the increasing magnetism of the great musical cities of Europe definitely came first.

As the concert grew closer she felt excited but a bit diffident. She ran through the programme with Adele several times. The latter made a few suggestions but on the whole said little and encouraged her to sing the programme as she had done previously in Oxford. She didn't want to give Detty conflicting advice about the presentation of these pieces. Perhaps the greatest excitement was the posters giving the programme with the logo of the NCH and underneath Orchestra of the Dublin Philharmonic Society conductor Albrecht Lowenthal and finally, unbelievably, in equal letters Bernadette O'Neill – Soprano. This made her feel professional and very proud. A few days before she had met Albrecht and had had a first piano rehearsal with him. Detty liked him immediately. He was old enough to be her grandfather but treated his young soloist with deferential middle-European courtesy.

'The *Abscheulicher* is a very difficult piece for such a young voice but I hear from all sides you sing eeit very well. Perhaps we should start with the *Lieder* however?'

He was encouraging and interesting to work with without being intimidating. Detty's good musicianship found no problem in adapting to a new conductor and she felt as confident as she could as they approached the great night. She decided to wear her green Indian silk dress which, fortuitously, was comfortable for singing. This time, not wishing to incur the wrath of her Prima Donna daughter, Peggy said nothing about it being too old for her.

On the afternoon of the final rehearsal she went through the John Field room, past the great aspidistra, up the double staircase and through the side gallery feeling awed by the presence of the spirit of so many great musicians.

The word had gone round Dublin musical circles that there was a new native talent of more than ordinary promise and the hall was packed. The long wait during the orchestral pieces of the first half had to be survived but eventually she was on the platform to warm applause. The voice was there and she thought that the Strauss songs probably sounded as good, if not better, than they had done in the Oxford competition. She was able to approach her greatest test confidently with her passionate cry of 'Monster' ringing out against the tyrant. The agony of love and the hope of justice followed. Her parents near the front of the hall were on the edge of their seats as she came to *'Komm Hoffnung'*. Their musical knowledge was scanty but clearly their daughter was achieving something spectacular and they sensed the electricity in the hall, which occurs only on the rare occasions when the beautiful is spiced with the unexpected. She had hardly finished when the applause swelled into cheers as she was led back onto the platform to words of congratulation whispered enthusiastically by Albrecht in his courtly Viennese English.

She had still been mulling over the concert when she made the fateful flight to London three days later. The reviews had been excellent but more than one had voiced misgivings about so young a singer tackling such mature and difficult music. She changed planes in Berlin and boarded the elderly Ilyuishin which was to fly her to Königshof. She had begun to think about her destination and the next three months. She had still thought mainly about the convent and her role in it. Would it be like her old school? How would she get on teaching? Would she get the language practice she needed? She needed to keep up her voice practice but wasn't sure whether there would be any music at the convent? Politics had hardly seemed important at this stage and previously in her mind had consisted only of the heroism of the Easter Rising and the moving but well-worn history of British imperialism. Now she knew how wrong she had been. In Moltravia politics mattered. She was living in an unstable and brutal country where the sudden disappearance after the knock on the door in the night-time had again become a source of daily fear.

The first sign of the real nature of her host country had occurred as soon as she landed at Königshof airport. The arrival area was bristling with hard faced men and women in dark green uniforms all carrying machine pistols and checking the papers of the arrivals against long typed lists. She was passed through by the expressionless officials, coldly but without difficulty, as her visa was in order. She was welcomed warmly, however, at the convent and began to settle in. In spite of the press control that the new government had introduced, she learnt from the foreign newspapers which were brought back clandestinely by nuns attending church meetings in neighbouring states that things were changing fast. The old KGB cadres started to reappear a generation later now labelled NAS (National Agency of Security) and seemed as happy with their new fascist masters as they had been with their old communist ones. They did not get it all their own way, however, as there were increasing stories of strikes in the struggling industrial centres. In the towns there were many demonstrations spearheaded by students some of whom were very young. The NAS sometimes made a lot of arrests but often did little to interfere but took endless photographs. Even in the small town of

Ziatow which housed the Sacred Heart Convent and school where she taught, there were student demonstrations some of which Detty had watched from a distance with her fellow pupils and teachers. She was anxious for her Moltravian friends but had no thought of her own safety being in question.

At the beginning of November the Government issued a proclamation which she ignored then but realised afterwards should have alarmed her. At the time she never even realised that it might apply to her. The decree stated that: Owing to the difficulty of establishing citizenship following the recent political upheavals, all persons resident in Moltravia on 1st November would be classified as citizens and, regardless of the passports that they hold, they will be subject to all Moltravian laws and decrees without redress to foreign or international agencies.'

Her teaching in English went on as usual and there was some secret debating at the school on the merits and demerits of parliamentary democracy and the safeguards the citizen should expect from the state. Free speech was flourishing under cover even as it was being strangled publicly. The sixteen-year-olds showed a lively interest and related the subject matter to events in Moltravia but showed no fear, at least in the early days for their privileged skins. There were rumours in the streets of mass detentions in larger cities and a decree reintroducing compulsory military service for young men was suddenly announced. Some said that this was to reduce the street protests. It all seemed rather distant, however, when viewed from within convent walls. Gradually, even during the first term though discussion became more furtive and subdued and then began to peter out altogether.

She shook herself out of her reverie and back to reality as the rickety bus drove into the village square of their destination. Detty little realised that she was about to discover firsthand the reality of Moltravia under Travsky and the NAS.

When they arrived their hosts from the school seemed cheerful and pleased to see them. The girls sang their folk song programme, which was politely applauded and Detty added Schubert's Forelle and the Last Rose of Summer which seemed somehow appropriate. The teachers at the village school remarked that she had a lovely voice and asked her where she had learnt to sing so well. Over lemon tea and local cakes she talked about her home and university in England and the students and teachers seemed really absorbed and asked her lots of questions. All the visitors from the Sacred Heart remarked what a warm friendly atmosphere the village had even in the depths of winter. This prompted one of the local teachers to mention that this had not always been so and the place had a dark side to its history. There had been a Nazi concentration camp just outside the village, which was still commemorated by a memorial to the victims at its site.

Detty, with her awakened interest in political history, was curious to visit it after they left the school. The other teachers, however, shuddered and said that they didn't think there was much there and anyway it was not a suitable to take the children without prior notice. If she wanted, she could go alone as it wouldn't take long. Detty was suddenly determined and set off by herself. She was wearing strong boots and walking briskly to keep the cold at bay. It didn't take her long to reach the site through the flat unfenced fields, which were bleak and muddy. She found it quite easily on a rough track leading into some sparse woods where the camp had once stood. After more than seventy years nothing remained of the camp but the memorial was there. It was a silestone on a plinth commemorating the 62,000 who had died there. Just as she was about to leave and walk back she noticed that under the plinth there was writing in fresh spray paint. It was very neat and not at all the usual type of coarse graffiti. Across the stone was written in German, *'Jetzt alles vergeblich – Travsky hat aus Hitler ersehen*[11] and below 'NAS=SS.' For a moment she looked and wondered what exactly Travsky had learnt from Hitler. Then she heard a vehicle approaching up the track. She didn't know what made her hide but she somehow didn't want to be discovered by strangers in this emotional place so she slipped behind a tree.

Men in green uniforms jumped from a minibus. One of them pointed to the memorial and spoke angrily to the officer who nodded. She couldn't hear what they said but after some discussion they got back

---

11 Now everything is the same, Travsky has learnt from Hitler.

into the truck and returned down the lane. She just saw them turn onto the road towards the village then they disappeared behind some trees. Detty looked at her watch and realised that by delaying she had missed the bus back to the convent. She didn't worry too much as she knew there was a later one and, as a teacher, she had no need to be back at a specific time. As she started her return journey she spotted a passage through the trees to the right that she had missed on her way out. Instinctively she turned down it; after only a few paces of the track there was a dilapidated chapel, half hidden in the undergrowth which, relieved of its canopy of evergreen had invaded the old building. A wrought iron gate hung by one hinge. She edged inside. The light just struck a massive, worn sarcophagus in ancient stone: '*Gustav Immanuel, Knight of St Nicklaus and Hero of the Hanse.*'

With difficulty she read the old gothic script. She shrugged her shoulders. Presumably this was another proto Nazi who had tortured the good and squeezed the poor until they starved. What a hellhole she had chosen to work in. She walked briskly back along the road and arrived at the outskirts of the large village a short time later.

There were a lot of people milling about the streets looking agitated at an hour in the evening when the winter cold normally drove most inside to their TVs and suppers. Detty approached the square in front of the hall where they had sung earlier. A flagstaff which she had hardly noticed before stood in the square bare in the searing cold. The space in front of the flagstaff was floodlit by lights apparently running from a generator in the minibus that she had seen at the memorial. She saw an elderly man who was standing smoking with a worried expression on his face and asked him what was going on.

'NAS – trouble.' he muttered.

At that moment the officer appeared with an electric megaphone. He launched into a long tirade about the insult to the nation and its great leader, President Travsky. A local monument had been desecrated and he asked that the culprits should be denounced. He said that they knew it was the work of local young hooligan rabble and if the perpetrators were not revealed there would be a random selection for punishment. Still silence from the anxious faces.

'Very well,' he shouted and then to his men. 'Round up everyone into the square.'

Almost everyone was in the square already but the police searched the houses.

'Nobody leaves the square! Hoist the flag and we will teach these youngsters to give it proper respect. Separate the fourteen to thirty year olds – no arguments about age or fitness we will have them all.' Two policemen hoisted the red and black national flag of Moltravia while the rest set about brutally cudgelling anyone within range and eventually the young people – men and women, boys and girls were separated into a group. Detty was winded by a random blow from a club and at one point a policeman grabbed her and started pushing her into the segregated group of young people. Fortunately the village priest who had been at the school earlier during their visit was standing behind her. He protested that she was a foreign teacher visiting from the Sacred Heart and got clubbed in his turn but reluctantly the thug let Detty go. Eventually they had about fifty youngsters in the separate group. These were then told to take off their coats and sweaters. Any who were reluctant were savagely beaten and amid the groans many collapsed bleeding on the icy tarmac. Eventually all were shivering and blue dressed only in thin indoor clothes. The two policemen who had hoisted the flag then drove a group of the youngsters to a nearby farmyard where they were told to carry galvanised cattle pen sides back to the flagstaff and erect them. They struggled back to the flagstaff and, beaten by the police, erected a crude pen round it. All the young people were then driven inside and the gates padlocked.

'This hooligan group will remain here until morning to cool their heels and learn proper respect. No one will interfere, there will be a guard on duty in the schoolhouse and he will shoot if anyone from outside gets within twenty metres of the fence.'

As he finished speaking a couple came forward and flung themselves at the feet of the officer, 'Please spare my little one, Sir, Katya is delicate and so young.'

The officer replied, 'Stop snivelling or I'll have them all stripped so they can really feel the cold while they are learning to behave.'

He kneed the woman hard in stomach and she was pulled back by her husband bleeding. A girl already bleeding on the ground cried out to the woman, 'Don't mother – or they'll hurt you too!'

Like the others the child was only wearing indoor clothes. She had clear blue eyes which, in terror, she seemed to turn towards Detty with an unspoken plea. Eventually the parents knew that they could do no more and they turned away into a neighbouring house porch while the unspeakable cold of the winter night intensified.

Detty was at first numb with distress as she realised that she too could do nothing to help. Miserable and helpless she slipped away to catch the last bus back. She wondered how long any of them could survive dressed like that in cold which defied thick thermal clothing. She thought that they would all be dead by morning. She thought and thought about what she had seen and her horror and sadness turned to revulsion and anger. Incongruously music came uninvited into her head accompanied by the idea of an unspoken oath, half formed, half seen which she would not come to understand until much later. The tortured eyes of the 15-year-old and her anguished mother and father continued to haunt her for long afterward and she often wondered how it had ended. She was ashamed to be glad the term was nearly over and in a week she would be going home for the very short Christmas break. She would be glad to leave this country with its dreadful rulers mixed incongruously with a people who seemed so kind and honest. In spite of herself she was beginning to love them and she knew she would return for the next term in spite of everything.

The Christmas holiday in Ireland passed in a flash. It was marred by a furious argument with her parents as to whether she should go back to Moltravia.

'I have promised so I must,' she said with such determination that they knew it was pointless to oppose her. Deep down she knew that it was not only her promise which was taking her back. She had a task to perform.

When she returned she concentrated on preparing her talk on 'Ireland Yesterday and Today' which she had agreed to give to the students and staff. She had to prepare it in secret. She knew it would be a bombshell and would be forbidden if its theme were known. The lecture produced even greater alarm than she had anticipated and clearly her days at the Sacred Heart were numbered but she had fulfilled her task.

As a relief afterwards, she tried to distract herself by preparing for the concert which she was still to give as part of the pre-Lent festivities. The Mother Superior was aware of her talents and had particularly asked her to sing before the devastating lecture. Afterwards it was agreed that she should leave in due order at the pre-Lenten holiday but meanwhile the concert was still to go ahead. It might be her swansong but she had to make it good. In spite of the circumstances it was to be a joyful affair in the face of all the uncertainties and growing fear. She had chosen her four songs carefully to suit her voice with good tunes to please the youngsters. She started with *Dove sono*, which seemed strangely alien after her recent experience. She followed this with *The Cliffs of Doneen*, which he silently dedicated to the youngsters of the village most, if not all, of whom she presumed had died. To lighten the mood she sang *Molly Malone* exaggerating her rich brogue for the benefit of the English classes and finished with Desdemona's *Willow Song* and *Ave Maria* to mollify the nuns.

2
ZUEIGNUNG

Einst hielt ich, der Freiheit Zecher,
Hoch den Amethysten-Becher[12]

HERMANN VON GILM ZU ROSENEGG

She was still asleep when the raid came. There was a thunder on her door and there was only a minute to grab sweater and jeans before she was pushed out into the convent courtyard by swearing police thugs with machine pistols. It was nearly the last day before the holiday and like those of the school who had somewhere to go, Detty had packed her luggage to return home the night before hoping to be able to sleep in a little longer in the morning. Most of the staff and students were already there, shivering when she arrived in the courtyard. The police then divided them into groups. The older teachers and the very young children were then sent back into the school and told to remain there. The older pupils still wearing only their nightclothes or anything else which they had been able to grab, were herded onto buses. Detty found herself standing next to the driver.

---

12 Once I revelled in freedom and held the amethyst cup on high

'Where are we going? she asked.

'Interrogation centre,' he growled.

They turned into a disused barracks and were allowed to disembark from the bus. Armed guards kept them together on the freezing tarmac and Detty thought of the villagers in the piercing cold. This time she was definitely on the receiving end and she wondered if she would suffer a similar fate. An officer with a megaphone came out.

'Listen carefully. You have been brought here because of hooliganism and socially destructive activity at your school. You will be interrogated in turn and expected to give full and truthful information about yourselves and others.'

The interrogators sat at long tables inside the disused gymnasium with files of papers and photographs in front of them. They started with the younger ones, asking them questions about family-friends and what had been discussed at school. Most of the youngsters were allowed to leave with the ominous warning that 'that would be all for the moment'. They were presumably sent back to the school on the buses which had brought them. A number of the others were sent into the disused changing room with armed guards on the doors. The number of the detained increased as the older students and teachers were questioned until there were about forty in all.

Detty was one of the last group to be ordered up to the tables. She was angry and shivering. Immediately she looked straight at the interrogator assigned to her and said, 'I am a citizen of the Republic of Ireland and the European Union and I demand that you inform my Embassy immediately. I have witnessed disgraceful scenes this afternoon, which are a gross breach of human rights. I am here as a teacher and also a guest of your country on a cultural exchange from a British university.'

The interrogator looked at her just as directly and said, 'You are also a known spy and an agitator. We know that you are one of the ringleaders. You can be grateful that you are in civilian not military hands. A military court would have convicted you outright and probably sent you straight before a firing squad. You will now answer my questions.'

The questions concerned her identity, teaching, opinions and friends and the content of her activities since entering Moltravia. Shaken by

126

the talk of summary execution she answered some factual questions but refused to be drawn on the others. After about ten minutes the questioner said half to himself, 'It really doesn't matter. We have more than enough already.'

Detty wondered what it was of which they had 'more than enough'.

'Take her to the changing room to wait trial.'

Detty found herself amongst a crowd of bedraggled sisters, teachers and students from the Sacred Heart. They were wearing sweaters, dressing gowns and anything that they had been able to grab although it was now the middle of the afternoon.

The man with the megaphone entered. 'Those of you who have been brought here are all to be charged with serious offences. Because there are so many of you the magistrate has come here and the trials will start in a few minutes. Guards, bring them out into the hall.'

They were herded out. The 'magistrate' was an NAS officer with gold braid on his cap. He sat on an improvised dais with, on one side, a small enclosure. At the bottom of the hall was a wire compound with a door in one end.

'As your names are called you will be taken into the dock by a guard. First Bernadette Niamh O'Neill.'

Detty was surprised to be first after the long wait of the afternoon and almost reassured to hear the familiar hash made of pronouncing her second name. The interrogator was reading the evidence: 'Instigator of public anti-government agitation and demonstrations, corruption of young people and children against the party, spying for a foreign power.' It almost flowed over her and she wondered which foreign power she was supposed to have spied for. She couldn't really think of Ireland as 'a foreign power'. It might be England she supposed but there was true irony in that. At the end the magistrate said, 'Have you anything to say?'

Detty stammered out her Irish citizenship and asked for the Embassy to be informed.

The magistrate replied, 'Your offences were against this country and you will be tried in this country. I presume that you were trained as a terrorist in your own country. It has a reputation for that I believe.

You should know that I could sentence you to death.' He paused, 'Your activities have shown you to be a serious menace. The public hanging of a foreign spy would help us to encourage other countries to stop interfering with our internal affairs. However, because of your age and the possible need to interrogate you further, I am sentencing you to ten years in a labour camp. Take her away! Next!'

With her knees giving way Detty was led from the dock and pushed into the metal enclosure. She collapsed on the wire in despair and only roused herself when three more prisoners were pushed in to join her. She had heard nothing of their trial but was conscious of the quick disposal of the accused, all senior students from the Sacred Heart who had been each sentenced to five years in a labour camp for incitement to civil unrest. From the enclosure, they were transferred to a coach by more thuggish security policemen with machine pistols. One of these came on the coach with them and stood beside the driver as they pulled off. On the dark journey Detty found that she was sitting next to a small blond girl. She thought that she recognised her as being in the senior form at the Sacred Heart and who had taken part in the folk dance display in the concert before Lent. For a time she couldn't recall her name but eventually thought that she had remembered it and asked her, 'You're Tamara, aren't you?'

The girl looked surprised and said, 'Yes, Frau O'Neill, Tamara Nicolaevna but I didn't know you knew me.'

Detty smiled, 'I've seen you about and some of your friends are in my English class.'

Tamara continued, 'I heard you at the concert. You sang wonderfully – if only I could sing like that or even dance properly.' She looked wistful and continued, 'I've no voice and I'm too fat to dance well – look at my hips they are vast but I don't suppose any of that matters now.'

Detty looked at the neat young woman beside her and said, 'There doesn't seem much the matter with your figure to me, Tamara, and I saw you dance, it was fine – full of vigour and expression.'

'Thank you I'm so grateful to you, Frau O'Neill.'

'Tamara, how old are you?' said Detty suddenly.

'Seventeen – eighteen in January,' was the reply.

'Well I was twenty-one three months ago and our situation and relationship has changed a bit, hasn't it? Don't you think it's time that we stopped the Frau O'Neill stuff. My name is Bernadette – all my friends call me Detty and I would like you to too.'

'Of course Frau… Detty.'

'Now tell me, as you know this country and the regime much better than I do, what on earth is going to happen to us?'

Tamara looked sad and serious beyond her seventeen years.

'I will tell you what I know but it's not much,' she said and after a short pause continued. 'After the fall of the Soviet Union there were several independent small states in this region. Moltravia was in what had been at one time or another, the USSR, Poland and Germany. We were poor and life was hard but at first we were free and democratic. My father was defence minister and tried to set up treaties with the West to protect us. The poverty was severe and the people got restless. The extreme right wing mounted propaganda campaigns persuading everybody that they were being bled white by Jews and westerners. The president was honest and fair but to be truthful Hoffman – that was his name – was never really strong. He was an idealist and a dreamer. Travsky, the Fascist leader, plotted and plotted and persuaded some of the people that he did have the key to a crock of gold. He promised prosperity for all. He mounted a military coup, which was shamefully easily successful mainly because the government was taken totally by surprise. He deposed the elected government and conquered some of our smaller neighbouring states forming what he called greater Moltravia. He suppressed all opposition at home – often brutally. NATO was powerless because he inherited a good stock of weapons-grade uranium, plutonium and old nuclear weapons and showed some readiness to use them.'

'Now we come to the present situation. Travsky realised that there was still a powerful opposition in the country who were ashamed at how easily they had been overthrown. He needed some of them to work for him, so he didn't want to purge them in the usual way. Most of the educated people of Moltravia sent their children to religious schools and colleges such as our Sacred Heart Convent. Travsky needed hostages so he proceeded to raid the schools, sending the boys into the army or cadet regiments where they would be under military control and subjected to military discipline. This left the women. Travsky is no fool and realised that in many cases he could control his enemies by keeping tabs on their whole families. The schools and colleges were raided and he made sure that all prominent women and the female relatives of key figures, plus one or two useful others, were sent to labour camps under trumped up charges. Other women outside the colleges are collected piecemeal and suffer the same fate. He thus has total power over his opponents – men in the army under military discipline, women in labour camps under the terrible new penal code. A few outsiders, like you, who were thought to be dangerous, were caught in the same mesh. The Sacred Heart was the most prestigious girls' school and was left to last but rumours of what had happened at the others were already widespread and I knew we were under constant surveillance. You saw earlier that the students whose families were favourable to the regime were released immediately and sent home.

'"Evidence" is collected for the convictions. In most cases it is found by taking younger children from the schools on one side and threatening them with dreadful things that will happen to them and their parents until they are so terrified that they sign anything put in front of them. A few of the young ones were more stubborn and they were taken away and "persuaded". All read out aloud and signed the statements in the end. The court trial is then held. It is a farce and everybody knows that the selected students will be found guilty. At my cousin's high school, which was raided a month ago, the magistrate came to the school and the extorted statements were read out with the charge. All were found guilty, some were taken to labour camps but the rest including my cousin were made to denounce their families at show public meetings which is both evidence against their parents and a warning to them. Video films of students behind bars in tiny custody cells are taken by the police and sent to their parents with the threat that worse may follow if the parents are "uncooperative". Tales of torture by the secret police – the NAS – abound and even if they were not always substantiated, would you chance it with your child? You imagine the effect that that would have on your father – or mine.'

'The bastards,' said Detty, pale and hoarse thinking of her previous experience of NAS methods at the village.

'That's not all,' continued Tamara. 'There are some members of the former government that are too important for the casual warning to be enough. Their relatives have received special labour camp sentences were they can be supervised and cowed at leisure. These camps are run by cadres of volunteers not chosen for their gentility and that, Detty,' Detty noticed she used the diminutive easily for the first time, 'is probably where we are going now. We may be fed clothed even heated and to some degree cherished, because we are important, but at the same time we will be terrified and possibly tortured – me because of my father, you because you are a useful foreigner and, forgive me, you have stuck your neck out. You are a counter in the game.'

'God, I never thought of myself as that,' said Detty.

'I hope and pray to Almighty God that I am wrong.'

The Farm labour camp had four dormitory houses around two sides of a quadrangle. The third side was open down to the wire fence and main gate where the approach road reached it. The fourth was closed by the great hall of a former mansion reached by a flight of steps. It was this they now entered. A man with a megaphone appeared as they formed a group in the hall. Unceremoniously they were sent for medical inspection.

Few of them were wearing more than a sweater and jeans or a dressing gown over their night clothes. Under the bored eye of a hatchet-faced supervisor, a permanent number tape was clicked round each of their left wrists. Detty wondered what it would be like ten years later. They were then lined up for photographs. She found the whole business revolting but before she could think too much she had to join the medical queue.

Army paramedics under the loose supervision of the camp MO who did very little except stare coldly at the new intake, carried out the medicals. Each detainee went first to the stool in front of the table and was asked routine questions about her health, family, childhood, immunisations followed by details of her personal and medical history.

As they got to the head of the queue Tamara whispered to Detty,

'Don't make a fuss – try to answer the questions – they may do horrible things if you don't.'

Detty had the distinct impression that she was being protected by the tiny youngster more than three years her junior. She could hardly believe her ears as she heard Tamara's interview. She answered the intrusive questions in a calm matter of fact voice that betrayed no hint of embarrassment. It worked as she was rapidly waved through to shower.

It was now Detty's turn to be questioned and she sat in front of the interrogator. She answered the main questions but when it came to the personal ones about whether she had extracted secret information from Moltravians by seduction, she saw red and threw her head back and refused to answer.

'You're the Irish spy girl – we know you are a slag and we just want to know who you've been with and where. Be careful because I don't think anyone here cares what happens to you. You think that you are too grand to answer our questions? It just might help you if you do.'

Detty firmly and truthfully said that she had no sexual experience at all and then bit her tongue as she hadn't meant to answer. She also realised that her undoubted virginity was not going to prove to be an asset in the present situation.

'You don't really expect us to believe that.' The interrogator burst out laughing and signalled to one of his colleagues. 'Sven, give me a hand with this foreign bitch who thinks that she can get away with lying to me. She wants to join the martyrs.' He leered at her as he said this and Detty felt herself shudder.

Sven, a dark greasy lout with a drooping lantern jaw, approached the stool from behind and pinioned her arms behind her back. Detty felt her shoulders being pulled back thrusting her chest forward. The interrogator said, 'That's good – keep her like that.'

He reached over and ripped her sweater up and her bra off. He then pulled a packet of cigarettes out of his top pocket and lit one slowly. Detty watched exposed and sweating as he gradually stretched out his hand holding the cigarette towards her. She knew what he was going to do and felt her stomach contract with fear. He stopped with his eyes fixed on her, withdrew the cigarette and took a long drag until the end glowed brightly, then he pushed it again slowly towards her chest.

'You have the last chance to answer my questions truthfully.'

Detty was mesmerised and could think of nothing but the cigarette coming slowly towards her. Then the lighted tip pressed against her and the pain seared out through her whole body accompanied by the sickening smell of her own flesh burning. She passed out for a moment. Then she noticed that one of the younger detainees behind her in the queue had vomited at the sight and smell of the burning flesh and was being cuffed and kicked for her pains.

'That will teach you to be so brave. We will come back to the questions later.'

Through the red mist of pain from her chest she hardly noticed the examination. Automatically she staggered outside to follow the tiny figure of Tamara down the steps to the showers. At the shower Tamara put her arm round her tall ex-teacher and whispered, 'The cowardly bastards they even had to hold you as they did it. Two men to burn one woman that's what I call really brave.'

She spat with a venom that surprised Detty.

'How does it feel?'

Detty said, 'OK.'

But both of them knew it wasn't. The cool shower helped temporarily but the throbbing started to get worse again as soon as she came out. They wrapped the rough towels round themselves and returned up the steps under the cold stare of the guards from the door opposite.

Once back in the hall they queued at the uniform counter. They were issued with boiler suits, shifts for inside and rough underclothes. Each was given a hanging basket for their own clothes. The supervisor checked off the list mechanically.

The whole process seemed designed to dehumanise and subdue. They were marched to their dormitories to stow their clothes on the hanger above the bed and in the simple stained bedside locker. At last they were allowed to dress in their prison shifts with FYERMA printed across them. They then went to the dining room, which was warm with a good meal soup, chicken rice and salad – well cooked and ample

133

being served from the cafeteria. As in so many things Tamara had been right – torture and home comforts mixed together. Today Detty had had both.

Assembly followed dinner. The governor was fat, sweating and had little pinched eyes, which Detty instantly feared and mistrusted.

'You are here to work, obey orders and learn to be good loyal citizens of our great state. Work is divided into outside work, inside work, physical training and instruction. Each is alternated on a rota with duties assigned which you will find in your dormitories…'

Her head whirled with the complicated, incomprehensible instructions. Worse, however, Detty felt she had lost her identity in the shapeless garments. She felt deprived of individuality and terribly humiliated. She had become just an amorphous uniformed number. Tamara, practical as always, said the uniform had two purposes one was humiliation but more important was to make them conspicuous outside the grounds.

The governor continued, 'Your behaviour will be monitored by all staff and you will be punished for poor turnout, poor work, sloth, inattention, disobedience and indiscipline. The award of these points leads to punishment. Minor offence may be punished by fatigues. Worse offences will be punished severely. I warn you that we have absolute power over you while you are here and absolute discretion as to when you are released. You will make life easier for yourselves if you are obedient, respectful and co-operative at all times. In case you think that this is an idle threat we will now show a short film to stimulate obedience.'

The hall was darkened and a large video projector switched on. The film showed a girl in her late teens sitting on a mattress in a cell alone. As it came up on the screen, Mara gasped. The girl wore a camp shift like the ones that they had just put on and was sobbing bitterly. Two men in the camp guards' uniform entered and she shrieked 'no' and leapt into a corner. They seized her roughly and marched her to the door still screaming and struggling. Sunlight swept the camp quadrangle surrounded by the grave faces of detainees on one side and soldiers on the other. In the centre of the quadrangle was a platform with a gibbet with a solitary newly-tied noose hanging from the centre of the cross piece. The youngster still struggling was dragged onto the platform as the noose was put round her neck by a giant with a bored expression.

The governor, recognisably the same man who had just been talking to them, then appeared on the platform.

'Prisoner Hoffman,' he said, 'you have been found guilty of spying while under Government detention. You are sentenced to be hanged until dead and this sentence will now be carried out. Have you anything to say?'

The young woman flung her head back in a momentary flash of defiance as she was manhandled onto a stool and the noose tightened. There was a horrific momentary pause while the victim stared at her executioner then looked around her for the help that would not be forthcoming. The governor kicked the stool away and stood watching. It took some minutes for her to convulse and die. The final shot was a close up of the body, lifeless, lying on the platform. After the film the governor spoke again, 'If you are in any doubt about how serious we are here, I hope that film will have convinced you. You may now go but I would like to remind any of you who should feel rebellious that the fate of the prisoner that you have just seen can be the fate of you or others.'

Many of the new detainees had fainted and several had vomited at this horrible after dinner entertainment. Detty felt that the world had stopped and turned towards Tamara who had sunk to the floor and had her head buried in her hands. Detty quickly pulled her up but not before a roving supervisor had taken her number 'for indiscipline'. After they had returned to the dormitory, Detty asked Tamara about the hanged girl. Tamara burst into uncontrollable weeping and told the story.

'Her name was Andrea Hoffman and she was my best friend. She went to our school – your school. Unfortunately she was the daughter of the prime minister – my father's prime minister. At the coup d'etat they shot her father mother and brother so she was no use to them as a hostage – unlike me. She was detained here for some months then the president trumped up a charge against her. Then they made that film of her being publicly hanged which could be used for propaganda – to warn others.'

135

'So he hanged an innocent young woman for a bit of publicity?'

Tamara nodded miserably and Detty put her arm round her and held her close, comforting her as she sobbed. After a few minutes Detty whispered, 'Mara, the history of my country, a little country which has seen cruelty and oppression, has taught me that martyrs light a flame which can never be extinguished. Andrea did not die in vain. She will be remembered and remembered and one day the example she has given will inspire your people finally to break free. When that day comes I hope I shall be able to remind you of this dark time.'

There was not much sleep – but it came late in the night to Detty. Then the shrill whistle and the cry, 'All out.'

They stood frozen at their bed ends. Mara stood pale beside hers until yelled at by the supervisor to stand in the middle of the floor.

'You're on an indiscipline charge,' she yelled, 'to the wall and into the *Verhör* position.'

Mara clearly had no idea what she was meant to do. The supervisor cuffed her hard round the head and dragged her over to within reach of the dormitory wall.

'Legs apart, on your toes, knees bent, bend forward, two finger tips only touching the wall and don't move until you are told to.'

Bewildered, Mara did as she was instructed. Her legs and shoulders were stretched tight as she leaned forward to balance herself against the wall with just two finger tips. It looked extremely uncomfortable but struck a chord in Detty's memory, which puzzled her. She thought *Verhör* – why *Verhör* – questioning, interrogation? Mara was being punished but nobody was interrogating her. Then she remembered. She had seen a TV programme years ago in Ireland about republican prisoners being made to stay in this position while being interrogated by the British. Torture without frontiers she thought grimly, very simple, no equipment needed but almost unbearable the longer it went on and extremely convenient for kicking, beating or making the victim crash forwards head first against the wall.

After only a few minutes Mara was clearly suffering a lot. She moved trying to relieve her cramps and the supervisor punched her hard repeatedly in the stomach and told her to keep still. Mara groaned.

Detty rushed forward to help her as she collapsed, exhausted. The supervisor fortunately had her back turned but Mara struggled back into position and muttered quickly, 'Go back! If not we will get another session each.'

Realising the sense of this, Detty reluctantly stepped back. At last the supervisor told Mara she could get up and dress. She was slow dressing because of the cramp and her winded stomach but finally she was ready. The supervisor stood by the door. 'Perhaps you will remember that. Get along now or you'll be late for outside work.'

Most of the day consisted of labour details and of these the majority were outside. Although there was a barracks and a men's labour regiment nearby, the women worked by themselves, presumably because it lessened the threat of escape or insurrection. As much of the work and equipment was very heavy and had been designed for men to use, it was backbreaking and the guards, male and female, were brutally callous. The main products of the Farm were cucumbers for pickling and timber from the conifer forests, which were round two thirds of the perimeter of the estate outside the electric fences. There was some work picking up root vegetables as well and small numbers were detailed to inside parties to do the domestic work. It was common knowledge that the much lighter work inside the buildings was usually given to favourites who co-operated with the guards. Sexual favours, at least to the men, were strictly forbidden but it was widely believed that ways were found round the rules particularly by the some of the lesbian women guards.

For most of the inmates and certainly for those who did not co-operate in such arrangements the physical labour was very hard. Parties working on the cucumbers were in the fields all day bent double until their backs shrieked with fatigue. If anyone fell below the high set picking quota, their aching thighs and calves received a rain of blows from the guards.

Timber parties, however, were even worse and, as they involved working far outside the fence, the chain gang system was used. The prisoners had to pile metre long logs onto the lorries by passing them along a human chain. Each was shackled at the ankle by a short length

137

of chain to the next detainee. They were given leather gloves to wear but their boiler suits became torn and the heavy logs scored their bare forearms and arms. By the end of the day most were raw and bleeding. The only detainee not attached to the chain in each gang operated the massive chain saw. This was the most feared job of all. The saw was of full-sized professional weight and most of the women could hardly lift it let alone control it safely. There were several horrible accidents. When it came to her turn Detty, being stronger than most of the women and used to riding exercise, could manage the saw better than most. Even for her thirty minutes or so at a time was the most she could do until her arms nearly left their sockets and she had to hand over to someone else and be manacled back into the gang.

Very occasionally later they got the lighter work of cleaning stalls and picking up vegetables. The first morning they got a lighter assignment picking up potatoes dug out of the frozen ground and stored in clamps – backbreaking work but out in the fresh air with fewer guards. The boiler suites protected them and, if they wore their shifts underneath, kept them reasonably warm. It was a lighter labour for those who were fit and able to keep up to quota but Mara's stomach bruises hardly allowed her to bend and it was clear that she was in pain at every movement. Detty herself had some pain from her burnt chest which rubbed painfully on the coarse canvas of the boiler suit. She wished she had had a bra or been less well endowed – she had come a long way from the stunning silk dress of the summer ball.

'There is no greater pain than to recall a happy time in wretchedness.'

She thought – she had heard that somewhere – Milton perhaps or was it Virgil? She couldn't remember but whoever it was, he had got it right. She dragged her attention back to the present.

She cared increasingly about Mara and worried about her a great deal. She admired the uncomplaining way with which she had taken her punishment before. She felt an anger mount inside her and a desire for revenge at any cost against this terrible regime with its cowardly predilection for the murder and torture of the defenceless. She therefore worked at breakneck speed to help fill both potato baskets – once leaving her own short and receiving a vicious cuff from a passing guard for her pains. She succeeded in giving Mara the breather she needed and her new friend thanked her with a grateful discrete kiss at the end of the session.

They were given a reasonable meal before showering and changing into fresh shifts. She looked round as they changed – many of the inmates looked cowed and already had the dull eyes of the hopeless. The fresh cool cloth, although rough, against her inflamed chest was a relief but the prison shifts were shapeless and robbed the wearer of dignity and individuality. Although she herself had been a teacher rather than a student at the school she was still not spared this depersonalising garb in the camp. The detainees got a lot of sniggers from the barracks next door and of course escape in such a uniform was nearly impossible. On the other hand, compared with the ever threatening punishments and hangings, it seemed but a small point.

As they were new arrivals they were given an education period by a young female commissar who went on endlessly and boringly about revolutionary objectives and industrial strategies of Moltravia in bad Russian. The benches were hard even for Detty and she wondered how Mara was coping after her treatment.

The following day produced their first experience of a cucumber party but the midday meal was a reasonable beef stew with bread. Their appetites had returned and they ate well. Mara remarked how hard the morning had been but warned Detty to be careful not to say anything out of place as there were microphones everywhere. She again had the strange feeling that she was being protected by her small young friend rather than the reverse.

At the end of the meal a guard appeared in the hall with a loudhailer and announced that that afternoon all detainees were to be employed on hygiene duties at the local offices, schools and barracks. As usual no transport was provided and detainees would have to run to their duties. The guard was a small man relishing his power. Detty thought about their predicament. She was inclined to curse men but felt that she couldn't. After all, the women at the Farm seemed even worse than the men. Anyway the men were not real men here only inadequate cowards. They were afraid of the power and fecundity of the women that they controlled and what they might be able to do if they were ever to break free from the tyranny in which they were held.

She learnt from the other detainees that these runs took place on days when detainees were used to clean the schools and the local barracks. They were also a public spectacle which served as a warning to the local people to show what their fate would be if they didn't toe the line. It was a popular source of entertainment for the soldiers from the surrounding barracks who helped at the check points and the lads from the town.

For the work run the detainees assembled in blocks in the quadrangle. The man with the loudhailer reappeared: 'You will each take a time ticket as you pass the gate. You will then run from here to the town school where you will have your time ticket stamped before starting work. You must complete the run to work within the time limit on the ticket. You will be detailed in the various tasks cleaning the schools and government offices. Your tickets will be stamped on completion. You must then run back to the barracks assigned to you and have the ticket stamped again. Again you will perform the cleaning tasks assigned to you and have your ticket stamped after satisfactory completion. You then return here to have your ticket stamped at completion of the run back. You must keep to time and perform your allotted tasks satisfactorily. Any detainee who is slow or slovenly will be punished. Is that clear?'

They set out for the town followed by a jeep with armed guards. Detty would have had no trouble in outstripping the field but hung back to keep an eye on Tamara. Although obviously still in some pain, the latter managed to establish herself in the middle group.

As they came to the time check there was a queue in front of a desk manned by army cadets. The young men started a great game taking the time cards and refusing to stamp them and hand them back to the distress of the detainees who saw the precious seconds ticking away.

'Will you get punished if you are late? We didn't know, what a shame then!'

This mean game made Detty's Irish temper flare and she screamed abuse and threats of exposure at the cruellest of the boys.

'You report me, you foreign bitch, and I'll see my father deals with you,' came the contemptuous reply.

'He will too,' muttered Mara after they eventually got their stamps.

'His father was an illegal drug importer but is now the new police chief commissar.'

Eventually each detainee got her card and set off to work as directed by the housekeepers. The cleaning work was menial and accompanied by threats from the housekeepers but not hard.

After a couple of hours they had finished and set off for their allotted barracks which happened to be the one next door to the Farm. The journey was straightforward although groups of young soldiers coming in and out of the barracks made suggestive comments most of them were at least fairly flattering. They vulgarly admired their feminine features and argued fiercely over which one they fancied most. Mara was a neat little piece of all right but Detty got most votes for her long shapely legs, firm figure and beautiful hair which had somehow survived her ordeal. It seemed more normal and the girls almost felt flattered as they ran past. Detty was honest enough to admit to herself that she would have felt aggrieved if she had shown off her spectacular body clad in the briefest of clothes to young men and nobody had noticed. Still expecting abuse she followed Tamara to the time check which was laid out on tables outside the barracks gate. She passed her card to a tall fair young soldier who stamped it immediately clicked his heels, bowed slightly and passed it back immediately. For a moment both were looking into each others' eyes and the card dropped to the table between them.

'*Entschuldigung Sie, gnädiges Fraulein.*' he picked up her card and handed it quickly back to her. Detty completed her final floor washing in a daze. She would have undoubtedly have been in severe trouble if Tamara had not pointed out that she had missed a large section and put it right before the orderly spotted it. They hurried back to the checkpoint. Detty made sure that she gave her card to the same young soldier and once more their eyes met.

'God protect you – you are a very beautiful young lady. *Auf wiedersehen. Gluck auf!*'

'*Danke gleichfalls!*' Stammered Detty blushing and immediately wondered if it was appropriate or even impertinent.

141

His words had been spoken in formal, courteous, old-fashioned high German with a slight southern sing-song but no trace of the flat local twang. As she turned onto the last leg of the run, there was a flow and bounce in her step that had certainly not been there before. She felt unbelievably that she had glimpsed something special and beautiful in the midst of this inferno. It could not be true. It had to be all her stressed and twisted fantasy. She had gone about five hundred metres when she realised guiltily that she was well ahead of the group and had lost Tamara who she was supposed to be helping. She slowed at once and found her companion again. Tamara smiled impishly although it was clear her legs and hips felt very sore.

'Well,' she said, 'You certainly made a hit there.'

'He stamped your card quickly too,' said Detty defensively.

'Sure but he didn't say I was very beautiful and address me as gracious young lady – that's not the kind of language you expect to hear in a labour camp.'

'He was just a nice bloke.'

'Yes I agree – very nice,' grinned Tamara. Detty felt she had lost that exchange and said no more until they reached the final check safely without penalty. They were in good time for a shower and change into shifts for supper which Detty found she enjoyed for the first time since the nightmare began.

The evening session was inside work and they changed into working clothes. They were set to work to polish the wood floor, panelling and tables of the Great Hall, which was part of the original old Schloss. A supervisor in a chatty mood explained the layout. Two doors led off the dais, one was the governor's rooms where he prepared for assembly and sometimes dined visitors. The other was the domain of the armourer who organised interrogation routines either for detainees in the camp or sometimes for prisoners sent for questioning from elsewhere.

At the moment the supervisor finished explaining, the armourer's door opened and the grim huge figure of Andrea's executioner emerged. He said, with a voice of authority, 'I want two detainees to do some maintenance jobs. They will do.'

He indicated Detty and a girl called Liese who was standing next to her and had been at The Farm already for some weeks.

'Oh my God,' muttered Detty's companion, 'that's the armourer. You want to keep out of his way.'

Detty thought that she didn't really have much choice but she still appreciated Liese's attempt to warn her of the danger. Her warm thoughts of the handsome soldier disappeared as they entered the large dark room dedicated to pain and death.

It was medieval and horrible. All round the wall were glass-fronted cupboards. Some displayed guns and others objects which Detty had not seen before but recognised from pictures as restraining collars, handcuffs and leg irons. There was a rack of various whips and other cupboards with objects that she couldn't identify at all. Some appeared to be short clubs and one was like an expandable telescope. One thing she recognised immediately. Standing on one side of the room was the dismantled gibbet complete with rope and noose that had been used to dispatch the poor young woman in the film. Alongside it was a stout oak trestle and several thick metal poles. There were miscellaneous other bits of ominous equipment.

'All the wood needs washing, the leather oiling and the metal fittings greasing. You start with the guns, and you with the trestle and post.'

Detty was presented with a huge glass case which was one of two. The one at the other end contained miscellaneous objects. Her case contained guns, which she began to oil under the terrifying instruction of the armourer. She was almost glad she had the guns. At least she understood these as she had used and looked after shotguns at home. Some of the other things in the room looked the more horrifying because she couldn't understand their use. She imagined that it was a kind of museum that the armourer had collected. She imagined they were being shown it to frighten them and send them back to the blocks with tales of horror. Deep down, however, she knew that a man who could casually organise a hanging would have no compunction about using this gear if the situation presented itself.

When they had been working for some minutes, the armourer walked over to a door leading out of the main armoury at the opposite end from the hall. He opened the door and crossed the inner room, which was much smaller. He picked up a buff detainee's file from a shelf and stood for a moment reading it. He had his back to Detty and she was able to look into the inner room without his seeing her. It had no natural light and the walls were lined with a grey irregular material a bit like carpet underlay. The only objects to be seen in the room were various brackets in the walls and some ropes hanging from pulleys in the ceiling. Incongruously the only detached object was a crude metal double iron bedstead covered in a heavy steel mesh. The room was spotlessly clean and smelt of the pervasive, government issue, pine disinfectant. At first Detty thought that it must be some sort of gymnasium then she shuddered and cursed her stupidity as its real purpose inexorably dawned on her. She was looking into an NAS interrogation and torture chamber where the ghastly tools that she had seen were put to use.

Liese had the job of cleaning and oiling some of the more grisly stock. The armourer explained what he wanted in the way of work. He kept a heavy brooding silence that forbade questions that in any case neither dared to ask. Finally, the work session was finished and the armourer dismissed them with a gesture of his hand but without a word. They scuttled out through the hall and into the light, with relief. They both knew that they had been in the presence of torture and death although nothing had actually happened to them.

*

After the first days, apart from back breaking work, little actually happened to disturb the new detainees further. It seemed that they had been punished, shown the armoury and made to watch Andrea's execution to scare them and now they were being left alone. Once the point had been firmly made, it was assumed that they were totally cowed and would be submissive to any order. In the main this was right as all of them had been humiliated and most were too terrified to voice independent thoughts let alone any pointless opposition. They just did their work tasks trying to avoid the casual beatings. It was sufficient to let them lead the life of half-frozen skivvies without doing much more. The video tapes which were sent back to the Moltravian families made it clear what their loved ones were enduring, without needing to show actual torture.

In a few detainees, however, some covert spirit remained. One clear morning seemed to hint of better things. For a miracle the day was bright and sunny and although it was still very cold, there was just a suggestion of warmth as the morning drew on. Detty had been lucky and had been appointed to some stock work. She was left alone as she was inside the perimeter electric fence. She was almost enjoying her solitary cleaning the outside cattle stalls. The sun hinted of a distant spring as it shone mistily through the stall doors. She had had no thoughts of music since she had been in the Farm but now she softly started singing, her voice hoarse at first after long silence. It grew in strength and unconsciously she chose one of her favourite songs:

Ja, du weisst es, teure Seele,
dass ich fern von dir mich quale
her voice strengthening in crescendo,
liebe macht die Herzen krank
habe Dank.[13]

She didn't know what love was making her heart sick. She thought ruefully that she had a number of preoccupations besides love, which was, in fact, far from her mind at that moment. It was a fine song, however, and she had enjoyed the sound of her voice in the raw air of the late winter countryside. As she finished the verse and thought about its meaning, the silence was broken by an answering voice coming apparently out of nowhere:

Einst hielt ich, der Freiheit Zecher
Hoch den Amethysten-Becher
und du nahmst die heilig' Karte
Habe Dank

---

13 Yes dear soul you know
    That I'm in torment far from you
    Love makes heart sick,
    Be thanked

After an astonished moment, she laughed with an explosion of young joy, too long absent from her life. Like an echo he laughed too and the air was filled momentarily with the sound of carefree happiness. As their laughter died down she began to sing again – joined immediately by the clear baritone:

Und beschworst darin die Bösen
bis ich, was ich nie gewesen
Heilig, Heilig ans Herz dir Sank
Habe Dank[14]

The moment gave a special beauty to the last verse of Strauss's song and they both savoured it for an instant in silence. Suddenly Detty said impulsively, 'I want to see you – and I am going to try.'

The side of the farm that bordered with the barracks was not as well protected as the outside perimeter. Both were high security areas and it was thought that no would-be escapee would indulge in the folly of swapping one for the other. Detty was therefore able to swing herself up onto the high shelf of the stall and edge along it till she came to an overhanging hoist arm at one end. From this she could jump into the hay loft on the barracks side. When she arrived the young soldier of the check point was already there waiting for her.

'You have a beautiful voice, Fräulein,' he said again using the old fashioned diminutive that he had used at the check point.

'So do you,' said Detty with a crinkly smile round her grey-green eyes, 'and a quick way of adapting poems. What are you called?'

'My name is Marc Retten and it is my native language, whereas, I may be wrong, but I don't think that it is yours.'

'Oh,' said Detty teasing. 'Is my accent that bad, Marc?'

He replied a trifle too seriously but with great feeling, 'I have never heard German sound more beautiful on anyone's lips.'

---

14 And you banished the evil spirits
    Til I, as never before
    Holy, sank upon your heart
    Be thanked

She dropped a curtsy in mock seriousness as he continued

'Anyway what is an English lady doing in this awful place? And please tell me your name.'

'I think that needs three answers,' said Detty still teasing. 'First, I'm not English, I'm Irish, second, I'm supposed to be teaching English on a university placement, third, my name is Bernadette O'Neill but, like Mimi most people call me Detty. Now tell me a bit more about yourself. I could tell you're not from Moltravia.'

'No I'm German – you could say I'm here on business.'

'I want to know more – much more,' said Detty, 'but I have to finish the stall and get back. I shall be here in three days time when the rota comes round. Can you get back?'

'Sure,' he said, teasing in his turn. 'There are not too many volunteers for refuse collecting and most people don't realise that you get a very lovely young lady included in the rubbish.'

Detty put her tongue out at him, instantly regretted the adolescent gesture and dashed back over her perilous route.

She was able to hang on to the cow shed assignment and they met very briefly every few days. She learnt that Marc had arrived in Königshof on a music scholarship on the eve of the revolution. He had got his residence permit to study Polish medieval music almost the same day that the fascist government had produced its edict that all males between 17 and 24 resident in Moltravia regardless of nationality should be treated as nationals and drafted into the army. The only exceptions were those with full diplomatic immunity. The official reason for the decree was that the turmoil that had existed in the area following the fall of communism had made it hard to know who were citizens and who foreigners. Though there was some truth in this, the actual motif was much more repressive and sinister. Young men of military age within the borders had to be controlled in case of counter-revolution in the face of the terrible repression that Travsky had introduced.

When they met again they talked about each other but also of the disasters that had hit the region in which they found themselves. First, the Nazi invasion, then oppressive colonial communism and then a few brief years of freedom dogged by economic deprivation. Because of the economic difficulties the Fascists had been able to seize power using the promise of full employment and prosperity to stifle opposition. Once installed they had shown themselves to be the amoral sadists that they really were and the country groaned in fear as more and more atrocities were perpetrated. Worst of all they had their hands on nuclear weapons and might well be prepared to use them to maintain power. Marc said that the condition of the general population was almost worse than theirs in the camp and the barracks. Detty said she found that hard to believe when she remembered the punishments that she had witnessed and Andrea being hanged. They lived under the tyranny of beatings and the threat of the gallows.

'Yes, I know,' said Marc, 'but look at it like this. Outside the NAS call and you disappear – you are probably killed, possibly tortured first, nobody knows anything – you are a nobody. At least here most of you are important women or like some of your fellow inmates are daughters – or wives – of important people. Most of the prominent people are in prison or at least under house arrest but having their sons in the army and their other relatives in a labour camp provides an excellent second line of defence against escape or subversion. You may wonder why they like the press and TV to show conditions in the camps. The reason is that they use these reports to frighten the relatives into obedience for fear of worse things happening to their loved ones if they step out of line.'

Marc paused and after a few moments silence Detty said, 'What about me – I don't have an important or even Moltravian family – why me?'

Marc replied thoughtfully. 'I've been thinking a lot about that. I think they worked it out like this and in a sense I think you are the most special of all – you come from a small respected country at the heart of the Union and in a sense you are a hostage for free Europe. I am very much afraid that they will not treat you any differently from the rest. At the right opportunity they will hurt you publicly as a gesture of defiance to a concerned but impotent European Union and NATO. I am very sorry to worry you by saying this but I think that there is just a chance that you can look after yourself better if you are prepared.'

Each meeting was very short because of the rota of duties but in between Detty thought a lot about the conversations and about Marc himself. She became convinced that he knew what he was talking about and her hatred, anger and frustration boiled inside. She was mature for her years, resourceful and intelligent – if only she – they – could do something. The younger detainees were often only children who had been dragged from their homes or schools to this dreadful place and were completely cowed by the horrible things that they witnessed or suffered themselves. They were petrified and no wonder.

Then there was the boy himself and Detty realised that she was tremendously attracted to him. He was very good looking, courteous in an old-world way, funny and serious when appropriate and behind all this was the ability to analyse situations and make decisions. She was sure that he was attracted to her but, in spite of the illegal 'Fraulein' he had never once patronised her and had treated her as a responsible equal from the first. From her convent upbringing, love was not a word which readily sprang to her mind but she knew that this young man was becoming enormously important to her. This was depressing and added to her frustration, given her hopeless situation. 'I shall be over thirty before I get out,' she thought to herself, 'and what good is that?' She knew deep down, however, that her predicament was likely to be resolved one way or the other, probably badly, before the end of her sentence. She had narrowly escaped hanging on arrest and the image of her standing like Andrea on a stool with a noose tightening round her neck while her executioners cocked a snook at NATO was all too real.

After another three days they met again. The last conversation and her later thoughts had made Detty depressed. The spring atmosphere and Strauss's songs of their first meeting seemed a million miles away.

'I felt very guilty after you left,' said Marc. 'You have enough to put up with without worrying you further. I did feel though that… how do you say? Forewarned might be forearmed but when I thought about it later I thought I was wrong and had just frightened you uselessly.'

'Rubbish,' said Detty forcefully, 'Warning is helpful and I should know – you were quite right.' She paused a moment, 'Marc – I know it may seem silly – but isn't there anything I – we – can do? I feel so helpless and angry. Can we set fire to the camp or something?'

'I don't think that would help much,' said Marc staring at the straw bale intently. He was clearly troubled and wrestling with something on his mind. There was a long pause before he finally turned to her, 'Yes, Detti, there is something you can do but I want you to know before you agree that it will require great nerve and courage. It will put you in enormous danger and you don't have to agree.'

'Try me,' she said feeling the great weight of depression replaced by excitement.

He went on, 'You must know that what I told you about my arrival here was the truth but not the whole truth. I have another role. I don't want to tell you any more than I must for the less you know the better – for both of us.' He paused again, 'Your governor is one of the most important men in the regime after Travsky himself. He is involved in major political decisions. We need copies of documents kept in his office. As you know the office is constantly in use during the day and guarded. At night, however, they have such confidence in the electronic perimeter fence that I think the office is only locked not guarded. Do you know whether that is so?'

Detty nodded, 'Yes, I think it may be. The Great Hall has four side buildings. At the front by the steps is the guardroom, which is always manned but they are often only a service platoon and are pretty slack. They drink beer and sleep a lot of the time – even on duty. The other side at the front is the punishment solitary confinement block and the Sanatorium. At the top of the hall the governor's office is reached through a door on the left.'

Marc nodded, 'What's on the other side?' he asked.

'That is the armourer's store. I have worked there. It contains a comprehensive collection of guns and other equipment designed to exploit every possible frailty of the human frame.' She thought of the ghastly collection she had seen. 'He is a right charmer but he's not there at night.'

'Bastards,' muttered Marc with a venom which showed Detty another side of his character – the strength of his anger.

He continued, 'Therefore they are correct in thinking that it would be very hard for anyone to break in from outside? The electronic guard at night even goes between the barracks and the camp. But it would be possible for someone already in the camp to break into the office?'

'Given the right equipment – yes.'

'OK,' he said, 'I want you to get into the office at night and photograph any strategic correspondence and orders that you can find and five files – fewer if you can't make all five.'

He was speaking precisely now, like giving orders, more like a soldier than a student of medieval music, she thought. He appeared to have pushed his doubts about involving her to the back of his mind.

'How do I operate the locks?' she asked.

'Electronic key built into the base of the camera that I can give you. You find the key next to the IR light – it should open both the main door and the filing cabinets – unfortunately we can't test it first. I will bring it to you next time.'

At the next visit he produced the tiny camera and showed her how to work it and the key mechanism in the base. She hid it inside her boiler suit checking that nothing showed.

'Now for the files,' said Marc 'As I said there are five – first in the small cabinet to the left of the governor's desk is one marked Labour Camps – Confidential Procedures. Photograph the first eight pages. Then there are two large filing cabinets behind the desk, one is marked Current Detainees and the other is marked Former Detainees. From the Current Detainees you need to photograph the first six pages and the records of the following, which I think will be in alphabetical order – 734 Natalia Malinova, 759 Liese Zahnsdorf, 986 Tamara Oblova,' and he paused — '987 Bernadette O'Neill,' he waved away her half-spoken question and went on 'from the Former Detainees file you need 305 Andrea Hoffman. Please it's better if you know as little as possible – one day I will explain – and you can guess some of it anyway. If you are caught try and dispose of the camera that will help us and you. Unless you are actually filming they may not suspect you have it. I will see you in three days. *Viel Gluck!*'

He had said all this in rapid clipped German but as he finished his expression changed to one of tenderness and great anxiety, 'I love you!' he said in English and then immediately added, '*Verzeihung* – I apologise!'

She felt choked and turned and left without a word.

She thought out her tactics during instruction and the afternoon work run. Today would be the day to act because that would leave room for two further tries in case of problems. She feigned a stomach upset during dinner and the lecture that followed it to help explain away any movement during the night. The first time she asked to leave the lecture room the female commissar agreed with a scowl. Half an hour later she asked again, and again was allowed to leave but was told she would be punished for disruption on her return. Re-entering the room she was ordered to stand in the *Verhör* position until the end of the lecture. At the end her shoulders felt as if they were falling out of their sockets and her hips burnt but she had the at least the knowledge that she had deprived the commissar of the satisfaction of beating her for moving. She was more angry and determined than ever and muttered to herself, 'Worth the effort.'

3
THROUGH THE FIRE

Durch das Feuer drang ich,[15]

WAGNER: SIEGFRIED ACT III Sc3

Before the night drink and roll call she made sure her boiler suit was easy to reach. She went to bed with the camera inside her briefs, which she wore to bed hoping no one would notice. After two hours, there was quiet in the dormitory and she slipped out to the lavatory carrying her boiler suit with the precious camera still stowed in her pants. The dormitories were not locked at night because the lavatories were by the main staircase and also because the electronic perimeter alarm was thought to be so good. Nobody seemed to take very seriously the possibility of a detainee escaping and hiding herself somewhere within the large building complex to escape at daylight. In fact so confident were the NAS that their terrified, de-humanised prisoners were incapable of resistance that in some ways security was amazingly lax. The authorities took the view that it was unlikely that young people cowed by cruelty, frightened out of their wits and with nowhere to go, would have much drive left to escape.

---

15   I conquered the fire

Although she was not trying to escape, Bernadette Niamh O'Neill took some pleasure in proving them wrong. The block door was locked but was easily circumvented from the inside by opening a window in the house kitchen which led immediately to the area steps and onto the quadrangle. Unfortunately, the moon was nearly full in a brilliant starlit, freezing night. She was able to move round the courtyard walls close to and under the shadow, blessing the dark grey of her regulation boiler suit. The worst bit was at the foot of the steps to the great hall when she had to cross the moonlit open door of the guardroom. She held her breath and slipped quickly across. Disaster struck as she reached the entrance to the hall. In her hurry she had not noticed a protruding stone block which she tripped over falling forward heavily on her face and stubbing her bare big toe agonisingly. She stood, slipped into the shadows and held her breath. Fortunately, as she hoped, the occupants of the guardroom all appeared to be asleep and snoring and didn't even hear her crash to the ground. She checked the damage to her toe, which by great good fortune was not bleeding. Then it took only a minute to cross the hall.

She found the governor's office door and pointed the key at the lock. It gave a satisfying click and she opened it. The files were exactly as Marc had described them.

'How the hell did he know that much detail when he didn't know the layout of the hall itself,' she thought.

She found the Confidential Procedures File on the governor's desk with some letters and opened it. She had little time but it seemed a guide to the real motives for running the camp. As she photographed she was able to read some of it.

'The detainees who are to be held in the camps are either subversive themselves or held as a surety for the good behaviour of their relatives who are actual or potential public enemies. The regime must therefore look after their physical welfare by seeing that they are fed, clothed and sheltered while at the same time ensuring that treatment is severe enough to be used to secure conformity from relatives and others. Where external *prominenti* are involved they must be made aware of the detainee's harsh treatment by public news and private bulletins. It must also be made clear to them that any lapse of behaviour on their part will result in swift retaliation upon their detainees. This retaliation will be officially formulated as punishment for some offence committed by the detainee herself…'

There was a lot more concerning treatment and observation of various types of detainees. There was also a note to the effect that 'since the unfortunate Hoffman affair, capital punishment and punishment producing considerable irreversible physical or mental damage to a detainee must have the consent of the president through the Interior Ministry.'

Detty completed the photographs and turned to 'Current Detainees'. She came to Natalia's file first. She was the 20-year-old daughter of a senior army general who was popular with his fellow officers and with the troops and loyal to the democratic government. He was under house arrest and it was feared that he might escape and could be a focus for an insurrection. Natalia had been given five years for inciting riot. The secret instructions were that she was to be kept healthy but subjected to constant fear of torture and execution.

It was expected that she would commit frequent minor offences which could be punished in such a way as to cause pain and frighten her without damaging her permanently. After punishment she would also be threatened with fearsome, detailed retribution on the next occasion. It was important that her father was supplied with photographs and video films informing him of the progress of his daughter's rehabilitation. Several copies of photographs, which had been sent to General Malinov were included in the file. They showed a tall thin girl with her long dark hair falling from a red velvet band in various states of distress. The general was also to be informed that any insurrection in which his name was implicated would result in his daughter being hanged, without trial, as a traitor immediately.

Liese, the subject of the second file, Detty had met already cleaning the armourer's quarters. She was the daughter of a high-ranking air force officer who the regime hoped to bend to their purpose. Her supposed offence was inciting riot in the university where she was a student. Her treatment was to be progressively harsher to help 'persuade' her father to assist the regime by reorganising the air force.

The file on Tamara was similar. Her father also under house arrest, was the ex-defence minister and therefore had dangerous or helpful contacts in the USA. He had been sent a photo of her first morning punishment cleverly showing the petite fair girl clenching her teeth in pain and exhaustion as she held the *Verhör* position. Detty had no idea that any photographs had been taken at this time and noted that there must be a hidden camera in the dormitory. She hoped sincerely that it wasn't a twenty-four-hour video camera that could have recorded her present exploit. She told herself to be extra careful in future. Her own file confirmed Marc's theory. She was hostage for a continent. Maximum publicity in the cheaper Western press was to be obtained. She thought of her parents and sister and their attempt to prevent her from returning to Moltravia. One more note caught her eye.

'Although it is improbable that O'Neill was actually spying for NATO when she was arrested, she is vocal, resourceful and intelligent and does represent a security risk. She may require more surveillance than most detainees and it may take harsher treatment to control her. This may be applied according to the governor's discretion if she proves too uncooperative. It would be wise to break any resistance that she shows and a high profile incident would provide valuable propaganda. For the moment, this should stop short of eliminating her. She may have further uses in several different ways.'

She shuddered at the cold-blooded language. As far as her character went, they've got it right though she thought and was suddenly fierce with anger. Then she wondered how the authorities could know her that well.

'Although she is already under sentence of death under Moltravian law, it is reiterated that she is valuable alive and such a sentence must not be carried out without the express authority of the president.'

Detty shuddered and finished photographing.

One to go – she opened the Former Detainees cabinet. She found Andrea Hoffman's file easily enough. She began photographing. Andrea's lively pretty face stared out reproachfully from her identity photo and there were various others of minor punishments and finally her hanging. Her death sentence was included in the file:

'Following the execution of the traitor Hoffman with his wife and son, the daughter, the detainee, Andrea can have no value as a surety and may form a dangerous focus of unrest. She is therefore sentenced to death by hanging on a charge of subversive activities. The sentence is to be carried out immediately with maximum publicity to ensure that waverers, who may doubt the seriousness of the government's intention in punishing traitors, conform.'

It was signed by the governor. Just as she finished a loose sheet headed from the Office of the President caught her eye. It was dated the day of Andrea's execution.

'Security forces operating abroad report that information probably collected by Andrea Hoffman has IN FACT been passed to foreign enemies. IT IS THEREFORE IMPERATIVE THAT HER PROPOSED EXECUTION IS STAYED UNTIL SHE CAN BE PROPERLY INTERROGATED TO OBTAIN FURTHER INFORMATION.'

Underneath was an unsigned pencil note marked 'Too late'. Perhaps Andrea had been fortunate after all thought Detty thinking of that awful room at the back of the armoury. Was this the explanation for Marc's knowledge of the locks and keys? Detty wondered as she photographed this sheet also and, making sure everything was back in its place, she left.

It had taken her about an hour and the night was darker for her return. There was no difficulty, the guards still snored and the courtyard was deserted. To store the camera was the main problem. She took care to hide it for the time being under a blanket while moaning with apparent colic. She decided it was best to make a small tear in the mattress as if it had caught on the metal bed strut and push the camera into the straw. The chances were that it would remain concealed for two more days and all would be well. If the tear was noticed she would be punished for damage to camp property but at the moment she felt elated and that the risk was worth it. Lying in bed sleepless she thought again of the man who had dropped into her life like a bombshell. So far she was glad she had not let him, or herself, down. She wished she knew more.

The 6am reveille came far too soon. Fortunately for Detty if not for them there was little time left for inspection as the staff were occupied hazing defaulters. One who was being treated particularly badly was the only daughter of a prominent businessman who had a contract for military clothing. Father was being slow in his deliveries and it was decided that he needed some encouragement to speed up. Anna had been arrested for hooliganism, for no apparent reason, on her way home from her college. She had led a sheltered and rather spoilt life and she became hysterical and abusive on arrest and was still trying to protest to the governor on arrival at the camp. This gave the authorities the excuse to treat her badly, which suited the political objective very well. Video clips of her treatment could be sent to 'encourage' him. She refused to get into the *Verhör* position and was persistently and ruthlessly beaten up. Then she was locked in a solitary room while the rest were sent to breakfast. Detty was grateful for the diversion but sorry for the child. She wondered what father would think of the video, which was even now being taken to his factory by dispatch rider.

The wretched Anna prevented much time remaining for inspection on the second and third mornings much to Detty's guilty relief. Before dawn Detty had recovered the camera and secreted it in her boiler suit. After breakfast she went to the stall and did a few minutes noisy work. Finally she swung herself across to the hay loft. Marc was already waiting. He asked how it had gone and Detty was able to reply with some pride, 'No problem.'

'Nevertheless,' he said, 'you have been in very great danger. I – and others – are more grateful to you than I can say. One day I hope that these criminals will be brought to justice and then you can know how much you have helped and be adequately thanked.'

'It really wasn't a problem,' said Detty, and for some minutes they looked at each other in silence.

There was a rustling noise and the sound of talking in the lower part of the barn. Marc quickly grabbed the camera and hid it under a loose board.

'Pretend we have been making love – then there is a chance they won't look for the camera – if they find it we are both dead or worse.' As he spoke he undid his belt and started taking off his trousers. Detty saw the point and unzipped her boiler suit and swiftly pulled her pants down and off. Quite naked on her boiler suit, she lay back unconsciously sliding one hand behind her long hair and draping the other across her stomach. Marc thought that she looked like a reclining Botticelli Venus. He said later that that was the moment when his feelings for her turned from respect and admiration to adoration.

There were steps on the ladder and in a moment they were surrounded by a military police patrol machine pistols at the ready.

'What a pair of turtle doves,' said the NCO. 'This is a good way of spending the morning fatigues, Retten, I can see why you volunteered. Take him to the guardhouse and her to the governor at the farm.'

She saw Marc gazing anxiously and forlornly after her as he was marched off. He told her later that guilt at what he had done to her overwhelmed him at that moment. He thought that if he could not right the wrong that he had done her, he had no further reason to live. She quickly pulled on her pants and climbed back into her boiler suit firmly but politely declining the assistance of the young soldiers who seemed only too willing to help her. She was then made to descend the steps and marched round by the road back into the camp and up to the governor's office with a burly military policeman on each side. One MP knocked and was invited to enter. The governor was there with his steely-eyed secretary.

'Good morning, Sir, we think that this is one of your young ladies. We found her in a hayloft on the barracks side *in flagrante delicto* with one of our soldiers from the barracks next door.'

'She is certainly one of my detainees,' said the governor leering at Detty. 'But I'm not sure about the lady bit. What have you got to say for yourself?'

Detty felt numb and very cold. She couldn't think of anything remotely helpful to say.

'Very well. Take her to the solitary confinement cells. We will decide what to do with her later.'

The soldiers marched her out across the hall and down the front steps. There to her regret, they handed her over to the thugs from the service regiment who were on permanent duty in the farm camp. Two of them took her to a cell, which consisted of three concrete walls and an iron grill with a door closing the fourth side. The only furniture was a shelf bunk with straw and a bucket. They roughly stripped off her boiler suit and handed her a prison shift. Shocked and cold she was left sitting on the bunk.

The parting shot of the guard was, 'You'll be by yourself here, darling, no fancy men allowed.'

Meanwhile the governor had picked up the telephone, 'Get me the CO of the barracks,' he said then, 'Good morning, Colonel, I would like to have a word. Your place or mine? OK I'll expect you shortly.'

The colonel arrived after a few minutes, 'Good of you to come, Colonel, I would like to discuss our two lovebirds. What do we do with them?'

'A few days in the glasshouse should suit mine – I don't know what you want to do with the girl.'

'I could probably persuade Travsky to let me hang her but it seems a waste and it would be over quickly. This is a good opportunity to make an example of her and I think the president would like something imaginative, something that will get into their newspapers. She is an arrogant young bitch and it would be just as satisfying to humiliate her thoroughly as to hang her and we would still have her in case of later need. I think I would prefer to have them both punished here. It would be good for control and good for publicity.'

He smiled at the colonel seeking agreement and approval. It wasn't forthcoming so he went on, 'I'll tell you why. They are both foreign. He's German and she's Irish. She is sentenced to ten years for spying for NATO with a suspended death sentence for incitement of revolt. She is valuable property but so far has kept her nose clean. Not a lot to feed the Western press with until now. With this offence, however, we can show righteous indignation and claim the right to punish her while showing clemency because we have not executed her for her offence – in fact I make it four offences. A spectacular double punishment of two lovers will certainly get the most publicity – probably more than executions and we still have them as bargaining counters, We may be able to extract some important concessions on the embargo from their governments.'

His little piggy eyes twinkled with sadistic enthusiasm.

160

The colonel paused for a minute. The governor hadn't said what he meant by spectacular punishment but the colonel knew his methods. Finally he answered saying,

'No – What's the point. There is no advantage in punishing him severely. Besides he is one of my best soldiers – in fact one of the only intelligent ones that I've got and I don't want him damaged. He must be dealt with by army discipline and the NAS don't have jurisdiction over the military. Besides there is another thing – he is an upright young man and probably very fond of her. He will feel responsible for getting her into trouble. I guess that if we give him a trivial penalty but he will feel very guilty on her account and it will be the worse for him. I can't influence what you do to her. So you don't intend to execute her, do you?'

'Wait and see – perhaps I have something else in mind – fitting the crime.'

They walked across the great hall together and down the steps. The governor put his head round the guardhouse door

'Oleg, please take the colonel and myself to the solitary block. The key clicked and the armoured door opened onto the line of cells closed with iron grills. The first two were empty. Detty was in the third with 'O'Neill' and her number on a cardboard label over the door. She lay curled up on a thin mattress with her back to the door and her knees pulled up like a baby with her hands over her head.

'O'Neill,' shouted the guard, 'Governor for you! Come and stand at attention at the grill.'

Detty didn't move.

The guard reached behind and took a long wand with a thick handle from a rack on the wall. He poked it through the grill towards Detty until the point rested on her leg. He then pressed a button. She cried out and jumped off the couch shaking with pain and clutching her leg.

'Now come over here at once and be respectful to the governor or I'll give you one in a much more sensitive spot.'

By way of explanation to the colonel, he said 'Electric cattle prod – very high voltage low current – we find it works well on two legged cows as well.'

The Governor explained, 'Oleg used to be a farmer before he joined the NAS. He calls this his new cow shed.'

Detty staggered towards the door and stood shivering in pain in front of the three men. She was very pale and her striking hair looked bedraggled. She looked at the floor silent half-angry and half-frightened and her athletic figure was only partly obscured by her simple prison shift. The colonel admired her and felt sorry for her. She reminded him of a thoroughbred racing filly – all grace with power.

'O'Neill,' said the governor. 'The colonel and I have just been discussing your little escapade and its punishment. I am having you charged with four offences. First, escaping from a labour camp. Second, unlawfully spying in a military installation. Third, soliciting for prostitution and fourth, seducing a soldier from his duty. The second and fourth carry the death penalty. We shall decide when it is to be carried out tomorrow morning.'

Detty gave a gasp and saw in her mind's eye her own body convulsing at the end of a rope like the other one.

'Have her ready to receive sentence at assembly tomorrow.'

They turned away and the colonel angrily said, 'You're a sadistic bastard – you know you have no intention of hanging her.'

'I know that but she doesn't and it won't do her any harm to spend a day thinking about it.'

'You're right about one thing,' said the Colonel, 'she's a smashing looker. Young Retten's certainly got good taste – I rather admire him.' Detty lay sleepless and cold. The cells were just warm in the daytime but freezing at night. She wept a little silently and wondered if she was spending her last night on earth. Though a good and devout Catholic, she felt paralysed and she couldn't pray. She seemed too detached. She thought she was going down to hell and tried to tell herself that she really didn't care if she was killed. Then she had an image of Andrea in her death agonies and realised she was deeply afraid. Besides she was just twenty-one and didn't want her life to be wasted.

Towards dawn she dozed fitfully. Breakfast was brought – substantial as usual but all she managed was a cup of hot sweet coffee. Then her dormitory supervisor arrived accompanied, to Detty's delight, by Tamara

162

carrying a basket of her own prison clothes. There was also a kimono, which Tamara had found somewhere and put round Detty's shoulders. The supervisor was attending to some papers with the guard.

'Mara,' said Detty. 'They're going to hang me – like Andrea.' she finished in a sob. 'I don't want to die.'

She put her head between her knees and wept.

Tamara put her arm gently round her shoulders and whispered in her ear, 'Rubbish, they'll never hang you – you're far too valuable.'

She showed at that moment, Detty knew, a knowledge and a wisdom far beyond her years, born of having lived through terrible times. She went on, realistic as well as comforting, 'They may hurt you cruelly but they'll never hang you. They'll look after you like one of their own.'

Detty was silent for a moment, 'Thanks, Mara, I think I even believe you,' she said smiling through her tears. They set off for the infirmary where the sick-bay showers were situated. Tamara was still carrying the basket with Detty's clothes and waited while she showered.

Her friend then had to leave to rejoin her house. As she dressed in the clothes Mara had brought, Detty wondered how on earth she had persuaded them to let her come to the solitary block at all. After the fear and cold of the cells she was glad to have been active again and hated returning to her cold, public but lonely cell.

She was surprised, however, when, without announcement, the governor reappeared at the grill, 'I have spent a lot of time worrying about what to do with you, O'Neill, you should be flattered.' he said in an ingratiating confidential voice.

He looked at her for some moments before continuing. She was conscious of a chilling mixture of cruelty mixed with lust in his face. He was obviously enjoying himself and his power over her. In spite of this she sensed a weakness in him.

'You are very proud and quite courageous but atrociously arrogant and you must be taught a lesson. However, I am not going to execute you. Instead I looked up some old laws and I think our ancestors may have helped me decide how to deal with you appropriately. My former opponents here, who ruined this country in pursuit of spurious democracy, used to be very enthusiastic about our Hanseatic past. I don't agree with them but on this occasion it has come to my aid. Read this – you are a German scholar you should be able to translate it.'

He passed over to Detty through the grill a photocopy of an old document. She was shaking with cold and despair and took some time to read the old Gothic script. Finally she got it fairly clearly.

Hansestadt Königshof
(by order of the Burgermeister
in Council for the Summary Punishment
of Wrongdoers within the City and its fiefs)

Enacted in the year of Our Lord 1346

For each offence of:

Robbery	*Death by Hanging to take place in the Rathausplatz*
Public Affray or Riot	*Exposure in the Stocks for such time as to allow Remorse and Repentance*
Swindling and Fraud	*Public branding with the letter by hot iron on the forehead*
Blasphemy and Witchcraft	*After the question has been put, Death by Burning at the Stake in an appointed public place*

In her bemused state, Detty couldn't see what any of these, horrific as they were, could relate to her supposed offence. She didn't think that she could be seriously accused of witchcraft. Then she came to the last item:

Whoring and Lewdness (except as provided in Stadische Bordell)	*Stripping and Chastisement with Birch Rods at the Cart's Tail throu' The Streets until the Miscreant be Bloody and Remorseful*

'Did you hold a license as a prostitute from the town brothel, Fräulein O'Neill?'

Detti shook her head, stunned.

'Which of these punishments, therefore, do you think should apply to a young woman found *in flagrante delicto* with a soldier as you were not, as you indicate, in the official town brothel?'

Detty, shocked and feeling sick and faint, said nothing.

'Well, as you don't seem to know the answer I will suggest it to you. You were caught whoring and certainly exhibited lewdness when the colonel's patrol found you. A hayloft in the barracks is not a licensed brothel. I shall have you punished in the manner prescribed by our old city law. You will be flogged with birch rods as prescribed, but as we don't have a suitable cart or suitable streets near here, a trestle in the courtyard will have to serve. Apart from that, as a scholar, you will be glad to know that the venerable sentence will be carried out to the letter in public "until you be Bloody and Remorseful" as the statute says.'

He paused savouring the words, *'Blutbefleckt und Reuevoll'* watching for her reaction. All Detty could think, horribly detached, was that it was odd that the medieval script capitalised the adjectives. Somehow she seemed floating, looking on from outside, and couldn't feel the terror and anticipate the humiliation and the pain as he expected and hoped. It wasn't courage. It was just that she had passed into a state of total depersonalisation. It was happening to somebody else. She wasn't really there. She would soon wake up and be herself again. The unreality was pervasive and momentarily total.

'We will see what the Western scandal sheets make of that. Aren't you going to beg me for mercy?'

He looked disappointed and in the last remark seemed almost to ask her to plead with him. She realised that it would be pointless and was determined to deny him that pleasure at least. Momentarily, it flashed through her mind that her refusal, albeit involuntary, had given her back a certain power and a certain influence over him. It was only later, much later, that she realised fully that this was the moment when the infernal tie that bound them had changed in her favour. Overtly, he still savoured his power but as he stood looking at her, there was that haunting look of uncertainty and pleading mixed with the sadistic pleasure.

He got nothing in return, not because of her courage, but because, at that moment, she physically could not respond. His ingenious but primitive sadism had stunned her and for the time being her flight from reality shielded her and she could say nothing at all. After a long pause he turned and left.

Two women attendants came for her and handcuffed one of her wrists to each of them. Detty couldn't imagine why as at this moment she hardly had command of her body herself and anyway escape in these circumstances was hardly possible. The handcuffs seemed part of the ritual, just for show and to strike fear into the other detainees. They led her up the steps and then stood on either side of her at the back of the still empty hall. Mistily she was aware of the hall filling with muted detainees.

The governor re-entered followed by the chaplain accompanied by two young soldiers acting as servers. They took their place on the dais and the chaplain said the Mass in German. Detty strove to call on her deep faith but found the numbness forbade response and the awfulness of the surroundings contaminated the service. The Catholic inmates, who were the majority, lined up to take the sacrament. Finally she herself was led forward and one hand was unlocked at the last moment to steady herself before the sacrament. There was an awful symbolism in this, a half-Mass, given to a half-Catholic who was at this moment half-human.

The chaplain finished and the two attendants remained with their prisoner at the front of the assembly. The governor now took centre stage. The pompous gloating cruelty was back in place after the moment of uncertainty. Maybe there had never been any uncertainty and it was all a figment of Detty's battered mind.

'I need to tell you that one of your number has committed several extremely serious offences. Bring Bernadette O'Neill onto the platform.'

The guards marched Detty, still between them, onto the dais.

'Bernadette O'Neill you stand convicted by summary trial of several offences. First, escaping from a labour camp, second, unlawful spying in a military installation, third, seducing a soldier by sexual lures from his proper duty and fourth, acting as a common prostitute.'

Detty wondered whether she was the first virgin prostitute – not currently important she decided sadly.

'Two of the offences constitute treason against the state and therefore carry the death penalty.'

He paused to let this information have its effect on the detainees in the hall and the offender. Detty thought for a ghastly moment that he had changed his mind and an image of Andrea's death agonies again passed before her.

'We have decided, however, to exercise clemency.'

She felt a wave of relief sweep over her but the governor was speaking again. This time he addressed her. 'Being a foreigner, you may not have known until this morning that formerly in our city, under its ancient laws, unlicensed prostitutes were flogged through the streets to preserve health and public decency and as an example to others. You have been taken as a brazen whore and convicted. Your will be punished according to custom. You will receive thirty strokes with birch rods. Do you have anything to say?'

There was silence.

'Very well. The sentence will be carried out at 5pm. Take her back to her cell to await punishment.'

She was accompanied back to her cell by the two female supervisors. She was examined briefly by the odious MO who pronounced her fit for punishment. She wondered what she would have to have had wrong with her to be found unfit to suffer in that hellhole. Then she sat and waited and waited until it seemed five o'clock would never come. She heard the clock in the courtyard strike every hour and half-hour. She remembered a record of Kathy Durkin singing a strange song years ago back in Ireland during her childhood. It was about somebody waiting for execution while the clock in the tower struck the hours. It took much longer in real life than it did on the record, she reflected ruefully but at least she wasn't going to the scaffold.

The news reached Marc when he was paraded with the defaulters in front of the colonel.

'Two days loss of leave and an extra night's guard duty,' was the verdict. The colonel seemed relaxed and added, 'Don't do it again but I can't say I blame you. A superb broad like that must have been a great lay! It's a shame she is going to have such a hard time.'

Marc just resisted the temptation to punch his CO on the nose for the first remark while cold fear clutched at his belly with the second.

'Hard time, Sir?' he queried trying to sound calm.

'Yes,' said the colonel, 'I got you off under military law but there was nothing I could do for her. She will be flogged this evening – thirty strokes with the birch. You have to attend with the rest of the unit. I gather that my neighbour the governor has found a medieval statute or something relating to the punishment of tarts which he is enjoying himself applying rather literally to your young lady.'

Marc was horrified – Detty – thirty lashes – his mind reeled – protect her – rescue her – it was all his fault for staging the sham lovemaking. How could any human soul give thirty lashes to anyone – but to a woman let alone to that perfect body? Oh God – his discipline – his mission – his fault – he would offer to stand in for her but he knew that was useless. He had no illusions about the sadism of the governor.

Dazed he followed his companions over to the Farm. He didn't want to go but realised that he had no choice. Anyway perhaps he could get some crumb of comfort to the woman he now realised that he adored at the cruel moment when she was to be tortured in front of his very eyes. He knew it was useless and that he could do nothing. The Farm detainees were standing down one side of the quadrangle leaving the other side for the soldiers. The end by the steps to the great hall was reserved for officials and VIPs while at the bottom of the courtyard were the press photographers and film cameramen. The floodlights were already turned on revealing the stout oak trestle in the middle of the yard.

After a few minutes the governor and his guests came down the steps from the great hall. He seemed in high good humour and they had obviously lunched long and well.

'Ladies and Gentleman,' he said, 'Welcome to the Farm Camp. The security guards have done well to uncover the activities of a particularly dangerous young alien who is already serving a sentence here as a foreign spy. She has been found guilty of the following offences.'

He read the list with obvious relish.

168

'This afternoon we are here to carry out her punishment according to the historical law of Königshof for the correction of vagrant prostitutes which we hope will not only teach her a salutary lesson but will discourage any other young person tempted to follow in her footsteps. Bring in the offender!'

Marc was awestruck by her courage. Her chestnut hair streamed over the cloak she wore over her shift. More impressive still was the way she walked with her head high, her back straight and her chin out as if defying them to do their worst. If Marc had thought her a Botticelli Venus when he had last seen her, he now thought she was transfigured into a martyr saint. Somehow Marc, on this worst day of his life, drew some strange comfort from her fortitude. He did not know of course that this valiant heroine had been a sobbing, despairing child until Tamara had given her back hope.

As she was marched across the yard, the victim herself tried to keep calm and tried not to look at the trestle or the armourer standing huge and grim as he had done when they hanged Andrea. She tried to get back that sense she was outside herself watching it all happen to someone else. What they were about to do would degrade them not her, she told herself, trying hard to believe it. She drew a crumb of comfort from the fact that, for whatever reason, she was to be tortured in the clean outside air not in the ghastly isolation of that awful sound-proofed padded room behind the armoury. She felt that somehow the onlookers would protect her from the worst that might have happened to her in private. Then she thought of her ancestor, the great O'Neill, and reminded herself again that she bore a King's name and must aquit herself with pride as a true daughter of Ireland, as had her national patriots. She would try to show them all! It distracted her from dwelling on her plight and the humiliation and pain that she was going to have to suffer to think of the troubles of her ancestors. She succeeded in distracting herself until she was observing the terrible scene from afar. Again it was happening to somebody else. She was conscious of the cold night air as the armourer took her cloak and shift off positioning and strapping her firmly but not unduly roughly over the trestle. She was numbed and unresisting. For a moment she

169

wondered whether the humiliation or the pain would be worst. After a pause of a few seconds wait, the pain began and she knew the answer. She coped with the first few strokes but then she tried in vain to fight the searing agony overwhelming her strapped limbs with merciless repetition. The pain ceased to be in time and place, it was always and everywhere.

Eventually everything grew misty and there were only flashes of fiery anguish in her consciousness. Later she thought she was being carried and she heard Marc's voice but was sure it was an hallucination. When she finally woke up and vomited, it was the night. She felt herself gingerly and every movement sent new stabs of pain shooting through her. Her back and legs burnt ferociously and the straw stuck to her wounds. She needed to get up but it hurt so much that it took her what seemed like hours to get free from the straw. Then her troubles really started as her legs wouldn't bear her weight and she had to half crawl to the bucket with every movement renewing the agony.

Some hours later the MO visited. He made a perfunctory and rough examination and left muttering his verdict, 'The pain is much as to be expected. It should have taught her a lesson. I hold, and the governor agrees, that the pains afterwards are part of the punishment and help them to remember. She has quite severe splintering though which will go septic if it's left. This could cause fatal infection. Has she a friend – female – I mean in the camp who would attend to them? We can't spare staff.'

The attendant turned to Detty, 'Have you?'

'Ask Tamara Nicolaevna,' she choked a whisper. 'I think she will come after duties.'

That evening the female attendant had been replaced by a male. The pain was worse as she was now more fully conscious. It felt as if she was enclosed in molten lead from the waist to the knees. Then suddenly there was Tamara smiling at her side like a small fair angel.

'Oh Detti. What have they done to you?' she said, and then with sudden resolve, 'We can't have this. I need to take the splinters out of your poor back. It will be sore and take a long time and you need a painkiller.'

'They won't let me have one – it's part of the punishment,' repeated Detty distantly and weakly. 'The doctor said there was no point in beating me if they eased the pain as soon as it was finished.'

'That sounds like his true bedside manner but I'll try again,' said Tamara and turned to the attendant.

'I would like some morphine, iodine and forceps.' She said with her sweetest smile. After this there was a long muttered conversation but eventually they were produced. Mara smiled at her friend and gave her an injection with surprising expertise saying, 'I've never done this before for real but they taught me at Red Cross on a cucumber and it seems quite straightforward. Tell me if I hurt you. It will relieve the pain and give you some lovely dreams, my poor darling. Then I'll get to work tidying you up.'

Gradually a rosy feeling came over her and the pain melted away like magic. She could feel Mara gently pulling and swabbing and occasionally there was a slight tweak as a stubborn wood splinter came out but the relief after the searing pain was heavenly.

Towards dawn Mara said, 'That's enough for tonight. We will finish tomorrow.'

She turned to the attendant and said, 'OK, I'm ready to pay as agreed.'

She then disappeared with him leaving Detty to wonder exactly how her friend was having to pay for the help that she had given to her.

After an interval she reappeared, saying to the attendant, 'Tomorrow?'

He took the equipment and morphia from her and said, 'As agreed, you can have it all back tomorrow… as agreed.'

She nodded calmly in assent and Detty, still free from pain under the morphine, worried again at the probable cost and marvelled at her friend.

During the day the doctor arrived and turned her over roughly grunting. She cried out partly from current pain partly from the memory of her ordeal brought back by the rough handling. The doctor remarked that she was a strong fit girl and doing quite well. 'No thanks to you,' thought Detty. By evening she was fully conscious but the dreadful throbbing had come back. She longed for Mara's return but hated the thought of the hideous bribes she knew her friend was paying to help her. As she lay she found she could pray and she petitioned her gentle stoical name Saint and the Virgin on behalf of all women.

She thought about the governor and how he had used her plight to feed his sadism. The ghastly charade of using the medieval Hanseatic town's punishment obviously gave him pleasure but it might also be a way of taunting his opponents in exile. One thing he had got wrong though – her whipping might have made her Bloody, as the statute said but certainly not Remorseful just Revengeful instead. She savoured the word, *Rachsuchtig*, in her mind spelling it in the capitalised Gothic script of the awful old document. In her present situation she did not know how, but one day she would repay the ghastly little man.

Without thinking about it consciously, she found herself remembering about that most beautiful of all prayers for hope which she had dared to sing so long ago at the university singing contest and again at her triumph in Dublin. She realised that she had not then had the experience to reach its full meaning. Now she had been through the fire and it came to her amidst her agony and despair. She remembered her conversation with Adele when she said it would be on her lips at the edge of hell. That was surely now – she began to whisper it over very softly to herself:

> 'Komm, Hoffnung, lass den letzten Stern,
> den letzten Stern,
> der Müden nicht erbleichen:
> O komm, er hell, er hell mein Zeil,
> sei's noch so fern so fern,
> die Liebe, sie wlrd's erreichen,
> Komm, o komm, komm, o Hoffnung!* [16]

---

16 Come, Hope, let the last star
    Not fade from the weary!
    O come make bright my goal
    however distant it may be
    Love will find it
    Come, o come, o come , my hope!

by the time she had finished she was actually singing it very softly and then she was aware of Mara standing beside her listening and smiling.

'That's very beautiful – what is it?' she said.

Detty replied, 'It's from *Fidelio* – Leonore's prayer for hope to save her husband who is dying in a dungeon.'

'Does he die?'

'No – he's saved.'

'That sounds like a good omen! Now lets get to work.' As she worked she whispered, 'I've got some news for you. Liese worked at the cow stall today and was able to speak to Marc who's back on his old duties. He asked if we knew how you were. Were you still alive? If so he sent a message to say that he knew he was responsible for your capture. He will never forgive himself for what happened to you and you will never forgive him – if you live. He can't face life with it on his conscience.'

Tamara was startled as, in spite of the pain that it caused her, Detty suddenly turned, to look at her with her green eyes sparkling.

'Get her to tell him that he's an idiot. I am a big girl and I take my own risks and am responsible for my own thrashings. I shall be with him soon to lift *'Den Amethysten-Becher'* – get that right because he will know that's really from me and,' she dropped to a low whisper, 'tell him that I love him.'

'You are really getting better!' laughed Mara full of relief. She gave Detty an injection and the latter again found herself floating out on a painless magic cloud. After several hours, Tamara said, 'I've finished. I think I've got them all – if I have left one you will feel it prick and we will remove it later. I'll just find an ice pack for you to help the swelling.'

She persuaded the attendant to part with some ice for the pack and then went with him into spare cell where Detty was aware she was paying the exacted bargain. She put her head round the door before she left looking pale and shaken but stoical. Detty found herself wondering how she could ever repay this small neat miracle, who had apparently willingly given such a shocking price and had probably saved her life. She prayed and made certain further vows wondering all the while if she would ever be able to carry them out.

Tamara's efforts seemed to lend Detty strength. It was almost as if she'd not want to let Mara down. In a few days she was up and dressed but very stiff and slow. Tamara massaged her scabbed skin endlessly and gradually it became more flexible. She was discharged from the infirmary and made to start camp routines, which seemed almost to help. The first work run was a challenge – she now knew what the fat slow detainees had suffered before, while she had been able to prance forward with her athlete's pride and arrogance. After the run she was desperately chafed and her hips throbbed but she had avoided punishment and kept with the pack. The guard was one of the decent ones and he gave her only a token slap with the strap as she struggled. She was desperately thin having lost many kilos following her ordeal but her appetite gradually returned under Tamara's constant coaxing and with it her strength and speed. Thanks to Tamara's meticulous hygiene all her skin healed properly but her back was heavily scarred.

She thought endlessly about Marc but for two weeks heard nothing. Then there was a brief message from Liese who had seen him for an instant at the stall. It was: 'Get fit as quickly as possible – important.'

Detty was a bit taken aback by the stark order after the love and remorse of the previous message. She thought long and hard and realised with a tingle that this command might be a prelude to some sort of action – possibly even the way to her devoutly craved revenge – even a call to arms. How much she wanted and needed that! She thought that she must still be confused after her ordeal and dismissed the idea as silly wishful fantasy. But she still threw herself into running, swimming and physical training and was rewarded by feeling her powerful body strengthening with the resilience of youth overcoming the dreadful injuries. She realised that anger was keeping her going. She began to feel in command of herself again and her spirits rose with her strength. She found herself thinking with pride of her fighting forebears and humming songs about the men of '98 and the patriots of '16. She was a modern Irish girl, European, co-operative and despised the cruel sectarian divisions that Ireland had known for so long but she was proud of her country's struggle to freedom and the heroism of the risings deeply affected and inspired her. Something of her own people's struggle resonated with the oppression she was experiencing herself. She thought of the cowardly fascist guards in the camp who regarded bestiality towards defenceless detainees as an everyday amusement and swore again to get even if ever she could. Determination, youth and confidence were powerfully recuperative and physically she was eventually back to full health. Psychologically she felt vengeful and angry and this was an antidote to the trauma. She was ready for anything Marc might want. Then her nascent confidence vanished with a dreadful crash.

Mara had always occupied the bed next to Detty's. Usually neither of them woke before morning but on this particular night Detty woke from a nightmare in which she was being chased into a furnace by a demon with a short club. As she woke she was aware that something was really wrong. She was just in time to see four masked, black clad figures carrying a fifth, gagged but silently struggling out of the dormitory. She leapt out of bed only to reach the door as the bolt slammed it locked behind the intruders. She banged at the door and roused the whole dormitory but for some time nobody came from outside. After about 15 minutes the supervisor arrived to announce that Tamara had escaped and the grounds and surroundings were being searched.

The supervisor stormed about what she called the riot and threatened punishment. They would each be punished for being involved in a gross breach of regulations. Detty hardly cared as she realised Tamara had been kidnapped and was desperately afraid for her. There had been something very sinister about the night raid on the dormitory and she wondered gloomily whether she would ever see her friend again. Why the raid? After all they were totally in the power of the NAS who could do anything they wanted to them. The only purpose that she could think of for the raid was to fabricate a false story, to stage manage something.

They had to wait two days to hear anything definite although rumour was rife. It was said that Tamara's father had escaped to America – picked up by a submarine with government defence plans from his old job. The president was furious and wanted to have the daughter hanged in revenge. Detty hoped against hope that the rumour was unfounded but, after Andrea's fate, she had to admit that it sounded all too plausible.

The worst part of all was that she could do nothing at all to help her heroic friend who had given so much to her when she was in need. She was almost sure that Mara was being held in the solitary confinement unit but this was now guarded under the president's special orders by a formidable military police detachment not the old slap-happy service battalion. Any form of access was impossible. She wished she could get a message to Marc, who she felt, somehow, could help, but there was no way of contacting him either.

On the morning two days after Tamara disappeared the assembly was hushed and expectant that there would be some news. Eventually the governor with one of the president's personal aides appeared on the platform. He looked flushed and breathless.

'You should all be aware,' he started, 'of the serious punishment for premeditated escape and most of you will have seen, either as witnesses or at least on film, the hanging of the detainee Hoffman for this offence in this camp several months ago.'

Detty felt her stomach turn over and held her breath,

'Some detainees, however, appear to be very slow learners and one of your number has again tried to escape and has been recaptured attempting to cross the perimeter.'

Detty controlled her strong desire to shout, 'lying bastard', knowing that it would do no good.

'Bring Tamara Nicolaevna Oblova onto the platform.'

Detty looked anxiously towards the back doors which opened to show a small blonde figure looking tiny and vulnerable between two police guards who marched her up to the platform. Mara was wearing her camp shift just as Detty herself had done before. She looked pale, anxious and haggard from loss of sleep but worse was the vacant distant look in those bright cheerful eyes. Detty was numbed by this dreadful sight. It was as if someone had drained Tamara's spirit. She realised that she loved this little creature more than she could tell and the thought that the bastards were torturing her was insupportable – far worse than her own ordeal. She felt silent tears well up and flow down her cheeks. Then she said to herself, 'Pull yourself together you're not going to help Mara by blubbing.'

The Governor was speaking again, 'Tamara Nicolaevna you have been convicted by summary court of an offence which carries a capital penalty. The president, however, has seen fit to suspend this sentence for the time being.'

Detty felt her heart leap with joy – irrationally as quickly she realised that they would hardly go to the length of framing Mara and then let her off – he was continuing, 'You have agreed to confess your guilt in trying to escape and to make an announcement for the benefit of the press and to condemn the treasonable acts of your traitor father. Read it to the Farm Assembly now and this evening you can read it to the news media publicl.'

Her hand shaking, Mara took the paper that was thrust at her and looked down at it. Suddenly with resolution she looked up at the governor and very deliberately tore the paper into tiny shreds and let them drop at his feet. The governor purpled with fury and struck her hard across the face knocking her to the ground where he stood looking down at her with virulent hatred.

'You think that you can make a public fool of me, you little bitch. Well, you will learn that you can't. We have six hours before the press and television arrive to make you see reason and we will make sure we use it to good effect. Pick her up and take her to the armoury.'

Detty noticed that there was now no pretence of taking her back to solitary confinement before transferring her to the armoury to be tortured. The reason that she was being taken to the armoury was clear to anyone detained in the farm.

'Bastards, bastards, bastards!' muttered Detty helplessly to herself as she made one futile attempt to get to Mara as she was picked up by the guards. Why not hang her and have done with it? – better than this slow death by the foulest of means.

She couldn't remember how she got through the hours to evening assembly. She had the awful sense of déjà vue as the press men, officials, soldiers and detainees gathered round the courtyard but this was worse. She had been hurt terribly, humiliated perhaps scarred for life but she had not been slowly, secretly and brutally tortured to death. She hung about near the entrance hoping to see Marc who finally appeared close

177

enough to speak to her in quiet English, 'God this is unbearable,' he said then, apparently inconsequentially, 'You must look out for the trash man.'

Before they were separated by the guards, Detty reflected that her punishment had almost been like a gruesome pantomime compared with this. This was different more serious – serious as death.

The governor appeared that evening in front of the reporters and the cameras in the great hall. He appeared with a look of satisfaction that boded ill indeed, 'Good evening, ladies and gentlemen, You may know that a traitor from the corrupt junta that formerly ruled this country has escaped with state papers to a tyrannical foreign power. Fortunately his daughter, who is a resident here, deplores his treason.

Detty almost smiled at the gross euphemism of 'resident'.

'She does not support his views and is here to make a statement to that effect. Bring out Tamara Nicolaevna Oblova.'

Detty couldn't look at first but eventually she peeped up at her friend. The first thing that surprised her was that Tamara was wearing a smart long loose black kimono, not the skimpy camp shift. Her hair had been set and her face made up. She looked like an awful grotesque doll. She took the paper passed to her by the governor and looked at it. For an instant her head half-jerked up and her hand trembled as if she was making the effort to repeat her act of defiance of earlier in the day. Then she convulsed for a moment and Detty thought that she was having a seizure. Finally, in a croak that was only audible because of a microphone hung round her neck she began to read:

'I, Tamara Nicolaevna Oblova sincerely regret the treacherous and disloyal gesture that I have made and thank the governor for exercising the right of mercy given to him by our wise and just President Travsky. I condemn wholeheartedly the treacherous actions of my despicable father, Nicklaus Oblov, and will assist in all ways that I can in bringing him to proper justice.'

The governor was speaking, 'Very well. Take her away. She will be brought here in front of you all to repeat her confession each week until her father is brought to justice. Please let me have the official film I want it to catch the flight to the USA.'

Detty realised that the film would show the wretched girl's father, Nicklaus Oblov, what was being done to his daughter as a result of his defection so that he might return to rapid execution in the hope that that might stop his daughter being tortured. Detty now knew why they preferred this to hanging. Tamara could be tortured little by little each week reopening her mental and physical wounds. It could be adjusted so she was not killed – at least not rapidly and her father could be sent each instalment including the torture itself, which they hadn't seen, but he would have to watch on video. This was far worse than hanging.

Detty watched the limp body being half carried to the infirmary. Again she tried to reach her only to be repulsed. She went back to the dormitory with no chance of sleep and then in the early morning drifted off into a nightmare about watching herself being dismembered. She supposed that Mara was almost part of herself now. Awaking again before the morning call she went out to the lavatory and there cold in her shift she prayed first to her own name Saint – the vulnerable, sad little girl from the Pyrenees for whom she felt affection but, truth to say, not a lot of respect. Then she prayed to St Joan of France, the girl warrior who was herself burnt at the stake. She would know the situation and help if she could. Finally with tears streaming down her face she prayed out loud to the Mother of God as the protectress of all women to save Tamara and to show Detty if there was any way she could give her own life for that of her adored friend.

As she finished and opened her eyes, quite suddenly the first shaft of early spring sunlight from the high window struck dramatically across the wash house floor. Was it a sign? At least it was an inspiring moment and for the first time in many days she went to start the day's work with a faint tingling of hope which, in the face of the facts, was quite irrational.

Feeling oddly comforted Detty returned for dormitory inspection. To her relief there were no detainees to be punished that morning and they were all able to complete the routine and go to breakfast with more appetite than usual. On her way back across the quad Detty saw the refuse cart accompanied by the familiar figure of the little old man. Remembering Marc's strange message she hovered near it.

179

In his thick flat local accent the old man said, 'Good morning, Fräulein,' using the old fashioned form and went on casually, 'What do you raise up high?'

Detty replied immediately, 'The amethyst chalice.'

He said very quietly, 'I have a paper for you. Pick it up and hide it when I drop it by the cart.'

She followed the instructions putting the cart between herself and the courtyard as she stooped for the paper and tucked it into her cleavage as the only hiding place available. She returned to the dormitory to change for inside work, which was in the hated sewing room. She had a moment to go to the lavatory and quickly read the paper. It read: 'Charity show in aid of Liu. Programme from the Smith's circle. First evening Act 1 conclusion, third evening first entr'acte, second evening Act 3 conclusion. Watch for the Wanderer and be ready on cue.'

At first she cursed Marc who seemed to be playing an obscurantist game. Then she thought again and realised that he had taken a chance to devise a code revolving round their common interest. He knew they shared this and it was unlikely to be understood by others in this inferno of a land. She began thinking hard as she put on her work tabard and went to the sewing room. All the clothes for the detainees were made there and it was loathed by the girls as the sadistic supervisors were unfortunately lesbians and were always seeking sexual favours and if denied were particularly brutal. Detty was usually picked out for a hard job and today she was having to stitch up the regulation shifts. She was no seamstress and anyway her mind was half on the job and half on Marc's message. The stitching in the first batch had left the seam line in several places.

The shop supervisor was furious, 'I would have thought that the public thrashing that you had the other day would have taught you a lesson but obviously it hasn't, you lazy foreign slag.'

So saying, she cuffed Detty hard across the face. Detty dried her bleeding nose and started to concentrate again. She had worked out Marc's conundrum by lunchtime and felt pleased with herself despite her sore cheek. Mara was Liu under torture. The Smith's circle was the Nibelung's Ring. She must escape with Marc like Siegmund and Sieglinde at the end of the first act of *Die Walküre*. Her heart leapt in spite

180

of herself at the thought of the double implication of this. They would then travel down the Rhein, i.e. to Germany as in Götterdamerung from there he would return as in the third act of Siegfried and break through the fire, i.e. into the camp to rescue Mara. She hoped Mara's role as Brunnhilde was a temporary one but jealousy was no part of her make-up. She must be ready for the Wanderer. She signalled her acknowledgement via the dustcart.

'Hope Grane is well. Is Nothung ready?'

In her anxiety over Tamara, Detty had forgotten that this was Friday, the day of the house assembly when the whole dormitory was to be detained for the disturbance the night Tamara disappeared. The detention took place in the guard room where they had to line the walls in the *Verhör* position in the biting cold under the eye of the particularly odious guard called Oleg and two of his companions. She had previously been propositioned by him and she had told him to get lost with some force. This was his revenge and he was particularly enjoying his power in supervising the punishment.

Afterwards she went up to him with her most winning smile and said she was sorry for her previous behaviour and now realised how wrong she had been. She explained that all girls loved being dominated by powerful men and although he was very severe to her, she wanted to thank them for punishing the arrogance out of her. She said that she felt he was now her master and she would like to please him. She went on saying that there was, however, one tiny thing he could do for her first. She did badly want to see her friend in the solitary block.

He was a stupid young man brought up on pornographic magazines and was gullible enough to believe this rubbish about all women being masochists at heart who looked up to men who hurt them. He half suspected a trap when the fierce arrogant girl appeared to be all submission and he was still dubious. At first it looked as though he wouldn't take the bait as he made every possible objection.

'Impossible. I would be punished. Was that what you want – to get your own back?'

Then she began to convince him he had conquered her and he was stupid enough to believe it and got more coarsely amorous. Eventually he agreed that he might be able to get her into see Tamara if she was nice to him. This was the crunch.

'What did he mean by nice?' she asked with her most innocent submissive smile. Finally they struck a bargain.

Clandestinely they passed into the punishment block. Detty noticed that Tamara was not in the ordinary cells but still in the infirmary at the end. Was this good because they were looking after her or bad because her injuries were so severe that she wasn't able to be discharged? They reached the infirmary. Tamara lay on a bunk with a wet dressing on her back. She was pale and had a fever but was conscious. She smiled and kissed Detty gently. She told her that an electric burn had become infected and the doctor had her on antibiotics and was frantically trying to make her better. She then added quietly that this was because they wanted to work on her back in the armoury to convince her father to come back. The doctor thought the governor would be furious if she wasn't fit enough to be taken back for further 'attention'.

Detty said with a conviction that she didn't feel that she was sure that they wouldn't torture her again while she was so ill. She then dropped her voice and said with some urgency, 'Mara, darling, we are going to get you out – Marc is and he knows how to. Whatever they do to you don't give up hope. Hang on and we will rescue you. This is a solemn promise. First we have to get out ourselves but that will be very soon and then we will be back.'

Mara said weakly that she wouldn't let them win although Detty didn't think that she really believed that they could rescue her. She looked very frail and Detty left even more anxious than when she had arrived. Would that little body be able to survive let alone stand a further dose of torture?

She walked down the corridor to be met by the grinning Oleg. The slave role that she had mapped out for herself was very tedious to say the least but worried by Tamara being in the power of this oaf she thought she had better humour him. He led her into the mess room of the guard house where several other young layabouts were smoking and drinking coffee.

'This is my personal slave, lads – bit of all right, isn't she?'

She paid the agreed price with hatred and revulsion. But there was vengeance in her heart but also a little relief that she had survived without rape – only because the guards knew it was illegal and severely punished.

4
ULISSE

Break, heart; I prithee break

SHAKESPEARE: KING LEAR ACT V

Between work periods she spent hours in the shower and hours washing her mouth out but the taste wouldn't go. She was in the middle of one mouth washing sequence when the duty supervisor came in and said, 'I've been looking for you everywhere. Report to the medical officer there is something he wants you to do.'

With trepidation she crossed to the revolting doctor's office beside the solitary block. She knocked and his voice told her to come in. He was sitting at a desk and looked up at her smiling, 'Ah, O'Neill – yes I have some good news for you. The governor would have given it to you himself but he has been called to Königshof. You are to be released.'

Detty couldn't believe that she was hearing this. It was all so matter of fact. Somehow, however, the cruelty was still in the MO's smile as he gave her this unbelievable news. Was it all going to be snatched away as a cruel joke? He was speaking again.

'You obviously have caused a stir in NATO and they want you back. I think that you may have embarrassed them by showing them how powerless they are. Anyway there have been some very high level negotiations and we have gained certain advantages in the form of conventional weapons to deal with counter revolutionaries and some of our hostile neighbour states while they are to have our mobile nuclear rockets and you. Please accept my congratulations. You will form part of a complete simultaneous exchange in a month's time at the German border.'

She couldn't believe it; it was all so simple – too simple. Then she thought of Mara and she realised that in three weeks she could do nothing for her. It would be too late. The MO was continuing.

'There is just one thing. According to our new eugenic laws where there is a history of moral depravity or where they or their families have an unreliable record, we send young people to the *Fortpflanzungsklinikum* in Königshof with a recommendation under law 76 section 8 to be carried out before they are released to their families. Do you know about the *Klinik* – it is always known as that for short?'

Detty's mind flew to wild stories that she had heard of forced breeding of babies brought up as state clones in some special unit but she said, 'No, Sir,'

'Well it's a misnomer really as you will see. There is a history of sterilising unsuitable people in this part of the world. The Swedes, Danes and Finns all did it and the Nazis developed it. They sterilised all the deformed, mental defectives and subspecies so that they wouldn't contaminate the stock with racially impure people. Later they also hit on the idea of sterilising young people with unsound views to prevent them spreading. After all we can't have hooligans breeding more terrorists and revolutionaries, can we? We could of course execute them and often do but they can provide a useful labour force once the operation has calmed them down and in the community they serve as a warning to others to behave themselves.

'Other countries sometimes sterilised by operation and sometimes used X-rays but we have to use the simpler methods. The men and boys are just taken to a small department whose slang name is the Lambing Pen where they are castrated by a ligature. For the first twelve hours they are detained handcuffed in cells. After that they are allowed

185

to go home as nothing they try to do will make any difference. Their testicles atrophy and come away. They are just made eunuchs. It is very simple.

'Sterilising the human female is more complicated so the women taken to the Frauenklinik need slightly more sophisticated treatment. As you will see when you get there that they are all operated on by technicians and students. It gives them good practice.'

'As well as not being able to have children, a spayed female of, say, how old are you? Twenty-one has a stormy artificial change of life which makes her wretched for several years. By twenty-five, however, she has settled down as a shrivelled docile old woman. Like the others, as you are being allowed out early, the governor and I think that you should be treated before you go.'

He smiled at her watching her face for the horrified reaction. She couldn't restrain her gasp of, 'Oh no', and then wanted to vomit. This was the plan then –to exchange her at the frontier apparently well but in fact horribly mutilated.

'We haven't, of course, made a big issue of this with our friends in the West but by the time they find out the exchange will be complete and they won't be able to do anything about it. Anyway the agreement just states that you are to form part of the exchange, they have not stipulated the, how do you say, state of the goods. So you'll be sent to the Frauenklinik to be sterilised yourself in two weeks time so that you will have recovered sufficiently when we exchange you. That should cure your arrogance and they can then take you back to – where is it? Ireland. You will be luckier than the ones who stay here because I dare say they will give you hormones when you get there. It won't make you fertile but you may be less wretched. I have already made out the order perhaps you would like to see it?' He passed her a piece of paper headed:

Republik of Moltravia Ministry of Home Affairs
Eugenic Department H
Medical Recommendation that:
Bernadette Niamh O'Neill, alien,

of no fixed abode but currently detained in the Farm Detention Centre is
certified as an incorrigible moral defective demonstrating antisocial
tendencies and sexual depravity.

Corroborating evidence: Convictions for
(1) Terrorist activities
(2) Common prostitution
It is therefore ordered that she be compulsorily sterilised under law 76
Section 8.
She is to be taken, under force if necessary, to the Frauendienst of
Fortpflanzungsklinikum there to be sterilised by surgical removal of the
gonads and associated organs as appropriate in the manner authorised
by the law.

The order to be carried out within 14 days.

There followed the MOs signature and qualification.

'You can keep that, it's only a photocopy. But as for today's trip, I just thought you would like to see what happens in advance. Eva Harting and Natasha Simonova are twenty-year-olds from your block who have similar certificates to yours but are for operation today so it would be quite appropriate for you to watch them being attended to at the Klinik. You will go as an observer and this time you will come back intact. The next time… Hurry the van is waiting. I'm off to go home to my children.'

Still clutching the photocopy and fighting the nausea at his cruel departing quip Detty went out into the courtyard to the van which already contained four terrified women.

It took half an hour to reach the Klinikum, which was an old converted tuberculosis sanatorium on the edge of the capital. During the journey the supervisor had chatted with the guard who sat with a machine pistol across his knee. Detty studied her four companions who knew what was in store from them and sat looking at the van floor silent and a pool of abject terror and misery. The youngest called Wanda was the daughter of an opposition lawyer; she was still in her mid-teens.

Detty's two contemporaries were very different. Natasha was a brunette not beautiful but big boned and vigorous. A typical healthy country girl thought Detty. Eva on the other hand was tall and thin with an elfin boyish elegance small bust and slender legs. She may have taken after her mother who was a famous dancer or her father who was a well-known poet. The state found both of them 'unsatisfactory'.

The oldest, Teresa, was in her mid-twenties with a dark complexion and tight black curls round her normally cheerful face. She was an accountant and had been married to a student leader a few weeks before she was arrested. He had been drafted into the army at the same time as she was detained. They had not heard a word of each other since.

Detty thought of trying to disarm the guard. It might have been possible as he was only one of the slovenly soldiers from the service battalion but what was the point? They had nowhere to go and would be rapidly hunted down, recaptured and tortured by the NAS. None the less she thought that if she was taken in a similar way next time she would have a go and she studied the layout of the van in preparation. There was nothing that could be used as a weapon inside and the farm shifts did not afford much in the way of concealment. A knife might be possible if only she could get hold of one. A lot would depend on whether the others in her batch would join in and help. Sadly she thought it was unlikely as they were generally paralysed by terror at this stage. She would give it a try, however – a quick bullet would be better than being hacked about like so much meat.

In front of the building was a car park with a notice pointing round the back indicating *Mannerdienst* and the breeding unit *Zuchtendienst (Fortphlanzung Züchtung Weiblich)* where women had the state babies. Another notice pointed to the main entrance with *Frauendienst* on it. A NAS police van had just driven up at the same time containing a couple of uniformed NAS guards and an attractive looking family of five. Father was a fit looking man of about forty; mother probably a year or two younger, good looking with a trim attractive face and figure. There was a tall athletic looking son of perhaps eighteen and very pretty identical twin daughters with fair complexion and blonde curly hair who might have been a year or so younger. They were well dressed in warm winter coats and obviously came from a prosperous background. They kissed an anxious goodbye to each other before the impatient policemen led the men off in the direction of the men's service and brought the mother and twins over to join the party from the Farm.

They entered the grim building into a reception hall a little like a bare hotel atrium with several clerks processing admissions. They were directed towards a short queue at the head of which behind the counter a plump but sallow shrunken woman who could have been any age between forty and sixty, was filling in forms. As they waited in the queue the mother of the twins turned towards Detty and said, 'Do you know what is going on here? The police told us there was nothing to worry about we were just needed for a social family study and we expected to be asked to fill in questionnaires and things. It's not what I expected here but perhaps these forms are the questionnaires, are they?'

Detty was shocked to realise that this family had come here with no idea of the sinister reputation of the place. She felt that it was pointless to explain now and muttered that she wasn't sure herself, which in a sense was almost true.

The mother continued, 'By the way I am Barbara Kolyashin and these are my daughters Anna and Saskia.'

'Bernadette O'Neill,' she murmured feeling that polite introductions were incongruous in such a place.

The mother went on, 'It's odd that we don't know as my husband – he was the one you saw in the car park works for the government as an engineer. He was in the contracts department until they moved him last week.'

Detty didn't know what made her ask but she said, 'Why was he moved?'

Barbara answered confidentially, 'He found his boss was taking bribes and tried to report him. Suddenly he was moved to another department. Bad really.'

Detty thought to herself – you don't know how bad. She was now virtually certain, having learnt something about the way the government cadres thought, that the visit of the family to the Klinik was directly connected with this incident.

There was no more time for talk as they had reached the head of the queue. The NAS woman pushed a piece of paper at the clerk and it appeared the Kolyashin family were to be dealt with first. The clerk filled out three forms, which Detty couldn't see to read except the large print title that read Republic of Moltravia Law 76 Section 8.

The mother said to the clerk, 'Can you tell us what is going to happen? I need to get home by 5pm as I have a dental appointment for my daughters.'

The clerk looked at her pityingly in amazement, clipped number bands on their wrists and said, 'Wait over there in front of those doors. You will be kept in one group with these four, indicating the Farm girls. They walked over to the doors and waited while the Farm party's forms were completed.

The supervisor said that she had brought four women for operation under Law 76/8 producing the four certificates. They had been booked in and there was one observer who the MO wanted to be made to watch it. The clerk made out a form with several sections for each of the four girls and put them one by one on the same clipboard as the Kolyashin family. Each form was headed with the woman's full name, civil status, date of birth and next of kin. She then turned to the box marked Cause of Admission and wrote sterilisation, circling compulsory as opposed to voluntary in the next box headed 'Procedure'. She laboriously copied out the technical name of the operation. The clerk slowly went on to the box marked 'Indication' and wrote 'moral defective/antisocial tendencies unfit for breeding' on each. Again it sounded just like cattle thought Detty. The form for the moment seemed complete and she copied the reference number from the top onto a wristband and clipped it round the relevant woman's wrist. She gave Detty a badge marked Visitor which drew glances of hatred from the others. She handed the clipboard to the nurse who motioned the party towards the Kolyashins waiting in front of the swing doors marked:

NO ADMITTANCE TO PATIENTS, RELATIVES OR
UNAUTHORISED PERSONS.

At this point the Farm staff woman left and the party under the direction of the nurse passed through the doors. The room was old and none too clean. It was tiled with coat hooks on one wall. Above these, incongruously, was a large photo of a laughing beach party playing with a highly coloured ball. Detty assumed that this was also displayed as a joke by some twisted mind. In the middle of the room was a small table with some papers with the NAS stamp on them and half a cup of cold coffee. The end wall had another pair of dark green swing doors like the ones they had entered by. The other side wall had steel shelving with piles of various items in the centre of a tiled arch which was the same size as the doorway in it. The room was cold, draughty and ill lit by a single electric light bulb in a very high ceiling. There were no outside windows.

The nurse went to the shelving and produced four thick plastic bags with Farm Detention Centre printed on them and three others marked Private Clothing. She then told the seven to undress. Detty's companions should put their Farm clothes in bags so marked. She explained that they would not need them again and they would be sent back to the Farm. They would wear gowns until their relatives collected them with outside clothes after their operations had healed.

The nurse turned to the Kolyashin family, 'You also will undress but put your clothes in one of these private bags. I will write your numbers on them and they will be returned to you when you are discharged after your operations.'

The mother became hysterical, What was happening? There must be some mistake. They hadn't asked for an operation. What operation anyway? She must insist on being allowed home.

The Farm party stood helplessly watching. Detty thinking, as the doctor had intended her to think, that in two weeks time she would be doing the same. Here there were no beatings, tortures or insults, only a desperately cold emotionless routine. Nobody seemed interested in the innocent young people whose bodies, minds and lives they were about to ruin. It was just routine and Detty wondered if she almost preferred the sadists at the Farm. At least they had some human emotion. The nurse looked impatient at the delay and said in a flat voice, 'You and your daughters are here by order of the State Department of Eugenics to be compulsorily sterilised under law 76 section 8 (Sterilisation of Moral Defectives). Now please let's get on.'

As her companions were being prepared Detty, wearing a gown marked visitor, was led away to a viewing gallery in the wall of a large hall where the operations took place. The scene below was that of a large, multiple operating theatre. There was not a lot of noise only muttered conversation from the working technicians and the occasional sound of distress as spinal injections were given. It was all clinical and as emotionally cold as the pit of hell. Detty realised with a start that if she had not known that these people were being mutilated against their will it could have been an emergency department after a major accident or a field casualty clearing station.

To her surprise there were a lot of other visitors in the gallery. It was quite crowded with spectators and Detty tried to decide why they were there. Some were clearly relatives who in spite of the large notice at the entrance had got passes to see their loved ones mutilated. They were very distressed and many were sobbing. There were a number of NAS and other officials who seemed to be there for kicks. Some of the onlookers were trainee paramedics and medical students learning how to do the job. Detty wondered whether in a week's time her own womb would be removed by one of these unprepossessing young men and women. The last and largest group were young people like herself. Some were individual and had visitors' gowns on. Like her, they were probably being frightened or taught a lesson. The others were groups of office workers, farmhands and students who were wearing outside clothes and had entered the gallery from outside. Each tour was in the charge of a woman NAS staff officer in an olive green uniform who was explaining in detail what was happening. Detty listened to the one addressing the nearest group of students.

'President Travsky is trying to help us become a happier, healthier and more industrious people. It is like being in a garden. It is important to breed healthier plants and weed out the defectives and prevent them spreading their problems. This clinic was set up for the humane sterilisation of individuals with inherited defects, handicaps or illnesses.

192

We also sterilise people with mental illness to prevent them handing it on to their children. These are the people you see in the second row and we attend to about eighty each day.

'The president realised, however, that these defects were only one sort of canker in our society. Wisely he knew that families or individuals who worked against the state and progress were an even larger and more serious problem. These people were liable to breed criminals, hooligans or terrorists and should be stopped. In the front row here, therefore, we sterilise a number of offenders each day who have been certified as moral defectives. A similar number of men are treated in the *Mannenklinik*. Some of these women have been convicted of socially damaging crimes like prostitution or drug abuse. The others have either given evidence of antisocial opinions themselves or come from families with such opinions. We want you to know that you have absolutely nothing to fear if you and your family are obedient, industrious and support the state. But the privilege of bearing the next generation of Moltravians will not be extended to those who step out of line or who come from devious stock.

'Those in front of you have all been certified as moral defectives and they are about to be sterilised by the removal of their womb and ovaries. This will mean that they lose not only the ability to have children but also their other feminine features and sex drive. Although they are all young, they will be made artificially into old women. You will now stay here for half an hour to see some operations being done. Then we will go up to the gallery wards so that you can talk to some of the patients recovering from their operations, most of whom are now bitterly sorry that they did not behave themselves before it was too late. You have the opportunity of getting it right. Take it and you will come to no harm!'

As the NAS woman finished, Detty was aware of the door to the outside at the back of the gallery being unlocked. Two male NAS came in accompanying two men wearing shorts and singlets. Detty thought they were familiar and indeed recognised them as the Kolyashins father and son. Both had their hands handcuffed behind their back and they seemed in great pain. The boy carried a steel bowl into which he retched. The NAS men who had brought them reattached their handcuffs to a rail in the gallery and started gossiping. At first Detty couldn't look, then a dreadful compulsion made her witness what was done to her companions and would soon be done to her. Time passed slowly.

The original nurse returned and asked if the batch had all been attended to. Detty nauseated and grey-white nodded then the nurse said, 'You can now go up and talk to them before your transport comes in an hour.'

She led her to the lift and they went up to the first gallery. Here there was no silence. As they left the lift a cacophony of moaning and shrieking assaulted their ears. Round the outside wall of the gallery were innumerable trolleys locked in position between lockers. Each trolley bore a figure on a mattress wearing the uniform white gown.

'These are all today's said the nurse. 'They get a standard pain killing injection when they arrive here but it often isn't enough as the spinal wears off so they shriek a bit.'

Many of the patients were moaning and restless with pain. A few just gazed into space with an expression of detached shock. The true meaning of their experience had hardly sunk in.

She found the four from the Farm still together at the far end of the bottom gallery. Eva who had been the first, was in great pain moaning, 'Oh God I'm on fire. Help me! Help me!'

Teresa was quieter but her face was contorted with distress. Natasha was the quietest of all but looked at Detty, intact in her pristine gown, with the bitter primitive malevolence of a wounded animal.

'Just you wait,' she said. 'You stuck up bitch. They will get you yet and I'll come back to help.'

Detty put her hand gently on her arm and said, 'Tasha listen! You are quite right. They are going to do me next week. That's why they made me watch today to give me two weeks to think about it. At least you didn't have that – I wasn't here to gloat – just to be terrified. I am so sorry. God go with you, Tasha – I shall always think of you. Pray for me.'

Slowly the words sank in and Natasha's expression changed, 'Oh Detty I'm sorry,' she whispered at last with her face flooded with tears amidst her pain. 'We didn't know. We thought you were here as a privileged foreigner, out of curiosity to gloat. How awful for you, poor Detty.'

'No worse than for you.' Detty replied but Natasha was overcome by a spasm of pain and Detty turned to Wanda.

The latter was deathly pale and her trolley and gown were stained with blood.

'That's not the real trouble,' said the nurse. 'She's bleeding inside she won't last long. Nothing we can do.'

Detty cradled the girl's pale face in her hands and whispered encouragement to her softly. She said, 'You are going to a place where there is no pain or sadness and everything is bright. Have courage. Would you like me to say a prayer for you?'

The pale head nodded slightly. Detty repeated the last rites and gave her absolution. She was of Polish origin and probably Catholic but Detty didn't think it really mattered. A few minutes afterwards the shallow breathing stopped. Little Wanda's agonies were over.

'Your transport has arrived,' the nurse told her.

Detty kissed Wanda's brow gently and with tears running down her face turned to go.

When she returned to the Farm she had a message that the MO wanted see her. She felt desperate and beyond hope. Her utmost ambition was to kill herself before they had a chance to 'attend' to her. She knocked through habit.

'Come in,' said the doctor who was drinking a clear liquid. 'Ah O'Neill. You're back. Come in. Sit down. Have a Vodka?'

She shook her head.

'Did you see your friends operated on then?'

'And killed,' muttered Detty.

'Oh dear,' said the doctor mildly. 'They didn't all make it? That was bad luck – doesn't happen so often these days. We must make sure that doesn't happen to you or else there will be nothing to exchange and we can't have that. Perhaps I had better get hold of a competent colleague. But what did you think of it? Are you looking forward to your turn? Do you think it will quieten you down – I think it will – no more soldiers in lofts and that sort of thing – eh!'

'I think I'll ask them to use the video room for you then you can take the film back with you to show your father. He's a colleague of mine, isn't he? He'd be interested to see our technique.'

'You filthy sadistlc bastard,' burst out Detty.

'Oh dear dear, talking to me like that won't save you. In fact I'll put it on the form of recommendation, aggressive females calm down too wonderfully after the operation. Go to bed now. Goodnight.'

5
RACHE

Sweet is revenge – especially to women –
Pillage to soldiers, prize money to seamen

BYRON: DON JUAN

The following morning she felt sick and hopeless but slowly her desperate resolution returned and she knew that she must try to escape quickly or kill herself. For the moment she didn't know how to do either. She must let Marc know the new danger and get his help.

'Hunding near. New horn calls. Can we do finale act I soonest?' she wrote quickly then, 'What about Grane? Very concerned re Liu. Urgent+++.'

She handed the note to the rubbish man telling him to say it came from one grappling with evil spirits. It was accurate and an allusion to *Zueignung*.

Still nothing happened and she began to wonder if Marc was in trouble himself or if she had misunderstood the message. Early the following morning she emerged after assembly thinking gloomily that she only had five days left and wondering how she could kill herself first. Then with a guilty start she realised that she was so preoccupied with her own fate that she had not given enough attention to Mara who might be back being tortured at this very moment. She had almost given up hope but cast a despairing glance at the rubbish cart which had given her a link to Marc but now, she felt, was no longer relevant. It rumbled in slowly as usual but, she noticed absentmindedly, the driver had changed. This was her last contact with Marc gone, she thought miserably. Instead of the little old man there was a much taller old man wearing an old hat and an eye patch over his left eye. She woke up with a start. Wondering if she was hallucinating, she looked again. 'The Wanderer!' she thought, remembering Marc's message and forgetting her misery with a rush of excitement.

She had no need to mention the amethyst chalice.

'There's a dustbin behind that service door. It's out of sight. Get into it', he said quietly. 'You will be tipped into the truck automatically then lie still whatever is on top of you, as long as you can breathe.'

She went behind the door and jumped into the large malodorous refuse bin. The bin was wheeled out and she felt the forks on the truck engage underneath it. With sudden panic she wondered if it might be one of those dustcarts that grinds up the rubbish and pushes it back. Then she told herself not to be silly and trust Marc. Anyway it would be quick and better than being butchered at the Klinik. She landed on her head. Sure enough she was half smothered by plastic bags, rotten vegetables and a foul smelling brown fluid that she couldn't identify, but nothing worse.

The cart moved off through the gates following the twice-weekly refuse route. Only with difficulty Detty pushed upwards through the contents of several more bins which were tipped in on the way. After some more minutes the cart stopped again. Peeping out she realised that they were next to the housing estate near to the barracks. She thought this was where the NCOs and officers from the barracks lived but wasn't sure. Peering further, Detty saw what had to be the back of the great hall of the Farm Schloss although she had never seen it before from outside. Was this freedom? There was a noise and she ducked low but it was only Marc adjusting the tailgate. He motioned her to stay inside and said, 'I am going to the front of the cart to immobilise the engine. I shall then leave a note saying it has broken down.'

His clipped precise *Hochdeutsch* voice was reassuring.

'I shall then get a motorbike that is here and belongs to a sergeant who is away for a couple of days. Have you ever ridden pillion?'

'No,' she said.

'You're going to now. Just hang on to me tight. If we are stopped you are one of the secretaries who is having a lift to the town. Talk bad Russian – your *Hochdeutch* is too good and easily identified. It might be suspicious. Get on when I bring the bike round the far side of the cart.'

She resented his implication that she couldn't speak the local *argot* but thought that this wasn't the moment to make an issue of it. Suddenly she heard Marc speak again, *'Gut' Tag'* he said reverting to the local accent.

Detty held her breath but the passer-by took no notice except to return the greeting and soon the footsteps got fainter. Eventually she heard the motorbike being wheeled round the far side of the van. One quick last look from the rubbish and she neatly flung her leg over the tailboard and ran the few steps to mount the pillion. Neither had helmets but this didn't matter as these were not the Moltravian fashion. Marc passed her a knitted Balaclava, 'We don't want your hair showing – it's far too distinctive and this will help you to keep warm.'

He waved to two soldiers on the pavement as they passed who waved back routinely. Then they were away, covering the short distance to the town, which they crossed slowly so as to avoid suspicion. As they passed the junction to the Sacred Heart Convent, Detty wondered how the school with its decimated pupils was surviving. Presumably it was now full of good little fascist children swearing loyalty to Travsky and the regime while saluting the flag each morning.

Once the main road on the other side of Ziatow was reached, Marc opened the throttle to over 200kph and the bike flew over the flat dreary road punctuated by occasional groups of trees, on the open stretches the road merged at its distant horizon into a grey flat sky. He turned round to her, slowing to make himself heard, 'How long before they notice you're missing?'

'About an hour, I hope.'

''That might be enough. How's your seat?' he shouted back.

'OK.' she yelled in his ear, although truth to tell when she thought about it, it was getting quite sore, although she hadn't noticed until he asked. He opened the throttle again, blocking any chance of conversation.

They took several side turns, then off onto another main road and then into more side roads. They were clearly trying to confuse the opposition and Marc had obviously taken some care trying to plan the route. Meticulous, she thought, just like bringing the Balaclava for her. Eventually they reached gently undulating wooded country that was different from the featureless plains around Königshof. Marc turned onto a very minor road where there was a narrow bridge crossing a medium sized river.

'Give me a hand,' he said and they both struggled to raise the heavy motorbike onto the parapet at the middle of the bridge. Eventually they were able to tip it over and it hit the water with a great splash that they both imagined would be heard for miles. Nothing, however, stirred and when they looked over the edge, to their mutual relief the motorbike had disappeared from sight under a swirling, muddy patch in the water.

'The next bit is on foot,' said Marc and they set off to trudge over ploughed fields with thick mud sticking to Marc's boots and Detty's unsuitable trainers. Marc kept checking the direction on a small compass.

'We go to that barn,' he said after they had trudged about seven kilometres and Detty's calves ached with fatigue from the weight of the clay. 'And we wait there until nightfall. We had better approach carefully although I think that the farm is abandoned. At dusk we make for the frontier – I hope that we can find some bicycles. Try and get some rest. I have brought some sausage and bread to eat.'

They climbed into the hay loft which immediately reminded Detty of that other one of the same type. Miraculously there were two tins of beer and some soup cans remaining from what had probably been a harvest workers summer bivouac. They drank the beer but didn't feel much like cold soup. They talked of their main anxiety, Tamara, and Marc confirmed that he had to get back to Germany to be able to help her but assured Detty that he would waste no time.

'It really is urgent, Marc,' Detty said tearfully. 'She's very weak and it's only a couple of days at most before they give her her next dose, if they haven't started already, and even with her courage she won't be able to take much more. Then there's her father – he may come back and then they will probably kill both of them.'

'I hope we have already helped a bit there,' said Marc leaving Detty to wonder again about that strange 'we'. 'I hope I have got a message through telling him on no account to return or else both he and Tamara are both as good as dead. The only question is whether he will believe me.'

Detty nodded.

'I am sure they will only keep her alive to bring him back – it must be very hard for a father to stay away and know what is happening to his young daughter.'

'We can only hope he sees the point. They say he's a very sensible bloke. In fact every ordinary Moltravian that I've talked to holds him in a sort of reverence as the antidote to Travsky,' said Marc thoughtfully.

'That bastard and his henchmen!' Detty opened her mouth to go on and tell him about her most recent hideous experience. A sudden inexplicable caution stopped her and afterwards she was very glad that she hadn't.

It was miraculously warm at last for an early spring afternoon in those northern climes with a warm southerly breeze and Detty went down to try and wash some of the filthier rubbish from her boiler suit at the standpipe tap. When she returned she left the wet garment to dry on the rail and lay down on the straw, slipped her coarse camp pants off and took up her position with one hand behind her neck and the other draped languidly across her stomach.

'I think we have some unfinished business,' she laughed to Marc. 'I hope that I am not tempting providence as I recall the last time I did this I finished up with a damn good thrashing. Quite right really, I suppose for a good convent girl who has behaved like a wanton. The worst thing, though, was that we were interrupted.'

Marc needed no second invitation and undressed quickly. They kissed hungrily then suddenly he looked very worried and said softly and awkwardly, 'Detti, are you... are you... all right?'

She looked straight at him very seriously but with her green hazel eyes twinkling mischievously. After a short pause she said, 'Herr Marc,

201

I am deeply offended. I have presented my personal assets as seductively as I know how. I have made you a very straightforward offer and you ask me if I am all right. I hoped that you might be able to tell me if I was all right, young man. Maybe you don't like my perfume!' she ended with assumed haughtiness of a woman scorned.

For a moment he took her seriously and said, 'I don't mean that – you know that I don't – I think that you are the most beautiful, wonderful creature that God ever created. But you have been hurt, very badly hurt… after all that you have been through… before we make love…'

'Marc, for a very brave and clever man there are times when you are an adorable sensitive idiot – yes I'm all right. I heal very quickly – my Aunt Deidre used to say so when I was a little girl and fell over. I know you will be gentle but there's no need to be too gentle because I'm ravenous for you.' She dropped her voice, 'In spite of all they have said about me it will be the first time – which is what I have wanted ever since you gave me that time ticket.'

Their bodies entwined as if they had always belonged together. Later Detty felt a sharp twinge and groaned aloud with pride and pleasure. Aunt Deidre was right as even when the blood rushed her to her climax, the pain was quite obliterated by the ecstasy. She whispered to him, 'If we never make it to the frontier it will have been worth it.'

He said with quiet determination, 'We are going to make the frontier, *Schatz*, I am greedy.'

At dusk they were on their way again towards the loom of *Altkirche*, which was a small town where they hoped to pick up bicycles. Providentially on the outskirts was a woodwork factory with some bicycles chained up outside. Marc was able to cut the chain with a mountaineer's knife and free two of them. Silently they rode off. They had gone about three kilometres when they saw very bright lights cutting fast through the darkness towards them. They just managed to roll into a ditch before a patrol car complete with searchlight swept past. Fortunately the searchlight was scanning the far side of the ditch. After that they had to go very carefully hiding in good time at any approaching light. After another half-hour of cautious going, they came upon a road-block at a junction of two roads which they had to spend some time circumventing. Soon the roadblocks became more frequent and Marc whispered that they were within a few kilometres of the frontier, which had clearly been sealed off.

The going then became very difficult with almost continuous patrols and blocks. Eventually Marc stopped and thought for a moment as yet another patrol flashed passed. Detty realised that part of the problem was that the spring dawn must only be an hour or so away. She felt bewildered and very tired. For the first time she realised that she was relying completely on Marc whose brow was furrowed and anxious. She looked around to the left and heard a noise like a small fast-flowing river or stream. Why not swim? She thought and then to herself, don't be ridiculous as the frontier was still quite a distance away and the river water in late winter would be freezing.

Strangely, however, Marc appeared to be thinking along the same lines and walked towards the river scanning the banks. Further along on their side was a dilapidated boat, which a casual inspection revealed had no bottom. Then a little further was a hut-like building with a small landing stage in front on the river bank.

Marc examined the shed, 'That's better,' he murmured to himself and set to work to cut the lock off the door with his knife. After a few minutes that seemed like an age it burst open and Marc smiled a smile of satisfaction.

'We just might have a guardian angel after all – have you ever done any canoeing?'

'No,' said Detty admitting another deficiency and feeling unusually inadequate after her lack of motorbike experience.

'OK, just take a paddle but don't do anything with it until I tell you. Let's have this one.'

He chose a double Kayak, which they carried to the river and gently dropped in.

'Hold on,' he said 'while I shut the door and get the paddles.'

He was back in a moment and showed her how to get into the stern seat without upsetting the delicate craft and then with a sudden confident movement he pushed off and seated himself in the bows. They were away.

'Two problems,' muttered Marc quietly. 'One is that they may spot us from the bridges, and the other is to decide where and how this stream goes into the Oder. How far up and whether there's any obstruction. We can only wait and see.'

He paddled and the canoe picked up speed. Detty was dying to help but knew that her inexperience would as likely capsize them as help them.

After about two kilometres Detty calculated their first question was answered and they found themselves in a much larger river with lights on the banks. They approached a bridge with more lights and a lot of activity.

'Put your head down and don't move,' whispered Marc. Silently on the current they edged up to the bridge and through. Apparently nobody was looking over the parapet. Marc spoke softly again

'So far so good,' he said, 'if we get the other ones right, my love, this evening we will be having the best meal Frankfurt can provide... if we get them wrong I hope we will be dead because otherwise we will be back in Königshof in the Winterburg having a very uncomfortable time.'

Detty was glad he didn't know exactly how uncomfortable her time was likely to be.

The second bridge loomed and seemed deserted, possibly it only carried a railway but there was a third one soon afterwards as the river began to curve steeply. This was covered in arc lights and they could hear the shouts of soldiers or guards. Marc took the canoe over to the inside of the bend and stayed close to the shore. They passed the bridge and were several hundred metres downstream before a light caught them. There was a crackle of rifle fire then a lot of arguing voices then a couple more shots one of which hit the top strake of the canoe but mercifully didn't hole it or hurt the occupants.

'I think that they thought that we were a drifting log,' whispered Detty.

'Yes,' replied Marc, 'I tried to keep into the shadows to look like one.'

There was silence and they completed the bend carefully and slowly. Suddenly they came into an even wider river with another broad long reach. Marc crossed over again to hug the bank to their left. They went on for about fifteen minutes then suddenly powerful searchlights flooded them.

'This is it,' thought Detty. 'I hope I'm shot. I'd rather that than they take us back to Königshof for treatment at the Klinikum and other charming games.'

No shots but a loud hailer ordering them to come alongside a landing stage. There, above them, were soldiers with submachine guns. Detty thought she would be dead at any second.

Marc spoke and sounded oddly calm, *'Wo sind wir, bitte?'* he asked.

'Neubrandenwald Standort,' came the reply.

'Deutschland?' said Detty, suddenly realising a glorious possibility.

'Ja, naturlich, Deutschland.' And to confirm the point he pointed his torch in the air to outline the red, black and gold tricolour flying next to the twelve gold stars on a blue background of the European Union.

'Gott sei dank!' shouted Marc at last losing his calm as his pent up emotion boiled over.

Detty threw her hands in the air in exultation at the last, nearly capsizing the canoe which had carried them to safety.

They climbed ashore. Detty could hardly stand up her knees were shaking so much with cramp from the boat and relief. Marc caught her and folded his arms round her and gave her a long deep kiss. The soldiers coughed and turned away tactfully but after some minutes when there seemed no immediate prospect of the embrace ending, the sergeant gave another low cough. Detty and Marc sprang apart guiltily looking embarrassed and the Sergeant asked quietly, 'Excuse me, mein Herr, might I ask who you are?'

'I'm so sorry, Sergeant,' replied Marc, 'Oberleutnant von Ritter, *Division Spezielle Operationen,* South Western Command, Stuttgart and this is Frau Bernadette O'Neill from Ireland – originally that is.'

The sergeant saluted promptly adding, 'Excuse me, Herr Oberleutnant, but do you have any ID?'

'No,' replied Marc, 'I have been on special service but if you take me to the CO, I think that I can satisfy him on that point.'

'Very good, Herr Oberleutnant, Corporal Weitz and Trooper Mann, please take the Oberleutnant and the Frau to Oberst Wenger immediately.'

They set out along the river bank with the early sun just beginning to appear over the wetlands and misty scrub. It was very beautiful, like the dawn of time. Detty was overcome by a mixture of emotions – joy, relief, love and not a little disbelief. It was all so unreal and she felt overwhelmed and confused by her feelings. She couldn't control her tumbling thoughts and without realising what she was doing, she softly started to sing:

Freude, schoner Gotterfunken,
Tochter aus Elysium,
Wir betreten feuertrunken,
Himmlische, dein Heiligtum! [17]

She realised that even out of practice as it was her voice had got steadily louder and that Marc had joined in. The two soldiers, sensing that their escort duties were only a formality, smiled and then started singing softly too. With the sound of the first verse of Schiller's hymn dying over the misty river Detty began the second. As they reached:

---

17 Joy, beautiful spark of the gods,
    Daughter from Elysium,
    We enter, drunk with fire,
    Heavenly One, thy sanctuary!
    Your magic binds again
    What convention strictly divides;
    All people become brothers,
    Where your gentle wing abides.

    Who has succeeded in the great attempt,
    To be a friend's friend,
    Whoever has won a lovely woman,
    Add his to the jubilation!
    Indeed, who calls even one soul
    Theirs upon this world!
    And whoever never managed, shall steal himself
    Weeping away from this union!

Wer ein holdes Weib errungen
Mische seinen Jubel ein

she felt Marc squeeze her hand and she turned to sing to him alone as sensually as she knew how:

Ja, werauch nur eine Seele
Sein nennt auf dem Erdenrund

before lowering her voice for the sad last couplet. With the third verse she allowed her strong soprano to lift over the men's voices to the river and the trees. As they finished they all laughed and Marc said, 'Anyway we can always go to the Staatsoper as a ready made ensemble if the army has no more use for us. Well done everybody!'

'The Frau has a most beautiful voic,' said the Corporal shyly.

Detty thanked him seriously and said how wonderful it was to be free on German soil. On an impulse she said, 'I shall sing my hosts' anthem,' and started to sing again to Haydn's grand old tune:

Einigkeit und Recht und Freiheit fur das deutsche Vaterland
Danach lasst uns alle streben bruderlich mit Herz und Hand!
Einigkeit und Recht und Freiheit sind des Gluckes Unterpfand
Bluh im Glanze dieses Gluckes bluhe deutsches Vaterland! [18]

'There you are, gentlemen,' laughed Marc, 'not only have you found a Lorelei in the river in the morning but she sings the correct verse of our national anthem. How on earth did you learn that?'

Detty greeted this by thumping him firmly in the ribs before replying,

---

18 Unity and justice and freedom
   For the German fatherland!
   Towards these let us all strive
   Brotherly with heart and hand!
   Unity and justice and freedom
   Are the foundation of happiness;
   Flourish in the radiance of this happiness,
   Flourish, German fatherland!

'The Nuns made us learn the anthems of the twelve on the anniversary of the European Union declaration. They weren't very successful as we struggled a bit with the Greek and the Portuguese. We objected to God Save the Queen as we were all right little Fenians then. Germany was OK though. I had always been fascinated by the country and that tune is hard to forget – I knew it would come in handy sometime.'

Marc was suddenly more serious, 'Detti, we should return your compliment by singing your anthem, after all you are our guest but I am ashamed to admit I don't know it.'

'I shouldn't worry,' laughed Detty, 'not many people do – certainly not in the proper language – but I shall give you a lesson,' and began to sing again:

> We'll sing a song, a soldier's song
> With cheering, rousing chorus
> As round our blazing fires we throng,
> The starry heavens o'er us:
> Impatient for the coming fight,
> And as we wait the morning's light
> Here in the silence of the night
> We'll chant a soldier's song.

The lilt of the tune in the morning air was infectious and after their experiences, appropriate. Then as she came to the chorus she changed language and the effect was electric – none of the three men listening understood a word of it but that didn't matter as her strong voice soared proud and true:

> Sinne Fianna Fáil,
> atá faoi gheall ag Éirinn,
> Buíon dár slua
> thar toinn do ráinig chugainn,
> Faoi mhóid bheith saor
> Seantír ár sinsear feasta,
> Ní fhágfar faoin tíorán ná faoin tráill.

Anocht a théam sa bhearna baoil,
Le gean ar Ghaeil, chun báis nó saoil,
Le gunna scréach faoi lámhach na bpiléar,
Seo libh canaídh amhrán na bhfiann.[19]

As she finished Marc said, 'Your native tongue?

'Not exactly,' laughed Detty, 'but the tongue of my ancestors.'

'What does it say – the chorus I mean?'

She translated it into German adding, 'It sounds better than in English.'

'Do you really hate the English – you have cause to. Strangely I don't think we ever have really hated them.'

'No, of course not. At Oxford with lots of English friends – how could I? But when I sing that song – particularly in Gaelic, the old Fenian rises in me and momentarily I really do.'

'It's a beautiful anthem. It suits you – proud and brave, fierce and strong. It should be better known.'

After a pause he broke the silence, 'You must be proud of your country – it came through in your singing.'

Detty thought a moment, 'Yes, I am,' she said finally. 'It is a little country and has achieved a lot. Now it is free, has been prosperous and pretty happy but it has not been all good. Not long ago we were blowing up our own people. Young English lads were shooting young Irish lads and vice versa, and the Lord knows what they were doing it for. All mad,' she added, and went on, 'what about you? Are you proud of Germany?

---

19 Soldiers are we,
    whose lives are pledged to Ireland,
    Some have come
    from a land beyond the wave,
    Sworn to be free,
    no more our ancient sireland,
    Shall shelter the despot or the slave.
    Tonight we man the "bearna baoil",[fn 4]
    In Erin's cause, come woe or weal,
    'Mid cannon's roar and rifles' peal,
    We'll chant a soldier's song

You should be but this morning, I am perhaps a little biased.'

He also thought a bit before answering, 'I feel rather the same as you. We are in the heart of Europe and that is good and right. In my time, we have worked hard for peace and justice and that is good too. But, and it's a big but, during the last century the horrors we have just left were refined in Germany and, worse, were done by Germans all over Europe. Travsky's thugs have modelled themselves on our thugs. No thinking German can forget that history but thank God it is history.'

'It was a long time ago,' said Detty thoughtfully and then added, 'The hope lies in that blue flag that we saw with such joy and relief this morning. That is the future.'

'Amen to that,' said Marc as they reached the HQ building and the mess. The corporal announced them to the guard at the HQ entrance and after a few words on the telephone they were escorted up to the COs office. Oberst Wengen was a bluff Saxon in his mid-forties. He shook hands with Marc who introduced Bernadette.

'*Wilkommen in Deutschland! Wilkommen in Freiheit,*' he said looking at her with admiration. 'We have heard something about your ordeal from the newspapers, Frau O'Neill, you are a very brave young lady and I am honoured to meet you and have you as my guest.'

Detty murmured, '*Danke schon, sehr vielen dank,* Herr Oberst'. Then feeling that this was totally inadequate impulsively rushed forward and kissed him on the forehead.

The colonel momentarily looked taken aback and then his broad face flushed with pleasure, he asked, 'Is Ireland full of beautiful young women who creep out of rivers in the early morning and kiss undeserving middle-aged men, Frau O'Neill?' he asked.

'Yes, Herr Oberst,' replied Detty. 'It happens regularly there. Come to Ireland and I'll show you.'

'If this continues,' said Marc laughing, 'I'll be tempted into insubordination.'

'Don't worry, Oberleutnant, I'm sensible like Hans Sachs – I don't want to share King Mark's fate. Forgive me for a moment, Frau Bernadette, while I make a call to establish the Bona Fides of this young scallywag who has dragged you out of Moltravia.'

He asked Marc for his identity code and picked up the phone. In a few moments the job was done.

'They seem to think that you are who you claim to be.' the colonel said as he replaced the phone.

Marc suddenly looked serious. 'There is something very important that I need to attend to,' he said and continued. 'We have a colleague still in Moltravia who is being tortured and who is in very grave danger. For security as well as humanitarian reasons I need to go back at once to try to get her out. It is urgent and I must act quickly.'

The colonel answered at once. 'That seems a bit of a tall order but I understand. How can we help? What do you need? I am afraid we don't have anybody here experienced in that sort of operation.'

Marc looked relieved at this ready co-operation. 'That won't be necessary, thank you, Sir, as I have access to a specially trained unit but I need to signal Stuttgart to get them up here as soon as possible.'

'No problem. Use our network.'

'There is one other thing, however, we shall need a light plane – about a twenty seater and a very skilled pilot who can do hedge hopping under radar in extremely difficult conditions.'

'I will ring my Luftwaffe colleague at once and see what he can sort out, meanwhile carry on with getting your men. Frau Bernadette, I am sure you would like to change. There is a guest house at the back of the mess. It's empty and at your disposal. We will try and find you some temporary clothes until you can get into town.'

Detty had been thinking furiously for the last few minutes. Startled she came out of her reverie and thanked the colonel. Then she turned to Marc with a look of grim determination,

'I must come with you,' she said plainly, thanking her good fortune that she had not yet shown Marc the crumpled photocopy still in her boiler suit pocket. Even without that, Marc was first stunned then furiously angry. Was she mad? Had she lost her senses? Did she want to be hanged by the NAS? What did she think that they had both been trying to do for the last few days? Didn't she realise that he had put her in terrible danger and cause her to be dreadfully injured already and now she made a stupid suggestion like this?

Finally, he calmed down and Detty began quietly, 'It's not as mad as you think. I shall have no existence without you – or Mara. But more practically you must be able to get into the farm without alerting the barracks next door. Once the barracks alarm goes off, any party you could muster which was small enough to act secretly and quickly, would be overwhelmed and captured in minutes. How can you gain entry with that sophisticated electronic fence? Even if you did get inside you would be extremely obvious as the only men in the women's compound apart from the guards. I, however, am the right sex, know the place like the back of my hand and even have the right clothes – although I wanted to burn them this evening. I could join an outside working party and easily get in unnoticed. After that I could let you in Trojan-horse style. The last place they will expect me so soon after the escape is there.'

'The other problem is Tamara herself,' she continued, 'she knows me but if she is suddenly faced with a party of strange men, the poor girl will think she is being abducted to be killed or tortured again and cry out – after that discovery is almost certain.'

The more logical Detty's argument became, the more sad and furious Marc looked. But before he had a chance to launch into another tirade the colonel interrupted quietly, 'Although I appreciate your anxiety, Oberleutnant, I think Frau O'Neill has made a important point. I am not an expert in Special Operations, however, it does seem that her presence would tip the odds substantially in your favour. May I make a suggestion which might help?'

Marc still scowled unhappily – a scene dancing before his imagination, which he thought was the most terrible that he could imagine. The colonel continued, 'Travsky, arrogant swine that he is, has a residual respect for German forces. He admires our armed forces for just the reasons that we would most like to forget and I am sure he would be a little reluctant to abuse an officer of the *Bundeswehr*. I suggest that I contact the GOC and obtain Frau O'Neill a temporary commission in the *Bundeswehr*. It might help to protect her in the event of capture and would give us a reason for intervening on her behalf in that unfortunate eventuality. It would have to be in the Music Corps but that is quite appropriate, although it will be a little unusual to have a musician attached to a special operations unit. I hope that this will help to settle your anxieties.'

Marc looked unconvinced but bowed to the view of his superior and eventually acquiesced.

'I will have some clean clothes sent over to the guest house as I am sure that you would like to go and change,' the colonel continued calmly to Detty. 'Meanwhile the Oberleutnant and I will begin to make the necessary arrangements.'

Detty made her way to the visitors' house accompanied by a secretary who miraculously produced clean underclothes, jeans and a sweater while apologising that they were not smarter. It was an old house but modernised with several bedrooms with adjoining bathrooms on the first floor. Detty noticed with some satisfaction that they all had double beds although inevitably two rooms had been prepared for their use. She carefully removed the photocopy from her pocket before she stripped off her filthy camp boiler suit. She had had the presence of mind to remember to ask the smart secretary if there was any chance that it could be washed and dried quickly. The secretary looked suitably puzzled. With a look that made it clear that it was not up to her to question the odd ways of foreigners she said that she was sure that could be arranged. Carrying the noxious garment in a plastic carrier she then left to allow Detty to wallow undisturbed in the best hot bath that she had ever taken.

As she lay, allowing the water to soak the aches out of her exhausted and abused body she gazed abstractedly at her toes poking out of the warm water. She thought about her man, for such assuredly he was after the last days. She loved him deeply and she was in heaven, but it was a heaven that might so easily, nay probably, become hell. There were heavy odds against their being able to free Mara and if they failed all her joy would be as nothing. Mara might be dead, moribund or so closely guarded that, with all their subterfuge, they couldn't reach her. The prospect of her own death worried her less; she surprised herself by realising that she actually didn't feel terrified at the thought of returning to the Farm. She knew that during her ghastly detention she had wanted so much to get even that her anger and thirst for revenge had probably saved her sanity. Now she sensed the opportunity of perhaps both saving Mara and pursuing her vendetta. The possibility of dying in the attempt seemed worth the risk.

She dressed and walked back to the mess feeling fresh, calm and confident. It had begun to rain but the grass still seemed preternaturally bright and the magnificent old Pomeranian church in the village behind the camp seemed to glisten in the wet.

Marc and the colonel were still together. Marc looked up and smiled at her half apologetically as if to say, 'you know it was only because I love you.' Detty smiled back. The colonel greeted her again. 'So, we have some progress. We have got the aircraft and we have got Ernst – wait till you meet Ernst – never was anyone less appropriately named but he's a splendid pilot – as long as you can put up with the music. We have also cleared your temporary commission with the *Geheimdienst* and the men of the special detail are on their way from Stuttgart. The Oberleutnant wants a planning meeting for you all tomorrow at 09.00. Meanwhile I am going to pull rank and issue an order. Oberleutnant, you will take Leutnant O'Neill into Frankfurt, buy her some decent clothes and the best dinner the town can produce. It's not as good as its namesake, I'm afraid, but the Ratskeller is not too bad and I'll ring the *Alten Oder* to get them to let you have rooms for changing.'

'*Jawohl*, Herr Oberst,' said Marc smiling, 'with pleasure.'

'Oh and by the way you will need money.' The Colonel passed over a bulging envelope 'Send me a cheque sometime – no hurry.'

After thanking him Marc went off to have a quick wash, leaving Detty the opportunity she wanted. 'Herr Oberst, may I ask you two favours?'

He looked up attentively realising that she was now very serious. 'Of course,' he nodded

'The first is an envelope.'

Looking a little puzzled he passed her one. She placed the photocopy of her sterilisation order inside and sealed it continuing, 'Would you be kind enough to keep this for me – perhaps you have a safe?'

He nodded again.

'When I return tomorrow, as I intend to, I will ask you to give it back to me unopened. The second favour is connected to the first. If by chance I do not return, whether I am dead or captured, I ask you to

214

open the envelope yourself and pass the evidence that it contains to the most appropriate German authority. When you have read it I am sure you will know what to do. Oberleutnant von Ritter does not know as yet of the existence of this document. I do not want him to as it might affect his judgement regarding tomorrow's exercise.'

As Marc re-entered the room the colonel murmured, 'Of course.' He put the envelope quickly in his pocket.

They left the mess and walked out into the pale sunlight. Marc turned to Detty very seriously and said, 'Let me see if I get the order right, hairdresser, dress shop, perfume and cosmetics then dinner.'

She looked up at him with unashamed adoration. 'Marc von Ritter,' it was the first time she had used his proper name and she enjoyed it, 'you are a miracle. Not one man in a thousand would have got that right, but it bothers me that you know so much about women – it must come from your secret past.'

'It's in the family,' said Marc laughing, 'one of my great great uncles had a notorious affair with an Austrian Empress and there have been numerous French actresses.'

'I'll have you know I am not a French actress and I'm certainly not an Austrian Empress.'

'But you are descended from the last rightful High King of Ireland and I guess that makes you a princess – for me anyway.'

They both laughed and got into the taxi.

The young hairdresser complemented Detty on her hair but asked what on earth she had been doing to it.

'Travelling,' she replied, accurately but laconically.

With a few 'Tut, tuts' he got to work and after much discussion and considerable time the transformation was complete.

Marc had waited on the corner for some time before she emerged. He expected a transformation but his jaw still dropped when he actually saw her. Her long high-lighted hair swirled round her smiling face in a profusion of red-gold. She was more beautiful than even he had dared to dream when he had fantasised about her night after night in his squalid Moltravian barracks. The first thing she did was to give him a long kiss to the scandal of several by-standing small-town citizens.

The perfumery was a success but the clothes more limited. Eventually they emerged burdened by a reasonably complete set of jeans, sweaters and lingerie together with a few things to keep Marc going until he could get home. Detty's final purchase was a black silk cocktail dress trimmed in gold which she intended to wear that evening. It was rather short but she had good legs and as she reflected she hadn't had much opportunity to show them off recently.

The colonel had been as good as his word and the concierge at the hotel expected them and showed them to a vacant room. Detty was amused that this time they were assumed to be a couple and nobody attempted to separate them. Once alone they made love long and hungrily before setting out to the Ratskeller for dinner.

Real champagne was found somewhere in the cellar after some difficulty. Marc proposed a toast to the two of them and Detty replied in English, 'Absent friends'.

Marc murmured, 'Yes indeed…to tomorrow… if only…'

There was no need to say it – a silent prayer was enough. Towards the end of dinner Detty finally felt the exhaustion that she had been fighting off all evening . This must have been her longest day, she thought, except perhaps tomorrow. They returned to the camp and to bed sleeping softly in each other's arms.

Detty was conscious of Marc getting up and dressing early. He whispered that he must go and see his men and arrange the meeting. She dozed on but finally awoke with a start just in time to ruffle her own bed guiltily before the orderly arrived. She bathed, more hurriedly this time, dressed in jeans and a sweater and went across the crisp frosty parade ground to breakfast in the mess. It was fine again but a very cold morning. She was astonished to find even the frost different here. She could only be a couple of hundred kilometres from the Farm but the frost sparkled and sang to her, whereas before it had menaced. She laughed at herself and turned in to the breakfast room of the mess. It was deserted but breakfast was laid out. She was finishing her yoghurt and debating whether to go straight for honey or have smoked ham first when she heard a loud but not completely tuneless voice requesting Argentina not to cry for it in the corridor outside.

The owner of the voice was short and stocky with a small fair bristly moustache. He appeared somewhat taken aback to find the mess occupied by a solitary unknown female but promptly introduced himself with a bow, 'Fliegerhauptmann Strauss at your service. Please call me Ernst most people do.'

Detty introduced herself not daring to use her temporary rank.

'You're English.' It was a statement more than a question – another followed, 'You must know Lord Lloyd-Webber.'

Detty wondered which of the inaccuracies in this statement to address first and finally said, 'No I'm afraid I don't – you see I am Irish.'

This was accepted and she didn't need to explain that probably rather few of the sixty million English knew Andrew Lloyd Webber personally.

'You see,' continued Ernst, 'I would like to meet him – I am a great fan.'

'I rather gathered that.' smiled Detty and he looked puzzled in turn.

'Don't cry for me, Argentina' – in the corridor,' she added by way of explanation and he nodded understanding.

They chatted about Andrew Lloyd Webber until Marc arrived, took a quick cup of coffee and hustled them off to the meeting. The atmosphere at the meeting was serious, a little tense but quietly professional. Marc introduced Detty to his men as Leutnant Bernadette O'Neill on special secondment. Unusually for the formal Germans, she thought, he added each of their first names after their rank and second name. Detty concentrated on remembering these – Nik the sergeant, Franz the explosives man, Karl the paramedic, Rudi the navigator and David and Sigi the marksmen – all were specialists.

Marc began by describing the mission, 'I am going to begin by giving you a brief outline of the operation and then hand you over to Leutnant O'Neill whose expertise we shall use to get into the target camp which she knows well. First, the mission. We are going into Moltravia to the women's compound of a labour camp called the Farm near Königshof to release one prisoner. She is Tamara Nicolaevna Oblova. She is the daughter of the ex-foreign minister of Moltravia who is now in the USA. She has also been a good friend to Germany and gave valuable assistance to Leutnant O'Neill and me on the mission that we have recently completed.

217

'She also has current strategic importance for reasons that must remain secret. Unfortunately we know that she has been extremely brutally tortured and we must expect to find her in a poor physical state. I must stress that, unfortunately, we are going in for Frau Oblova and Frau Oblova only. There are approximately two hundred and forty other women in the Farm, many of them *promenenti* or the relatives of *promenenti* but whoever they are we must leave them there. Secrecy is vital as there is an army barracks next door as well as the men's compound opposite and, if discovered, we could never fight it out against overwhelmingly superior forces. Even if we succeeded in releasing the other detainees, they would have no means of leaving the country and would be bound to be captured and subjected to further atrocities.'

'Fliegerhauptmann Strauss will fly us to a landing strip seven kilometres from the camp. We will be met there by a local contact from the antifascist resistance group, the *Freiwehr Livonias,* who will take us to a copse 500 metres from the perimeter of the Farm. After that Leutnant O'Neill takes over. Leutnant O'Neill please continue…'

'Gut' Tag, meine Herren,' said Detty trying her hardest to sound cool and efficient in these unfamiliar surroundings as she smiled round the table.

'May I say first how very honoured I am to serve with you, I will try not to let you down. As Oberleutnant von Ritter has said I have a good knowledge of the Farm as I was a detainee there until recently. My knowledge was learnt the hard way!'

She smiled again and the tension relaxed further – most of them would know something of her story from the press coverage.

'My plan is really quite simple. If we arrive at dusk I can join one of the outside working parties in the fields, with luck without being recognised. I still have my regulation detainee's boiler suit and I can slip in behind one of the other detainees so the count will still be OK. While I am doing this the rest of you will make your way to the single door on the north-eastern margin of the perimeter fence. This is the gate used by senior staff when they enter and leave in the evening or at other times when the electronic surveillance system is switched on.

A single guard inside the gate operates it manually. I will disarm and immobilise him and open the gate with the electronic key that he carries. This should not be too difficult as they will not be prepared for an attack from *inside*. Once you are through the gate I will move forward to the solitary confinement block, which also contains the sanatorium. Frau Oblova has been, is being, seriously injured, possibly very seriously, and she is almost bound to be held in one or other section of this building.

'Now detainees often run errands for staff so I can probably trick my way into the solitary block. Again I will immobilise the attendant, hopefully only one at that hour, find Tamara and tell her that help is coming. After fifteen minutes two of you follow me in leaving the others to secure the retreat. Two points – medical help will be needed and probably carrying gear.'

Detty looked at Karl, a massive Bavarian who had worked in the family forestry business before joining the army. His huge hands were evidence of his former trade. He nodded and said, 'No problem, Frau Leutnant, I have a skiers rescue harness which should do the job.'

'And I will be the second man inside,' added Marc, 'the rest guard the retreat.'

'The other problem' continued Detty 'is getting the three of us past the guardroom door which is right opposite the solitary block and usually open. Fortunately the guards are low quality except when there is a security alert so if we come without warning there is an evens chance they will all be drunk, but extreme care must be exercised. Also there is a possibility that there is still a high security warning in force after my escape. Fortunately, I think that that is unlikely now as they will know that I have got away and they will not expect me or anyone else for that matter back at the Farm. The governor is not a military man and currently he is too concerned with politics – and sadism – to give proper regard to security. He thinks that he and the NAS are untouchable. I hope that we will be able to put him right. We need two pass signals. I suggest the Oberleutnant whistles '*Zueignung*' to let me know that it is safe to open the gate and taps the sword motif for admission to the solitary block.'

She grinned at Marc while several of the men looked puzzled at the reference to the sword but said nothing as Detty finished, 'That is as far as I can help.'

'It seems well thought out,' said Marc. 'Thank you. Does anybody have any questions for Leutnant O'Neill?'

Sergeant Nik said, 'Forgive me, Frau Leutnant, but suppose it doesn't go according to plan?'

'I've thought of some snags and can overcome some of them, I think,' said Detty, 'but the critical part is my getting to the back door. Give me three hours at most. If I don't arrive by that time assume that I have been captured, abort the mission and get out as fast as you can.'

Detty looked round several of the men as she spoke but deliberately avoided Marc's eye. He himself broke the silence.

'If there are no more questions we will come to hardware and logistics. We take a full medical travel pack, stun grenades, silenced small arms and usual personal gear. Leutnant O'Neill, what do you need?'

Detty blessed the foresight that had made her work through her requirements in the bath that morning.

'A small automatic – close range but manoeuvrable, a commando knife, three pairs of strong light handcuffs and some nylon cord – ten metres should be enough.'

'We can get you a Beretta 92FS, which is small but adequate at close range. Can you use it by the way?'

'No, I am a fair twelve-bore shot and not gun shy but I have no experience with handguns. Can I practice here after the meeting? Is there a range?'

'Sure, I'll get the Oberst to ask for an arms instructor.'

'Are there any points about the flight, Fliegerhauptmann?' he turned to Ernst.

'It is not the sort of journey I'd do on a Sunday afternoon,' said Ernst grinning, 'but I dare say we will manage. The Moltravians tend to ignore their radar and most of their MiGs haven't been serviced since the fall of the USSR and the last May Day parade but they would still outgun us. In fact we don't have any guns at all. We will go in under the radar and hope that they are all drunk. Getting back may be the tricky bit.'

'OK, *meine Herren*, muster at 16.00 ready for take off. Leutnant O'Neill we will fix your pistol practice.'

As they departed the huge Karl said quietly to Rudi and David, 'She is stunning.'

'Are you talking about feminine beauty or her grasp of military strategy?'

'The first – but the second isn't bad either. I wouldn't mind having her plan a sortie for me.'

'You can forget that,' said Sergeant Nik overhearing them 'She's out of your league and anyway I rather suspect that the Skipper has first call there.'

'Spoil sport,' muttered the others.

The firearms instructor was a senior sergeant who clearly enjoyed the novel experience of having an attractive girl as a trainee for a change. He was impressed with her aptitude and after a couple of hours with a break for lunch he said she had mastered the 92FS well. She had certainly learnt a lot about side arms including their types and uses with a bit of history thrown in. She avoided Marc who in any case seemed busy. After that the time dragged endlessly. She couldn't settle to anything and the mess magazines seemed somehow irrelevant. She was glad when she could return to the guest house to change into her newly laundered Farm boiler suit and join the others in the briefing room prior to take off.

*

The morning frost had disappeared as they walked across the damp misty tarmac in the late winter evening, silent apart from Ernst who was quietly singing, *'Turn you face to the Moon'*.

The pre-flight checks over, the engines of the small Fokker roared and at last they were off tearing across the runway to take off. They gained height going north along the ribbon of the Oder and then at the appointed place dived to treetop height and re-entered Moltravian airspace across deserted fields. It gave Detty an odd feeling to be crossing back into the country they had left with so much difficulty two days before. She patted the 92FS in her pocket.

They appeared to pass no habitation, presumably thought Detty, this was pre-arranged, and after about thirty minutes Ernst landed the plane skilfully but not without bumps in a field that appeared identical to many that they had passed over in that flat, desolate land. They taxied under the edge of a copse and were greeted by a repeated owl hoot. Mark jumped down and a shadowy figure came out of the trees to shake his hand. Quickly they found the lorry and jumped in. Detty was sitting next to the driver as he manoeuvred round the wood and onto a rough track, which Detty thought was faintly familiar. Eventually they were on the metalled road. Detty sitting beside the driver said quietly to him in Russian, 'It's very brave of you to help us.'

He almost spat as he replied, 'It's you that are helping us – anyway I would give my life willingly for revenge on the bastards.'

'Have you suffered much?'

'They took my youngest daughter and penned her to a flagstaff overnight until she froze to death. That's what they do here – no firing squads or gas chambers – much simpler they just let the winter do the executions then bury the corpses in lime pits. My girl had done nothing – a sweet child who never harmed anybody.'

Suddenly a scene flooded back into Detty's mind, 'When was that?' she said choking and trying to look at his features from the side.

'Last December in the village over there.'

Now she was sure.

'I was there,' she said quietly, 'from the Sacred Heart – I saw it – I am so sorry – I could do nothing.'

'Nobody could. You must be the tall foreign girl who sang like an angel to the school – everybody remembers your visit – I thought I recognised you. Why are you here now? You should have stayed safe.'

'No,' said Detty decisively. 'I could do nothing then but with God's help I will do something tonight to avenge Katya.'

'You even remember her name – God make you prosper and keep you safe.'

He used the courteous elegant old form of speech which made Detty wonder again about these strange attractive people she had come to know and love.

While they were talking they had turned off the road up a track besides a wood which hid them from the Farm. Detty leapt down first and made her way back towards the fields that lay behind the buildings. As she crept out of the cover of the wood she hit the first snag – there was not a working party in sight. Dark had fallen quickly under the lowering cloud and the working parties had gone in early. They were always anxious about escapes in the twilight. They must have just missed the return of the last parties. She thought quickly and headed for the main gate limping as she went. As the guard stopped her she was thankful there were no dogs. Perhaps they had not been let out for the night yet.

'Sorry, Sir,' she said 'I twisted my ankle and couldn't keep up – the supervisor didn't see me in the twilight.'

She produced a winning smile. The guard perked up from looking bored and quite liked the idea of being merciful to such an attractive girl.

'OK – go on in. You may get punished if they spot you from inside but I won't report you.'

'Thank you, Sir,' she said with another cringing smile and slipped inside.

As normally as possible she walked round the courtyard trying not to think about its associations and concentrate on the job in hand. There was no challenge and with her heart still pounding she reached the steps to the hall. So far so good. It was not an assembly evening and the hall was empty but at the far end a shaft of light came from the open door of the armoury. She crept up and looked round the door. There, before her eyes, was one of the three people she hated most. The still newly healed wounds on her injured back tingled as she looked at him. He was inside crouched over some papers. The door creaked.

'Yes,' he growled half looking up.

She could not carry out her plan safely with him there. She made an instant decision and walked quickly into the room.

'Excuse me, Sir,' she said in the Farm detainees obsequious whine. He looked up, recognised her instantly and exclaimed, 'You!' and lunged for the alarm button. Detty's first shot hit him in the shoulder and spun him round. She then fired full into his chest at point blank range and he dropped choking as the blood soaked through his clothes. He gagged twice, a further breath came which was half whistle, half rattle and then he lay still with his eyes open staring at her. For a moment she stared back, an incongruous memory was at the back of her mind. Finally she remembered what it was, *'E avante a lui tremava tutta Roma,'*[20] she said aloud to herself as she re-loaded her gun. Then she turned and walked out quickly. She was surprised that she felt quite calm and without a scrap of remorse, only deep satisfaction.

The postern guard was dozing in his sentry box. She went up to him and said, 'Excuse me Sir, I have been told to bring you this,' indicating an imaginary object at the side of the box. He fell into the trap and as he got up to look round she stuck the Beretta in his back and grabbed his rifle. She warned him that he was dead if he moved or shouted. She then handcuffed him to a convenient lime tree. As she took out her knife he looked terrified but seemed relieved when she only used it to cut his shirt off to use as a gag which she tied behind the tree binding his head firmly. She felt in his pocket for the key, heaved a sigh of satisfaction when she found it and walked over to the gate.

She whistled *Zueignung* softly breaking off after two lines. To her relief after a very short pause she heard the whistled reply completing the tune and opened the gate for the men to file silently inside. They crossed back through the hall pealing off men at their appointed places. When they arrived at the far end, only Detty herself with Marc and Karl were left. Detty crept forward alone the last few paces to the top of the steps. There was the sound of angry voices, 'I told you she was severely injured and that you were too clumsy with her in the last session.'

'You said another session would be all right and we stopped after four hours.' Detty winced in the darkness as the voice went on, 'You never said she would croak.'

Terror gripped Detty for the first time. Supposing it was all in vain.

'If there is any chance of saving her she must go to a major hospital – and it's a slim chance at that.'

'We couldn't do that and maintain security – particularly not after the other break out. The Klinikum is under NAS control and it's the only possible place.'

---

20 Before him, all Rome trembled

Detty shuddered.

'But they couldn't provide the care she needs. They only do one thing and turnround is more important than quality even in that.'

'She's not much use to us dead but we could keep it a secret from her father and send him old clippings. Anyway we can't have her going to a civilian hospital and let every Tom, Dick or Harry know exactly what goes on here or worse have her rescued by that young Hun from next door. We had better let her die here – I'll sort out some story with old film that will get her father back.'

The governor laughed callously and the doctor murmured agreement.

As soon as they were gone Detty slipped down and rang the door bell with her heart pounding. The guard answered through the grill and she recognised the voice of the loathsome Oleg. She disguised her voice and whined, 'Excuse me, Sir, one of the junior's has cut herself in the kitchen and the supervisor has sent me for a bandage and some dressings.'

The door opened and with a single movement Detty stuck the Beretta in Oleg's chest and slammed the door with her back.

'You!' she heard for the second time that evening.

'Yes, me,' she said between her teeth. 'One word and you're dead!'

She pushed him towards an empty stall.

'Stand on that chair and drop your trousers.'

He obeyed cringing and shaking. She handcuffed his wrists behind the high grill rail and tied his ankles below the bottom one with the cord. She then pulled his Y fronts down and pulled out her knife which she lay beside his shrinking genitals remembering the mortification of her fumbling blow job at their last meeting.

She looked at his puffy, quivering and trembling face. Then she said, 'No I'm not going to – I wouldn't stoop that low but one sound out of you and I'll be back with pleasure to make sure that there's not enough left on you to ever abuse and humiliate another woman.'

With that she kicked away the chair leaving him struggling to get a foothold on the lower bar to take the weight off his hands.

She turned away and hurried to the end of the solitary confinement block that she remembered so well. The sanatorium was deserted and at first she thought that there were no patients there either. Finally in a corner she identified a tiny hunched bundle on a bunk. Fearing the worst she crossed over. She hardly recognised the emaciated, dehydrated figure of her friend but the eyes although sunken were Tamara's and she was at least breathing. Detty bent over her and whispered, 'Mara, it's me, Detty, and I've come with Marc to take you out of here as I promised.' Tamara looked up startled scanning Detty's face.

Eventually she seemed reassured and smiled weakly whispering, 'But how…?'

'Never mind, we have skilled people who will help and an aeroplane waiting. I'll be back in a minute.'

Looking at her watch she hurried back to the main door to hear the soft tap in the rhythm of the *Nothung* motif, the second pre-arranged signal. With Oleg's electronic key she opened the door and the huge Karl followed by Marc slipped inside. As they walked rapidly down the corridor Marc nodded towards the precariously perched half naked Oleg struggling for a foothold on the bars and said, 'Who's that?'

'Oh,' replied Detty with a broad grin. 'A young man learning to ask nicely and say please.'

There were no further questions and they reached the infirmary. Karl took Mara's pulse and felt her skin and looked grave. Saying nothing he lifted the tiny figure onto his rescue harness and not waiting for the officers muttered, 'Lets go.'

They crossed the block swiftly and slipped out of the door closing it silently behind them. There was still no movement from the guardroom opposite. They crossed the hall, passed into the perimeter passage and out of the back gate past the still-tethered figure of the guard.

It was now pitch dark with the copse making a jagged silhouette against the night sky. They were just able to see the outline of the truck as they approached. They moved off as soon as they were aboard. It all seemed childishly simple and they were just heaving sighs of relief when they heard the shriek of the alarm sirens and the first rockets hissed into the sky, filling it with light behind them.

With Karl still carrying his fragile bundle like a baby they crossed quickly to the plane. Ernst,imperturbable as ever, was still singing *Music of the Night*. He taxied across the field and began his take off run as the

226

first jeeps appeared on the rough track, machine guns rattling as they came. One bullet hit them as they gathered speed but there was no obvious damage. After what seemed like an age the bumping stopped and they were airborne.

'If you think it's feasible can we go back over the sea to the north. They are bound to have fighters on the direct line and when we get to Ronne we can turn back to Barth. It's not safe but it's the best chance we've got.'

'OK, boss, as you judge best.' agreed Ernst.

Karl was busy getting an infusion line up on Mara and Detty turned to try and help, watching with impotent admiration as the huge hands confidently guided the needle into the tiny arm.

'She's very dehydrated – she might be quite a lot better with some fluid on board.'

Detty did what she could to help Karl and cursed her lack of first aid knowledge – what was the good of a soprano voice with her friend's life hanging by a thread? Thinking of this she suddenly remembered something and began to sing the *Abscheulicher* softly as she had sung it to herself in her own crisis. She didn't know if Mara recognised it or even heard it in the bustle but at least it made Detty feel better.

'She's stable but very very weak,' said Karl, 'but she has courage and we could make it.'

He took her blood pressure again and gave a gruff grunt of satisfaction.

There was no more to do for Mara for the moment and Detty turned her attention to the an anxious conversation between Marc and Ernst.

'It's definitely company,' said the latter, 'and as they are coming from behind I don't suppose they are here to wish us *"Bon voyage".'*

'No,' added Marc, 'and they seem to be gaining pretty steadily,'

'About 10 minutes I reckon,' said the pilot, 'I'll give the NATO emergency signal but I don't suppose it will do much here – even Bornholm's some way off. Pity, we nearly got away with it.' he added phlegmatically.

For the second time in recent months Detty realised that she was about to die but was grateful that at least she would die intact and with dignity. What a waste, she thought, they had done so well up to now. Suddenly Ernst pointed at the screen again.

'More company,' he said, 'this time from a different direction – I wonder…'

Sure enough there were two more bips closing them fast with every sweep from the front. A moment later a streak of light flashed past them on either side in view from the blacked out cabin. Back on the screen, as if to order, the pursuing dots reversed direction and began to recede. They held their breaths until Ernst, listening to his cans, whooped with laughter.

'Cheeky bastards these Danes,' he said, 'one of them has just told me that if his papa knew he was helping the Luftwaffe he would get sent to bed without his supper. Actually he just happened to be airborne and patrolling Danish airspace. I told him that we were out of role too – seven Germans rescuing a Polish girl wasn't exactly in the old script and that we would buy him a beer to make up for his supper. He answered that it would have to be Tuborg as he was allergic to German beer. I guess we owe them a drink for all that. They know (unofficially) what we have been up to and they have said that they will escort us to Barth just to make sure that we don't get any more Moltravian callers.'

There were smiles all round and messages of thanks to the Royal Danish Air Force who providentially had been doing an airborne exercise at the right moment. While the others discussed the coincidence, Marc whispered to Detty, 'Well done the boss! When he said he couldn't do anything to help us I knew that he had something up his sleeve – Stuttgart/Kobenhavn… He wants to meet you.'

Detty found herself wondering if the coincidence might not have taken a bit of planning after all.

They landed at Barth and a Luftwaffe MO came on board. He assessed the situation, congratulated Karl, gave Mara some antibiotics through the line and suggested that they flew straight on to Berlin and arranged for Tamara to be transferred directly to the university plastic surgery and burns unit. Minutes later they were circling over the *Tegelsee* with the cheerful lights of Berlin below them. The Spree wound through the city a bit like her own dear distant Liffey but twisting with much more dark water on either side. Suddenly she felt a profound warmth for this strange great historic town with its chequered history but which was welcoming them to safety and whose medical skill might yet save the life of her dearest friend.

The ambulance was waiting as they touched down at *Schönefeld* and Detty held Mara's hand as she was loaded onto the stretcher out of the aircraft.

'I must go with the others – see you at the mess.' shouted Marc and they were on their way across the city in the ambulance. Tamara was taken immediately to a single room and examined by the duty surgeon. Detty supplied what details she could and explained to the ward clerk that Oberleutnant von Ritter would fill in the gaps tomorrow.

The surgeon emerged and spoke to Detty, 'I have been a surgeon with relief organisations all over the world. I have seen torture victims before but none alive more severe than your friend and to think it happened right next door to us. She has been brutally treated and is very severely injured. She needs her fluids watching very carefully and she has a dangerous infection of her wounds but your colleague has made a good start. She will need several plastic operations when she is well enough and the infection has settled.'

With a ray of hope at this last remark, Detty asked, 'Will she be all right?'

'She's a tough young lady and with our care she should make it. But, Frau Leutnant, you look to be dead on your feet and unless you look after yourself you will be as ill as she is. Sister, please get someone to call Leutnant O'Neill a taxi.'

Detty remembered nothing of the drive to the mess, which was deserted apart from the waiting Marc.

'I think a civilian hotel will cause fewer raised eyebrows,' he said. He lifted the phone and ordered a taxi to go on to the Grand Hotel on the Friedrichstrasse. Detty hardly noticed her surroundings that night and struggled with her numbing tiredness into the lift to their luxurious room where two triumphant but exhausted *Bundeswehr* officers fell gratefully into bed together.

6
FREEDOM

Der ist's allein, der sagen kann:
Wohl mir, ich bin ein freier mann[21]

J.A. BLUMAUER

It was after nine before they awoke. Detty walked out onto the balcony of their room. It was a cold clear morning and she gazed over the *Unter den Linden* towards the *Museum Insel* and the cathedrals. She felt a hand round her waist and Marc was beside her.

'This must be the most marvellous city in the whole world,' she muttered, 'but then it would be this morning, wouldn't it?'

'Heh,' he snorted, 'You just wait until you see Munich.'

She turned round to him and laughed, thoroughly amused at this first hint of Bavarian jingoistic pride. She was learning more and more about her handsome soldier with every minute that passed. By the time they had had breakfast in their room it was late. Detty rang her parents and talked to her mother who was overjoyed that she was safe and delighted

---

21 For himself he lives
    No other serves
    He alone is truly free

to hear her. There was a surprised pause when Detty told her as casually as possible that she wasn't coming straight home. She explained, looking mischievously towards Marc, that she had some unfinished business to settle with the German authorities but that she was free and well after her troubles, which she knew had been well-publicised in the western press. Peggy O'Neill tried to protest but eventually had to be satisfied with the promise of further 'phone calls and 'see you soon'.

Detty was having another luxurious bath when Marc called through the door to say that he was going downstairs for a breath of air but he would come up and collect her in a little while.

'Don't worry,' she shouted back. 'I can see you in reception in half an hour.'

She finished her leisurely bath and realised that she had nothing to wear except her Farm uniform of the day before. She was just about to ring, diffidently, for room service when she heard the sounds of the key in the door. She assumed it was Marc but, he hadn't confirmed he would come back to the room. For an instant her mind drifted onto the first act of *Götterdämmerung* and she wondered, if stark naked from the bath, she was in danger of being raped either by an intruder in the likeness of her lover or anybody else.

All was well as Marc appeared smiling and obviously pleased with himself. In his hands he carried two bags one marked Galleries Lafayette and the other marked Lehrendorf. The second bag he opened producing an eau-de-nil slub silk trouser suit with a cream blouse. It was gorgeous and clearly not cheap. The extras came out of the Galleries Lafayette bag, everything was there. She spent some minutes hugging Marc. He began to caress softly the contours of her body which inevitably led to them spending some minutes entwined hungrily on the bed.

When she had collected herself Detty began to dress, preening herself to his satisfaction, in his purchases. Finally, together, they stepped out into the great circular gallery of the hotel. She had been too tired to notice the splendour of her surroundings the night before. Now she looked round in wonder, first at the galleries of rooms circling up three stories above them up to the glass dome. Below her was the elegant first gallery with its magnificent staircase reaching down to the foyer. She gasped.

'Do you approve?' he said.

'It's incredible. I've never seen anything so elegant,' she replied, remembering that the previous pinnacle of her hotel experience had been the homely Randolph in Oxford when her parents came to visit her at university. Marc went towards the lift and to her surprise pushed the button for the first floor.

'Aren't we going to the ground?' asked Detty, puzzled.

'Yes,' said Marc, and then as they left the lift on the first floor, 'but there is something we have to do first.'

He took her arm and together they walked round to the top of the great staircase before Marc went on to explain, 'I came here as a lad many years ago while the city was still being rebuilt. They had just finished restoring this hotel which oddly was built originally before The Wall came down. When I saw this staircase I was overawed. I said to myself – one day I will walk down that staircase with the most beautiful woman in Berlin on my arm. Today, Miss O'Neill, you are going to fulfil that ambition for me.'

'Herr Graf,' replied Detty trying to hide the real emotion that she felt, 'how could any woman refuse an invitation like that?'

They came slowly down the centre of the broad staircase and heads of Americans, Chinese and a few Europeans turned from reception to watch the handsome young man with the beautiful, tall, chestnut-haired girl on his arm as they arrived in the foyer. A rather over-loud American lady with a grey-blue rinse remarked to her corpulent submissive companion in a stage whisper, 'They must be film people, Chuck.'

Detty found herself wondering what they would have thought if the onlookers had known what this handsome couple had been doing two days and even more two weeks before.

There was then some obligatory shopping as all their previously purchased clothes were still at *Niederbrandenwald* and Detty made a further visit to a hair salon. Marc remarked that at this rate every German town would have a hairdresser and dress shop marked: 'By appointment to Frau Bernadette O'Neill' – like the ones in London used by the British royal family. Detty pouted and said that of course if he only fancied her when she looked scruffy or half-naked she would try to understand. Predictably he replied that the half-naked bit was all right as long as she kept it only for him in future and that unfortunately he couldn't stop fancying her whatever she wore. Perhaps they had doctors in Ireland who could cure him of this serious malady but please to make sure he never met one.

Abandoning the banter for the moment they took a taxi to the hospital only a few blocks away. Detty went into Mara first while Marc cleared up some of the details left over from the night before. He told the ward clerk that Tamara's address would be care of *Graf Max von Ritter, Altes Schloss, Oberdorf, Bayern* and that her father could be contacted via the German Embassy in Washington. The clerk looked suitably respectful.

Detty, meanwhile, had found Tamara propped up and pale but smiling, the drip still going in her arm. A huge bouquet of spring flowers dominated her bedside table. In their hurry they had brought nothing with them for her. Detty was puzzled and had no idea of the origin of the flowers. She was a little suspicious. As far as she knew there was nobody in Germany apart from themselves who knew Mara at all, let alone her whereabouts. The patient watched Detty looking thoughtfully at the flowers and then weakly smiled her old teasing grin, 'You didn't know about them then?'

'No,' said Detty truthfully. 'I'm intrigued. Who did they come from?'

Without answering, Mara pointed to an elegant card on which was written: '*An Frau Tamara, eine treue holde Heldin*'.

It was signed with six signatures and underneath was written *2nd KSK Kommando.*

'Aren't they splendid?' said Tamara beaming and Detty, readily agreeing, didn't know whether they were talking about the flowers or the donors.

She echoed something Tamara had once said to her, 'Nobody has ever sent me flowers saying that I am a truly beautiful heroine.'

'You're getting your own back, aren't you?' said Tamara weak but with a hint of triumph remembering her teasing remark months before.

'But it is rather different.'

They giggled like the couple of children that they almost were in age although sadly older in experience.

Detty thought to herself that Mara was not only better in body but was also miraculously recovering psychologically. At this moment there were six men she wanted to hug in gratitude for so many things. She wondered whose idea the flowers had been in the first place – possibly Nik- but it could have been any of them. She had been treated as a piece of meat herself – no worse – as a helpless plaything to be hurt and humiliated for the sordid gain and perverted gratification of others. So had Mara and she knew just how important those flowers had been to Mara's self respect. She marvelled at the insight and tenderness shown by a bunch of young soldiers doing one of the world's toughest of jobs. They had retained their sensitivity to understand the profound ordeal that Mara had suffered and respond in this way.

She went out for a moment to look for Marc who was finishing the paper work with the clerk. He looked up, 'Is she OK? I'll be in in a moment.'

'She's better by the minute,' said Detty, 'the staff are great and she's just had a tonic.'

Marc looked puzzled in his turn and Detty added, 'From your lads.'

'How?'

'They have only sent her the largest bouquet that you've ever seen with a wonderful inscription. Any girl is going to get better with six gorgeous chunks of manhood caring that much about her.'

Marc went in to see for himself and in front of Mara he said to Detty, 'I knew nothing about this. Sorry, you've only got me – second best indeed.'

Tamara laughed which was obviously still very painful and they apologised. Marc then explained what he had done about giving them the Oberdorf address and contacting her father. He had arranged for Mara herself to phone her father from the hospital that evening. Mara couldn't thank him enough and her startlingly blue eyes filled with tears. Through her tears she said, 'You have all been so good to me. This is a wonderful place and I'm so happy to be here. How lucky your people are. How I wished I really belonged here. I have no country now. I've been

234

Russian then Polish then Moltravian and now I don't belong anywhere – a displaced person, I suppose. Though my mother was German once – she was born in Königsburg in 1944, which just made her German.'

'A different time and a different Germany,' said Marc, almost to himself, as Detty comforted her.

The nurse came in and asked them to go so that she could attend to Tamara's back. As they got outside Marc turned to Detty and said, 'I have an urgent task. I must have word with my boss and perhaps my father also.'

'What are you going to do?'

'Try and start to get a charming young lady something she longs for' he teased.

'You know that Knights Errant have to have more than one maiden in distress.'

'Right,' said Detty, 'but watch it – this maiden isn't distressed anymore and come to think of it, I'm delighted to say, she's no longer a maiden.'

To emphasise the point she dug him in the ribs with her finger.

'Don't I know it after yesterday. You seem to have forgotten that I watched you out-manoeuvre and outgun the NAS. You're a one girl Panzer division as well as the most beautiful woman in Berlin.'

She dug him again and he cowed away in mock terror. Suddenly more serious she said, 'Can you do it? It would be great.'

'I don't see why not – Germany owes her a lot, she once had a German mother and we do have some influence.'

'Go off and harness your swan then.'

They drove back to the hotel and Marc picked up the telephone and pretended to ask the concierge to send a swan up immediately. Then he began to phone in earnest giving his CO a potted history of Tamara's family and her exploits. Following this he rang his father and gave him the same story adding at the end that the girl in question was tiny, pretty and brave as a lioness and he hoped that he would meet her soon. An hour later as they were preparing to go out for dinner Marc's father rang back saying that bar the formalities he was pretty sure he could get everything fixed.

'It's not what you know but who you know,' muttered Detty to herself in English.

Then she explained the saying to Marc who replied also in English, 'How do you say it? I think I can live with that when it's for Tamara. Anyway she deserves a medal not just citizenship.'

Detty looked at him and said, 'I think she would prefer a passport to a medal but if it was anybody other than Mara I would be extremely jealous by this time. You can get her a medal too later if you like.'

After some days Tamara was sufficiently strong to go to theatre, have her dreadful electrical burns thoroughly cleaned and her first skin graft done. As soon as she had recovered enough Marc produced some papers for her to sign and a photographer.

There were two more grafts in the next two weeks and the day after the second, Marc and Detty arrived to find her sitting up in bed with an envelope by her bedside.

'I think that this is the proudest day of my life,' she said pulling a small red booklet from the envelope. The booklet was a *Reisepass* that proclaimed that Tamara Nicolaevna Oblova was a citizen of the European Union and the Federal Republic of Germany.

Sure of Mara's eventual recovery and determined to stay in Berlin until it was further accomplished, Detty now had some time to herself. Marc, who also stayed in town, was often busy with his military contacts. The first day by herself she drifted towards the *Kurfurstendamm* and the shops. As she reached the shopping streets and headed towards the *Ku'damm* itself she was turning over in her mind all that had happened. Suddenly, incongruously, she felt a yearning need for peace and prayer. Ridiculous, she said to herself, amongst all these people as she threaded her way through the cosmopolitan crowds. Hardly knowing where she was going she lapsed into a daydream to awake some moments later in profoundly peaceful surroundings suffused by deep blue light. The light scintillating from the glass walls of the shimmering octagon brought her to her knees where she prayed long and hard in thanks and hope. Later she realised that the *Kaiser-Wilhelm-Gedachtnis-Kirche* was Lutheran but it made no difference. To her, the sudden appearance of this sanctuary, in the most unlikely surroundings, seemed miraculous. She learnt later that this very special place had been built in the aftermath of cruelty, slaughter and destruction. This seemed to make it still more appropriate for her prayers for the current victims of torture and oppression whose ordeal she had both witnessed and shared.

She did not know how long she knelt in prayer before she reluctantly got up to leave, crossing herself before the shining sculpture of the risen Christ. A notice in the lobby announced that that evening the Choir and soloists were singing the Bach Cantata no 176 *'Es ist ein trotzigund verzagt Ding'*. Suddenly she wanted to sing with them and tentatively she asked the woman in the book and information stall.

'The Kapellmeister only comes shortly before the service,' she said, 'but you could ask the organist – he has just arrived to practice.'

She approached the young man explaining that she knew the cantata and had sung it in Oxford (she didn't add as the soprano soloist) and wondered as a special favour whether she might join the choir for that evening. He looked a little doubtful at this unusual request and mentioned that, of course, she had missed the rehearsal. He then brightened up and said that if she knew the work and was an experienced singer he felt sure it would be in order.

She went back to the hotel excited and warmed up properly. The feeling of letting her voice out of the prison which had held it for so long was wonderful. Considering her lack of practices it felt very good. After seeing Mara in the afternoon, she returned for the six o'clock service and somewhat diffidently introduced herself to the young Kapellmeister. He seemed much more relaxed than the organist and said how much he admired the church music traditions of Oxford and that it would be a great pleasure to have her join them in the chorus that evening.

She felt very nervous as she realised that she must not let Oxford down. She needed to contain her powerful instrument, particularly as it was still not entirely reliable with the lack of regular practice. Also she did not want to appear conspicuous amongst her new amateur colleagues. It went well and she was pleased when she was asked to come back.

She returned the following week to sing in another cantata. Talking with the conductor afterwards she now felt brave enough to mention

237

that she had sung solos in Oxford. To her pleasure and amazement he asked her to sing the solo in the next service. The thrill of being able to harness the riches of her voice to Bach's immortal music in that moving building was deeply satisfying. It was an experience that she would never forget.

Marc was busy with military debriefing meetings for quite a lot of the time. Each day she went to the *Tiergarten* to walk and then she went on to explore the museums. She had begun keeping a journal and after her walk she went to write it up and drink a beer with a snack at *Zur Gerichtlaube* in the *Nikolaiviertel*. In the evening she would meet Marc and they would visit Tamara together. She looked with longing at the concert and opera programmes but at this stage Mara had to come first. There would be time for the *Staatsoper* and the *Philharmonie* later.

The emotion surrounding Mara's passport suddenly reminded Detty that, although her own citizenship was not in question, her passport was still in Moltravia. The day after, she presented herself at the Irish consulate in the *Ernst Reuter Platz* to find that she was already something of a celebrity. The women staffing the reception were Irish and about her own age. She found it really strange after all she had experienced to be talking in English about home for the first time for months to her own compatriots. The formalities proved no problem as her story was already well known and her temporary passport and duplicate driving licence were issued without difficulty.

A week later, after her sutures had been removed, the doctors said that Tamara was fit to go out for a few days but stressed that she would have to come and have the graft dressed the following week. Detty had bought her some basic clothes in advance thinking that she would give her a chance to choose others for herself later. Marc had had to return to the base at *Niederbrandenwald* with his men. He had left her with a fistful of money for Tamara and had borrowed a car for them from the *Bundeswehr*. He was to meet them later on the road south.

Detty drove cautiously to the hospital feeling anxious in the heavy Berlin traffic and strange to be behind the wheel again after so long. She managed to negotiate the journey and felt pleased with herself when she found a parking place relatively near the hospital. Mara looked pale and very thin but cheerful as she collected her final medical instructions. As the staff wished her on her way, she turned to Detty and asked, 'Does Berlin have a hairdresser and a dress shop?'

'One or two,' said Detty laughing and hailing a taxi, asking for the *Kurfurstendam*.

The first stop was the hair salon that Detty had patronised on her arrival in the city. They went through the same routine of telling Tamara that she had wonderful hair but how had it come to be so sadly neglected?

She answered that she had been in hospital for an operation on her back which explained both her hair and the necessity for caution as she sat in the chair. They got to work discussing styles and an hour or so later a shy looking Mara walked out into the outer area where Detty was waiting. The latter was leafing absently through a bridal magazine to her friend's silent amusement. Mara made no comment but simply said, 'How do you like it?'

Detty put the magazine aside guiltily and looked up with genuine astonishment at the metamorphosis. The neat pretty schoolgirl had gone and in her place, aided perhaps by her recent weight loss, was a petite elegant young woman whose finely carved features were framed in a cascade of golden ringlets.

'You look really wonderful,' she said in unfeigned admiration. 'Good enough to eat. I shall have a hard time fighting off the young men of Berlin.'

'Why bother?' said Mara, pleased at the reaction.

After a quick first coffee there was a short but devastating attack on the shops of the *Ku'damm* followed by the *Ka De We*, which produced a wardrobe for Mara and a lot of laughs followed by further coffee and *lebkuchen* at *Kranzler*. Detty was anxious that her convalescent charge didn't get overtired and Mara worried a bit about spending money. This had always been short in the Oblov household in spite of her father's rank. Detty had to tell her that Marc would be very cross if she didn't spend enough and she in her turn informed Detty that she felt strong and well. They both thus overcame their doubts and had a riotous shopping spree.

Mara finally found the right moment and remarked with mischievous ingenuousness, 'You are spoiling me but I suppose I ought to look nice to visit your future parents-in-law.'

Detty swallowed the bait and rounded on her, 'They are not my future parents-in-law... yet,' she finished lamely, giving the lie to her righteous indignation.

'I know – you will tell me he's just a nice bloke soon – you did that once before and I wasn't convinced even then.'

'You're impossible – you ought to respect your former teachers and seniors – I should have left you in hospital.'

'You told me to treat you as an equal and anyway if you didn't marry him you would be stark raving mad and make me very miserable, *gnädiges Fräulein*.' Tamara finished with a wicked grin.

She was teasing and the old fashioned formal phrase took them back to the punishment run where Marc had first used it to Detty. The latter was pleased that Mara could refer to the hell that they had left. She had to acknowledge to herself that her friend had recognised their instant love even before they did themselves.

Eventually Mara had everything from jeans to formal dresses as well as accessories. Detty bought her an exotic perfume from Givenchy and blushed at Mara's innocent-sounding remark that perhaps they should look at the bridal department 'just for interest'. If it been anyone else she might have been truly embarrassed. As it was she just relished the fun and the evidence that Mara was back to her old self was heart warming. Eventually they staggered back to the car park accompanied by a young man from the store who seemed pleased to give the foreign girls a hand with their parcels but rather sad to know that they were leaving town.

To Detty's relief they were just in time to drive out of the city before the evening rush began. They passed through the *Berliner Forst* and arrived at the *Beclitz Rasthof* where they were to meet Marc. The latter was already there, smiling and relaxed as he kissed them both. He asked how the shopping had gone.

'Gone is about the word,' said Detty, 'have you seen the back of the car?'

'Good,' said Marc inspecting the overloaded Volkswagen adding in his military style, 'That was the idea.'

They discussed who should go with who and Marc eventually decided reluctantly that it was best for the two girls to go together and follow him. As they drove south the spring sun sank gradually over the gentle Brandenburg countryside. They crossed into Sachsen Anhalt passing the junction for Leipzig. Then they passed through Thuringia giving Detty the chance to tell Mara the story of *Tannhaüser* and how *Lohengrin* was first performed at Weimar just down the road.

Mara listened to the old romantic yarns and then said suddenly, 'Detti, do you know when I knew I was really going to be all right?'

Detty looked puzzled and enquiring.

'It was when you sang your song to me on the plane – I had been resigned to die and just wanted it to be quick and before they could hurt me too much more. I even thought you were an hallucination or the angel of death when you arrived at the Farm. As I heard your voice on the plane, I was still half-conscious but suddenly as you sang, in my confusion, I saw hope springing out of a cool sky like spring rain. I knew that I would live and was safe at that moment, with a great certainty.'

For a moment Detty still looked puzzled and then remembered singing *'Komm Hoffnung'* when she felt so helpless that she couldn't do much to help Karl. At the time she didn't think Tamara had even heard and how wrong she had been. Aloud, she laughed, 'At that moment the rest of us weren't so sure!' she said thinking of the pursuing Moltravian MiGs.

As the countryside became more hilly, they crossed the bridge over the *Saale* and passed the sign announcing *Freistaat Bayern.* Just afterwards Marc pulled off the road into the service area. He jumped out and hugged them both.

'Herzlich wilkommen in Bayern', he said, then in English, 'Welcome home!'

Detty still knew relatively little of Marc's family, apart from their address on Tamara's papers. She knew that Marc's father was in banking, that his mother was a musician and ran the family's forestry business. Marc had a younger brother called Wilhelm, always known by the English nickname Bill, who was studying economics and psychology at Munich University. She knew from the odd remark like the joke about the Austrian Empress that they had been around some time and surmised that the family had been of some importance in the past.

241

As they turned off the Autobahn into the *Frankenwald* she felt nervous with a tingling anticipation at the coming meeting. They passed through several neat simple villages each with its church and *Gasthof* and a cluster of white houses with grey roofs. Detty tried to work out why some of the churches had elegant spires and some small onion domes. Was it significant of the Catholic – Lutheran divide? She wasn't sure. Eventually they reached the yellow sign reading '*Oberdorf*'.

The village consisted of a large cluster of houses and two or three shops, as well as an onion topped church and a couple of *Gasthofs*. It was clearly a minor centre and of more importance than most of the others they had passed through since leaving the Autobahn. They came to the far side of the village and Marc turned left past a gatehouse in some conifer woods then up a carriage drive and there was the Schloss. It looked mainly eighteenth century stone with the usual grey roof but some parts including the tower at one end were probably older. Detty thought to herself – half-country house – half-castle. Marc drew up to the porch and jumped out. The door was opened before he reached it by a broad beaming woman who was soon joined by an excited couple who embraced Marc in turn. He turned to the girls, 'This is Bernadette who is always called Detti and Tamara who everyone calls Mara. This is Hildegard who keeps us all in order and my mother Sophie and my father Max.'

Detty was pleased with herself at returning the greeting with Frau Gräfin and Herr Graf. A knowledge of Richard Strauss made it easier. She thought that she must have been wrong about Germans being formal. The atmosphere was so friendly and relaxed that it really could have been Dublin.

Marc made a great fuss of Hildegard who was obviously delighted at his return and insisted on telling him most of the local gossip even as she showed them all to their rooms in '*Jungflugel*' under the tower.

'Do you know that Gertrude Meyer has got into the Conservatoire at Munich to study for a Performer's Diploma. Pauline at the *Schwarzer Adler* has had twins but poor Kurt's nice young wife from Freiburg had a miscarriage – poor thing she looked so pale and sad afterwards…'

The light on the late winter evening had been failing as they drove up to the Schloss and by the time they got to their rooms it was almost completely dark outside. Hildegard drew the curtains and switched on the lights. Detty noticed that the shaded chandeliers gave a warm creamy glow without any electric harshness. Some thought had obviously been given to the rooms that the two girls were in. They were on one side of the passage in adjacent rooms with a bathroom in between and Marc's own room was slightly beyond hers on the other side. Detty thought that it was unlikely that Marc had had the chance to explain his exact relationship with the two young women that he was bringing home but his mother had come on a tactful solution which implied nothing but equally made nothing impossible.

Her room had warm burgundy hangings, comfortable chairs and a bookcase with a mixture mainly of novels, poetry, history and art books in English, French and Italian as well as German. On one wall was a modern still life of fruit and flowers, a second had an oil painting of a boy and a girl in eighteenth-century costume. The boy, Detty noticed with amusement, was strikingly like Marc and was presumably an earlier von Ritter scion. The last wall had a sixteenth-century woodcut, which she gazed at for some minutes thinking that it was quite wonderful – the lordly poet and lady of the manor stood outside a castle gate and inside were groups practising all manner of arts and sports. There was music, dancing, jousting, hunting, fishing and even a boxing match. Detty made a note to ask Marc or his parents about it.

She knocked and went through to Mara's room, which was similar to her own but furnished in old gold. She looked at her friend's dressing which to her relief seemed clean and dry after the long journey. Her legs were now healing fast and the dressing only covered the side of her chest and back where the burns had been so badly infected. She was able to stand in a bath and wash but full bathing or showering was still impossible. Detty helped her and took a quick shower herself. They had a leisurely discussion on what to wear and decided on ankle length woollen skirts – Detty's was turquoise, Tamara's peach coloured. They then chose cream silk blouses. Normally Detty had a liking for low neck lines and backs but she was pleased that by chance this time she had bought a high collared blouse which was similar to Mara's.

Marc knocked and asked them if they were ready to come down. He led them down the wide staircase and ushered them into the drawing room. Graf Max was standing with his back to the great log fire and presiding lovingly over a magnum of Krug, still corked in an ice bucket:

'Sophie is panicking in the kitchen with Hildegard,' he said with a smile, 'but she will be here in a minute. Tell me, Marc, do you have room for elderly recruits in your unit. We were told that you were on a highly dangerous and top secret mission and you suddenly reappear with not one but two beautiful young ladies. I rather fancy that type of dangerous mission – how do you do it?'

Before Marc could answer, Detty laughed,

'It was quite easy in my case, Herr Max, Marc found me in a rubbish bin – though Mara took a good deal more effort.'

Sophie arrived before Marc was required to explain and the Krug was softly and expertly opened. The toasts of welcome were drunk. Detty's nervousness had relaxed enough for her to be able to really enjoy the fine steely wine which seemed to bubble down the throat forever. She must find out more about this she thought. Champagne had not been part of the O'Neills' cellar and this wine seemed light years away from the supermarket brands that had passed for the height of luxury at university balls.

The talk drifted on to music.

'Marc tells me that you have a very beautiful voice.' said Sophie, 'What have you done so far?'

Detty sketched her career finishing with the National Concert Hall concert in Dublin and Sophie nodded her approval, 'My cousin Bernhard is *Leitung der Festspielchor* at Bayreuth, I am sure he would like to meet you and hear you while you are here – if you feel up to it that is'

'I certainly feel up to it but I don't think that I am in that class,' said Detty and cursed herself for the unwonted modesty as soon as she had said it.

'Truly you must – he is always keen to hear young singers – we will fix it up.'

'I'd really love to,' replied Detty, correcting her previous diffidence.

The talk moved on to domestic life in Moltravia before the crisis and then the history of the Schloss. Detty asked about the woodcut in her room and Max told her that it was a sixteenth-century work from Nuremburg called *Die Freuden der Welt* – the Joys of the World – by an artist called Christoph Zell.

'From the city and time of Hans Sachs himself?' asked Detty.

'Exactly. It was a wonderful period in Nuremberg,' replied Max looking impressed.

'I shall look at it with even more interest then,' she said.

They went into dinner still talking and Detty felt that she had known them for years. They started with foie gras deliciously accompanied by *Trockenbeerenauslese* from the Rheingau followed by trout fillets and dark bread with a fruity Franken Steinwein from the family wine estate near Wurzburg.

The main course was venison, also from the local estate with sour cream, red cabbage and *Klosse* – the dumplings characteristic of Franconia and Thuringia. Sophie introduced them to the girls saying that Hildegard always criticised her for making them too small – '*Nicht echt!*' – she would say, but Sophie stuck to her guns and served modest versions in defence of her guests appetites and figures. They talked of the traditions of rural food in their various countries as the *Klosse* and venison were demolished with relish. Sophie said she always hesitated to serve Franconian dishes to newcomers as they had a reputation for being heavy amongst other Germans. The girls replied in chorus that they had never eaten anything more delicious and Sophie smiled contentedly. Max was also apologetic as he served a *Cornas* saying that he didn't think the German reds were up to a rich game dish.'

The delicious deep violet-flavoured wine was also new to Detty who decided that, as well as the elder son, there were many other good things to learn about in the Altes Schloss. Marc remarked that he had dined with his CO before going away and had had a very full Merlot from *Ihringen* on the *Kaiserstuhl,* which really was full enough for rich meat. His father instructed him to find out exactly what it was the next time he saw his Oberst.

For coffee accompanied by home produced *Obst* they returned to the drawing room. A little later Detty drifted in a cloud of wine and contentment, as if magnetised, towards the piano looking at the pile of music on a side table. Amongst the piano pieces was an album of Schubert songs, which she started to leaf over. Max caught sight of her wistful glances and asked her whether she would sing for them adding that he couldn't think of a greater pleasure after dinner. She said that she would love to but apologised that she was lacking practice although she had been doing exercises daily since arriving in Berlin.

Marc got up and joined her seating himself familiarly at the Bechstein. He looked at Detty who nodded and he began the accompaniment to Goethe's *Liebhaber in allen Gestalten*. Detty started singing the couplets and was relieved that in spite of her long silence and limited practice, her voice, albeit wayward in places, was still there. As she got to the final *'Ich bin nunt wie ich bin; So nimm mich nur hin!'*[22] two ideas flashed through her mind.

The others asked her to sing more and she gave them two other Schubert songs – Holty's lovely *Seligkeit* and *Rochlitz Alinde*. Finally as a joke and after a struggle with a reluctant Marc, Seidl's *'Die Männer sind mechant'*.

At the end Sophie cried, *'Brava*, great sentiments and wonderful singing – you do indeed have a very fine voice. Men may be bad but I agree with Marc's judgement on that!'

Detty was pleased that her last song seemed to cap the relaxation of the evening. Tired but very happy they all said goodnight.

As she woke, Detty was conscious of a great sense of peace as if God had at last remounted his heaven. She leapt out of bed as the light filtered through the curtains and looked over the back of the house. A frosty lawn ran through a small formal park, merging at the bottom of a slope into the still winter woodland on the steeply rising hills of the *Frankenwald*. How she had missed hills in the last six months! The village and the Schloss she guessed must already stand fairly high – both from their name and from her impressions of arriving the night before. There were, however, higher wooded slopes behind the park on both sides and she thought that there must be a small stream or river in the valley. The

---

22 I am as I am

    Just take me as such

morning sun had a misty opalescent quality that heralded spring. It was very beautiful as well as peaceful and she stood for some time looking at it and then said a short prayer of thanks for her deliverance.

She started to shower with last night's Schubert running through her head. She dried herself, put on her dressing gown and went into Mara's room. The bed was empty and Mara was standing by the window looking out over the view.

Seeing Detty she said, 'I think that this must be heaven; it is so beautiful and to think I sort of belong here. It's now my country – and I owe it all to you and Marc.'

Detty put her arm gently round her and said softly, 'Just think what we owe to you – but I'm glad it's good.'

They went downstairs to the dining room. Max had already left to go to his bank in Wurzburg. Sophie was at the estate office working on the forestry, which apparently she was developing with considerable success.

Marc was reading the *Nordbayerischen Kurier*, which he put aside when he saw the girls. The lavish Bavarian breakfast seemed a little soon after the banquet the night before and they did scant justice to the smoked ham, boiled eggs, cheese and sweet breads concentrating on fruit juice and local honey. When they had finished Marc suggested a walk to the village but warned them to wrap up as it was still very cold for all the bright sunshine.

As soon as they reached the first houses they began to meet people. There was clearly some puzzlement that Marc should reappear with two foreign girls in tow. Old Eberhard, the forester, met them on the road. He was heard to mutter to his friend Wolf in their earshot that two girls at once seemed more like Graf Bill than Marc who had always been the serious one.

The three of them then got a fit of the giggles, which they had barely controlled when a woman in her early twenties with long brown hair came round the corner on a bicycle. Marc hailed her shouting, *'Meinen Gluckwunsch, Trudi!'*

The girl stopped and smiling with pleasure, thanked him.

'This is Gertrude who has just got into the Munich Conservatoire to study piano performance and composition. May I introduce Tamara and this is Bernadette from Dublin – soprano amongst other things.'

Gertrude found herself wondering just what other things the tall beautiful Irish girl represented to her childhood sweetheart but she had grown up enough not to be unduly jealous. After all, her passion for Marc had begun to decline at about fourteen and anyway she liked Bernadette's smiling face and slightly mischievous eyes.

After a few minutes chat about music and Munich, Detty, who sensed an ally in Gertrude, remembered her ideas of the night before.

'Could we possibly do an Easter concert when everybody is here?'

She looked from Gertrude to Marc with her head on one side questioningly and back again. Marc adopted his best military manner, 'Right! Coffee at the *Schwarzer Adler* and we will talk about it – you can spare the time, Trudi?'

Trudi nodded and they went into the *Gasthof* and ordered coffee. The inside was larger than Detty had expected. It featured a comfortable wood-beam roof and brass fittings. The latter were old, she judged, but the building had probably been rebuilt in the traditional style. At the back was a small *Biergarten* still firmly under its winter raps. Across the other side of the garden was a long building with steel barrels stacked outside it. There was a sign marked *'Brauerei'*.

Detty surprised, asked if they actually made beer on the premises. Marc replied, 'Indeed they do and it's very good too but this is the person to ask about that.'

He indicated a dark plump woman in her late twenties who had just entered from the kitchen area. After the introductions there was an obligatory break as the dark girl, who turned out to be Pauline, the hostess, brought her three- month-old twin boys down to show them off.

When the coffee finally arrived they started planning in earnest. The available forces seemed to be the local *chorverein*, choir, and the village brass band, which doubled as an orchestra when supplemented by strings and was led with vigour by Graf Max. Trudi and Sophie were the pianists and Marc (baritone), Bill (tenor), if he turned up, Detty (soprano) and Max (bass) – if he wasn't too occupied with the orchestra. Trudi and Marc thought that they could get other soloists if necessary either from outside or from the choir which had several members capable of solo parts. It was agreed provisionally that the programme should consist of an opening chorus, a piano piece from Gertrude, various lieder and opera arias and perhaps a whole scene with soloists and chorus to finish. Marc and Gertrude would make some contacts and they would meet again in a couple of days.

They returned to the Schloss after midday for a salad lunch. As soon as it was 3pm Mara rang her father in New York. She came back looking excited and saying that he was arriving in Munich in two weeks time and that she must book a hotel for them. Marc looked worried and glanced at his mother who was just back from the estate office. Sophie knew Marc was worried about security for Oblov who was a top risk terrorist target.

On cue Sophie said casually, 'Please Mara, would your father consent to come here? We would love to meet him and you could have the lodge to yourselves so you can catch up on the news.'

'But, Frau Sophie, you have been so kind already I really can't impose on you for more.'

'Nonsense it's our pleasure and much safer for your father.'

So it was settled.

Sunday dawned with snow falling fast as they made their way on foot to their first Mass since their return. Somehow it would have been wrong to use a car for a pilgrimage. The little Roccoco church with its onion dome had a light dusting of snow. Over the door was the inscription *Pereunt et Imputantur* and Detty paused struggling with her little convent Latin to try and understand it. Marc laughed when she asked him what it meant.

'It's from Martial and means time passes and is booked to our account. It's our family motto – I think it's supposed to encourage you to stop wasting time and get on and do something useful. I used to tease my brother with it – his account is quite a long one – particularly rich in young ladies and brewers!'

Inside there was an essential peace. The whole party felt the need of a special thanksgiving.

Detty knelt between the man she adored and her beloved companion. She prayed silently for the victims who would never see the rejoicing, the lovely young Andrea, Katya freezing in the village, Wanda abused to death in her childhood and the Kolyashins, alive possibly, but permanently mutilated. She thought and prayed sadly for them all for some minutes. Then rejoicing at His goodness to her and hers she poured out her heart and thanks in prayer to God, the Virgin and the saints who had enabled her to reach this earthly paradise from a grotesque inferno of hate, torture and fear. She shuddered as she thanked God for sparing her a future without love or hope. She offered particular thanks for the saving of Tamara from the verge of a horrible death. She felt that her own strength on that mission had been given to her by the intercession of her saints. The survival of the tiny figure kneeling beside her, now sadly scarred but otherwise was almost healthy again, miraculously in mind as well as body. She was sure that it could not have been achieved without divine intervention.

The young Father Dieter offered thanks for the reunion of the von Ritter family and salvation of the two young people that they now welcomed in their midst. As the family walked back to the Schloss, Detty's eyes were still filled with tears of emotion. She sensed the same emotion in the quiet gratitude of the rest of the party and recognised fortitude also in Sophie. It could not be easy to have a son who took enormous risks as part of his job – or a husband either she dared to think.

The day after, Marc had to go north to arrange for his men to return to Stuttgart. He left saying that he would be back for the evening and then would have some extended leave due to him from his tour in Moltravia. Sophie divided her time between the house and the saw mill office and had a good deal to organise in both. She told the girls that they should do exactly as they wanted and please would Detty use the piano and any of the music that caught her fancy.

After breakfast Detty telephoned the colonel at *Niederbrandenwald.* He offered his congratulations at the successful outcome of the mission and it was arranged that her envelope should be returned to her by post to Oberdorf.

That accomplished she went with Mara into the drawing room and began to look through the many scores and sheets of music that occupied the large bookcase beside the piano. As well as a great deal of

Chopin, Liszt and Brahms piano music which she assumed belonged to Sophie, there were considerable numbers of chamber pieces and vocal scores of operas. Detty sang a few scales and spent some time talking to Mara about the life and works of various composers illustrating her points on the piano. She then got on to some serious practice on Schubert and Brahms Lieder, before stopping when Hildegard brought them coffee.

Afterwards she studied and practised music from *Ariadne auf Naxos*. Before lunch she had time to go further into the opera of *Tannhäuser* with Mara. Accompanying herself she sang Elisabeth's greeting. It was the first time since the concert at the Sacred Heart all those months ago that Mara had heard her friend sing an operatic aria in full voice and she sat spellbound and silent for minutes after the music died away.

After the pause she said, 'It's so much more thrilling with a live voice than the radio or a record.'

Detty, aware that she still wasn't fully warmed up, said laughing, 'You ain't heard nothing yet!' in English which left Mara looking puzzled. Detty quickly explained and they went and had lunch.

Marc was as good as his word and arrived back for dinner looking pleased with his day. He had taken his men a card of thanks from Detty and Mara and the arrangements for the transfer back to Stuttgart had gone smoothly.

Detty said that she missed them all and Mara agreed. 'It would be great to have a party for them – would it be improper?' she asked Marc.

'I don't think so,' said Marc. 'We are pretty informal these days.'

He smiled as he thought of something and went on 'but if you are going to invite Ernst I had better go out now and scour Munich for Lloyd Webber records.'

They laughed and Detty said, 'Perhaps we should invite the great man himself.'

There was another after dinner concert that evening. Sophie felt more relaxed with a less formal meal and played several Chopin Studies and Nocturnes. She played with great feeling and made special play with the fact that it was in honour of Mara who was Polish in culture if not by nationality.

'I've been a bit of everything at one time or another but I'm very proud to belong here – thank you again Herr Max for all your help and of course, Marc.'

Marc was in strong voice with sections of the *Winterreise* and Detty sang Wolf's *Heimweh* and Strauss's *Traum durch die Dammerung*. Then she asked sheepishly, 'Are you all feeling strong?'

They nodded and she passed the score of *Ariadne auf Naxos* to Marc at the piano.

'*Es gibt ein Reich,*' she murmured to him and he started to play the music of Ariadne's anguished haunting scena, which she hadn't sung since her visit to Adele in Ballsbridge an age ago. She started very quietly in front of her small audience of sophisticated listeners and gradually the emotion built from the grief-laden call for release by Hermes until the final tumbling intervals as she prays him to take her burdensome life from her. After she had finished Sophie and Max muttered *Brava* quietly and Max added, 'I heard Lisa della Casa sing that when I was very young at the Prinz Regenten. Your voice reminds me a little of hers. It takes a very fine soprano to do that scena justice and tonight you have done it justice.'

Detty felt as thrilled with that one comment from a man steeped in the music of his land as she had been by the university prize or the plaudits of Dublin.

Every third day, Detty set out with Mara back to Berlin for dressings and at the end of the first week for another skin graft. The normal visits required Mara to stay in hospital overnight and she had to stay for three nights for the graft. Usually Detty took a hotel room and stayed with her. The time of the last visit before her father arrived coincided with an appointment that Graf Max had in Berlin and he offered to take her and bring her back.

Detty and Marc said goodbye and watched from the porch as the tall and the tiny figures set off towards the big Mercedes deep in conversation about Polish piano music and the culinary traditions of Pomerania.

'They don't seem to be missing us,' said Marc as they turned and walked back towards the Schloss.

Instead of going inside Marc walked on round the side of the house and into the garden with Detty beside him. For a long time they walked in silence but when they were halfway towards the wood he turned to her and said in English, 'Detti, will you be mine, really mine, mine forever? Will you marry me?'

Her answer was out in German before she thought at all, *'O Siegfried! dein war ich von je'* [23]

They kissed long and deeply until neither could breath. They walked on in silence thinking about each other. Marc broke the silence and said, 'You will be marrying a captain. I had my promotion through this morning with a year's added seniority and a posting to the Staff College in England next year under the NATO arrangements.'

Detty turned and saluted then kissed him again.

'A German officer with an Irish wife – that ought to set the British army by the ears – we shall have to be good diplomats!'

'You always have to be good diplomats in that sort of post but it should be a bit easier than our last joint assignment,' he said, and went on, 'The CO wants to meet you to say thank you. He has invited us to lunch in Munich tomorrow. I thought that might work as Mara is in Berlin with my father so I've booked a hotel and tickets for *Der Rosenkavalier* at the Nationaltheatre in the evening.'

'That sounds wonderful,' said Detty excitedly as they walked on. 'Can we get married here?' she said suddenly.

'Yes, of course if you want to but won't it upset your parents?'

'No, they do as they are told – usually,' she said laughing, but suddenly serious again she added, 'It would be lovely here with the village church which is so special and the Schloss but there are other reasons – first it is probably safer and… and…' she hesitated not knowing how to say it and then out it all rushed, 'You remember what I was accused of… punished for in Moltravia? Well, Ireland is still a funny old fashioned country in a few ways and too near to England for its own good. What with the nuns at home thinking I was a whore and the English tabloids raking up all the titillating bits, it might spoil it all and that wouldn't happen here.'

At last she paused for breath. Marc realised guiltily how deeply she too had been hurt. Perhaps they had concentrated on Mara too much. He agreed readily.

---

23 Siegfried, I have always been yours

'When do we announce it?' she asked.

'I must talk to your father first.' he said.

'What rubbish. Don't be ridiculous,' she flared and then grinned.

'All right if you must – you old stick-in-the-mud. Can they come for Easter? If Dad can get away. It won't be too much for Sophie and Hildegard?'

'No they will thrive on it and after all there is plenty of space.'

'Marc, there is another thing – something that I haven't told you about but I must do so now.'

She pulled an envelope out of her pocket, took out a piece of paper and handed it to him. She watched him go a pale shade of grey green as he read:

Republik of Moltravia Ministry of Home Affairs
Eugenic Department H
Medical Recommendation that:
Bernadette Niamh O'Neill, alien,
of no fixed abode but currently detained in the Farm Detention Centre
is certified as an incorrigible moral defective demonstrating antisocial
tendencies and sexual depravity.

Corroborating evidence: Convictions for
(1) Terrorist activities
(2) Common prostitution

It is therefore ordered that she be compulsorily sterilised
under law 76 Section 8.
She is to be taken, under force if necessary
to the Frauendienst of Fortpflanzungsklinikum
there to be sterilised by surgical removal of the gonads and associated
organs as appropriate in the manner authorised by the law.
The order to be carried out within 14 days.

Signed: F Kovacs MD
Authorised Medical Officer

There was a long silence. Eventually Marc said in a strangled voice, 'And you went back into Moltravia with this hanging over you?'

Then Detty broke down in sobs and again it all tumbled out.

'He gave me a copy to taunt me and then sent me off to watch other girls from the Farm, who I knew, having it done. It is worse than a death sentence, isn't it? I wonder why – they had already sentenced me to death but that didn't seem to matter as much as this. It's so horrible isn't it? I saw them doing it to others – it was nauseating – so cold blooded – so cruel – so permanent. It's the one thing that is always in the nightmares. I couldn't tell you before we went back. You wouldn't have let me go – you would have been killed and Mara would have die – so I had to take the chance. I left this sealed with the colonel to be opened if I didn't come back. I reckoned with the Beretta I could virtually always shoot myself before they could capture me – anyway I comforted myself I could. I wouldn't have minded dying but that...'

'My poor darling,' whispered Marc, 'and I never knew and you still went back – my God.'

He cradled her head and cuddled her like a baby while she sobbed uncontrollably. Finally she looked up and smiled through her tears.

'But I'm OK. I had a protector stronger than that rotten bastard.'

'You did,' he agreed.

7

ALLES, WAS ICH BIN!

Will er Gemahl mich heissen
Geb'ich ihm, was ich bin![24]

WAGNER: LOHENGRIN ACT I

The autobahn passed through woods and hills with signs to Bayreuth and *Nürnberg*, city of so many associations, and after a couple of hours they entered Munich glimpsing the Olympic Stadium on their right. Marc pointed out *Schwabing* with its Bohemian associations and the *Englischer Garten*. They parked at the *Residenz* and took a taxi to an unobtrusive address off the *Nymphenburger Strasse*.

When she was introduced, Detty was surprised to find Oberst Kramm so young. He was a cheerful man, broad shouldered with bushy eyebrows. He was in his mid-thirties and wore a grey suit. He spoke with a little of the long vowels and sing-song accent of the south west. He excused himself and said he must get Marc to sign some papers but it would only take a few minutes. He saw that Detty was comfortable

---

24 If he will have me as wife,

   I will give him all that I am

and then took Marc into a back office. They returned in ten minutes and he sent for coffee. He then turned to Detty, 'Frau O'Neill, I am authorised to express the gratitude of the *Bundesrepublik* for your great service on our behalf.' He smiled 'I would also like to express my warm personal thanks and admiration for the resourcefulness and bravery that you have shown in helping us both before and after you became a temporary member of my service – I sincerely wish that you could become a permanent one. As is proper in a mission report, von Ritter has told me confidentially about the horrible activities in Moltravia and the threat that you were under when you first escaped. The bravery that you showed in going back to face that threat again was well-nigh incredible. That was courage at a level seldom seen in any service and it deserves the highest form of recognition.'

He smiled at them both continuing, 'I fully realise that it must have been almost equally difficult for you, von Ritter. I know, however, that you, Frau O'Neill, actually also suffered a great deal in addition on our behalf. The services rendered by Frau Oblova and yourself will not be forgotten. How do you feel now? Are you better?'

On being assured that she was fully recovered he went on, 'As you know von Ritter has been promoted and received a prestigious appointment and we were able to be of some service to Tamara Oblova in the matter of citizenship, but for you, as yet, we have done nothing. I would have dearly liked to recommend you for a German decoration for bravery. Because of the delicacy of the operation, the possibility of international difficulties with the neutrality of your own country and in addition the sensitive nature of your mission, we must bide our time for the moment.'

He smiled, 'There might also be a few questions here in Germany about why a female musician officer was attached to our unit. Although, I hasten to add, I think that my colleague, Oberst Wengen did brilliantly in obtaining your commission. It would certainly have helped you to have been in the Bundeswehr should you have proved yourself less capable than you were in coping with Moltravians.

'There is no reason, however, why you should not receive a gratuity for your service under our colours. I would like you to accept this on the understanding that it is merely routine and in no way is intended to be a fit reward for your courage or service.'

He handed her an envelope that she opened. It contained a draft on the German Overseas Development Fund for €100,000. It was more money than Detty, who came from a modest background, had ever seen before. For a moment she was silent and then said, 'Thank you, Herr Oberst, for your remarks and for this very generous gratuity. I would always do what I could for justice and freedom which I believe are the most important things in life.'

Dropping her serious tone, she smiled and looked at Marc who nodded imperceptibly.

'1 think that I may have got more, much more, from our adventures than perhaps you realised.'

'Perhaps I should explain, Sir,' said Marc, becoming very formal again, 'that I have asked Frau O'Neill to be my wife and that she has done me the honour of accepting. I hope that you will have no objection.'

'First, my heartiest congratulations and second, of course, we have no objection. Not only have you chosen a partner who has served the unit with such distinction, but the posting in England is usually reserved for married officers with English speaking wives. There is a social dimension as well as a purely professional one. I must, however, ask you one thing, Frau O'Neill, and I hope that it won't seem intrusive or impertinent but I am sure you will realise why it is necessary.'

He coughed, 'You will not have any… eh special problems getting security clearance in England?'

Detty laughed, 'I think that you mean, Herr Oberst, that, to use a well-worn phrase, am I or have I ever been a member of an illegal organisation? The answer is no. I am a patriotic Irish woman but no more and I promise that I won't sing rebel songs at a British Mess Dinner – although I do have a good repertory of them.'

'And very good songs they are too,' said the colonel laughing. 'I have heard some of them in Ireland on holiday fishing – perhaps you will come and sing them at our mess dinner… but perhaps that wouldn't be ideal for the solidarity of NATO.'

He became more serious again.

'Splendid, anyway. It couldn't be more suitable. When will you be married?'

'We hope to announce the engagement at Easter and to be married in July. This will give us time for a honeymoon and to find a house in England. Bernadette was half way through her degree at Oxford when she went to Moltravia and we hope that she can finish it while I am at Shrivenham.'

'That sounds feasible – good luck to both of you. It is good to have friends in Europe, Frau O'Neill, and if the future of the Union depends on young people like von Ritter and yourself perhaps we may have some hope for times ahead. You understand the difficult position that we are in. We know the risk of the evils of Moltravia spreading throughout the East but what can we do? We are Germans and if we interfere in politics to the East, what will be said? With our history? After all it is only in the last few years that our troops have officially been permitted abroad at all. All we can do is to gather information, publicise and keep track of their gruesome work, raise public awareness, keep our allies informed and do a little, very little undercover work with the highest degree of security. Your recent mission was an example of this and as I have said it was extremely well done although we are sensitive that the cost to you was high. We are, I repeat, very, very grateful.'

'And you don't think a German officer with an Irish wife in the British army will strain diplomacy too much?' Detty asked.

He smiled again,

'I couldn't possibly comment on that except to say that if we didn't think von Ritter was up to it we wouldn't have appointed him. As for yourself, I cannot see you being other than an asset and after all the Irish have had a lot of practice at handling the English, haven't they?'

'Nearly a thousand years, Herr Oberst, but not always successfully, I will do my best not to let you down – my Oxford background may help a bit.'

He laughed, 'I am sure you will succeed – now – lunch.'

A short walk took them to *Boettner*. The Oberst looked at Marc out of the corner of his eye but addressed Detty, 'The Bavarians can't rival us Swabians for food, Frau Bernadette, but they say that this place isn't bad for fish.'

The atmosphere relaxed with the use of Detty's first name and Marc replied to the wind-up with a smile. 'That's unfair, Sir, I mustn't be insubordinate but I'll let the food speak for itself.'

And so it did with pike soufflé followed by lobster garnished with crayfish securing an unspoken victory for Marc and Bavaria – at least on the day.

The conversation at lunch ranged over the wider aspects of European politics, Detty's aspirations as a linguist and a singer together with the finer points of fly fishing on the Loughs of western Ireland. As they shook hands at the door, Kramm whispered to Marc, 'You've got something very special there – look after her.'

'I will, Sir, never fear.'

After the colonel left they walked hand-in-hand across the *Maximilianstrasse* to a small street where Marc led the way into a tiny shop with an almost empty window. A small man peered myopically over the counter.

'Ah, Herr Graf, you have come to see the stones.'

He produced diamonds, emeralds, rubies and sapphires and poured them onto velvet mats. 'You see it really depends upon the design.' he said.

For over an hour they looked at designs and stones. Marc made it clear that it was up to Detty to choose anything that she wanted. After her initial astonishment she set to work with her usual energy. Eventually she decided on a Celtic cross with a central emerald and four arms of graded alternating diamonds and emeralds.

'It has really got to be emeralds, hasn't it?' said Detty rhetorically.

The little jeweller extolled the glories of sapphires and rubies until Marc explained, 'You see my fiancée is Irish and green is the national colour of Ireland.'

Detty felt a quick thrill at hearing Marc refer to her as *meine Verlobte* for the first time while the jeweller commented at length on how well the Frau spoke German and how unusual this was in a young Eng… Irish lady.

Detty smiled, thanked him and said could she ask a very great favour.

'Of course nothing would be too much trouble for the *Gnädige Frau.*'

260

'Would there be any possible chance that the ring would be ready by Easter as we want to announce our engagement then?'

'It will be possible, difficult but possible – the intricate design takes a little longer but of course the Herr Graf will have the ring by the beginning of *Passionwoche.*'

As they finished, the jeweller gave Marc a small box which he put into his pocket without comment. Detty was puzzled but said nothing about it. When they left to walk to the Englischer Garten she said to Marc, 'I want you to keep the ring until the Easter concert. You will know when to put it on my finger.' And then almost to herself. 'It will fit beautifully.'

'Of course it will fit beautifully. What are you talking about, darling?'

'No – something different – promise that you will keep it until the moment is right.'

'Of course,' said Marc again, 'but can't you explain – you are beginning to sound like *Erda* – all wisdom and riddles.'

He didn't understand a thing and was wondering anew about this captivating, mad Celtic girl who had flashed so unexpectedly like summer lightning into his ordered Teutonic world.

'As long as I don't look like her I don't mind,' laughed Detty.

'You don't – you don't sound like her really either – you couldn't reach *"Mein Schlaf ist Traumen, mein Traumen Sinnen, mein Sinnen Walten des Wissens".*'[25]

'No – that is the contralto passage I envy most.' She started to sing quietly, '"*Ein Wunschmadchen gebar ich Wotan: der Helden Wal hiess fur sich er sie kuren".*'[26] She broke off, 'It doesn't sound the same when you transpose it.'

'*"Kuhn ist sie und weise auch"*,'[27] he finished, 'you're Brunnhllde not Erda, the description fits you to a tee! We had better go back: we need plenty of time to change.'

---

25 My sleep is dreaming
    My dreams have meaning
    The meaning leads to wisdom
26 A wish maiden I gave to Wotan
    Battle heroes she chose for him
27 She is brave and wise as well

'You wouldn't be thinking of having your wicked way with a simple Irish country girl before going out – would you, Herr Graf?'

'It had crossed my mind.'

'Good,' she said and bobbed a curtsy. 'Thank heavens, as we say at home, that you can never trust the gentry.'

They shared a shower and made love. Detty dressed in the indigo silk sheath that she had bought in Berlin. She wondered whether it was too low cut and clingy, but one look at Marc's face as he sat staring at her reassured her.

'You're more beautiful than ever,' he said finally. 'That dress is fabulous. It dazzles the eyes of a simple soldier.'

'But is it good enough for a Bavarian Countess elect?'

'Good enough for a daughter of the High Kings of Ireland.'

She slapped his bottom and produced a theatrical pout. 'You're never going to let me forget that, are you? Remember I'm also the girl that you tipped into the trash cart.'

Detty's excitement rose as they entered the Nationalstheatre. Over the months, they had sung together and talked endlessly of music in all sorts of improbable situations. Now she was actually in a theatre with the man she loved. And what a theatre! She insisted on going into the beautiful galleries and then the auditorium early and sat drinking in the atmosphere. This, although it had been restored after its destruction, was the birthplace of *Die Meistersinger, Tristan, Rheingold* and *Die Walküre* to say nothing of so many Strauss first nights.

They held hands through the arrival of Ochs, the levee and the capers of Mariandl until the Marschallin's existential angst ticked the act to its close. Over an interval coffee, Marc said that Detty would make a wonderful Octavian. She was thoughtful for a moment and said after a pause, 'I know that I do have a good voice – but to try for a professional career – it's so chancy and there are so many sacrifices. I think I would prefer to sing for pleasure, finish my language degree – and look after you. Doesn't sound very ambitious or modern – does it really?'

The curtain went up on Faninal and Sophie. The great orchestral climax announced Octavian. As he handed over his rose, Marc slipped the box he had collected from the jewellers into Detty's hand. For the rest of the act she clasped it tight containing her curiosity. Once Ochs had had his spirits revived by the assignation with Mariandl the curtain fell and after the applause Detty was able to open the box. Inside was an exquisitely sculptured silver rose.

In the middle of the stalls she kissed Marc to the horrified astonishment of the serious Bavarian ladies.

'What the hell if they are shocked?' she said to Marc as they went out. 'This show is supposed to be about love.'

The final trio cast its spell, Detty collected her coat and they walked out into the fine cold night.

'I'm thirsty. I want to drink beer,' she demanded to his astonishment.

'Munich style – complete with ompah?' he asked.

'Of course! Munich style.'

They walked the short distance to the *Hofbräu Haus* through the frosty March night. He ordered *zwei Masskruge* and watched while she was presented with hers. He waited in vain for her astonishment. Not a bit of it, to his further surprise she set about the huge mug with relish only pausing from the task to tell him it was great but he hadn't really lived until he had drunk Guinness on the banks of the Liffey. She would put that right soon. He assured her that she was now a real Bavarian entitled to '*Grüss Gott*' with the best adding, 'I can't wait to see you in a *Dirndl.*'

'I bet you can't,' she grinned, 'but I would wear one for you.'

'I would have to make sure your knot was on the right.'

She looked askance at him.

'It means that you are married or engaged.'

'You mean that you have to announce it publicly to put off the competition – that spoils the fun. Surely that doesn't happen at the *Oktoberfest?*' she exclaimed.

'*Sei ein richtiges kleines Luder!* You really are a proper little hussy,' he said laughing and eyeing her curvaceous figure with unfeigned admiration. He added, 'anyway I'm not taking you to the *Oktoberfest* wearing a *Dirndl,* I'll have to put you on a lead. Anyway, the *Dirndl* isn't traditional in *Franken* only in *Oberbayern,* I haven't brought you all this way to lose you at the *Oktoberfest.*'

'You've changed your tune. Shame, I was looking forward to it,' she laughed.

A leisurely breakfast in their room was followed by an extended shopping trip. Detty opened a bank account and deposited her gratuity. They let her draw cash immediately as she had paid in a government draft. With money of her own for the first time she bought a pale cream silk evening dress for the concert. As with any singer the main consideration was whether the dress was right for the voice. She eventually decided that it was and it was arranged that it should be sent to Oberdorf. After some time on the obligatory shoes and accessories they went off on a browse round antique and record shops.

Suddenly she left Marc's side and dived impetuously inside an antique shop and gesticulated to the owner indicating the window. He opened the safety window and produced a small silver goblet with a gilded onlay in which were set some blue red stones. Detty inspected it closely and then asked the shop owner about it. He said it was a late medieval chalice about 1460, which almost certainly came from the treasury of a disbanded Dominican priory near *Miesbach*. He produced a certificate of its later provenance.

Detty asked the price, looked appropriately crestfallen and asked if there could possibly be any reduction. The green hazel eyes and pleadingly beautiful face, together with the knowledge of the original generous mark up, induced the proprietor to say gallantly that he would sell it without profit for a smile from such a beautiful *Auslanderin*. Detty didn't entirely believe him but she parted willingly with a hefty slice of her gratuity and presented the cup to Marc saying, 'To the finest, bravest man in the world on our betrothal – your own amethyst chalice from a besotted fiancée.'

They returned home to greet Tamara who was glowing from an excellent progress report from the hospital and Max who seemed to have enjoyed showing his appreciative surrogate daughter more of the sights of their despised capital city.

*

264

The weather had broken. The approach to Franz Josef Strauss airport was misty and soaking wet in the early spring morning. Awkwardly Detty and Marc tried not to intrude in the anxious thoughts of their waiting companion. The impersonal announcement board indicated that the 11.53am American Airlines flight from New York had landed and then that the baggage was in the hall. Several times Tamara jumped like a startled rabbit as parties of travellers came through the arrival gate only to settle again to wait. A small man in a collar and tie and a smart grey suit finally appeared. His silver hair was receding and only in his piercing blue eyes and firm determined jaw did he resemble his daughter. Nonetheless, Detty realised that the moment had arrived even before Tamara leapt forward.

'*Oh, Vati!*' she cried and buried her face in his chest. For some moments they were locked together.

At last he said, 'But are you all right?'

She released herself from him, nodded tearfully and turned towards Marc and Detty. 'Yes, I am,' she said, 'and I want to introduce you to the two reasons why I am safe and well. Hauptmann Marc von Ritter and Frau – no perhaps I should say Leutnant,' she smiled through her tears, 'Bernadette O'Neill – my rescuers and my dearest friends.'

Nicklaus Oblov turned towards Marc and said, 'Herr Marc, I was brought up as a Pole and we learnt to hate Germany and the German army. Today I owe the safety of my dearest treasure to an officer in that army. I cannot begin to tell you what that means to me but please accept this embrace as a symbol of my heartfelt gratitude and may it also be a symbol of reconciliation between the nations.'

Marc murmured, 'Amen to that,' and stooped to enfold the little man in his arms.

Choking on his tears Oblov at last turned to Detty, 'And to you, Frau Bernadette, what can I say? When I learnt what you had achieved in rescuing my Tamara, I came here expecting to find you immense and powerful but now I see that all that faith, loyalty and courage came from someone very young and so beautiful. In Poland as children, we always knew that Ireland was the land of the saints and the Martyrs. Today I have met a living Irish saint and I wish to pay homage to her.'

He bent very low to the astonishment of the airport passers by and kissed her hand reverently. Detty gently raised him up again and said in a firm low voice, 'I owe more to the courage of your daughter than she owes to me but, of course, she won't have told you about that.'

She kissed him on both cheeks and they slowly moved off back to the car.

The Oblovs travelled together in the back leaving Marc and Detty silently in front. The air was laden with powerful feelings and not much was said until they were approaching Nuremberg when scraps of news began to be exchanged between father and daughter.

'I thought that you might be safer at the Sacred Heart when I left.' he said in great pain. 'But I knew that it would take a miracle if you were to survive. It was only the men then who had been forced into the army. At first I thought that he wouldn't touch the women – certainly not young girls – but soon they put me right about that... I should have known... I of all people should not have underestimated Travsky. Finally I realised that you were in as much danger if I stayed as if I went – possibly more. If I went they might use you to get me back that might have kept you safe. But I didn't know the terrible things they would do to you and to your wonderful friend. I should have guessed – nothing is sacred to him – you have heard nothing of Gisela?'

'No, Vati, I'm sorry.'

Finally they arrived in front of the lodge and saw the newcomer settled in. The daughter that he never expected to see again, acting as his hostess in the home which had adopted her.

Hectic days of rehearsals for the Easter concert followed. It was all accompanied by a lot of laughter. Marc and Detty practised their duets accompanied by his mother and Graf Max took the village band with its grafted string section in hand. Chairs were borrowed from the village school to increase the capacity of the hall to about two hundred with a few extras possible in the gallery. The concert would be in the late afternoon of Easter day followed by supper – a joint effort with the *Schwarzer Adler* and the village. Finally there would be music and dancing into the night. It was all arranged and settled.

In the evenings, there was more music and talk. Nicklaus Oblov had talked long with Tamara about the future of Moltravia. He was careful to keep their domestic concerns out of the happy general chat but occasionally it was made clear that everybody was interested and he talked to them seriously and willingly.

He had now become officially the leader of the government in exile and he had many responsibilities. First, he wanted to avoid useless pain and bloodshed. There had been several revolts, all of which had failed and had been brutally suppressed. However, eventually they had to strike if they were ever to free the country. There was some evidence that Travsky's bloody purges were weakening the country both by removing some of its more able people and by creating an opposition desperate even in the face of torture and murder. But was revolt really more feasible now? Would there really be any more chance than previously? Could it be successfully organised – a greater effort would bring greater penalties if it failed? His thoughts trailed off as he said, half to himself, 'What we really need is the resources and courage of the Hansa against Waldemar.'

Detty, not surprisingly, had harboured a deep loathing for all things Hanseatic since the governor had claimed that her unspeakable punishment was legitimised by Hanseatic statute. Hearing the hated name, without thinking, she uttered her disgust and Oblov looked up quizzically at her. She felt ashamed of her impulsiveness, and, feeling that she owed her friend's father an explanation for her rudeness, she explained the circumstances of her birching and its supposed association with the Hansa. She added, 'They must have been as bad as Travsky if all they could think about was hanging and branding people and flogging women.'

Nicklaus Oblov smiled at her very gently and replied, 'After what you have told me I am not surprised that you feel like that but what you say is not true. Konradin was just trying to justify his unquenchable sadism. The Middle Ages was a cruel time and all society used cruel punishments – human life was cheap and the rich and powerful exploited the poor and weak. The Hansa, however, although it did have these punishments on some of its members' statute books, certainly didn't invent them or even use them often. The Hansa was a league of decent merchant cities trying to protect the rights of the citizen traders against the crime and the viciousness all around them. The feudal princes and, I am sorry to say the Church, had a callous disregard for truth, law or human life, which was awesome. In addition the countryside was littered with bandits who enjoyed the protection of the princes and treated ordinary people with a fearful cruelty. Burnings, beheadings, slave labour and torture were widespread.

'Against these crimes the Hansa stood as a protection. In a Hansa city nobody was convicted without trial and a citizen always had the right of a defence. The eventual punishment may have been severe but at least it was just. Citizens under the protection of the league could travel the roads without being daily in fear of robbery, rape and murder. We stood for the defence of the merchant and his trade but also for the defence of the common man. Königshof represented the citadel of freedom and justice between the Scheldt and Novgorod and our brother cities stood with us from great Lübeck to the smallest. The tyrants trembled at our judgement! How dare Travsky and his vermin henchmen quote the Hansa as justification of their crimes!'

The little man's eyes blazed with a holy rage that was fearful. Detty had noticed how he had slipped the personal pronoun into his explanation. At that moment she wished the floor could have opened and swallowed her up.

'I am sorry. I have been wholly wrong. I didn't know – but that is no excuse. I have more remorse for my idle talk tonight than I suffered under Konradin's birch.'

'Detti – please! It is not your fault. What they did to you in the name of the League was an abomination so of course you feel bitter about the Hansa. How could you know when they distort everything with their lies? You have served us valiantly but think well of the Hansa, it may yet be our model. Beside,' he broke off and smiled at her, 'I would make more mistakes about Irish history.'

Detty pondered deeply on what he had said. In her spare moments she searched for books about the Hansa and, fascinated, learnt more and more about its true history. How the league of free cities had defied the feudal despots. How Hanseatic outposts were founded in all the great trading centres of the then known world. How piety and justice

268

flourished alongside the prosperous trade of the merchants. She also came to respect deeply the conviction of the chief of the Moltravian government in exile and to understand the love of the old League, which had stood so bravely and successfully against a corrupt Church and the unscrupulous might of princes.

*

They left the autobahn and headed down the Nürnberger Strasse towards the town. Detty felt a tingle of anticipation. She tried to decide whether it was due to the visit to the theatre of so many sepia prints and record covers or whether to the prospect of meeting a major luminary in the operatic firmament. More probably it was the chance of singing, however briefly, in front of somebody who had listened to more great voices than she had had hot dinners.

They came upon their first goal suddenly on the left. Through the trees Detty read with awe the inscription carved across the front of the house which she had first seen as a photograph long ago, as a schoolgirl in Ireland:

 'Hier, wo mein Wahnen Frieden fand-
 WAHNFRIED
 Sei dieses Haus von mir benannt. [28]

Athough it was out of season and everything was quiet, the house museum was open to the public. Marc said quietly to the concierge that Professor Dr Meisl had said that he would telephone to say that they were coming. They were introduced to the Direktor who greeted them, explained about the reconstruction of the house after the devastating bombing in 1945. He showed them round some private rooms before tactfully withdrawing saying that he was sure that they would like to look round in their own time.

---

28 Here where I find succour from my madness
    Wahnfried
    I name this house

In spite of the reconstructions, Detty relished the pungent aura of nineteenth-century high art in the home of one of its apostles. She had to keep reminding herself that the composer of the *Ring, Tristan* and *Die Meistersinger* had lived here – had walked down those staircases, visited the children's bedrooms, dressed in the room on the strange mezzanine floor. Last but not least here he had rehearsed *Götterdämmerung* and worked on *Parsifal*.

Possibly the powerful presence of Cosima who had ruled here for so much longer contributed even more to the atmosphere. They toured the basement collection of miniature theatre sets before walking through the garden to the joint tombs at the edge of the park behind. They stood there silently for a moment. Detty thought it would be good to be buried in her own home and wondered if you could still do it. Then she remembered that the Church would probably not approve, after all Wagner had been brought up a protestant, if a rather complicated one.

They had time for a visit to the Markgraf's opera house whose shimmering baroque had first brought Wagner to Bayreuth before crossing down the road to the *Eule* to meet Cousin Bernhard for lunch. The *Eule* is a simple enough *Gaststatte* made famous by the artists of Bayreuth whose photographs line the walls and date back to the very first festival in 1876. Once frequented by the family and famous soloists, this had sadly become less usual during the festival in these media and publicity conscious days.

Bernhard Meisl, broad featured and grey, came forward to greet them with a warm smile. Marc shook hands and introduced Detty who noticed with amusement that she had again become his *'freundin Bernadette'* and that the exciting *'verlobte'* of Munich was still not for family consumption. Bernhard smiled and shook her hand, remarking that they were namesakes. He apparently knew something of their recent history as he teased Marc about finding such a beautiful lady on active service. Then he added with a wink to Detty that his only disappointment was that an Irish princess coming to Bayreuth should surely have been called *Isolde*. Over lunch he talked about the festival, its past and its future plans. As they took the short drive up the Green Hill to the theatre, his anecdotes continued.

The forecourt and the facade looked warm in the bright but chilly spring sunshine. Detty looked at the loggia seeing in her mind's eye the musicians appearing to recall the audience to their seats with a motif from the forthcoming act. The sides of the building seemed a jumble and reminded Detty irreverently of the DART side of the old Lansdowne Road Rugby ground, without the railway tunnel but smarter. The inside, however, was all that she had ever imagined with its steep, severe amphitheatre of seats leading down to the orchestra cowl in front of the cavernous stage. Even though it was early spring there was some activity in the theatre. Bernhard amused them with an endless stream of details and stories about the theatre and its past spiced with anecdotes of the Wagner family and the artists who had appeared there over the years. They were shown the famous conductor gallery corridor, the inside of the sunken pit and the rostrum graced by so many famous names.

Eventually they reached a door inscribed 'Professor Doktor Meisl'. They entered, sat down and were served coffee by Bernhard from a white Nymphenberg service. At one end of the room was a Steingraeber grand piano. As she looked at it Detty felt suddenly mesmerised. In her mind she saw Siegfried learning fear from the sleeping Brunnhilde on her rock. She had been through trials, terror, humiliation, torture, hopelessness and faced death itself and worse. She had dealt death to a monster a thousand times more sinister than Fafner. Now she sat in the company of the man she loved and his charming friendly cousin and felt near panic because in a moment the time might come for her to sing. Her own singing had been mentioned only briefly over lunch when Bernhard had recalled that Sophie had said that she had an excellent voice. This hadn't terrified her but after their tour of the theatre with its potent ghosts of Lehmann, Nordica, Leider and Flagstad to say nothing of Richter, Toscanini, Furtwangler and Knappertsbush real fear gripped her. This wasn't Dublin or Oxford – this was Bayreuth. It was almost as if Bernhard had suddenly donned a beret and developed piercing eyes and a long hooked nose. She tried to calm herself but found that all she did was to keep licking her lips and swallowing.

271

Perhaps it was his long experience with singers but Bernhard seemed to notice that she suddenly seemed silent and tense and quickly turned to her saying, 'Sophie told me that you have a beautiful voice that we should hear. Would it be at all possible for you to sing for us? Whatever you like.'

'Of course – if you don't mind.'

Detty smiled, got up and crossed to the piano. Marc followed her and sat on the stool. She started with Schubert's *'Im Fruhling,'* still feeling very nervous. Her voice seemed disembodied – it belonged to someone else she heard it as from afar. Then as she tried to listen to herself, she began to believe it was all there – true and clear – with a gentle sensitive *legato*. She began to enjoy herself and forgot her nervousness. With hardly a pause she nodded to Marc and they went on to Strauss's *'Erfreit'* confidently with the sense of occasion helping her to express great feeling. As she finished she heard Bernhard say softly almost to himself, 'Well done.'

On a high, she spotted the vocal score of *Tannhauser* on top of a pile on a table.

'May I?' she said to Bernhard who answered,

'Of course – please.'

She passed the score to Marc saying, 'Act 2 – you know.'

He played the introduction and she swept into *'Dich teure Halle'* her young voice compassing accurately the thrilling intervals and she knew it was good. Her companion had not let her down and she filled Elisabeth's greeting to the Hall of Song with ecstasy.

As she finished there was silence in the room. Suddenly the confidence drained away – had she made a fool of herself – after all it wasn't a formal audition? To have sung that in front of him – here! What arrogance, what stupidity.

Just as the doubts were taking over he turned to her smiling. 'Frau Detti,' he said, 'that was superb and reminded me so much of a young lady that I heard in this very room many, many years ago. Like you – forgive me – her technique was not yet perfect but the beauty of tone, excitement and the quality... to have a similar experience is a rare pleasure. Frau Detti you have a fine voice and you use it very well.

It is a soloist's voice – yes, even for this theatre. Sophie was right, even here you could sing leading roles. You need more maturity, although it is wonderfully mature already for one so young, and some more professional training to perfect it, but the voice, the musician and most of the technique are all there. If you wish I could arrange for your final training at Munich or also we could do some work together but perhaps you have other plans?'

She thanked him adding that at the moment she was planning to finish her degree in England. If he would really be prepared to teach her, of course that would be wonderful. She was intending to continue her serious lessons would think hard about Munich.

As they left, a man in his late thirties came out of a neighbouring room, 'Dr Berni,' he said, 'why were you auditioning *Tannhäuser* this afternoon? The new production is still three years away.'

Bernhard smiled at Detty. 'I thought I might have found an Elisabeth for the future. What did you think?'

'Good, very good – a young voice but true, very powerful and well phrased. Who was it?'

'This young lady. Frau Detti, may I introduce Maestro Anton Meilin who is conducting the Ring next year in the new production. Maestro, this is Frau Bernadette O'Neill and my cousin, Marc von Ritter.'

After they shook hands, Meilin said, 'The Herr Professor only allows me to hear his protegés through the wall but I enjoyed what I heard very much. Are you available next year? We have still not cast Gerhilde and Helmwige – or Woglinde – the first one dropped out – and a small part might enable you to get the feel of the theatre before taking on larger roles. Please let me know if you will be available to audition.'

Detty's mind was in a whirl. She could not believe it but she thought that she had just been offered the chance of a part at Bayreuth. She stammered her thanks and said that she would certainly let him know. As they left, Bernhard was serious once more. He said, 'Frau Detti, thank you for coming. I hope it was worth it. You really have an exceptional voice but please don't sing too many *Abscheulichers* and *Liebestods* yet. You must cherish a fabulous instrument and, forgive me, but you are very young still.'

She smiled and thanked him for his advice. She was silent in the drive back to Oberdorf and Marc left her alone with her thoughts.

That night she dreamed of standing over a valley of light singing into the warm black chasm beyond. Then the dream became confused with hideous images from the past. The theatre became a vast hall of tortured cripples with hyenas in human form shrieking derision and obscenities from tiered galleries. The conductor was the armourer standing over her with blood on his chest. She tried to cry out and found that she couldn't. Then she awoke to find Tamara, who had suffered so much more, comforting her as she had done once before. The consoling familiarity of the Schloss and her dear friend were around her. She assured Mara that she was all right. Eventually, reluctantly, her anxious friend returned to her own bed. It was still dark and Detty lay awake thinking of the previous day. Could it really be true? Had she really been so casually offered the chance to sing at Bayreuth – the temple, which she had not dreamed of ever being able even to visit?

*

At breakfast Bill appeared looking bleary eyed from a long pre-Easter party which had clearly made the Munich brewers work overtime. The presence of the two girls appeared to improve his hangover. He was at his most gallant to Detty who assumed quite correctly that this was merely an opportunity to try and wind up his brother. She turned the tables by getting him to agree to do a tenor solo at the concert and sing the final scene *Florestan* opposite her *Leonore*. Muttering good humouredly about Irish charm he agreed to both but only on the condition that he could choose '*Che gelida manina'* as his solo with Mara as Mimi in full costume.

'But I can't sing,' objected the latter.

'That doesn't matter,' replied Bill. 'You only have to inspire me by letting me look at you.'

He then started to sing '*Gern hab ich die Fraun gekusst'* in a suprisingly true tenor voice looking yearningly into Mara's eyes. She clearly found the whole experience very satisfying and looked distinctly weak at the knees.

Marc and Detty watched this side show with increasing amusement.

'*Er ist wirklich shrecklich*' muttered Marc to Detty then aloud, 'Bill, you might at least let us finish breakfast before trying to seduce my guests.'

'Jealousy won't help, brother,' answered Bill still gazing at Mara. 'You don't have exclusive rights on all these fabulous creatures that you seem to stumble over. Now I must have your answer on the *Boheme* tableau or else I shall have to go out and fall on my sword.'

Mara blushed very charmingly and agreed demurely. 'Minx', thought Detty seeing a new side of her friend for the first time and muttered to Marc, 'I reckon she will get as give as good as she gets.'

Gertrude was waiting for Detty to rehearse. They were now becoming close friends and Trudi was able to say that she sensed a new authority in Detty's singing. After the session had finished they sat over coffee and Gertrude asked how the visit to Bayreuth had gone. Detty hadn't meant to talk about it but suddenly she blurted it all out – musician to musician – girl to girl.

After Detty had finished Gertrude said, 'It is a great honour, Detti, but I am really not too surprised. You have a magnificent soprano, near perfect articulation and a professional technique. I could see you as a thrilling Elsa or Elisabeth at Bayreuth and they must love your figure and looks. They rarely, if ever, take singers who don't look good as well as sound good. But don't hurry. You will hazard your voice if you use it too much under too much pressure too soon.'

'Everybody tells me that and I think that when I'm in a sensible mood, I agree, but somehow the big parts thrill me and I can't wait to try them.'

Marc met her in the village to walk back to the Schloss. When they were safely in the country out of sight of the village he said to her solemnly, 'I hope that you realise that as the *Intendant* of the Oberdorf Easter Festival I will have to terminate your contract.'

Detty looked at him wide-eyed in puzzlement.

'We can't possibly afford Bayreuth soloists' fees.' he said.

She turned and punched him viciously in the midriff and said with mock fierceness, 'You tease me again or say a word about yesterday to anyone and I shall have a real Prima Donna's tantrum.'

So saying she hugged him and kissed him equally fiercely.

The long awaited arrival of the O'Neill family for Easter was scheduled for the following day. The only reasonable flight again came to Munich. Detty and Marc set off in the big family Mercedes down the now familiar road through the forests past Nuremberg to the airport. Although she had telephoned frequently since she had been free and had written two or three lengthy letters, it still seemed an age since she had seen them. It was even longer since she had seen Nuala. She had been still in France on the late August day that her father and mother had left Detty at Dublin Airport under a leaden sky, to travel to Moltravia. She had reassured them that, in spite of what they had read about her in the press, she was well.

She thought it prudent to add that she had experienced some difficulty in getting out of Moltravia. She felt guilty that she had been in Germany for over six weeks now without going home. She had tried to explain to her mother over the phone about her responsibilities to Mara and her involvement with activities at Oberdorf but she feared, correctly, that it sounded somewhat lame.

Rather to Detty's surprise, they had not seemed upset and had agreed readily to come and spend Easter with an unknown family in a Bavarian Schloss. Brian had not even seemed to mind the expense of a locum at short notice, which in normal times would have caused a tirade about not being made of money and the need for economies.

Such is the blindness of love, that it had never occurred to Detty that her parents and sister might have guessed that there was more keeping her in Germany than music and the need to care for Tamara. It had not taken Peggy or Brian O'Neill long to realise that the young German officer who their elder daughter had mentioned with studied casualness in letters and telephone calls, might have something to do with her remaining in that country.

Sister Nuala summed it all up with the forthrightness of a sixteen-year-old convent girl when she said that it seemed that sister Detty had probably 'got the hots' for this Marc. Her mother had told her not to be so vulgar but had not disputed her conclusion.

Marc felt extreme trepidation about meeting his future Irish family.

Detty, in turn, felt a little apprehensive about introducing Marc, who up to now, she had tried to portray as a casual acquaintance and colleague. She knew that once her family saw the two of them together that fiction could not be sustained.

Both of them, therefore, awaited the arrival of the Ryanair flight with some anxiety which increased as the other passengers came through the gate. They need not have worried. The O'Neill family arrived in such a flurry of hugs and chatter that it was some moments before Detty could even get an opening to introduce Marc and allow him the opportunity to welcome them to Bavaria. Then the catching up on gossip interspersed with information about the Easter festivities at Oberdorf continued.

Much to Marc's relief nobody mentioned Moltravia. He had found Mara's father's arrival deeply moving but somehow felt pleased that this time round cheerful Irish banter seemed the order of the day. He realised that the O'Neills must have felt deep shock and anxiety at the piecemeal news that had reached them of their daughter's captivity and ordeal but he sensed that they felt that this was neither the time nor place to relive the experience.

As the journey home progressed, Brian and Marc became involved in an animated discussion about the problems of game conservation in Ireland and Bavaria while Peggy tried tactlessly to persuade Nuala to speak to Marc in German. Much embarrassed, the latter declared that she couldn't see the point as Marc spoke perfect English and anyway Detty would be bound to correct her.

As was their custom the entire von Ritter family accompanied by Mara and Nicklaus Oblov gathered in the porch to greet the arriving party. After the introductions Peggy asked Tamara how she was feeling, to which the latter replied that, thanks to Detty, she was feeling great. Bill remarked mischievously in fluent but richly accented English that Nuala was even more glamorous than her sister. This led Detty and Marc to exchange meaningful winks. Tamara caught herself casting a sharp glance at Nuala but then felt ashamed of herself for reacting to this flirtation with a schoolgirl.

From the Olympian superiority of her eighteen years she assured herself that there was nothing to worry about and relaxed. Nuala on the other hand thought that she was quite looking forward to spending Easter in this company as long as Detty didn't get too pompous. Bill, she decided, was definitely a good prospect as a brother-in-law. Was a brother-in-law's brother still a brother-in-law? She didn't know but was keenly aware that she risked death or mutilation from her sister if she asked, so wisely she kept quiet.

Thursday was bright and clear and Detty came down to breakfast early. Only Marc was there looking tense and pacing up and down, like a caged tiger. She realised that he was trying to find her father alone and, although she regarded all this as charmingly archaic in the twenty-first century, nonetheless, she thought that she had better help him with a little stage management. She left after a quick breakfast and went to her parents' room.

'Da,' she said to him as he was shaving, 'I think Marc is trying to have a word with you alone – please try to help the man – won't you?'

'Is he then?' her father replied. 'Leave it to me, I will give him a chance, for sure. I might have to warn him off.'

His elegant daughter's only repost was to stick her tongue out at him, mutter something that she wasn't supposed to have learnt at St Conleth's Convent and disappear rapidly.

Soon after breakfast the deed was done. Brian was rather taken aback at being addressed as Dr O'Neill after the informality the day before but assured Marc that he would be very proud to have him as a son-in-law. He now felt able to thank Marc for getting Bernadette out of Moltravia. Marc looked at him very seriously and replied, 'Dr O'Neill, as you know, I am deeply in love with Detti, and therefore I am biased, but there is another side to this. I am also a professional soldier trained to judge men in action and under stress. Your daughter has the courage of a lioness and is extremely resourceful. She would fight for freedom and justice with the last breath in her body, which, I confess, sometimes worries me. I served with her briefly as a fellow officer and I never had a finer military comrade – even if she was there ostensibly as a musician, although, as you know, she's pretty good at that too. I can't believe my luck.'

Brian nodded, shook his hand and wished him every happiness. Marc thanked him and asked for his help in keeping the engagement secret a little longer. Detty contrived to run into Marc a moment later and asked:

'How did it go?'

'He told me that I was a n'er do well scallywag and not worthy of you and never to cast eyes on you again or he'd chase me out with, how you saay eet, ze horses vhip.'

He put an elaborate Mittel Europa accent into his flawless English.

'Liar, I can't get any sense out of the males around here,' she said thinking of her father's comments earlier and laughing. 'I shall go and flirt with Bill.'

They rehearsed the finale of *Fidelio* that evening. Max led the village orchestra and contrived to sing Rocco's line from the leader's desk. Bill produced a bright if somewhat inaccurate *Florestan* and Detty, free from all her preoccupations about the difficult task that would come later, allowed her majestic young soprano to soar freely over the others. She enjoyed the serious murmurs of approval from the orchestra about the quality of the young Irin's singing but she kept saying to herself, 'You know you can do this – this isn't the real test.' All in all though it went well and everyone was happy at the end of the evening.

On Good Friday it snowed and they attended a performance of Bach's *Mathaus Passion* in Bamberg. Detty drove her mother back alone in Sophie's VW which gave them their first opportunity to talk together. The roads had been cleared and the drive through the darkening Easter peace of the *Frankenwald* was romantic without being too difficult.

Peggy had been much moved by the performance in Bamberg and had found time to say a prayer of thanks for her daughter's safety. Detty said quietly that she had said many prayers and told her mother about her prayer to Mary and the ray of light across the washroom floor. After that she said she was able to face the later trials with hope. Gradually, even in danger, she began to feel safe and even strangely powerful. She added how important Tamara had been – and was – to her.

'And Marc?' asked her mother.

'Wait a little and soon you will know – anything that you haven't already guesse,' was the reply.

At Mass on Easter Day Detty gave her thanks to the Virgin again. This time it was joyful and she had the feeling that she herself and her companions had been part of a triumph over evil.

In the afternoon everybody left the lunch party to change. The men performers wore evening dress with Marc in his mess uniform. Detty wore the dress with its gold silk skirt and cream low-cut bodice that she had bought in Munich. Mara had a ankle-length patchwork dress with a puff sleeved blouse and shoulder shawl. She looked the complete pretty Bohemian for her *tableau vivante* with Bill.

As they changed Detty said to Mara, 'This is the second most important day of my life so far – make me look right.'

Mara rushed around attending to Detty's dress and her long chestnut hair with the same attention that, seemingly aeons before, she had cherished Detty's wounded body under very different circumstances. Finally they were both satisfied that they looked as good as possible and they went down to the hall.

Sophie was acting as Mistress of Ceremonies, flushed but capable. She was surrounded by numerous musicians and choir asking 'Frau Gräfin this' and 'Frau Gräfin the other'.

At last everything was in its place and the orchestra started the *Vorspiel* to *Der Freischutz*. It was played with gusto and not a little skill and Detty found herself thinking that perhaps only here in Bavaria could you find horn playing of that quality in what was essentially a village band. Bill then gave a vigorous *'Che gelida manina'* and the audience swore that he never took his eyes off the tiny pretty Polin whose hand he held throughout the entire rendering.

Detty and Marc sang *'La ci darem la mano'*, which got a special reception, particularly when Marc said to the audience afterwards that perhaps he and Bill should reverse roles. Detty added that she was quite happy as an innocent peasant girl. The locals who knew what was in the air between their young count and his beautiful foreign girlfriend, who did after all speak *'echt Deutsch'* enjoyed it and applauded loudly.

Gertrude then played a virtuoso performance of the Chopin second scherzo. The hall roared into applause for the local heroine and Detty found herself calling *'Brava'* louder than anybody – amusing her father but scandalising her mother. They broke for drinks and canapés. After the short interval, Sophie played three Brahms waltzes and then announced to the audience that Frau Bernadette had a something special to say. The latter went up onto the platform and Gertrude again took Sophie's place at the piano.

Detty then spoke to the hall, 'Frau Sophie, Herr Max, *teure Freunde*, this is a wonderful night and a very important one for me. I owe my life and my happiness to two people who are here tonight. I ask you to allow me to express my feelings for them in song in the presence of you all. The first song I will dedicate to Frau Tamara. Many of you have got to know her here as a wonderful person but nobody can know, as I do, the strength and courage which she can produce in dire adversity. Hers is the spirit of this song from the great work, which started this concert.' She nodded to Trudi who began to play and Detty started her recitative:

'Du zurnest mir?
Doch kannst du wahnen,
Ich fahle nicht mit dir?
Nur ziemen einer Maid nicht Tranen!'

As she began the aria she tried to make her voice dance lightly and accurately over the notes.

'Trube Augen,
Liebchen, taugen
Einem holden Freundin nicht.'

She knew she was working hard on unfamiliar territory but the song had always reminded her of Mara and she wanted to sing it for her so much. She began to feel more confident, the trills were coming off – her faithful companion was behaving well even if it was being asked to jump some strange hurdles.

She was enjoying herself as she started the last section and her big voice felt under control and was rippling over the runs almost, she thought, like a proper soubrette. As she came to the final repeated line:

she turned towards Mara who was flushed and happy in her Bohemian dress and sang directly to her. With the instinct of an artist she knew it sounded right, and she also knew that Mara understood it as a public and sacred token of her thanks and her love. As she finished and the audience applauded she left the platform, went over to Tamara and kissed her on both cheeks before returning to bow to the audience.

She gave no introduction to the next piece, just waited for silence and nodded imperceptibly to Gertrude. This was home territory, far from easy and very important, but she knew that she could do it well. The hushed visitors realised that something very special was happening. She stole a glance at Marc who understood something, but not all, of the scenario. He looked very handsome in dress uniform, rooted immobile, listening on a high stool to the left of the platform. She hoped that he had remembered – too late to do anything, if he hadn't now anyway.

'Einsam in truben Tagen', she began softly and sadly describing Elsa's sorrowing vision mirroring her own despair captive in an infernal land. She followed Elsa's description of the growing intensity until the lament filled the skies and she falls asleep at last. Trudi's fingers floated ethereally over the notes. With the excitement and hope swelling in her voice Detty continued:

'In lichter Waffen scheine ein Ritter nahte da,
So tugendlicher Reine ich keinen noch ersah;'

She looked at Marc who was gazing at her bemused. On she went until with:

'Des Ritters will ich wahren Er soll mein Streiter sein!'

---

29 Are you vexed with me
    You can't really doubt how I feel for you
    But you are not made for tears
    The eyes of such a lovely girl
    should shine with happiness not be troubled
    Dear friend have no more pain

She turned fully towards him and continued:

'Hort, was dem Gottesandten Ich biete far Gewahr:'

gradually as she sang she crossed the platform towards Marc with her voice gently softening until she reached:
'Will er Gemahl mich heissen, Geb'ich ihm, was ich bin!' [30]

For months she had planned this moment and she put her entire soul into it. She dropped her head low before him with her gold silk skirt flowing behind her and her red gold hair glinting down her back. She held out her left hand towards him. He knew his cue, as she had always known he would, and deftly slipped the ring onto her outstretched finger. The beautiful emerald Celtic cross flashed green fire in the lights. He pulled her to her feet and kissed her. There was a brief pause as the hall drank in the scene, then they went wild with applause and congratulations. Detty said afterwards that she didn't know if the cheering was for her singing, the romance of the occasion or the affection that they all felt for Marc and the von Ritters. Her own family looked slightly stunned as the clapping and cheering broke out.

Finally Marc led her out by hand onto the centre of the platform and Detty was able to thank and applaud Gertrude, her faithful collaborator, who was herself standing and smiling by the piano. Marc raised his hands for silence, which was slow in coming, 'Dr and Mrs O'Neill, *meine Eltern*, Nuala and Mara, *sehr teure Freunde,*' he said. 'As you have seen Frau Bernadette has just asked me to marry her and in a spectacular manner entirely typical of her genius. No one argues with Frau O'Neill when she has made up her mind. I love her deeply so you have witnessed my instant obedience.'

---

30 Alone in my saddest days
In shining armour a knight appeared to me
A man of such splendour as I had never seen
I shall wait for the knight, my champion.
Hear what reward I offer for the one sent by God. If he will be my husband, I shall give him all that I am.

They laughed as he went on, his German very correct and serious, 'I have only one reservation. She has cast herself as Elsa, which is just because she is true and beautiful and fortunately she knows my name already.'

The audience laughed again.

'But many of you will know, as I know, that she has other qualities which are more reminiscent of *Brünnhilde* – *die Walküre*. She is as fearsome in battle as she is beautiful in love.'

Detty hung her head down half in mock, half in serious embarrassment.

Tamara enjoying herself in the front row cried, '*Hört, hört!*' scandalising her father in turn.

Marc continued, 'I found her in a rubbish bin and then we had many adventures that ended in her performing a single-handed act of bravery which amazed my commanding officer, my veteran troopers not to say myself. Before that Bernadette had been subjected to a series of ordeals so terrible that I cannot bear to think of them on this happy night. But she came through these full of courage and thirsting for justice and revenge. I must however, pay tribute to someone whose own courage helped Bernadette to survive, Tamara Nicolaevna, whose cheerful fortitude in the face of abominable evil has already been celebrated by Bernadette in song this evening.

'Tamara is now one of us and we are proud to have her but she still feels deeply for Moltravia. I would like to pay a tribute to her and her father. Further I want to say that if Moltravia, free and united, could produce men and women like them then we can look with joy and gratitude at one of our eastern neighbours after so many terrible years of conflict. Herr Oblov was born in Krakow and studied at the Jagiellonian University and as a tribute I tried this evening to find someone who could play the great trumpet call from the *Basylika Mariacki*. Sadly I failed – Helmut has a trumpet but nobody knows the notes.

'Finally, before we break for supper, Detti and I would like to sing for you the song that brought us together on the rubbish dump – Trudi – please.'

They sang *Zueignung* as they had sung it those months ago – first her then him then both of them together. Yet again the hall stood and

284

cheered. As they prepared to go to supper, a small figure climbed onto the platform and waved his hands for silence. In very correct high German, Nicklaus Oblov said, 'Frau Gräfin, Herr Graf, Meinen Damen und Herren, it has been a long and very moving evening but I would like to keep you a moment longer. Graf Marc has been very generous about my daughter, my one-time country and its ancient historical capital city. In the last week I have realised that it would be my proudest moment to see my Krakow twinned with your Nuremburg as they both represent the best and the worst in the history of our world and would symbolise our hopes for the future. This may be difficult but I know that both here and there the best will triumph eventually. At present, sadly, this cannot be but if Herr Helmut will do me the honour of lending me his instrument...'

He took the trumpet and played the magical haunting notes of medieval Krakow. He broke off suddenly as always. This was at the moment when the trumpeter watching on the church tower had been struck in the throat by an enemy arrow. Somehow moved by the experience if not understanding its true significance, many were dabbing their eyes as they went to supper.

Afterwards they all became one as they joined in the hymn of hope and freedom which is the finale of *Fidelio*. Detty was touched and pleased to note her father and Nicklaus Oblov on the platform amongst the basses. These represented what she loved most – with Ireland, Germany and the eastern lands rejoicing together was anything impossible?

8

KILDARE AND ENGLAND

When I first came here you were always singing

SEAMUS HEANEY: FIELD WORK, THE SINGERS HOUSE

The runway at Dublin Airport glistened in the drizzle. Detty gazed at the familiar scene bemused as she watched her father push the baggage trolley to the car in the airport car park. Surely it had never happened, she had never been away or rather she was just coming back from a normal term at Oxford. The last nine months – both the horrors and the glories – seemed a dream. Only the aching stiffness of her back after the flight told her it was real. If Marc or even Mara had been able to come everything might have seemed more connected but Marc, although still theoretically on leave, had been called back to Stuttgart and Mara had stayed in Oberdorf to keep her father company and try to negotiate her university place at Munich. They were to come together to Ireland in a week's time.

The M50 with its bordering factories joined the M7 with still more industry in ugly evidence of the Dublin economic miracle. Eventually they reached the green fields – still that startling intense green of the cliché. She looked out on the Kildare countryside, which was sodden but homely and gentle and realised the truth of another cliché, like many of her exiled fellow countrymen, she had never thought to see it again. The white and grey bungalows shone damp in the rain. It was a complete contrast to the riot of colours in Oberdorf that she had left a few hours before but for all that it gave her a warm feeling of belonging. They turned off the motorway by the racecourse at Naas and soon left the main road before Athy to reach Ballyinch. As they rounded the last bend, the grey rendered family house was there. It was as she had always remembered it, with its extension at one end, once her father's main surgery now a branch accommodating the consulting room and waiting area which he still used, although the main medical centre was in Athy. The walls here too wept in the wet and the sodden path squelched under their feet as they left the car with the spring, rain-soaked light already fading.

Detty kissed her mother and then went straight to her bedroom somehow urgent to see that nothing had changed. Sure enough the same childhood mementoes and teenage tokens – photographs of set dancing competitions, and later the pipe band. Then there were horses with all the rosettes, pictures of pop stars mingled with classical musicians and holiday souvenirs. Prominent was a signed photograph of Henry Schliessen, the young handsome American Heldentenor, who for several years now had set all Europe and America ablaze. '*To Bernadette with all best wishes, Hank.*' She remembered vividly the thrill when it had arrived through the post. She didn't dare share her excitement with the other girls in the convent as, after all, Schliessen wasn't a rock star and wasn't even Irish. They wouldn't have understood. All the treasures were still there. Another life, another age almost another planet – ruefully Detty thought that she would spend some time rearranging things before Marc arrived. She didn't really know why she felt that she had to hide her childhood from the man who already knew so much about her but somehow the nick-nacks and the gangly little girl in her kilt didn't quite fit with Special Operations and Munich high life. She looked at the latest of the photos from only the previous year. One showed her triumphant behatted self on a fine hunter belonging to her Uncle Christy. She had just won the Ladies Race at the Kildare Foxhounds point-to-point. It was a day that she had savoured. That photo would remain near the front of the shelf when Marc arrived.

She had left a lot of her clothes at Oberdorf but she still had massive baggage, which she had to try and accommodate in this modest room. Her new clothes highlighted the contrast between the impoverished student of last summer and the not-so-impoverished near-countess of this one.

She went downstairs to join her mother. Peggy was already in the kitchen grumbling to Maire, the woman who helped her from the village, that in the excitement of meeting Detty she hadn't remembered half the shopping. She was therefore woefully lacking in ingredients for the welcome-home cake. Maire spotted Detty in the doorway and rushed over to hug her kiss her.

'Darling Detty, isn't the finest thing that you're home. Joe and I thought that you'd never be seen again. Such dreadful stories there were of what had happened to you. Are you all right now?'

'A lot of the stories were true, Maire, but I'm better than ever now.'

'That's great and I hear you've got a lovely man but I reckon he's the lucky one. Joe was quite jealous but he says he'll forgive you if you'll come to the bar again. He says *The Fields of Athenry* has lost its soul since you've been away.'

Joe, Maire's husband, was the fluter of the village and long ago had started to accompany Detty when she sang the old songs in The Victory Plough which was Terry Boyd's bar. There had been an O'Neill family row when her father first realised that Detty was going to the bar in her school holidays. Brian had said that it was intolerable, out of keeping for a young girl let alone his daughter and that she would become a drunk, learn bad language and be in moral danger.

Her mother, however, had come to her rescue on this occasion saying that Detty should be encouraged to learn Irish things. It was the tradition of Aosdána and anyway he had always grumbled at the amount of time Detty spent on 'that heavy German music'. Brian had snorted and said in Detty's hearing that that was all very well but liking

Irish music was no reason for his daughter becoming a barroom tart. At that Detty had exploded and for the first time since childhood really stood up to her father. In an outburst of righteous anger she said with force and reason that Irish traditional music had no connection with immorality. Father and daughter went at it hammer and tongs for some time. Eventually Brian realised that he had gone far too far. He had been surprised at the adult contempt his adored elder daughter was able to throw at him. She was a child no longer. Peggy again had to step in as the peacemaker and had pointed out that it really was the music that Detty loved. She only drank apple juice and that anyway the entire male population of Ballyinch would go to the stake sooner than see a hair on her head harmed. Brian apologised to Detty, and father and daughter eventually agreed a contract and calmed their Celtic tempers. Detty was allowed to go and play her banjo and sing at The Plough as long as she was back by 10.30. He hinted that she shouldn't tell the nuns that she had been frequenting pubs when she got back to school.

She thought of all these schoolgirl troubles as she headed towards the bar, banjo in hand, after supper that evening. The music was clearly audible several houses away down the close-packed village street. She started humming the *ceili* tune before she pushed through the door. Conn, the accordion, Barry the fiddler, Kevin the pipes, Joe and a couple of others were hard at it. Nowadays Terry thrust a glass of Beamish into her hand rather than apple juice, as soon as she entered but the money was waived away as usual, making her feel rather guilty given her changed financial circumstances. She waited for the pause and the welcome, tuned the banjo and joined in. It was all so familiar that the last year and all its events seemed never to have happened as the music flowed on.

It was her turn to sing and her reputation earned her a hushed expectancy. She started with her more cosmopolitan favourites. The first, appropriately, was '*Did you miss me?*' with the others all joining the refrain '*Yes, we missed you*'. Then she joined in a jig before making a rather unsuccessful attempt to convince the company that she was '*a poor little beggar girl*'.

The music got more serious with Detty singing two ballads to the hushed barroom. They all clapped and Barry who had teased her unmercifully since she was a schoolgirl said, 'Hi Detty, that's not the sort of thing you sing for those fine Dublin people, I bet.'

'Sure it is and the next time we want a decent fiddler we'll send for you too!'

They paused and Detty announced that she would like to bring a special visitor with her next week – the man she was going to marry. There was a general groan of disappointment. Barry asked anxiously, 'He's not a Dub is he?'

'No, he's German. He's called Marc and sings.'

There was general interest, surprise and questions. Joe summed it up that if she couldn't marry a decent Irish lad he supposed it was not too bad and at least she wasn't marrying a Saxon from her university. She sweetened the news by adding there would be a second visitor in the form of a very pretty friend that she had met while she was away. This finally secured the vote of approval.

Barry then serenaded Detty with the *Rose of Castlerae* with the words suitably modified to Ballyinch and Moltravia at the appropriate places in the song. Detty knew what was expected of her next and there was a hush of expectancy as Detty started to play the haunting introduction of *The Fields of Athenry*. She sang the ballad, amid flash backs of Moltravia adding deep emotion to the words that she knew so well, and had last sung at the Sacred Heart lecture. She almost allowed her emotion to overcome her professionalism and was near to tears as the ballad faded away and the applause and murmurs of congratulation broke out. She told them, by way of explanation, 'Somehow the last year has made it mean even more to me.'

The final jig session warmed them up before they all said they would see her next week 'with your man'.

*

The high-speed ferry slid into Dun Laoghaire quay. Mara had forced Marc to remain on deck until the last moment to watch the sweep of Dublin bay from Bray Head and the mountains round to Howth and Ireland's Eye. This was special, as in their different ways, they were silently paying homage to the person who had brought them here, and meant so much to each of them. This was Detty's adored homeland. Marc knew that she had made no secret of how much it meant to her from the first moment that she had said to him, 'I'm Irish,' when he committed the unforgivable sin, as he now realised, of accusing her of being English.

Marc thought of his preconceptions of Ireland – catholic, beautiful – bad food, bad roads, friendly people and perpetual rain. It wasn't raining today and the soft light was indeed beautiful – the more so after the harsh contrasts of Moltravia and the colours of his own summer Franconia. Mara was looking entranced first to the mistiness of Wicklow then north to the rising bulk of Howth.

'We must go,' said Marc, realising that holding up the whole Anglo-Irish contingent at Dun Laoghaire with a large German registered Mercedes wouldn't be diplomatic. They rushed down to the car just as the others were about to move.

As he drove off the pier, he saw the tall silhouette of the figure he adored standing a trifle anxiously at the side. He searched desperately for a place to stop, leapt out and kissed her.

'Get in,' he said.

'But it's only a couple of steps,' she protested with her Irish accent stronger on her native heath.

'To be sure,' he said, mimicking her with not a bad imitation of the Irish brogue beloved of English music halls but he was rewarded by a solid punch in the midriff from his beloved.

'You'll behave yourself here or I'll call the *Fianna* out from the Hill of Allen to chase you back to Nibelheim' she said mixing her mythologies happily and grinning with that open smile which had first melted his heart. They headed towards the restaurant at the head of the town pier.

The oysters were sublime, the Cloudy Bay Sauvignon rich and complex, as always. The following seafood platter with Dublin Bay prawns, which Marc would have called langoustines, mussels and the finest turbot fillet he had ever dreamed about, melted in the mouth.

As he left the restaurant, he looked reflectively round the bay finally gazing at Bray head opalescent in the misty afternoon sunshine and said reflectively, 'Detti, why do you tell me – what is it the Londoners say – porky pasties?'

Detty collapsed with uncontrollable giggles.

'Pies!' she said not knowing whether he had done it deliberately. 'Porky pies – has to be to rhyme with lies and anyway pasties are Cornish not cockney.'

'I see,' said Marc with a mannered Teutonic seriousness, which she was now certain was part of a wind-up.

'But you said that it rains all the time here and the food is awful, Detti? You could have travelled the length and breadth of Europe and not eaten anything as good as that. And now we have the sunshine!'

'Did you really like it?' said Detty warmly holding up her face to be kissed and basking contentedly in the middle ground between love of the man and love of the land. Then with a start she remembered Mara whose English, although improving was not up to word plays and rhyming slang, looking mystified at their side. She switched into German and lamely tried to explain the joke. It didn't work but Mara smiled happily all the same.

'We aren't in a hurry.' Detty made a statement rather than asking a question adding, 'I'll drive then you can both look.'

Marc nodded and she slipped comfortably into the driving seat. They set off amongst the white seaside houses past Joyce's Martello tower. In a few minutes Detty was struggling to find a parking space in a crowded road lined with restaurants and small, interesting looking shops. She eventually turned into a side street and found a narrow space, easing the big Mercedes between two vans.

They got out and Mara struggled to get her tongue around Glastule Road written on the street sign. Detty headed purposefully to a shop marked Caveston's and Mara tried her pronunciation again this time out loud. Detty nodded with approval and they went inside.

Marc again revised his unspoken prejudices about Irish food. There were counters of fresh delicious cheeses, featuring the Irish but with some good continental examples. In the back was almost the finest display of fish that he had seen. It reminded him of the display of an improbable merchant outside Lübeck that he would always remember.

'Great to see you, Detty. It's been too long. How are you then?' said the young girl who served them from behind the counter. Mara reckoned that she must have been about her own age perhaps slightly older. Detty introduced Mara and then Marc as her fiancé and they chatted for a few minutes about their families and Marc and Mara's origins. Detty left laden with a selection of Cooleeney, Carigaline, Milleens and Cashel Blue – unfamiliar but seductive looking cheeses and a deep succulent side of smoked wild salmon.

They headed south. Mara saw the countryside dominated by great dramatic hills and valleys. She wondered how it was possible not to be overwhelmed by such wild beauty within a few kilometres of the ferry and urban life. To their left was a great lake, more dramatic than anything that she had ever seen in her fractured native land. Detty told them with assumed nonchalance that these were the Wicklow Mountains, 'A bit of a cliché really but worth seeing as it's ye' first visit.'

Mara, who knew her friend well by this time, detected the bursting pleasure and pride that Detty tried to hide when showing the breathtaking beauty of her homeland. It was not for nothing that the casual suggestion that they were 'not in a hurry' had been made at the ferry dock. They turned off the road and parked. There, they were told, was Glendalough and the beehive hut of St Kevin with his cave in the rock above the Lough. Mara was having her first glimpse of the places of those great Irish saints whose feats in saving Christendom she had heard at her father's knee in a far away country.

As they walked, Detty was nestling at Marc's side. 'Do you know what St Kevin did when a seductive girl followed him to this place?' Detty asked, looking wide-eyed up at Marc. He shook his head. 'He picked her up and dropped her in the lake and she drowned.' Detty was still eyeing Marc quizzically and seductively.

'I knew that I would never make a saint,' replied Marc, seizing her round the waist and lifting her high.

'This is more like the fighting and dancing they held here later.' squealed Detty and Mara suddenly felt lonely that there was nobody to squeeze her and lift her high. They got back in the car and drove on. There was a particularly luscious piece of woodland that Detty told them was Avondale, remarking enigmatically and without further explanation that it was the home of the last real High King of Ireland. They were off onto the country roads past Aughrim with its battle site until, facing the westering sun, they crossed over the hills to Tinahely and stopped for glasses of the deep dark brew called Guinness at Murphy's Hotel. If truth be told Mara, when she first tasted it, wasn't sure she liked it. Soon the general enthusiasm for the rich bitter draft was infectious and swept over her. For years afterwards a flavour, any flavour, that recalled that unique taste brought back the aura of Detty and that magical evening in the Wicklow Mountains. The mountains were now moving behind them as they passed into Carlow skirting the lower hilly farmland, still twisting through country lanes on a route that Mara thought it would take a millennium to learn. She was entranced by this narrow winding, hilly country so very different from her flat wide desolate and desolated homeland. She noticed a signpost to Castledermot and a moment later Detty pulled to the side of the road and leapt out, smiling she kissed first Mara and then Mark greeting them with, *'Failte go Cil Darra* – Welcome to Kildare.'

Echoing Marc's proud welcome to them both at the borders of Bavaria three months before. Again Mara, proud as she was of her adopted country, wondered what it must be like to welcome guests in freedom to the land of your birth.

'It's not a *Freistaat,* though come to think of it, I suppose it once was. However, we have a lot of saints, horses and soldiers to make up for that – to say nothing of the whole nation of the *Fianna,* the old magic people, living under the Hill of Allen.'

Welcome at home was tea, barmbrack and Peggy fussing. Marc, however, laid into the rich fruit bread saying that it was quite wonderful – rather like the stollen of Nuremberg but, tactfully, even more delicious, he thought.

Peggy decided that he would do as a son-in-law and that perhaps Germans were not that different from other young men. When it came to appetite, this one didn't seem hard to please at all.

The following day they set out exploring Kildare town and the countryside after a leisurely breakfast. A heavy shower took them into The Silken Thomas for coffee and introductions and gossip took a good chunk of the morning. Feeling a bit guilty and with the sun trying its watery best to break through they decided to work up an appetite by walking beside the golf course towards The Curragh. They had gone several kilometres on the old back road when the two visitors stopped and gasped.

Detty had been brought up with the countryside and around horses all her life. She loved and knew them with the easy affection born of complete familiarity. Marc and Mara, looked at the great expanse of green of The Curragh with the running rail white against green sward sweeping from the mile start angling slightly away towards the distant stands.

'That is fantastic,' he said. 'I have never seen grass anything like it. How do they fertilise it?'

'They don't. It has just grown here undisturbed for several thousand years.'

'Do they often have race meetings here?'

'Oh, every two or three weeks here in summer but of course there are lots of other courses quite near so we never go short. This is the home of Irish flat racing – they run the Derby here and lots of other famous races. Would you like to go to a meeting one day?'

'Yes, please!' Mara and Marc almost shouted in unison with an enthusiasm that came from the heart.

'That's easy, at least. My aunt's married to a trainer and he's bound to have a runner soon. I'll give him a ring as soon as we get in.'

The visitors enthusiasm took them to Naas the following Sunday to meet Deidre and Christy who had a five-year-old in a novice hurdle. The colt, called Pantelin, had won at Clonmel the previous week and carried a five pound penalty. Christy was not optimistic about him with this disadvantage but had decided to let him take his chance. Marc, who had ridden a bit and been to the races at Baden grasped the situation and Detty, switching into German, did her best to explain the finer points to Mara. The latter was filled with enthusiasm but her face fell a mile when their runner could only manage a creditable third place. He had run a clever race under the big weight and quickened well at the distance.

Mara's morale improved when she discovered that this result, far from being a disaster, entitled her to a small but satisfactory dividend on her Tote place ticket. She returned from the windows beaming and clutching her ten euros unbelievingly. Deidre whispered to Detty that her friend had clearly got the bug and was well on the way to becoming a high roller.

As they parted after a successful day, they were invited to visit Christy's stable at the end of the week for lunch. They arrived at coffee time and Christy started to show them round. They looked at the horses in training and then went through to the attached stud. As they walked across the yard Christy said, 'There is someone here that I would like ye' to meet.'

Detty looked at him quizzically. He walked straight to the furthest box and pointed inside. The legend on the door said, 'Filly Foal Illumined out of Phoenix Light by Norway's Mast 13 March 20--.

'We all call her Firebrand,' said Christy looking at Detty who was transfixed by the young foal. Two thoughts ran through Detty's head, the first was that this youngster had the look of eagles in her eye and the second was that in some way the filly would become part of her life. She hardly heard Christy's next remark.

'She was born on your birthday last year. I think that was what gave her name. It was after you. She's growing well.' He grinned.

'Who does she belong to?' asked Detty.

'Why us at present,' said Christy. 'We bred her and we own, the dam, Phoenix Light – she's over there.'

Marc stood in the background looking thoughtful

Much later, the day before the wedding, Christy and Deidre appeared at Oberdorf and gave Detty an envelope. It contained a simple card with a photograph of a beautiful foal on it.

'*To Bernadette and Marc with love – she's your wedding present.*'

'Marc tells us you can afford her training fees.' Added Deidre as she arrived in Obersdorf.

'Darling Deidre – if it's for Firebrand. I'll do a strip show and record phoney Irish ballads to pay for her. Now tell me can we come back and talk to her as soon as we are back from honeymoon?'

'Of course, she will be most put out if you don't, she likes a chat.'

The eastern sun woke her early, perhaps too early. Although they had broken their journey at the *Vier Jahreseiten* in Munich, it was not until they arrived in Venice that Detty was able to throw off the feelings of unreality that had attended the last two days. Memories flooded in. First, there was the civil ceremony at the little *Standesamt* in Bad Steben. Simple but thrilling and leading up to the great day. She remembered waking in her familiar bedroom at Oberdorf with the Lanoure model dress with its dramatic line hanging in the corner. There was hair dressing and getting ready, with Hildegard more agitated than Detty herself. There had been a quick glass of champagne with her two bridesmaids, Nuala mightily impressed and vulgar as ever and Mara pink and silent with joy and emotion. In the fortunate sunshine, with the girls, she took the short walk across the park to the little onion-domed church carrying her salt and bread.

In the German tradition, she met Marc at the church door. Then she had a complete surprise. As they walked to the altar, they were accompanied by the traditional music of Barry the fiddler, Joe the fluter and Kevin playing wonderfully as always on the Uilleann pipes, she was hearing the old familiar sounds of her Kildare musical childhood. Marc had not wasted his time getting to know her friends at the bar. This had to be the work of the fantastic man that she was here to marry. Her own family wouldn't have dared and only Marc amongst her Bavarian family knew of the happy hours that she had spent making music with these special friends. As she stood beside him she squeezed his hand and whispered, 'Thank you – but I've forgotten to bring my banjo.'

'First things first,' he whispered back.

Cool from the burning light of a scorching summer day, they had celebrated their marriage Mass. Trudi had mobilised the vocal resources of the district to sing the seven part Bruckner Ave Maria Motet as the musical centrepiece. The bride had tears streaming down her face as she listened and cared nothing for her make-up but she did remember to hold out her right hand for her wedding ring and change her engagement ring over. They came out into the porch into the sun as dazzled by the light and their happiness they received blessings in five languages. Marc kissed his bride and both his bridesmaids to the pleasure of the onlookers and the delirium of the photographers. Detty put on a theatrical pout when he seemed to spend rather too long cuddling his senior bridesmaid and the onlookers loved it all.

She had loved the homely music that greeted her at the church but there was another surprise in store. As they crossed the *Hofgarten* back to the Schloss a double choir sent the noble melody of Orlando Lassus' *Gloria* rising into the summer air. Trudi had worked with her usual enthusiasm to get the double choir perfectly acoustically arranged under the old walls of the garden. The Oberdorf band, happy to be back with wind music on the great occasion, had produced miracles for Trudi who directed the entire ensemble from an improvised podium under the great lime tree. They all gave a good account of themselves. As they stopped to listen, Marc wondered if they knew they were singing in front of the director of, perhaps, the greatest opera chorus in the world. If so it certainly didn't seem to put them off. Detty was so moved at the end that she was still in tears as she dragged Marc over to them to thank them.

Dinner at the Schloss followed.

They had danced the traditional dances, first together then with the parents. Bill had produced a scurrilous speech in English in the form of a *Heldenlied* with references to dustcarts, motorbikes and canned beer. By the end both the Irish and the German contingents were fairly puzzled but they all roared with laughter at the bits that they understood and it didn't seem to matter. The dancing and singing had gone far into the night with their many friends.

They didn't leave until late into the following morning. Jan, from the local bus service had volunteered and drove them to Munich. By the time he drove into the *Maximilianstrasse*, it was nearly dawn.

Sleep and love took them to an hour the day after when breakfast was no longer an option. They just made the Tiepolo Express for Venice which left at 11:30am arriving at the *Hauptbahnhof* with much more fluster than anticipated.

Even at 6:30pm the persistent private motor boatmen from Santa Lucia still had to be fought off. Eventually they were able to catch the

Vaporetto Uno, as Marc had decreed, to go down the Grand Canal slowly, past the *Palazzo Vendramin,* as the light faded to evening in the west behind them. They looked at the *Palazzo* in silence both thinking of Wagner and the oft told tales of his death there. They left the boat at the Schiavoni and walked the short distance to the Hotel. They scandalised the doorman of the *Danieli* by arriving carrying their own hand luggage.

Morning flooded *St Giorgio Maggiore* sweeping on to the *Redentore.* Detty stood at the window musing about the inequalities of life passing so swiftly from horror to bliss. That quotation about the pain of recalling a happy time in wretchedness came back to her as it had on that terrible day at the Farm. She had never looked it up or found out where it really came from. Fortunately, this time it was in reverse and the feeling was blissful. The *Redentore* – the Redeemer – it was a strangely unusual name for a church and the theme of redemption – of saving – preoccupied her for some minutes.

She was determined to visit this church with its unusual votive name. Saving wasn't just about souls, it was about institutions, about freedom, about values and about suppressing horror and cruelty. These things had a different meaning when you had been so close to them and suffered them yourself. She thought how lucky she had been. She might have been destroyed by the horror and humiliation of her experience. The terrors of her dreams and sudden recollections made her realise how close she had come to her personal precipice. Her love, her Faith and indeed, she had to admit it to herself, the triumph of her revenge had, she was sure, saved her. She wasn't very proud of the part that naked vengeance had played in sustaining her but she could not deny it.

She wondered about Mara who had not only had to suffer torture herself but had seen the certainties of her childhood, including her mother and her childhood friend, destroyed on a wave of beastliness. Mara still couldn't talk about some of it and never mentioned her mother. She had every right to be terribly injured psychologically as well as physically. Detty thought and hoped that she also had survived, nourished by the love and respect that she enjoyed in her new surroundings. She knew that Mara had not finished with Moltravia. How could she with her father as the focus of hope of the exiles and oppressed? But somehow she needed her German home and her Bavarian friends to sustain her for whatever lay ahead. Detty had another barely formed worry. For all the joking and the horseplay, she had seen an attachment grow between Bill and Mara and deep inside she had wondered if her friend might one day become her sister-in-law. Now Detty loved her new brother-in-law dearly. They laughed and joked endlessly together but she was aware that he was a rolling stone with a roving eye and she was desperately afraid that Mara might get hurt once more in love as she had been by the NAS.

She sighed realising that this was not the moment to think of such things and was drifting towards the bathroom. A discrete knock at the door arrested her. She took one look at her new, sleeping husband. She realised that yet again they had over-estimated their capacity for morning rising and decided that it would be up to her to respond. A uniformed boy carrying a large silver tray loaded with coffee, croissants and that peculiar overcooked dark jam, which the Italians value as *marmelata artigianata*, stood in the doorway.

'*Buongiorno, Signora Contessa,*' said the youngster. '*Permesso, dove vorebbero metterli?*'[31]

Taken aback, Detty was struck dumb for a moment before indicating the side table. She had partially prepared herself to be referred to as Gräfin or Frau Gräfin although no one had used the title yet and she would still, for some time to come, think that it referred only to Sophie. *Contessa* however was a new experience and she realised guiltily that she rather enjoyed it. Joining in the spirit of the moment, as soon as the door had shut behind the boy, she went over to the half-awake Marc and whispered in his ear, '*Cafe, Signor Conte Capitano?*' and then wondered if she had got the three titles the right way round.

They took the *vaporetto* to the *Giudecca*. Detty pulled Marc up the steps into the Basilica of the *Redentore* half expecting an anticlimax. In a dream she paid the tourists' fee to the sacristan, her eyes fixed on the shining interior. She led Marc up through the church there they knelt in prayer and silence. Their eyes slowly turned upwards past the two

---

31 May I, where should I put it?

guardian saints to the shining marble altar, which ascended in stage after stage to the Cross and the Crown. There they stayed for some timeless instants then they lit votive candles with personal silent prayers. Then they turned, reluctantly, past the fresh flowers to come again into the splendour of the misty Venetian sunlight.

*

Term finished at the beginning of December and she drove back enjoying the winter hills but sad that she knew she was going to be alone. Marc had gone on exercises somewhere in Norway and would not be back until just before Christmas at the earliest. She could have returned to Ireland but decided instead that she wanted to get to know the new home that they had instantly loved, but had hardly occupied. She spent a couple of hours dreamily arranging things in the house. It had once been a pub and the metal rod that had displayed the inn sign was still to be seen on the front wall. Their living room was the old bar lying slightly below the level of the road outside. A half stairway led up to the library, it was a good size, but was made smaller by the upright Bechstein and piles of study books and scores eating into the space. The dining room and kitchen were at the back down another half staircase. The house had the advantage that, although right in the middle of the town and a few metres from the river, no one lived in the adjacent buildings so there was no one she could disturb by practising. The garden was a paved courtyard half covered by a pergola which ran along the side of the house dividing it from the brewery road. Upstairs was reached by a wooden staircase behind where the bar had been and consisted of two rooms, the bathroom and then there was an even smaller staircase leading to the tiny gabled attic rooms.

Up to now they had only had the odd weekend and night together in the house when the demands of university and Shrivenham permitted. She had not done much work on these flying trips but she had planned a serious assault on the books during the Christmas vacation as she knew Marc had to be away for much of the time. She also had a good deal of leeway to make up after her long absence, caused by the extraordinary happenings of the previous year. Eventually she was satisfied with the books that she had arranged round the desk in the library. The computer table that she had brought from Oxford was at its side and all was ready for work.

After a final look raound she went downstairs and slipped out into the darkening December afternoon. She ran quickly towards the bridge along the riverside road with the lights of the clubhouse shining across the cold river. As she reached the junction, she took a quick look past the church up the busy Hart Street. She turned away onto the pedestrian solitude of the winter bridge. The river was beginning to look misty and from somewhere on the Berkshire side there came the sweetly acrid smell of a garden bonfire, which was somehow always England. It was an essence different from the peat smoke of her old home and the pines and meadows of her new one. Never entirely comfortable with the English, she nevertheless loved the countryside of England and in her more generous moments could appreciate its part in producing the smug detachment of its disdainful people.

The towpath was deserted; apart from a dark bird that she couldn't identify which swooped in a low arc in front of her. Trying to follow the bird as it disappeared in the darkness, she thought about the strange, tortuous path that she herself had followed since she had completed her first years at university. She had been to the threshold of death before returning to this comfortable, prosperous yet still alien life in southern England. She walked quickly thinking of all the heroes of Britain who had passed through this sporting town on their route to rule the Empire and who had so often become the oppressors of her own and many other people.

Then she began to rethink her own story. With Marc and Mara she had enjoyed the further two weeks riding in the Wicklow hills, travelling into Dublin for plays and concerts and visiting old friends around the village. Marc had fished and played golf with her father in between their trips. Brian made no secret of the fact that he liked Marc and thought he would make an ideal husband for his adored, if headstrong, elder daughter. She sensed that he had been deeply disturbed by the horrors that she had endured although he never mentioned it aloud. Rightly or wrongly he felt Marc would 'be a proper husband' and shield her from further disasters of this kind. She was greatly relieved by this as, although they had had many fights, she loved her father dearly. In spite of her professed indifference, it was, in truth immensely important to her that the two most significant men in her life liked each other.

She reached the island with the Temple, white in the surrounding darkness and turned to go back flashing her pocket torch to guide her over the cattle grid. A moorhen, startled, scudded over the water. There was time for tea and she would do a bit of work before the rehearsal so she hurried on past a deserted Remenham Club and a now sparsely lit Leander back over the bridge.

The little house warmed its welcome as she made a pot of Assam and tucked her feet under in an armchair pressing on with Gogol's *Myortvye dushi* and making sporadic notes in cyrillic. She woke suddenly with Gogol on the floor and the clock chiming six. She combed her hair straight, fastened it back grabbed her score and set out for the church. Fortunately it wasn't far and the cold shook off the sleep.

As she walked she felt unusually resentful and a bit mean. She didn't really know why she had got involved in this *Messiah*. The local Catholics had been asked by the parish church to join in a joint performance for Advent. June Keleher, who was a solicitor in the town and a good friend from the Catholic Church, knew vaguely that Detty sang from casual remarks in the pub. She had put Detty's name forward for the chorus in her absence. When Detty had arrived back from spending a weekend in Ireland, June had asked her if it was OK and she had agreed readily. After all, she enjoyed making music of any sort and this seemed a good ecumenical exercise. She had therefore found herself in the ranks of the soprano section of the chorus. At first she had enjoyed it. The music after all was fabulous, if well used, and it was fun meeting new people in the town particularly as they were there so rarely. She understood that young professionals, three of whom lived nearby, had been engaged for the solos but as is usual for these productions they would only appear for the final rehearsals after the chorus had honed itself to a suitable competence.

They were now having the last choral rehearsal before the soloists arrived on Thursday for the performance on the following Saturday.

During the last few rehearsals, Detty had to admit she had found it a bit of a strain. This was partly because the parish church contingent, who, although outwardly charming, seemed to regard the smaller Catholic party with patronising condescension. More important, however, was that Detty was not enjoying her own efforts. At first she had regarded the task of stopping back her voice to blend with the local amateurs, a challenge and a good exercise but now she was beginning to find it tedious and a strain. More worryingly she was also beginning to wonder whether confining her strong, trained, dramatic soprano so strictly was actually doing her demanding alter ego any harm. She realised that she actually wasn't singing very well. It almost seemed that her voice was complaining about being treated in this demeaning way. At all events, she entered the rehearsal that evening feeling pleased that the ordeal was coming to an end and that Saturday would soon arrive.

She met June at the church door as a flurry of sleet swept down Hart Street.

'Hi,' they exchanged. Then June took Detty aback by saying, jokingly, 'You don't feel like singing the solo soprano, do you? Apparently there are big problems as our local girl has dropped out with glandular fever and we can't afford any of the possible replacements. You might have to do it.' June laughed and added, 'I'm only teasing.'

'I'd have no quarrel with doing it,' said Detty spontaneously.

'You're not serious?'

'Yes, Sure I'll do it.'

June looked astounded and somewhat abashed, 'If you're certain you can manage it, we will go and talk to Phyllida.'

'OK,'

Mrs Castle was the inspiration for the performance and the conductor. She was head of music at a local girls' public school and an able musician. Secretly, Detty felt that, although highly competent, she was a bit pedestrian and lacked the divine spark. She told herself, however, that you can't expect to find a Bernhard Meisl conducting a small-town choral society. Detty had kept her profile very low since joining the chorus and Phyllida Castle knew her only as an army officer's wife who was a conscientious but unexceptional chorister. She was therefore surprised and, at first, embarrassed by Detty's offer.

'It's very kind of you, Mrs von Ritter, very kind indeed, but it's a difficult part and – well – I don't want to be insulting or disparage your kind offer but we had hoped to have soloists of – eh – professional standards.'

'Of course, I understand your reluctance but I think that I might be able to do it. I have done some solo work and although I admit the soprano part in the Messiah doesn't lie quite right for my voice – it's not really my ideal tessitura – I would like to try.'

'Well, really I don't know but it is kind of you. We are in a bit of a fix. Do you really think you can? What is your *Fach* by the way?'

There was still a hint of condescension as she looked at Detty dubiously clearly regarding the unknown Irish woman as a last-ditch option with an inflated ego. Detty was now getting a bit fed up and was tempted to reply to the last question by saying *hochdramatische sopran* but thought better of it and contented herself with saying mildly, 'Oh, mostly nineteenth-century stuff – something a little more dramatic – but I do know the part and have sung it in Ireland. Could I perhaps audition for you after the rehearsal? If you don't think that I am up to it, I shall quite understand and you won't have lost any time finding somebody else.'

'Yes, of course, if you really feel you can do it,' replied Mrs Castle still obviously doubting but feeling that she could find no reason to refuse such a logical request and anyway there was no one else in sight.

Detty retired to the tower with a score to prepare, reminding herself and practising the tricky passages. She had no time to really school her voice into the light accurate touch that Handel needed. It was indeed a whole different world from the Wagner that morning. She wasn't satisfied when it was time to go down again. At least the work, which she had known backwards from her schooldays, was firmly at the front of her mind again. It had, after all, first been performed in Dublin and it was always a favourite there as elsewhere. She wondered what Mrs Castle would think if she realised that her new aspirant soprano soloist had been doing the previous day. She had in fact been at Haydn Roberts' house in Oxford being coached in Brünnhilde's awakening by one of the country's leading private voice teachers. That was all very well but now she still had to try to deliver the exacting Baroque vocal line which was very far from all the Wagner that she had been working on recently. She felt quite nervous.

The rehearsal came to an end and, like the congregation in the *Katarinenkirche*, the choristers began to drift out chatting. June and a group of friends from the Catholic contingent lingered by the door, trying to hide their curiosity to hear their companion in her audition. Paul Evans, the organist, was talking to Mrs Castle. Detty walked smiling up to them, 'Is it OK?' They nodded. 'Then I'll sing either '*Rejoice O daughters of Sion*' or "*I know that my Redeemer liveth*", whichever you like or anything else that you would like – as long as I know it that is.' she grinned.

Paul went back to the organ loft and Detty stood at the side of the altar. Paul started the introduction and there was a hushed expectancy from the little group in the doorway. They cannot have had any idea whether triumph or humiliation would follow. A moment later the church was filled with a gentle pure sound flowing miraculously through the tricky intervals and modulations with silky assured beauty. Paul finished the accompaniment and Phyllida Castle stood silent for a long time and then shook herself out of her reverie.

'Mrs von Ritter, that was beautiful, very beautiful indeed. To think that you have been singing in the chorus here – you should have said…'

'Said what? Well I hope it was all right – as I said it doesn't lie exactly right for my voice and, of course, I haven't practised it at all. I hope you understand – I did say that I had done some solo work.'

'Some solo work! It was wonderful. But tell me who is teaching you and what are you doing?'

Her patronising manner had now turned to a deference that was almost obsequious.

'I am studying with Haydn Roberts at Oxford at present and I have studied with Adele O'Mara in Dublin. You are very generous with your praise – I don't think either of my teachers would have been quite so forgiving about the wrong notes or the phrasing errors.'

306

She thought it best not to add that she was also studying with Bernhard Meisl at Bayreuth.

'Phrasing errors and wrong notes? But seriously I don't think that we can afford you. You are a trained soloist with a wonderful voice and professional technique – your fees...' she trailed off embarrassed.

'There's no problem. I live here and haven't I joined the choral society anyway? As a member there will be no fees – it's a pleasure as long as you've no quarrel with my singing.'

'Certainly not – it was glorious – we are so lucky to find you.'

'Singing has one problem for me, it makes me thirsty. Can we go for a drink?'

They were joined by the eavesdroppers and crossed the road to the Angel, June whispered:

'Detty, you are a dark horse. It was wonderful but you obviously knew it beforehand. Where did you learn?'

'For a school festival in Maynooth when I was seventeen but it's not something that you easily forget. Now, what'll it be?'

Detty, still feeling exhilarated by the adrenaline surge that singing always gave, her clasped a pint of Brakespear's old ale and toasted success to the performance. She added that the beer was beautiful even if you had been brought up on Irish stout and that she'd converted her Bavarian husband to it within two hours of arriving in Henley.

'I don't know how you keep your figure drinking that stuff,' said June and added, 'will Marc be able to come on Saturday to hear you?'

'No, he's away in Scotland on exercises for another two weeks – worse luck. But we sing together a lot so he knows what I get up to. He's got a very decent baritone. In fact we first really met when he heard me singing.'

She remembered the day at the Farm when they had made *Zueignung* into an impromptu duet and smiled to herself.

On the Friday she rehearsed with the other soloists. The alto was a performance diploma student from Manchester who lived in Wargrave called Amanda Ewing. She reminded Detty a bit of Trudi Meier – quite academic and serious but with a nice twinkle and a sense of humour. Detty said she always envied the alto part in the *Messiah* which seemed to be richer than the soprano solos. Mandy agreed that perhaps that was so but it made a change from being an also ran in almost everything else. They talked about the Royal Northern College and particularly its reputation for stagecraft training which, having been taught privately, Detty felt she lacked.

The performance, successfully over, they agreed to keep in touch and Detty went back to her house to bash her books for a fortnight until Marc returned for them to go to Oberdorf for the family Christmas.

It was a week after the *Messiah* and started like any other day. Detty got up at seven, dressed in a tracksuit and walked across the bridge before beginning her run along the towpath to the Temple and back. As she entered the house she saw that there was an email. The message read:

'Coming home unexpectedly. Back this evening. Tickets for *Rigoletto* at Covent Garden. Booked in at the Palmerston Hotel off Sussex Gardens for the night. Change there if you want to. Meet you there at 5pm. All my love, M.'

It sounded fun and was all very natural and all part of the life that they had lived together… and yet… and yet.. There was something indefinable that bothered her and aroused her sense of unease. She checked that *Rigoletto* was really on at Covent Garden – it was – and she rang the Palmerston Hotel, to see that it and the booking really existed – it did. Convinced that her fears were only one of her many flashbacks to past horrors she told herself not to be stupid and packed her overnight bag and put the dress bag with her black silk cocktail dress in it over her arm. She walked past the Angel, just discharging the later lunchers, to the station. It was a bleak cold afternoon and she was glad of her thick leggings and woollen knee length dress covered by her Bavarian leather topcoat that had been a present from Marc.

She changed at Twyford and was on the London train before she remembered, to her distress, that she had left her engagement ring on the bathroom shelf back at the house. She never travelled without this precious, symbolic ring that had been the centre of her declaration of love for Marc that Easter. She felt really upset that she was now going to meet him without it. Later she wondered whether it was providence that made her forget it, so that it remained safe or whether rather it was a guerdon that protected her and caused her without it to become exposed to danger. She relished the thought of seeing Marc again, although she admitted to herself that *Rigoletto* wouldn't have been her first choice and by the time she got into London her fears had almost disappeared.

It was raining when the train arrived at Paddington and she abandoned her first idea of walking the few yards to Sussex Gardens and decided to take a taxi. The driver was a cheerful London cabby of the old school.

'Up for the night, Miss?' he said.

Detty replied, 'Yes, I am meeting my husband. We are going to the opera.'

'What are you seeing?'

'Rigoletto.'

'Hope you enjoy it – we were once taken to it by my wife's sister when we were staying in Manchester – all about bodies in bags – I didn't care for it much.'

She didn't know why but Detty shuddered at this inoffensive comment.

'It's not one of my favourites but there are some good tunes.' she answered still wondering why she felt strange.

They arrived outside the hotel and Detty again fought back a sense that all was not right. The place was respectable enough. It certainly wasn't one of the tarts' parlours of King's Cross or even the cheap tourist hotels littering Bloomsbury but somehow it was an odd choice for Marc. He liked to stay at the best and could afford it – the Vier Jahrseiten in Munich, the Maritim Grand Hotel in Berlin, the George Fifth in Paris and in London it was usually Brown's or the Savoy, so why the sudden turn down market? It was true that he also loved simple country places full of character but this didn't fall into that category either – it really seemed strange that he had chosen it. She would ask him what the attraction was when he arrived but it didn't seem important and reasonably content she walked up the short flight of steps to reception.

There was a woman behind the counter who was slightly short and forbidding.

'Good evening, I am Mrs von Ritter. I believe my husband has booked a room for us tonight. Has he arrived yet?'

'Good evening, Madame,' came the reply, 'No he hasn't arrived yet but the room is ready. You are in number 212. Gordon will show you the way.'

9
SCHONDILIE

'Ach Reiter, zieh aus dein Oberkleid
Jungfrauen blut spritzt weit und breit.' [32]

Schondilie Anon. Old German ballad
(with 19th century text)

The corridor reeked of dark respectability as she followed the young boy who carried her bag. She was still carrying her own dress bag, which, she reflected, was not quite what she was used to. Then she remembered her convent upbringing and almost heard the voice of a Mother Theresa telling her that she had no natural, given right to expect another of God's creatures to wait on her at every turn. She felt increasingly uncomfortable but still couldn't order her thoughts or decide what was disturbing her. The boy eventually stopped in front of number 212 and Detty noticed that it was opposite a recess with a fire escape platform in the open area between it and a room across another landing opposite. He unlocked the door, deposited her bag, waited for his tip and disappeared.

---

32 'Oh, knight take off your outer garment,
Maidens blood spurts out far and wide

The room was dark in the winter's afternoon. She just had a chance to take in the double bed, TV and desk/table when she heard a click behind her as if the bathroom door had suddenly opened. She froze and in an instant felt her elbows gripped fiercely from behind. She struggled but it was too late. Her arms were dragged powerfully behind her. As she felt the handcuffs click on her wrists she started to scream but at the moment her mouth opened she felt hands at the side of her head and a firm sponge wedge forced into her mouth gagging her far back over her tongue. A rough bag of coarse material like canvas was pulled over her head. She did the only thing left to her and struck out with her feet and had the momentary satisfaction of hearing a pained gasp. Then a rope tightened round her ankles and she felt her left arm pulled straight followed by a sharp stab and darkness.

She awoke aware that she was uncomfortable and very cold. She had a merciless throbbing headache. The air was filled with rattling and her hands, tied behind her to a piece of wood, were being pulled this way and that by the jerking of the vehicle. Fortunately she was wearing her woollen leggings that she had put on that morning before leaving the cottage otherwise she might have already suffered severe frost bite. She was still gagged and her feet were tied together. The irregular motion of the truck stopped and she heard conversation in English. Then the truck started to move forward slowly climbing and rocking with the occasional shout from a workman outside. Then the motion stopped again completely and Detty was conscious only of silence and of a smell which, innocuous in itself, produced in her a great feeling of dread. It was the smell of pickled dill cucumbers. Apart from the illicit export of drugs, explosives and weapons quality plutonium, Moltravia's virtually only legitimate foreign trade with the European Union was dill cucumbers grown widely on the subsistance and slave farms of the Fohn plain and then packed and sent to European luncheon tables. Around the bottling stations that were scattered throughout Moltravia, the smell of dill and vinegar permeated everywhere. It was amongst the products of the Farm and the associations flooded in on her as, desperately, she tried to think of other, more encouraging, explanations. Reluctantly she came to the conclusion that there was no doubt that she had been kidnapped and was being transported, cleverly concealed amongst the empty returning pallets, into Moltravia.

This realisation made her stomach turn to stone and her mouth go dry. She had escaped from Moltravia, killed an ogre and had been safe in the European Union – whether Germany, Ireland or England – it didn't matter much. It had never crossed her mind that she had made bitter enemies, one in particular, who would go to any lengths to get their revenge. She had worried about Mara and her father but not about herself. She was now Gräfin Bernadette von Ritter, the adored and pampered daughter-in-law of one of the oldest families in Bavaria. How could anyone touch her? She was furious with herself that she had been so stupid and it had all been so easy. Where had the sharp wit and keen alertness that had got her out of the Farm in the first place gone to? Several things should have alerted her. The false email with no need even to disguise a voice, of course Marc would have telephoned or used the answer phone which would have said more about the message origins. The curious hotel with its conveniently situated fire escape, was so different from their usual haunts. Even *Rigoletto* seemed an improbable choice in retrospect, early Verdi was not a passion for either of them and surely Marc would have chosen a concert, play or the ENO rather than an opera with a routine cast which neither of them really liked. She had been so nearly alerted for all these reasons and yet she had taken the bait hook, line and sinker. Her anger added to her discomfort and her deep fear to produce a sense of desolation and misery.

After a period of some time, perhaps an hour, the jerking started again. Detty presumed that they had been through the Channel Tunnel. There were more shouts this time in French and the jerks were downwards. She tried shouting again but nothing happened. The lorry moved off and for several hours there was no sound except the drone of the engine and the piercing icy draught. Not only desperate in her misery but increasingly physically distressed, Detty wondered if she would be gagged and handcuffed to the crate the whole way to Moltravia. The motion of the truck increased her discomfort and just as she despaired of being able to retain a semblance of dignity she felt the vehicle slow down and stop. After a few moments a thickset woman appeared with a gun in one hand and a bucket in the other. Without saying a word she undid Detty's handcuffs and indicated with a gesture that she could use the bucket. Detty reacted as she had learnt to do in her previous months of captivity. Stumbling with cold she used the bucket and immediately the taciturn guard relocked her handcuffs through the crate wall. The guard then left carrying the bucket and closed the side door and left her in darkness. Detty had no idea where they were, presumably in a motorway parking place somewhere in Belgium, Holland or Germany. At any rate there was no chance of getting help, she was still gagged and hobbled and without any means of attracting attention. The lorry moved off again and Detty, physically more comfortable internally but intensely cold, began to think more about her predicament.

She was almost sure that she was being taken to Moltravia. The thought did nothing to improve her gloom. This time there would be no Mara to comfort her, no Marc to help her escape, she would be totally on her own. In addition she faced a suspended death sentence held over from her last visit and an order for compulsory sterilisation which she had only narrowly escaped before. In addition, since her last sojourn, she had returned as part of a military raiding party and had personally killed a senior officer of the regime. She reflected that they could only kill her once but that gave her little comfort as she knew full well that it was in the power of the NAS to see that she did not have a quick or easy death.

This brought her to the most disturbing thought of all. Whoever had arranged her kidnap had gone to considerable trouble. This had been no random or casual exercise. She knew of only two people in Moltravia who would have gone to that sort of effort. One was the ex-commandant of the Farm who she had heard was now vice president of the country, second only to Travsky and his son, Andreas. Travsky the original dictator was old and rumour had it that he had had a stroke. This had left his considerable capacity for evil impaired. Power now rested with Andreas and Lev Ilitch Konradin. Detty had good cause to remember the latter as, when he had been Commandant of the Farm he had ordered her flogging, after she was discovered with Marc.

Even Konradin's involvement, however, was not the most gloomy possibility that crossed her mind. The other Moltravian with special

314

interest and knowledge of her was the Farm's former medical officer who now, rumour had it, had given up any medical activities and had become commandant general of the NAS. Detty realised that her abduction was most likely a NAS operation and certainly her recent visitor, her of the revolver and the bucket, had NAS stamped over every inch of her. During her last few days at the Farm she had realised that Dr Frederick Kovacs was fascinated by her and in a certain sense strangely attracted to her. Here was the rub, however, his attraction did not appear to manifest itself in a sexual interest which had even the vestiges of normality showed by Konradin but by the desire to overcome her by slow planned humiliation and degradation.

At this point the wild fantasies of her imagination combined with the arctic draught through the lorry to plunge her into despair so deep that death itself would have been a marvellous relief. Even this, however, was out of reach and unattainable. She thought of Marc, her family and all the totems that had helped her before but they seemed to belong to a different planet, a different life. She tried to pray but was unable to say even a Hail Mary. Finally, exhausted, she drifted into a half sleep waking frequently when the handcuffs or the gag became unbearably uncomfortable and the gloomiest of thoughts rushed back into her mind.

As the sky, just visible through the palette stack and a crack in the side panelling, lightened in the direction she knew must be the east she was confirmed in her worst thoughts, that Moltravia could be their only destination. Her misery was tinged with self-anger as she reviewed again the errors, caused by her complacency, which had landed her in this state. She also remembered that she had taken the email printout with her to London thus removing the last possible clue for anybody trying to trace her whereabouts. It was true that the hotel receptionist knew her real name but the receptionist could have been planted there by the kidnappers. Alternatively she might have known nothing of Detty's abduction and merely have been left a message at reception that the von Ritters had changed their mind about staying.

All day the lorry thundered across a flat, seemingly endless road. They stopped twice, presumably for fuel, but nobody came near the crated prisoner. Once in between, presumably at a suitably isolated spot, the bucket and the revolver reappeared. The gloomy half-light in the lorry faded again with the short winter day and still they thundered across the long flat road. Detty thought about the suffering of her fellow human beings who had crossed that terrain to their deaths in the camps. She wondered what they had thought about, if their misery permitted them to think at all, in their cattle trucks on that terrible journey. Her fate was likely to be no better but they had had to do without even the scant respect for human dignity that she had been shown. The short day passed and it was night again and still the journey continued endlessly and monotonously.

Eventually after a seeming age the truck stopped, moved off again for a few minutes then stopped again. The stocky attendant reappeared, undid Detty's handcuffs and removed the gag.

'Get up,' she said in coarse Russian. Frozen rigid with cold and cramp, Detty staggered to her feet and edged between the piled palettes, which had hidden her. The backboard of the lorry had been lowered and gingerly she crabbed her way down onto a strip of dimly-lit tarmac. On one side of the lorry was a police van with high windows. Standing at the side were two men and a woman wearing a uniform that extinguished Detty's last lingering hope that she might be wrong. It was the bottle green of the Moltravian NAS. Her second living nightmare was only beginning.

The stocky woman was talking to the uniformed NAS, 'This is the special prisoner that the director is expecting – take us straight to the Winterburg.'

Detty entered the van and sat on the long side bench between the armed guard and her long-term plain-clothes warder. The Winterburg had been mentioned a number of times during her detention at the Farm. It was the NAS headquarters at Königshof. Built by the Russian KGB around an ancient fortress, the NAS had recommissioned it from derelict after the Travsky revolution. It had many functions. It was the administrative and decision-making headquarters of the NAS, a maximum security prison and also an interrogation centre infamous for its tortures and executions, some secret some public, of the politically dubious who were considered to be a threat to the regime. Mara had spoken often of their friends and her father's colleagues who had disappeared into it, never to come out. Few prisoners who entered the Winterburg were ever seen again but occasionally one or two were sent out to the penal regiments or detention centres like the Farm and whispered of the appalling things that they had witnessed.

After about an hour the van entered the outskirts of the capital and stopped in front of a grey steel portcullis, which lifted automatically upon an electronic signal. The van stopped again outside a low building that Detty imagined must be a reception area. She realised that her journey from the tranquillity of an English country town to one of the most feared prisons in the world was complete.

A bored looking clerk in NAS uniform received them.

'Name?' he said.

'O'Neill, Bernadette,' said Detty in these surroundings automatically reverting to her maiden name.

'Previous?'

'Absconded from the Farm detention centre,' said the plain-clothes officer who had been with her throughout.

The receptionist raised his eyebrows, 'Well, that won't make it any easier for you – and people don't abscond from here – except feet first.'

The two NAS laughed at the joke.

'There will be other charges as well, I expect. You wouldn't think so to look at her now but this young lady is supposed to be a dangerous terrorist,' added the woman.

Tempted though she was, she realised the uselessness of flaunting her citizenship or shrieking about civil rights. She got the feeling that in spite of their play-acting, the officials knew exactly who she was, who had ordered her abduction and why she was there.

The form fully completed she was led away to change. To her surprise there was no brutality, not even real humiliation. She was presented with a simple shapeless calico shift of an indeterminate off white colour, cotton pants and canvass slippers. She was even left alone to change, although she had no doubt that there was a spy hole or an observation camera somewhere. After a few minutes her special attendant, who had come with her from England, returned with a basket, demanded her watch, crucifix and wedding ring, which she put into an envelope. She then packed the clothes and the envelope into a wire basket. She motioned Detty to leave the changing room and led her along a dark green corridor, pausing only to pass the basket with Detty's possessions through a hatch. They reached an iron staircase and climbed two flights of stairs to the second floor. She unlocked a reinforced door with the number 231 on it and indicated that Detty should enter. The door slammed shut and the lock, which was the old fashioned key type, turned. Detty had for the moment reached the end of her journey.

The room was a sparse cell and not particularly terrifying in itself. On one side was a low breeze block shelf covered by a thin plastic covered padded mattress. The only other 'furniture' was a stone commode with a bucket under the padlocked perforated steel lid. The walls and floor consisted of a ribbed, sprayed-on, plastic compound with an irregular finish. Detty had no doubt that cameras and microphones were hidden in this so that the occupant was under constant surveillance. The only other feature was a barred vertical slit-shaped window that looked across a bare deserted courtyard to the other three sides of the building. It was drizzling with rain and the concrete was damp with a few irregular puddles. For the moment the whole atmosphere was mournful and dreary rather than terrifying. She noticed that the second and third floors of other dull grey blocks all had vertical slit windows like hers. The ground floor and the fourth and fifth floors, however, had normal windows and presumably contained offices and administration rooms rather than cells.

Detty took all this in and then sat on her bunk, overwhelmed by despair and loneliness. What would she have done for a companion – Mara of course but anybody from the grim dormitory at the Farm. Not that she would have wished anybody that she knew in this awful place. She then became aware too that the cell was cold, not unheated which would have been impossible in a Moltravian winter, but cold enough to make her shiver and her legs look blue under her shift. She tried to pray and this time managed something. Feeling slightly more comforted she rolled herself up in her single blanket and, exhausted, fell asleep.

She was awoken by the door being unlocked again. This time it was a different wardress – a tall blonde girl about her own age wearing a wrap-around pinafore in NAS green. It reminded Detty of the uniform worn by air stewardesses when they served meals. The girl carried a bucket with some water in it and a bowel of grey mush with a plastic spoon sticking out of it, which steamed slightly in the cold air.

'Wash and food,' she said in Russian. 'Look tidy – the commandant general is coming later.'

Detty tried to eat the mush, which tasted like sodden newsprint, but didn't get very far. She regretted the good food that had been a surprising part of the Farm regime and which clearly didn't extend to the Winterburg. She tried to wash in the freezing water but with neither flannel nor towel it was hard and bitterly cold. She eventually had to dry herself with her bed blanket but doubted whether this in turn would ever dry out again in the dank air.

After dressing she sat on the edge of the bunk and waited. She calculated that an hour had passed but she had no watch and no real idea of the time. At last she got up and went over to the window to look out. The rain had stopped and the courtyard was full of bent figures shuffling slowly round with dragging feet. Most were men in calico shirts and trousers but there were groups of women dressed in shifts like hers, who were kept segregated from the men in their own groups. They circulated with their heads down and their faces expressionless. It reminded Detty of the prisoners in *Fidelio* but there was no *Leonore* or even *Jacquino* or *Rocco* to display a shred of humanity. There were only NAS guards male and female with faces as expressionless as the prisoners, each wore a leather belted jacket with a revolver holster on the right. To the left, several had a short thick leather whip, clipped onto the belt at its handle with the free end tucked in so that it looped over the wearer's hip. A few guards had their whips out and flicked them idly in the direction of the cringing prisoners. There was really no need, however, as the whole body seemed cowed and incapable of resistance.

Detty was drinking in the gloomy scene when the cell door was unlocked again. The tall blonde stood deferentially to one side to allow the familiar figure of the man Detty loathed and feared most in the whole world to enter. He stood smiling triumphantly at her.

'Ah, Countess,' he said in English, 'this is indeed a pleasure. I am so glad that you were able to accept my little invitation. I am sorry that we cannot provide you with a better appointed room but this is a poor country you know. I hear that you have done really well since we last met – a beautiful public heroine, a splendid aristocratic marriage and a glittering singing career in front of you. My congratulations.'

He was enjoying himself hugely.

A flash of anger made her forget her good intentions.

'I demand to be freed at once. I have been abducted. I am the wife of an officer in the German army. You have no jurisdiction over me. Have you any idea the reaction my abduction will produce in the international community?'

She immediately regretted having been goaded into a useless outburst.

'No, and I don't really care,' replied Kovacs. 'The international community has never been friendly towards us and it is unlikely that they can do us any further harm. Also you forget one thing, please don't flaunt your German connections here, my colleagues and I are unlikely to be impressed. Neither your husband nor the international community have any idea where you are. No one has seen your face since you left London and no one will see it with the exception of two senior women officers of mine who are utterly trustworthy and who I have appointed to look after you. They will see to your every need.'

He paused for the theatrical effect to allow the cruelty of his irony to sink in.

'Never fear we have covered our tracks well and you won't be doing much socialising here. However, I hope that you won't be bored, I will come back and tell you the full programme that I have arranged for you. In the meantime you will be able to watch some entertainments in the courtyard, and so that you won't be too lonely, you will be also be able to hear from some of your fellow prisoners when they visit the room next door.'

Stung to anger again Detty made one more attempt, regretting it again as she did so.

'My detention here is entirely illegal and I must ask that I am released at once.'

'My dear young Countess,' came the answer, 'do I have to remind you that you are already under a suspended death sentence in this country. You have also been convicted of being a criminal moral degenerate for which you have been properly sentenced to corrective measures that have not yet been carried out.'

Bernadette shuddered in spite of herself and he relished her despair before continuing remorselessly, 'But in addition to these old charges there is the question of your absconding from a Moltravian penal institution, taking part in a terrorist raid in this country and brutally murdering a very senior security officer.'

He paused, 'In fact there is some irony in the last action of yours. When Vice President Konradin, who you will remember with affection as the commandant of the Farm, took up his higher office, he would have undoubtedly appointed the armourer to command the NAS. Thanks to you, he did not have that option and I had the good fortune to be appointed instead. I was able to use our best overseas agents to ensure that you returned here for a visit and I have complete freedom to arrange for you a leisurely course of education. There is no hurry about this and while I work out a programme for you, I will leave you to enjoy your surroundings. I shall return in due course.'

He turned to the tall artificial blonde who was smirking appreciatively at her boss's performance and indicated the door, which she opened and locked behind them both.

Detty collapsed on her bunk and curled up hopelessly in the foetal position. She could hope for nothing, plan nothing as he had cleverly left her in limbo. She had no more idea exactly what was in store for her than before he came in. She only felt that her most gruesome fantasies might be realised or worse. It was far worse than anything that she had experienced at the Farm. All she could do was to sit there in cold, silence and uncertainty and wait for the worst that that devil incarnate could plan for her. When she awoke the following day she felt slightly more positive and after another bowl of newspaper pulp she decided that she would work out on the damp floor in order to try and remain reasonably fit. She had just started when the screams pierced the silence. Initially the cries were male punctuated by pleas for mercy both male and female. It did not take her long to work out the meaning of the commandant general's cryptic remark about entertainment. The room next door was being used to torture inmates under interrogation and a special sound system had been installed to transmit the sound through the wall with outstanding clarity. She vomited the nauseous mush that she had eaten for breakfast into the slop bucket.

Nobody came near her and she was left with only the agonised sounds from next door for company. Very late, when it was already completely dark, the stocky NAS woman who had escorted her from England appeared at the door.

'You will put this on and come for exercise,' she said, and tried to pull a canvas hood over Detty's head. The latter was so much taller than her keeper that she couldn't reach. Detty, however, didn't see the point in senseless obstruction and eventually bent forward to allow this malodorous object with its small mouth and eye slits to be fitted. The Director was clearly taking no chances that she might be recognised. Thus equipped she was led down the stairs and into the dark freezing cold exercise yard. She walked briskly round the yard trying desperately to keep the Baltic cold from penetrating her thin shift. Frozen to the bone she was pleased when the statutory number of circuits were completed and she was allowed to return to the cheerless partial privacy and lesser chill of her cell.

In this way the days passed varied only by the differing cries of the victims next door. She tried to keep a scratch mark record of the days and in the quiet moments did mental exercises like trying to remember chunks from the bible, the winners of Olympic gold medals and finally as much as possible of the text and scoring of The Ring. Gradually the meaning of the commandant general's other cryptic comments about 'entertainment' became clear. Each morning the shuffling procession of white-clad lost souls circulated the central courtyard. At least they had better conditions than during the exercise period that Detty was allowed because the morning temperature was slightly higher and they gained some small warmth from each other. Conversation, however, was clearly forbidden.

After midday the courtyard had a much grimmer function. A few days after she arrived she noticed workmen erecting a platform with a long wooden beam supported by two verticals over it. Two nooses were tied over the beam. After a short interval two men with their hands tied behind their backs were brought in to the courtyard. They were stood on stools while the noose was tightened round their necks and then hanged in front of her and presumably every one of the two hundred other odd inmates of the Winterburg, whose tiny cell windows overlooked the courtyard. No attempt was made to remove the gibbet or the bodies for twenty-four hours after the execution. The following mornings exercise was completed with the prisoners circling the still gently swinging bodies. Detty had no idea who the men were or why they had been executed and clearly it was pointless to ask.

Later the following morning the monotony was broken by the tall blond NAS woman arriving carrying the hood. Detty imagined that she was being taken for the promised further interview with the commandant. To her surprise, however, she was led to the reception area and a waiting car. Her jailer motioned her to enter, then got in herself and sat beside her. The car was not an ordinary police van but a plush official looking limousine. The drive only took a few minutes. They swung through a set of imposing wrought iron gates and round to the back entrance of an equally imposing looking building. There they got out and were met by a male official who was obviously expecting them. He ushered them into a lift to an upper floor. Down a short corridor they passed through an unmarked wood panelled door into a very large luxurious office. It was empty. The jailer motioned to Detty to sit down on a leather chair in front of the desk and sat on a similar one at the back of the room herself. The desk had a large brass inkstand and a stack of trays containing papers. The object, however, that immediately caught Detty's attention was a photograph lying on top of a sheath of papers in the middle of the blotter. She recognised it immediately. It was a photograph of herself on her wedding day wearing the Lanoure dress. The photograph had appeared in many newspapers and almost every society and fashion magazine in Europe so she was quite used to seeing it but it still shocked her to see a finished print of it in this place.

She heard a discrete cough behind her and turned to stare straight into the face of Konradin. He turned to the jailer and told her to wait outside before sitting down opposite Detty behind the great desk.

'You don't know how hard I have had to work to see you,' he said, his podgy face smiling while the small hard eyes darted restlessly over Detty. She had the unpleasant feeling that she was being spiritually eaten up by this fanatic.

'You see the Commandant General arranged for your visit to this country and kept it very secret. My agents found out, however, and after some very hard bargaining, I got him to agree to this visit. I have no direct jurisdiction over the NAS, but I became, how do you say, very attached to you after our last meeting and that's why, as you see, I keep this beautiful photograph of you on my desk. To come to the point, if you agree to come to me I will try everything in my power to get you out of the Winterburg.'

Detty looked at him in silence for a moment, coldly angry, 'You seem to forget that our last meeting, which made such a deep impression on you, certainly made a deep impression, literally, on me. You had me flogged.'

'That was regrettable but you had committed a serious offence which I couldn't ignore for the sake of discipline but this time the situation is different.'

Amazed, Detty realised that he seemed to be almost pleading his suite with her as he went on, 'And anyway you must realise that I could, and according to the law should, have hanged you. I also had every opportunity to take you by force but I refrained because that was not the way that I wanted it. Now it is in the past and we should forget about it.'

'Regrettable! In the past! Forget it! I suggest you try being birched. The humiliation and the atrocious agony at the time are only the beginning. The splinters left under the skin stab every time you move and in a few days fester. Some victims die of blood poisoning. I was lucky because I had a devoted friend who removed the splinters before they did too much harm. Then you had her tortured too, literally to within an inch of her life, which was saved but not due to your mercy. Her punishment was far more brutal than mine and her only offence was being her father's daughter. And you expect me to have a relationship with you! I would rather trust myself to the tender mercies of the commandant general!'

'Very well,' he said with a sigh. 'I regret it and you may not find his mercies very tender. Whatever happened in the past, I genuinely admire you and would try to treat you well if you allowed me too. The commandant general is increasingly obsessed with power and loves ingenious cruelty. You knew him before but he is much worse now. Be warned!'

With these chilling words the interview ended and Detty was left to ponder them as she was driven back to the Winterburg. She did not have long to wait for more evidence of the truth of the vice president's warning. The following afternoon the workmen reappeared carrying a grating in the form of a thick trellis. They fixed this to the high gibbet platform facing Detty's cell. After a short time the commandant general himself appeared followed by a group of warders leading out five figures in prison dress. There were three men and two women and in turn they were tied to the grating and their clothes torn to their waists exposing their backs. Each was given two dozen lashes from the jailers' whips. Bleeding copiously they were then taken inside. It reminded Detty of her own earlier flogging and she wondered when her turn would come again. Trying to comfort herself she thought that there were worse things than physical pain and if that was all she had to suffer, agonising as it was, she could probably survive. In the case of the beating that she had just witnessed she noticed that the women seemed to bear it better than the men. They were calmer and more controlled.

Days passed and to her increasing surprise she was neither given electric shocks nor flogged nor hanged. True she witnessed the sights and sounds of these things being done to others with horrifying frequency until she thought that she would go out of her mind. Eventually she was able to pray and after one particularly horrible mass hanging she knelt and sobbed to the Virgin. Suddenly as once before a shaft of sunlight struck through the slit window and she felt her strength returning and knew she was not alone. She felt her guardian angel whisper to her, 'Wait, hold on and your chance will come.'

That night she had a curious wild dream. She was in the courtyard surrounded by a crowd but somehow they were not prisoners, they were cheering and happy. Suddenly Mara appeared and dragged her off to a great theatre and she was listening to the *Fidelio* trumpet call. Then she awoke in her cold cell but instead of it's being a great disappointment, she still felt inspired even after she was awake. 'I will lick 'em, she said to herself. 'I don't know how but somehow I will do it.' She felt that fierce determination that she had last felt on the tarmac before setting off for Mara. The strange thing was, though, that there was no outlet for her determination. She puzzled hard to find a solution but there wasn't one. Certainly there was no way out of the Winterburg she was sure of that.

Two weeks later her misery and hopelessness had returned when the stocky warder told her that the commandant general wanted to see her. This time she was taken by the lift to the fourth floor and the warder took her down a long corridor to a room marked in Russian commandant General. Inside this were a group of NAS girls in green tunics doing office work but on the far side was an unmarked door, which her warder approached and knocked on. A familiar voice told them to come in and Detty found herself standing in front of the erstwhile medical officer.

'Ah Countess, please sit down,' he said sarcastically.

Automaton-like Detty obeyed. The director paused and Detty was able to look round the room. Behind the director's chair was a large picture window overlooking the courtyard enabling the occupant to witness the executions and tortures that he, presumably, had ordered.

Her attention switched back to the commandant general who was speaking, this time without titles or niceties, roughly in the local Russian dialect. 'You have attempted, young woman, to make a fool of this country, its police and its government. We have shown you by what you have heard and seen in the last weeks that we are not to be scorned or made to look like idiots lightly. I have considered long and hard how best to deal with you. It would be extremely simple to flog the hide off your elegant back but that would be too quick and too simple. Anyway you have shown in the past that you are not a coward as far as physical pain is concerned. It would also be simple to hang you this afternoon but that would also be very quick and make you a martyr and a rallying point. We have one of those already and we don't need

326

another to encourage our enemies. Neither would be sufficient and I would prefer another way.'

His voice softened again into a quiet menace.

'Your many admirers – and I have been amongst them – recognise that you have three outstanding qualities, great beauty, a magnificent singing voice and high intelligence. You are indeed extremely blessed by all those attributes. I am prepared to offer you an opportunity and a way out of your difficulties. I would like you voluntarily to make all your talents available to me personally and our regime in the manner that I direct. In other words you will become my mistress, yielding your body to me in any way that I choose to use it, you will appear and sing in the patriot rallies and concerts and make recordings of patriotic songs. In addition you will put your brain at the disposal of the NAS, particularly helping them in encouraging and persuading dissident elements, some of whom are known to you personally, to return here and face a fair trial and just punishment for their treasonous crimes. If you help to capture for execution the traitor Oblov and his daughter, you will be freed on the day the sentence is carried out. Otherwise you must remain here with me permanently.'

He paused and looked at her questioningly. She felt for the moment strangely detached, reflecting that the two most powerful men in the land had propositioned her during the last few weeks. Distantly she tried to calculate which was the worse of the three chasms of hell, allowing herself to be physically abused, prostituting herself and her beloved art or betraying her friends. It had to be the last and she came out of her reverie.

'I'll see you in hell before I do any one of those things.'

To her dismay the director smiled, 'Exactly what I expected you to say although I think it will be you who will see hell not me. I will therefore outline my alternative programme that will address your great talents in a leisurely fashion one by one. First, you will make a return journey to the Klinikum where the sentence that you have already received for moral degeneracy will be carried out. Because of your importance and the need to see that you survive for the remaining parts of your – eh – education you will receive special privileges. The operation will be carried out under spinal anaesthetic in the usual way, I personally will be present. As you will be fully conscious we can chat. A further privilege will be that the operation, in your case, will be performed in a private room by the country's leading gynaecological surgeon. He was a little reluctant but when I pointed out that he had a daughter… he saw sense. We will allow you some time to get over the operation and I shall enjoy talking to you about your new feelings and ambitions in your altered state.

'You will then be ready for the second stage. This is a very small though delicate operation. Another skilled surgeon will sever the nerves to your larynx. After that you won't be completely voiceless. They tell me you can usually croke out some words. We will then allow you some weeks to relish your life as a voiceless, sexless crone gradually shrinking into senescence before we come to the last item.

'This is also a medical procedure and one in which I, as a doctor, have found particularly fascinating. In the room next door to yours here, as well as using electric shock as a routine aid to interrogation we have developed a technique adapted from psychiatric electrical treatment. If the electrodes are placed in a certain position and the shock is given for long enough we are now able to destroy both the memory and the intellect of the subject without of course killing him… or her. We have just completed treatment on a series of university academic staff with unhelpful opinions. The treatment has been very successful and they are now able to work usefully emptying the slop buckets and clearing out the Winterburg latrines. You won't have met them as unfortunately their treatment leaves them sexually rather disinhibited so we don't let them into the women detainees' quarters. It would be interesting to see if this happens to women too but in your case you will of course have been made safe previously.

'Once you have completed your programme and you have joined the ranks of this intellectual elite, we will really have no need to keep you here and we will agree to the request that you have made for release. We will release you somewhere in Western Europe as a croaking gibbering imbecile. You won't be able to tell anybody what has happened to you. They may find out who you are eventually and your husband and the authorities will rant and roar but it won't really matter to either of us then, will it? We will start on you the day after to-morrow meanwhile enjoy yourself. We have a hanging this afternoon to take your mind off your problems. I will see you on the operating table.'

In deep shock she lay in her cell contemplating her future, or lack of it. Her greatest ambition now was to achieve a good death and that gave her a sort of odd, desperate strength. She had the beginning of an idea of where her best chance lay of getting killed quickly.

Two days later in the afternoon the tall expressionless blonde wearing her NAS captain's outdoor uniform with revolver, but no whip, unlocked the cell door and without saying a word, put the canvas mask over Detty's head and led her down the iron staircase to the ground floor. She noted that even on this journey the orders were that nobody apart from her two female warders was to see Detty's face. The prison van was waiting beside a loading platform with the side door open. Detty looked about but realised that the steel main gate was still shut and that escape was impossible. Resigned, she entered the van sitting on one long bench while the NAS woman, after locking the door, sat opposite fingering her revolver. Detty was in half a mind to go berserk hoping that the expressionless girl would shoot her and thus release her. Somehow she held on and the van moved off and for the next fifteen minutes the two women stared silently at each other. As the van stopped Detty recognised the silhouette of the Klinikum.

This time she was led in through a side door. Still looking, hope against hope, for the supernatural help that she had once felt that she had been promised. She changed as ordered into the Klinikum operating gown under the supervision of her policewoman warder who had curtly dismissed the Klinikum nurse. Presumably to prevent the surgeon recognising his victim, the canvas mask was put back over her head as she was led into the operating room. At least it was not cold here, she thought. The surgeon was waiting for her and stood to one side while the policewoman ordered her up onto the operating table and prepared her for examination. She fixed two steel poles in sockets halfway down the table, took a nylon cord about a centimetre thick and about half a metre long and wound it viciously tightly round Detty's ankle which she then raised and hung from the hook at the top of the pole. She then did the same the other side. The cords hurt a good deal and Detty wondered why they didn't use canvas stirrups which she thought were the usual method. Presumably it was because in this setting the co-operation of the patient couldn't be assumed and it made it more difficult for her to kick out at an awkward moment. The policewoman then lowered the end of the table and said curtly, 'She's ready.'

The surgeon approached her and began to examine her, as he did so he whispered, 'You know what is going to happen to you?'

Detty inclined her head slightly inside the canvas mask.

'I am truly sorry, young lady, you know I had no choice. If I hadn't agreed to do it it would have been done anyway by one of those butchers outside.'

'I know,' whispered Detty. 'I know that you will be careful and gentle – I forgive you.'

'Stop talking,' barked the blonde girl adding to the surgeon, 'I have just spoken to the director general and he will be about twenty minutes. He is particularly anxious to be present at this operation and we must wait for him. Go and get a cup of coffee after you have finished.'

As the surgeon completed the examination, he raised the end of the table and unhooked the nylon cord and wound it off first one ankle then the other. He eased her legs down inside the steel poles, which he then removed and laid down on the table at her side. Through her slits Detty then saw him leave the room looking distressed.

She lay on the operating table waiting for the next terrible act in the drama. Suddenly like a bolt from the blue an idea struck her. The nylon cord, which had been used to tie her feet as she had been examined, was still attached to the poles, presumably waiting for her feet to be reattached for the operation itself. The policewoman was looking through the windows of the double doors into the anteroom. Detty had been so docile so far that the NAS woman clearly thought that there was no problem and she was dreaming of her next night off with her boyfriend in Königshof. Silently Detty sat up and slipped the nylon cord off the hook. Fortunately it didn't rattle. She hid it under her gown. Restlessly turning on her side she knocked the detached metal pole off the couch and sent it crashing loudly onto the tiled floor. The policewoman turned with a curse, called Detty a stupid cow and bent over beside the table to pick up the fallen pole.

It was the half chance that Detty needed. Summoning all her diminished strength she leapt over the side of the operating table, passed the cord over the stooping girls head and pulled for all she was worth. For a few minutes that seemed like an hour the girl struggled and gurgled. Finally, to Detty's immense relief she felt her go limp and with a gurgle slide to the floor. Determined to finish her off, Detty pulled the ligature even tighter before relaxing it to check that the girl's breathing had indeed stopped. Certain that the policewoman was at last dead, Detty worked with breakneck speed spurred on by rushing adrenaline and faith in her prayer. She stripped the jacket and blouse off the dead girl followed by her belt and skirt. With difficulty she lugged the body up onto the operating table and slipping off her gown placed it over the semi-nude body of the policewoman. Then she drew her canvas mask over the girl's head. Keeping the revolver well within grasp she quickly put on the uniform blouse, jacket, skirt and finally beret of a captain in the NAS. Unfortunately the operating theatre had two doors, one from the main mass operating hall of the Klinikum, and the other from the side anteroom by which they had entered. Thinking of her instructor at Frankfort, who had taught her well, she checked that the revolver was loaded – it was. She picked the best position behind one door and with her back to the other. She was much the same size as the dead policewoman. She hoped that, with the help of the director's canvas mask on the body, the swop would pass unnoticed at least until she had the director, and any companions that he might have brought with him, covered by the revolver inside the theatre.

It was astounding how, once engaged almost by a lucky chance in action, all her resourcefulness and determination had returned. The docile young woman hoping for death but submitting to mutilation a few minutes before had become a fierce and determined warrior. Her first inclination had been to escape immediately but for two reasons she knew she must wait. First, if she dealt with the director and the surgeon, the added time would help her make good her eventual get away and, second, she knew that she had some unfinished business to attend to.

Aided by her panic energy she had finished her jobs in good time. After a seemingly interminable wait she heard a familiar voice approaching from the direction of the main hall. 'I'm sorry,' he was saying, 'but you will have to work by yourself. I do not want any other witnesses. You say your nurses are trustworthy but nowadays nobody is to be trusted. There are too many hooligans and terrorists about. This girl is important and she has powerful friends in the West. Nobody must know she is here until I have finished with her, do you understand? You are sure though you are capable of doing the spinal anaesthetic as well?'

'Yes,' came the reply, 'it was always part of our training so we could work without help in remote areas.'

'That's all right then.'

He had paused in the doorway with the door half open.

As soon as they were both inside, Detty turned from behind the door and without wasting a second levelled her gun at the director's chest and fired. It was still early evening and there was considerable noise in the road and the main hall so she thought and hoped that the noise of the shot would pass unnoticed. The director slumped to the floor, bleeding but still alive.

'Hands up and face the wall,' she snapped at the surgeon who had blanched to a pale grey obeyed. She took no chances with the director and muttered to him, 'This is a great deal kinder than you deserve.'

She hoped he had heard as she put the revolver up against his temple and fired again. This time he was surely dead. Turning to the surgeon she told him, 'You are lucky in a sense. You were gentle with me a few minutes ago and therefore you have nothing to fear – at least not from me. Co-operate and I will tie you to the operating table and gag you and that may save you. I ask you not to try and move until they find you – I hope that you – and your daughter are not punished. This is the best that I can do.'

He nodded agreement and she got him to sit on the floor and tied his hands to the heavy operating table with the same cord that she had used to strangle the policewoman. She gagged him with a bandage, picked up the gun again and with a final glance round left the room by the side door, which was only locked by a simple key on the inside.

Outside the Klinikum, the director's car was still waiting with his chauffeur inside. Detty walked briskly up to it and said, 'The Herr Director needs to send some papers urgently back to the Winterburg. You are to take me back. He will phone you at the Winterburg if he wants you to return to collect him later.'

She held her breath for a moment before she got a very satisfactory, *Jawohl, Frau Hauptmann*, please get in.'

The fifteen-minute drive passed in silence. The driver parked in front of the main entrance of the Winterburg and Detty got out. She went through the outer gate flashing the dead girl's pass, which was unrecognisable in the dark as she entered. Inside she walked behind the gatehouse, paused, and waited until the driver had moved over to the official parking lot. He walked away from the car presumably in search of what passed for coffee in that benighted country. Once he was out of sight, she then walked back through the main gate and was saluted by the gate guard without a challenge. He took little notice of the familiar uniform.

She walked rapidly away from the city centre. It was a poor area and the road was lined with small food shops and others selling miscellaneous goods. Eventually she found what she wanted – a second-hand clothes shop. The shop was dimly lit and heated by a malodorous oil stove in the middle of the floor. It was attended by an old lady who looked tired, wrinkled and very thin. Detty hated to see the fear in her eyes on catching sight of the dreaded uniform she was wearing. She seemed to relax when Detty treated her courteously and she realised that the intruder only wanted to buy something. She used the dead NAS girl's wallet to pay a few thalers for a long shabby overcoat – warm but definitely nearing the end of its days. As she left, the old woman offered her a warm drink from the back of the shop which Detty refused with thanks. She then said that she hoped her visitor hadn't got too far to go as it was such a cold night and wished her a gentle good night. The crinkled eyes once filled with fear now smiled warmly in spite of the terrifying uniform. Detty had to restrain herself from offering some more money from her former captor's purse but decided that it wouldn't fit in with the character of a NAS officer and refrained.

She left the shop with the coat over her arm but a little further on she paused in another shop doorway and put it on over her very distinctive uniform. She then strode rapidly towards the central bus station straining to remember her Königshof geography. She knew where she was heading and eventually found the right bus which, to her relief, left almost immediately.

The village of Zublinsk was much as she remembered it as she got off the bus. The flagpole that had been the centre of the atrocities was still there. She knew that she needed to go to the south of the village – but which farm was it? A mistake might be fatal. She walked for about two hours in the bitter cold until it was past midnight. In spite of a bright frosty moon she could find no clue to guide her to the right place. There were three farms in what she judged was about the right location but they were all dark and it could have been any of them. She found an open barn on the side of the most easterly farm and for the moment decided to give up the search. She covered herself almost completely with hay for warmth and camouflage and went fast asleep.

She awoke at first light and savoured the smell of earth and woods garnished with a whiff of wood smoke on a bitter cold morning. The change from the odour of human pain, dirt and fear in the Winterburg was exhilarating in spite of the cold. Then suddenly she had the sensation that she was being watched. She began to look round and heard a movement. She turned and looked out of the front of the barn. To the right was the path down to the farmhouse but the sound had come from the stone ruins of an older barn on the opposite side. Then she saw the watcher. She was a beautiful peregrine falcon perching proudly on the stones, her white throat gleaming through the half light. A moment later she flapped her powerful wings and flew off towards a neighbouring copse. This had to be a good omen. Just as she was flying away an old man and two teenagers approached the barn from the house. These couldn't be from the family that she was seeking so, as silently as possible, Detty slipped out of the barn towards the west.

She reached the second farm in about twenty minutes, running as fast as she could in her heavy coat across the fields, iron rutted with frost. Breathless she hid behind some trees to observe. At first she thought that this couldn't be the right farm either as the only person to be seen was a very elderly woman feeding pigs. She was about to leave to try her luck at the third farm when a much younger woman appeared at the back door and walked towards Detty's sheltering trees, presumably to let the chickens out from a coop that was only thirty metres from her hiding place. As the young woman got nearer Detty recognised the features of the girl who had died at the flagpole. This must, she thought, be her elder sister.

Manoeuvring behind the trees, Detty moved alongside the path of the approaching figure. Just as the girl passed she moved quickly out behind her and clamped one hand over her mouth and with the other pinioned her arms quickly whispering, 'I won't harm you – take no notice of the uniform I'm wearing. I'm a friend. Take me to your father. He will recognise me.'

Petrified, the other girl looked Detty up and down until realising she had no choice in the face of her armed assailant, she turned and led them back to the house. On the way Detty explained who she was and how she had met the girl's father.

They walked through the outer door into a lobby full of muddy boots then through a second door into the kitchen. The driver of the lorry that they had used in Mara's rescue was sitting at the long wooden table eating a kind of porridge and drinking chicory coffee. He looked up startled and looked again with even more surprise as he recognised the young German woman officer who he had escorted previously.

'You are welcome,' he said in the old fashioned Russian dialect of the Moltravian peasantry. 'Sit down and allow me to offer you a cup of coffee. You will forgive me if I am surprised to see you unannounced.'

Detty took a seat and answered in the dialect, 'I ask you to forgive me for startling your daughter but unfortunately I had no alternative.'

'She has been very nervous since her sister was killed – you must forgive her. But please tell me how we can help you?'

'I am in desperate trouble or else I would not have come to you.

335

For some weeks I have been a prisoner in the Winterburg prison in Königshof. Yesterday I escaped by killing my guard and another NAS officer.'

She thought it wise not to reveal the exact status of 'the other NAS officer.'

'In order to escape I stole the uniform of the woman guard. Now I have to leave Moltravia with great speed, because it is only a matter of time before they catch up with me.'

'I have never met anybody who escaped from the fiends at the Winterburg before – I suppose that is a matter for congratulations but you are indeed in very great danger so let's be practical. How can I – we – help?'

'I know that at one time you had the means of getting messages to the German security service in Stuttgart. I was hoping that you would be able to send a message to them so that they could get me out by air or even by sea as I imagine that the land routes will be impossible.'

'I wish I could,' said the farmer sadly, 'but unfortunately I no longer have the means. After the young German officer – your companion – left I was told that the line was no longer required by Stuttgart and as it was a danger to me I was to destroy the equipment. The NAS were getting nearer to me all the time – I didn't care for myself but for the sake of my wife and my remaining daughter I was glad to destroy the equipment. I am so sorry.'

There was a long silence. Detty realised how stupid she had been to suppose the service would still be available and rely on it so much in her plans. The farmer's wife broke the silence, 'My husband is stupid, young lady, you are not welcome here. You are a terrible danger to us all. We have already lost one daughter, casually murdered by the fiends from hell. What do you think that they would do if they found out that we had been harbouring you? Please go at once and trouble us no more.'

Detty nodded, but before she could answer the farmer said, 'Mara, you should be ashamed of yourself. This brave young lady from a strange land is doing all that she can to combat the evil which stalks this accursed country and you can show her no care or gratitude. I am ashamed to hear you.'

Detty broke in, 'Do not be hard on her – your wife is right. I will put you in no further danger and go at once. Thank you for your hospitality and your kindness.'

She got up to leave.

'Wait,' said the farmer, 'There is one slim, very slim chance. You have seen the pickled cucumber trucks that trade our pathetic surplus with the West.'

Detty nodded 'and how!' – she thought.

'Well, my cousin is in charge of the local loading station and he is one of us. If you wish, I will try to get you loaded in a sealed crate. In this way, you might, just might, get back to Germany undetected. Sometimes the crates are checked at the frontier, sometimes not. At the moment they will probably check thoroughly because of your escape but there are so many of them it is still difficult to check them all. My cousin is quite skilled in loading and has occasionally got things through for us before. If you wish to try this way it is important that we go at once. Today is loading day and we must get you sealed up before the international driver arrives from Königshof. He will be an NAS man and in addition their families are always kept hostage for their return and good conduct. I will burn your uniform as that will not help you now and Katrina will lend you some woollen trousers and a sweater. It will be cold but with your coat that should be enough. The lorry should be in Oranienburg by nightfall but they often search very thoroughly particularly if somebody is missing. Change quickly now.'

The mention of Oranienburg, which she thought was a semi-suburb of Berlin and not the sort of place she would usually have found entrancing, seemed like a hint of bliss to Detty in her peril on this dark Moltravian morning. She thought of the falcon again and irrationally it comforted her. She turned to the terrified Katrina and said solemnly to her, 'Thank you for the clothes. I shall return them to you one day. That is a solemn promise. The day will come when...' she didn't know what made her hesitate and use the old, proscribed Hanseatic name '... Livonia is once more free.'

Katrina smiled but still said nothing. The farmer suddenly smiled, 'Thank you for that. Hearing that name on your lips is an inspiration that makes me believe it will be true. I am ready for it. That day I shall fly this.'

He lifted a floorboard and searched underneath finally finding the polythene manure sack he sought. Diving inside he proudly displayed the white and green flag with the falcon and golden chalice motive of Hanseatic Livonia. His wife and daughter looked even more frightened and he quickly put it back in its hiding place.

They walked out to the same lorry that they had used to get to the farm for Mara's rescue. Detty climbed in the back and the farmer put sacks over her. These would be no help if they were searched but might be sufficient to hide her from nosy passers by. The drive seemed to take hours but in reality it was only a few minutes. The truck stopped and Detty heard a few words of a whispered conversation about special cargo and a spare crate. Then they moved on a few metres and the farmer signalled Detty to get out and into a open crate beside the back of the van. They had presumably moved the truck to a private place behind the main packing station so this extra crate could be loaded secretly. The crate itself was fairly large and standard like the others with the markings of the Republik of Moltravia Agricoop on the side. Inside, however, was another crate resting on and surrounded by a double layer or bottles of dill cucumbers. Clearly this equipment had been used before and was designed so that anybody opening the crate and carrying out a cursory inspection would find what they expected – boxes containing bottles of dill cucumbers.

One of the men handed Detty a strange looking rubber mask, 'Put this on if you think that you are near to the frontier. It is an old gas mask from World War II but we have renewed the activated carbon. They use CO_2 detectors at the frontier. This will absorb the gas that you breathe out.' After she had climbed in the other man, who had not spoken previously, threw her a hammer and chisel muttering, 'Just in case you have to get yourself out,' adding with black humour, 'you don't need to lend them to the NAS. They have their own – amongst other things.'

Detty smiled. She was beyond being frightened by that sort of quip and she was fully conversant with the NAS tool kit.

'Don't let them rattle or it may be suspicious,' he added, and began to nail her up. The crate was dark but there was straw and adequate air holes and it didn't feel all that cold but of course the truck was still stationary. The nailing complete, she felt the forklift collect the crate and take it to load onto the lorry. Then for some time there was nothing except the noise of other units being loaded around her and on top of her. It was a good thing she wasn't claustrophobic she thought as she savoured the same pervasive smell of dill and vinegar that she had had on the outward journey. At last the loading noises stopped and she waited and waited and waited. It was dark and smelly but there was plenty of air, which filtered through the crack in the cases from the space under the palate. She could move but didn't like to too much as she wondered if the noise was detectable outside. It seemed unlikely but at this stage she didn't want to take any chances.

She was just wondering if there had been a change of plan and they were not going to leave that day at all. All at once there was a slamming of car doors followed by some rapid conversation outside and in a moment the engines of the lorry tractor started with a reassuring roar. They moved off and she prayed to her saints and the Virgin. This time the prayers flowed, the blocks had all gone. She submitted herself gratefully and humbly to the faith of her fathers. After she had finished praying she curled up on the straw and for the first time since she had left London she relaxed fully and went into a dreamless sleep.

She must have slept for some hours exhausted as she was. It was only when the lorry stopped she woke. She grabbed the gas mask and put in on with her heart thumping. She heard the driver talking to an official who might have been a frontier guard but who could have been part of a random roadside police check. The side of the truck was open and she could hear noises and see the shadows of people passing the cracks. Occasionally there was the splintering of wood as they forced open crates. If they contented themselves with a visual inspection she thought that, deep inside the load as she was, she was probably safe. The problem was that the police and customs all had electronic inspection gear and carbon dioxide detectors and if they used them there was no way that she could remain undiscovered. Under those circumstances she was as good as dead or worse. The likelihood was that they would make a thorough inspection as the death of the governor of the Winterburg and her escape must have been discovered by now.

She tried to comfort herself as the noise went on by thinking that at least the director was dead and that it was probably unlikely that the others would carry out his personalised sadistic programme on her which had been for his own private gratification. She thought about the three men at the centre of her hell. The doctor/director had been, she thought, the worst. Not only did he twist his medical training but his whole life seemed to revolve round gratuitous cruelty. The armourer, on the other hand, was just a violent savage brute, sadistic yes, but in a more straightforward and less perverted way. And the governor – now the joint leader of the country and the only one of the three left alive – what of him? Detty felt she despised him as well as reviled him. He was a little man spiritually as well as physically – cruel and revolting but essentially little – good at torturing and executing enemies and flogging men and women when there was no risk to himself, cunning but devoid of the courage which to an extent the other two had possessed. There was something horribly twisted about his strange obsession with her. He was utterly repulsive and quite old enough to be her father but there were others like him. The image of his leering face made her shudder but somehow he frightened her less.

10

THE TRAVELLER

Ich geh' durch deine Strassen
nach mancher langen Reise[33]

(HAMBURG FOLKSONG)

The noises stopped and she thought that she heard the soldiers, or whoever they were, jumping down. Then, to confirm her relief, the lorry moved off only to stop again a few minutes later. Detty hoped against hope that they had crossed the river and she tried to listen for conversation. At first she couldn't make out anything but after a time an official passed close to her and sure enough he was speaking *hochdeutsch*. For the second time in her life she literally jumped for joy to hear the language. This time she hit her head hard on the roof of the crate but it didn't matter one bit.

She realised, however, that she must be careful. She was still in a Moltravian lorry with a NAS driver. Several hours more passed and she slept again to awake when the lorry stopped and started manoeuvring. To her relief she heard someone shout in German, *'Wir mussen dieser*

---

33 I go along your roads to many long journeys

heute enladen.[34] The driver needs to get back and some of the goods require onward shipment immediately.'

The noises of moving crates started again and eventually she felt her own crate being lifted off and then lowered. She concluded that they must be in a transit warehouse. As her crate came to rest there was a chink of light through one, presumably the free, side. Time to leave, she thought, and she cleared the jar boxes out of her way. Not wanting to use the tools she had been given, she put her feet against the side of the crate where the light showed and pushed with all her might. Eventually the side gave way and she heard the crash of broken glass as the covering layer of boxes of cucumbers and the wooden slats of the crate crashed somewhere beneath. As she crept to the side to look out the ghastly truth dawned. Some ten metres below on the warehouse floor were the leaking broken boxes and wooden slats that she had dislodged. Not being familiar with warehouse practice she had assumed that she would be unloaded onto the ground whereas in fact she was on the top of the sixth layer of crates. Fortunately tragedy had been averted. It would have been the ultimate irony to have saved herself from the NAS at the Winterburg only to be killed falling from a cucumber crate in a German warehouse. As bad, would have been to kill or seriously injure the warehouseman who stood pouring out a stream of not very *hoch deutsch* at the cause of his near fatal accident. His companions, meanwhile, gazed, jaws dropping at the open crate high above the concrete floor which stood open displaying the apparition of a dirty, dishevelled figure wearing an antique gas mask. She tore it off revealing an undeniably attractive auburn haired girl stuttering rather incongruously, *'Entschuldigung Sie,'* as if she had just bumped into somebody in the theatre foyer.

After a pause, the whole party, girl and all burst into uncontrollable laughter which only gradually subsided. Finally the girl called out, 'Aren't you going to get me down then?' and muttering more *'Entschuldigungs'* one of them went to fetch a long ladder. Detty climbed down and to the further astonishment, not unmixed with pleasure, proceeded to kiss

---

34 We must unload this today

each and every one of them on both cheeks while tears of joy and relief streamed down her own.

At last she pulled herself together enough to ask, 'Do you have an office where I might use the telephone?'

The Burodirektor was pleasant enough and sat her down and gave her a cup of coffee but he was clearly troubled and Detty realised that he was the sort of official who did things by the book. She repeated her request to telephone and he said he was sure that would be possible but still sat looking at her dubiously. After a further pause he said, 'Excuse me, meine Frau, but I must ask you some questions.'

'Yes, of course,' replied Detty.

'First' the manager continued, 'I assume that you are Moltravian and have no right of entry into Germany and I must therefore tell the police of your somewhat – er – irregular – arrival.'

Detty smiled at him, 'You make three points, mein Herr,' she said, 'I will answer them. First, I am delighted to say that I am not Moltravian. At present I think I would rather belong to any other country on earth – in fact I am Irish by birth and German by marriage. Although, currently, I do not have my passport or other documents on me, I do have the right to enter the European Union and I think that I can prove it.'

He gave her a rather patronising, dubious smile. '*Wirklich?*'

She smiled again with as much charm as she could muster, 'I am also *die Schwiegertochter* of Graf Max von Ritter of Schloss Oberdorf, Bayern, and as my husband is currently on military service in the Bundeswehr with NATO in Norway and England, I would like to let my father-in-law know that I am here and am safe. With regards to the Polizei, I would be delighted if you would tell them and I would be extremely happy to talk to them as I have just been the victim of an outrageous international crime.'

Detty spoke with authority and obviously seemed convincing. It was now the turn of the Burodirektor's jaw to drop and he lost his stiff formal air, '*Bitte schon*, – please call the Herr Graf – er – Frau Gräfin.'

He stumbled to the formal mode of address, in spite of the inherent improbability of its applying to the dirty, dishevelled young ragamuffin that he saw in front of him. He didn't think that he had ever met a real

Gräfin before and like many of the petit bourgoisie he assumed they were all over forty and only to be seen with blue-rinsed hair and wearing mink coats on the Friedrichstrasse in Berlin.

Detty rapidly dialled the Oberdorf number. As usual the familiar voice of Hildegard answered, '*Hildegard, ich bin Detti, ja,ja alles OK – wirklich.*'

Finally Max came to the phone and she explained that she was safe and well in a foodstuff warehouse in Oranienburg, 'I will explain later – can you find Marc?'

'Yes, he has been to Moltravia under cover looking for you but found no trace. He came back to join his unit worried sick. We thought that they must have murdered you already. I have his number I will ring him.'

The senior Kommisar at Oranienburg was a kindly, rather overworked and overweight, man.

'You must be very tired, meine Frau, I will try not to keep you for too long. Now tell me exactly what happened.'

'From the kidnapping in London?'

'Yes, from the beginning.'

She told the whole story only leaving out her conversation with the director and the nature of the operation she was to undergo at the Klinik.'

When she had finished he sat completing his notes and then looked up.

'They must have had some reason for kidnapping you. Do you have previous connections with Moltravia that you have not told me about?'

Obviously, reading the daily papers for recent news was not his forte. She really didn't want to go on and wondered how much she should say so she looked him straight in the eyes and said, 'The answer to your question, Herr Kommisar, is yes, but I will need security advice here in Germany before discussing it further with anybody.'

'That makes it a bit more understandable. Thank you, Frau Gräfin, for your candour. Under the circumstances I do not think that I need ask you anything more at present.'

At that moment the phone rang, it was Marc now back in England. The conversation was short but the relief almost audible over the line. He realised there were others present and left it for later.

'Would it be more comfortable for you to await the arrival of the Herr Graf at the Polizeirevier?'

'Yes, thank you. Perhaps you would be kind enough to send him round when he arrives, Herr Direktor, I imagine that it is not far.'

'Less than five minutes.'

*

A few days after the audition, a white envelope addressed to Frau Bernadette O'Neill arrived at Oberdorf. Across the top was the insignia *Bayreuther Festspiele* complete with the famous sillouette of the Festspielhaus. Detty opened the envelope with clumsy fingers and stood gazing at her contract to sing *Woglinde* in the Ring cycle the following year.

Beside herself, like a small child, she rushed into the dining room where Marc was finishing his usual large breakfast yelling in English, 'I've got it, Marc! I've got it!'

Marc, who had already spotted the envelope and guessed at its contents, hugged her tight and whispered, 'I am so pleased – I never really doubted it – they are lucky to have you.'

'That's nonsense,' she said. 'I wasn't perfectly prepared and two months solitary confinement in the Winterburg isn't exactly the ideal preparation for a Bayreuth solo. I must start practising and see Bernhard – now.'

She then dashed over the entire house like a small child anxious to tell everybody, Hildegard, Sophie, Max and anybody else who would listen.

Later she walked with Marc through the late winter woodlands enjoying the freedom and the air. As they turned along the brook, she said to him, 'I suppose this is the realisation of an impossible dream. When I was at the Convent my first music teacher played me occasional records of strange, wonderful music from a place in a far away country where it is played as nowhere else. From that moment, I always had the ambition to go to Bayreuth but I never dreamed that I would be part of it and sing there.'

Marc couldn't take his eyes off her and then joking said, 'You usually seem to get the things you want, Detti.'

'Well, I got you didn't I? That was the most important thing.'

She kissed him and they walked on happy and silent. Eventually, as they turned back towards the Schloss, he said, 'You will get your degree this summer.'

'That's if they let me take it.'

'Somehow I think that they will, you have influential friends and however disapproving your tutor may be, it is known at Oxford that you couldn't help your absences and that you haven't been gallivanting.'

'I still think that I was stupid,' she replied.

'Anyway, after you come down from university you will be free to concentrate on your singing. What do you want to do eventually?'

She stopped dead in the path and turned and looked at him anxiously but very seriously. 'I want some first class teaching. If you don't mind I will talk to Bernhard Meisl about that then …' she paused, '…I want to sing *Leonore* in Königshof.'

Marc realised with a dreadful flash what she was really saying. He was stunned then furious and the idyll was shattered.

'Detti, don't even joke about that place. They have kidnapped you, tried to kill you and very nearly mutilated you and you can say things like that. You're mad! Are you determined to get killed or tortured? I don't understand you. Never mention that place again. I know what you went through but what do you think it was like for us? Not knowing, guessing, we were nearly out of our minds.'

'So was I,' said Detty very, very quietly.

Marc stopped in the middle of his tirade and looked at her again thinking hard. In silence they walked back to the house. The subject wasn't mentioned again and in the evening they sang Lehar and Johann Strauss and the old house was filled with music and laughter. Later in bed Marc took her in his arms and whispered, 'I'm sorry, Detti, but I love you so much and I was so scared for you at first then I thought that I had lost you forever. But I have thought about what you said and I think I understand now – at least the symbolism. Maybe it is the Will of God. Perhaps I should tell you, for you will hear anyway, that there is a rumour of a big revolt, which may happen soon in Moltravia with the support of the FWL and Nicklaus Oblov's Liberation Movement. It will probably end in mass slaughter like all the others but resistance is still alive in Livonia and who knows... one day...'

His voice tailed off and in a few minutes he was asleep.

She, however, tossed and turned. Her thoughts tumbled and in front of her eyes were images of a young girl handing over her only sweater and a farmer with tears in his eyes fondling a white and green flag with a falcon and chalice motive.

*

The Gaudy took her back in time. It seemed like a million years. Most of her year knew some of her more recent history and several had been at the wedding but it didn't seem to make any difference. It was good to see them all and just chatter about good times and absent friends. This was the best part of England she reflected. Ben Charles was still chatting her up and offering to take her with him to the south of France. He said it was no trouble at all as he was off there the day after tomorrow to visit growers in Burgundy and then spend a month in a friend's apartment at Roquebrune. Apparently he was working for Nutt Bros, the St James vintners, and this was part of the job. She pointed out that she was a respectable married woman with a fierce soldier of a husband who would run him through with his sabre for making such a suggestion.

Feeling relaxed and contented she arrived back at Henley in the small hours and casually checked the answerphone. There was only one message. She listened to a loved and familiar voice sounding anxious, 'Detty, its Mara – It's all going badly. Ring me if you can. I've got out to try and raise help. Please phone me I just want to talk to you.'

She then gave a number beginning 00 48 85. Detty was now more than suspicious of odd messages but it was undoubtedly Mara's voice. She quickly checked her code book finding that the number referred to northern Poland not far from the Moltravian frontier in the part of the south where the uprising had started. Detty thought for a moment and then decided that, under these circumstances, time of the night probably wasn't important.

347

'Detty! Thank God,' said Mara answering immediately. 'I shouldn't have 'phoned you but I was desperate.'

She was stuttering in her hurry. 'We are running out of food and can't get enough weapons and we're having a job treating the wounded. We must cross the river but I don't know how. The people are with us and are fighting amazingly bravely but without a breakout what can we do? Father is out all the time with the soldiers and they willingly die for him but gradually Travsky's thugs will strangle us. The Poles are sympathetic but terrified of another war and very poor themselves. They are willing to let supplies through but often there aren't any. Somehow I thought of you and Marc – once before you did a miracle...'

'Mara, I don't know about miracles but I will let Marc know and I will come to you.'

'Oh Detty – I shouldn't even ask. What will Marc say?'

'Leave Marc to me. Now how do I get to you?'

'Don't come through Germany all the entry points are watched and be careful how you leave England. The NAS tailed you once before, they know about you and they will do it again – they're mad, brutally, fiendishly mad. I will get another call to you early tomorrow when I've checked with our intelligence.'

Detty put the phone down and thought for a minute. She then quickly dialled Stuttgart and asked that Hauptmann von Ritter should ring her on a scrambled call from Norway. In a few minutes the call came through and she was able to explain to Marc what had happened.

He understood at once but sounded troubled. 'We will have to be very careful. As you know interfering with another country's internal affairs is always mucky and for Germany in the East, it's explosive – even after sixty plus years – but I'll talk to the boss and we will try to do something.'

He now sounded anxious, 'and, Detti, I know you too well to try and stop you going but please be careful – you know what they will do to you if they catch you again and you can't always bank on getting away with it.'

'I know, *mein Schatz*,' she said 'but don't worry – I don't intend to let them rob me of my life with you. *Toi, toi, toi.*'

The warning on the scrambled voicemail was terse but somehow convincing. The voice was male and just said, 'Listen,' then, 'Don't go through Berlin or you will never arrive. Go south avoiding Germany and on land – no airports. Do not appear to be going east when you leave England. Head through France towards the south or Spain and change your direction later. You will be followed, for certain, even from England. Try to first identify and then lose your tail. Choose your own route, be unpredictable and don't tell anybody but eventually get to Vienna. Then head north of Warsaw and cross the frontier at Zurstyn and say you seek the *Weltesche*. Allow seven days and we will expect you. Good luck!'

There was no more but somehow she was inclined to believe it was genuine – it didn't ask her to give herself away – only told her what not to do. Detty sat down in the comfortable old barroom and considered her next move. She was certainly frightened but alert and excited as well. She comforted herself that this time at least she had the initiative. If Moltravia was going to receive its unwelcome guest for a third time, at last, she would call the tune. Nevertheless, she realised soberly that the stakes were very high. She had been desperately fortunate to leave Moltravia alive and intact the last two times. The consequences of being captured again, particularly with her increased media profile, were too horrible to contemplate. For a moment she thought about Marc away in Norway. His anxiety was enormous, of that she was sure, but over the years he had come to realise her dedication to this cause. Whatever it cost him he would not stand in her way.

She returned to thinking about the instructions she had received. With regard to the unpredictable bit, she thought that she wasn't really the predictable type but that still didn't give her any indication as to how to follow that particular instruction. She considered leaping from moving trains and buses and escaping through the back doors of hotels. It all seemed very melodramatic but none of it made a lot of practical sense. Anyway, how did she know if she was actually being tailed? She must try to find out. On an impulse she left the house carrying a small empty suitcase and headed purposefully towards the station.

There was nobody obviously following her but a small queue formed behind her at the ticket office. She, loudly, booked a single to Paddington and went through onto the single platform of the little station inspecting the short queue as she did so. There were four businessmen impeccably armed with the *Financial Times* and two young women about Detty's age dressed in jeans and sweaters, probably students, she thought. The other two passengers were more interesting; one was a short middle aged woman and the other a balding man in a sweater and grey trousers.

The woman had to be the most likely suspect, as a tail of the same gender as the quarry was an obvious advantage, and clothing had to be inconspicuous in a variety of settings. This ruled out the businessmen and probably the students. Detty took a good look at Wargrave station, as they stopped there, to confirm her memory of the layout. It wasn't difficult, there is only a single platform for both up and down trains. They then went on to Twyford, where the branch line ended, and she got out.

Suddenly, as she left the train, the last part of the solution to her problem struck her. Instead of going to the booking office to get her return ticket to Henley, she got out her diary and her mobile phone then she crossed the station seeking a better signal. Satisfied she dialled a number from her diary.

'Nutt Brothers, Good morning. How can I help you?' answered a young woman's cut glass voice and Detty put on her best Oxford English:

'Could I possibly speak to Mr Charles,' she said.

'Which Mr Charles did you require?' came the reply.

'Mr Ben Charles.'

'Who shall I say is calling?

'The Countess von Ritter,' said Detty feeling deliberately wicked.

'Please wait one moment, My Lady, and I will put you through.'

The tone had perceptibly changed and now sounded impressed. Suddenly a familiar voice was on the line, 'Detty, how wonderful to hear you – but you don't usually use the posh handle.'

'It's for the posh wine merchants, now, who wouldn't want to be talking to simple Irish girls?' replied Detty, using an exaggerated stage brogue before she reverted to her normal soft accent, 'but, listen quickly – were you really meaning what you said about taking me to France?'

'Not 'arf' came the reply.

'That's grand – please don't ask any questions just say if you can do it or not. Can you pick me up at Wargrave station tonight at 10.45? Don't wait outside the station – as you leave the station and turn left past a little lane alongside the railway you find a road called Waterman Way, it leads to Bushnell's Marina, if you can put your lights out so that the car looks parked. What is it by the way?'

'Blue BMW coupe.' He gave the number.

'Good – I will meet you there. Then can we go straight to Dover – ferry – better than the tunnel?'

'Detty, I will willingly do as you say but I am intrigued. Why all the cloak and dagger stuff? What on earth is going on?'

'Too complicated to explain now. I'll explain as we go if you really can do it.'

'Of course, I will,' he said, completely serious. 'See you there.'

Back at the station, Detty noticed that the shopping bag was sitting on a wall outside the little station trying to look inconspicuous. She looked at shopping bag as the train back to Henley waited and hesitatingly looked at her watch. With a sudden gesture of decision as if she had changed her mind about something she abandoned the London platform and leapt back into the Henley train. Shopping bag waited some minutes and then also casually reboarded the train. Now she was sure.

She felt satisfied as she walked back from the station to the house going past the old parish church door, where she had sung in the Messiah, and along the almshouses. Once inside she fetched the Beretta from the gun cabinet where it nestled illegally amongst Marc's legal twelve bores and put it under her pillow. She set the alarm for 9pm and slept.

She woke before the alarm went off and had a quick shower. She thought long and hard about the Beretta, weighing up the chances of it being discovered before it was any use to her. Eventually she stuffed it into a shoulder holster which she donned and then put on one set of thermal underclothes under her jeans and sweater while packing another set with some more sweaters and other necessities in a backpack. Finally she put on her leather bomber jacket and a woolly hat and left closing the door softly and quickly behind her. She wondered as she did when, if ever, she would open the door of their comfortable English house again. She walked quickly to the station seeing no one but not looking in any great detail. This time she booked a single to Bristol.

The train was already in, making it much harder to spot a tail, who would have had time to board the train in front of her. At Wargrave she waited to the last minute and squeezed through the automatic door as it was shutting. She got out of the train just as it pulled out and ducked through a doorway. She caught a glimpse of a woman staring intently out of a window in the last coach as the train gathered speed. She hurried out thinking all the time that there might be another watcher already stationed there but spotted no one. Ben was waiting in the darkened car as arranged.

'Thanks a million,' she said. 'Get to the M4 as quickly as you can then we can talk.'

As they drove she looked over her shoulder several times to try and identify a following car. The traffic, as always, was heavy and she realised it would be near impossible to distinguish a tail. Ben drove fast and said nothing but once they were heading towards London on the motorway she began to explain.

'You know of my connections with Moltravia and you will have heard about the rising there. It isn't of course the first rising but it is the most serious so far and, for two reasons, it has a better chance of success than the previous ones. The first reason is that conditions in the country have deteriorated so much that Travsky's government is passionately hated even more than previously. They are only holding on by fear, torture and the Kolashnikov. The second is that this revolt has the active support and participation of Nicklaus Oblov, the greatest living Moltravian democrat, who has refused to take part in the previous risings but now realises that this is the moment to act.

'So where do I come in? Well, through chance, since my first visit to Moltravia as a student language teacher at the time when we were together at University, I have been drawn into the country. I love the people with their kind, stoical suffering and detest the Travskys – for there is now a son as well who seems to be worse than the father – and their henchmen, the NAS who are successfully modelled on the Gestapo. Twice I have nearly lost...' she hesitated '...my life in Moltravia at their hands. By chance and good luck I escaped and in addition in doing so I removed from the scene two of Travsky's most trusted henchmen. I now have the honour to be bracketed with Nicklaus Oblov, Air Marshall Zahnsdorf and General Malinov as one of the four chief public enemies of the regime. After the outbreak of the revolt, therefore, I have been under surveillance by the NAS, even here in England. They are afraid that I might return to help in Moltravia – or Livonia as the democrats prefer to call it – and that is exactly what I am doing – hence the cloak and dagger stuff.'

Ben's face had changed and now looked anxious and serious. 'I knew that you were a tough cookie, Detty, but I didn't know it was quite as serious as this. What did you mean when you said that you had removed from the scene two of Travsky's most trusted henchmen?'

'Exactly that, I shot and killed them.'

'My God! but why on earth are you going back? You must be mad.'

'You know that I am an incurable romantic and I am passionate about those people – I couldn't let them struggle without me – even if it is the death of me. I suppose that I am a bit like Lord Jim. More than that, Moltravia – Livonia, as I pray it will be again, is to me a symbol of the struggle between good and evil, between God and the Devil. In the modern world, Livonia is what we should strive for, Moltravia is the pit of hell from which Europe has emerged but which could so easily engulf us all again. There is one thing more, Oblov's daughter is my dearest friend and two nights ago Mara rang and begged me to come.'

'Mara!' said Ben startled. 'Your very pretty blond bridesmaid at the wedding?'

'The same.'

'I thought that she was stunning at your wedding but I never realised that she was Oblov's daughter – I never knew her other name.'

'For security reasons we seldom use her other name, not that it probably makes any difference as their enemies know it well enough. Both the Oblovs were at Oberdorf for our wedding laced with a comforting sprinkling of solid Bavarian security men – you know shoulder holsters and Lederhosen – that sort of thing.'

They both laughed which broke the tension.

'What can I do to help?' said Ben after a pause.

'Take me as far as Burgundy via the Dover Calais ferry. It's a less probable route and less easy to watch than the Shuttle. Treat me as your girl friend,' she smiled, 'up to a point. I will then take the train cross country to Vienna and creep into the rebel held territory from the local trains. I will pose as a student with a Eurorail pass – not so far off the truth really. Just wish me luck. I must come out all right. I have a wonderful husband and a contract to sing at the Bayreuth festival in the summer. I am not passing either up.'

'Much as I love you, Detty, I don't think I would sit through hours of Wagner, even to hear you.'

'Don't worry, you wouldn't get a ticket anyway,' laughed Detty.

The Dover Motel was suitably impersonal and Detty gratefully had a short dreamless night before showering and dressing on a piercingly cold morning. She was glad of the thermals as they left at 5.30am. She had only worn thick gear to save carrying it but now she was glad of it. The Channel was grey flecked with white horses and the winter dawn was overcast with a biting east wind and drizzle. Detty found herself wondering that if it was as cold as this leaving temperate England, what it was going to feel like on the bitter east European plain? The drizzle continued as they headed south, petering out after Rheims and allowing a weak sunshine to filter through the clouds. The talked of old university friends, Europe, wine and music and the long road passed comfortably enough. During the silences, Detty reflected on the strangeness of this old continent with its civilised way of life and peaceful countryside which yet could have horror and barbarism hidden round the next bend in the road. She thought of the century that had only just finished, the Great Wars, Russia, Spain, Hungary, Poland, Czechoslovakia, Ulster, Bosnia and Albania. The list was endless and now Moltravia as they passed through the first years of the twenty-first century. The pattern repeated itself yet again.

As they passed Troyes, Ben broke the latest silence, 'I am at least going to give you a good lunch.'

Her mind was not on lunch but she acquiesced and thanked him graciously enough.

Shortly afterwards he turned off the autoroute and headed down some side roads finally drawing up at the *Hostellerie du Cerf*, timbered and ivy covered on the banks of the new-born Seine. Ben was greeted as a long-lost friend by the *aubergist*.

'Monsieur Ben, Bon retour! What a pleasure to see you again and with such a lovely lady!'

Detty didn't feel very lovely in her student clothes with her hair scragged back and her back pack. She panicked in case Ben should get his own back by introducing her by her full name and title which would be embarrassing, but more important, bound to be remembered if enquiries were made later. She didn't think that they could be traced but if they were the last twenty-four hours carefully planned work might be undone at a stroke. To her immense relief Ben, who she had always known was far from stupid, had thought the problem through and only introduced her, with a knowing glance, as his friend. The Frenchman was thus confirmed in his supposition that the tall striking redhead was indeed Ben's chosen companion for frolics on the Cote d'Azur. This fitted well with Ben's former reputation. The landlord, however, remarked to his chef as he went out into the kitchen that Monsieur Charles' taste appeared to be improving but, '*Mon Dieu*, the clothes Englishwomen are seen about in! *Incroyable!*'

At Ben's insistence they ordered the *Carpes en Meurette* and the landlord suggested a *Civet de Lievre* to follow, explaining that hare was a traditional dish in Burgundy where the feudal landlord's relaxed their hunting laws once a year for the Eastertide feast. After *un flute de Champagne*, Ben chose a *Mazis Chambertin 1990* from one of his own suppliers to accompany the meal. He said it was a wine that was like her – beautiful but strong. Under the enthusiastic guidance of her father-in-law, Detty had come to know and love great wines and she cherished the complex bouquet and deep-layered grandeur of this venerable classic. At the same time she couldn't help wondering if this bottle might be her last. They relaxed contentedly over a leisurely coffee fighting off the landlord's insistent offers of the house *Marc de Bourgogne*.

As they set off south again, the afternoon of the early year was beginning to fade into evening. Silence reigned as the dark silhouette of the Cote d'Or passed to their right. Detty woke out of her reverie to notice the signpost to Citeaux, the citadel monastery of Bernard of Clairvaux, her earlier name saint, who had created the warrior orders and destroyed Peter Abelard while declaring his own devotion to the Virgin. He seemed the right saint for her mission and she prayed silently to him for fortitude adding a little rider that it might be tinged with compassion.

They left the road at Macon and at Detty's insistence Ben reluctantly delivered her to a country auberge before travelling the few kilometres down the road to his hosts who were *vignerons* at St Amour. As he left he kissed her very caringly saying, 'Detty, look after yourself. You're very special. They don't make many like you.'

Before she could reply he swung the car round forcefully and was gone in search of the wines of Burgundy and no doubt the solace of the girls of the Cote d'Azur. Turning to go back into the auberge, Detty thought about their relationship. He was no Marc and could never have handled her, but she knew he adored her and his kindness and dignity, as well as his restraint, over the last day and a half convinced her that he had grown into a fine and generous man.

Now she was alone with the nose of the great rock of *Solutré* towering symbolically menacingly over her. It seemed oddly appropriate that she was here as she set out on her strange obsessive and as yet goal-less journey. Under its shadow, redolent with the echoing passions that it had witnessed since the first ages, it was somehow easier to understand the illogical yet compelling nature of her mission. She had nobody to talk to now and she felt nothing stood between her and her impulsion towards a weird, ill-understood destiny, which would involve the crisis of her life in that strange country where, paradoxically, the worst and the best could happen.

But what could she, a young foreign woman really do to help Livonia and its patriots? In fact, would it not be exactly the opposite, as with her high-profile, wanted-person status, would she not be a liability to a brave people defying modern weaponry and all the odds for freedom? Sure she could bandage wounds and help orphaned children. She was not gun-shy and could fire a rifle from a foxhole but then so could many others and there was nothing special about that. And yet Mara had desperately wanted her to come and she felt so strongly that her journey was special. As she tried to analyse her thoughts she still had the overwhelming conviction that with her, Livonia stood a chance, without her the abyss yawned, but why and more important, how?

She abandoned her reverie and went to bed. In the morning she caught the workers bus into Macon while it was still dark. The bus had that unmistakable reek of garlic and Gauloises that is so characteristic of early-morning working France. She looked round the bleary faces and wondered how they would be spending their day. At least she was now fairly certain that she was not being followed. She caught the train at Macon and by means of several changes reached Basle and travelled slowly through Switzerland reaching the Austrian border and Innsbruck at nightfall.

Several times she looked wistfully north towards Bavaria – for her the magical land which had given her so many things, sanctuary, a beloved partner and the exciting beginnings of a career. It hardly seemed possible that two hundred or so kilometres to the north, this warmth and tranquillity still existed. Meanwhile she travelled east and soon north into the unknown of a country in Hades. She prayed quietly to the Mother of God that she might live to enjoy all that peace and joy again. She booked in at a very plain pension in Innsbruck, inconspicuous and near the station for the early-morning train. The accommodation was spartan with a simple hard bed and shared lavatory and bathroom. It didn't run to a TV but there was radio clock, which Detty turned on almost unconsciously.

A glorious stream of orchestral sound, as rich as it was unexpected, seized her attention. The piece swelled to its conclusion in a majestic melody that she found deeply moving. She trawled her memory desperately but unsuccessfully to recognise it and could not. She thought that it had to be Slavonic but she couldn't place it. Smetana, Dvorak, Martinu? No, they were all somehow wrong and yet it stirred her to her very depths and she desperately wanted to know what it was and who had written it.

The announcer's voice cut in, 'You have been listening to the tone poem Hansa by Gustaf Waldhuter.'

She went on to fill in some extra time by talking about the composer. Apparently, he was little known and now almost never performed. He had been born and spent his early life as a Russian imperial civil servant in Königshof. The announcer reminded the listeners that this was now the capital of Moltravia. Apparently the composer had been involved in the 1905 rising and had narrowly escaped with his life into exile in Mexico. He lived miserably in exile and died in his mid-forties. He dreamed endlessly of his return and of his native city, free and great, as it had been in the days of the Hansa when it stood as the principal and powerful trading station linking Bruges and Lübeck with Novgorod. He poured out all his emotions in the tone poem that was never performed in his lifetime and very rarely since.

At this critical moment in her journey, it was a shattering coincidence to hear the heartfelt music of the exiled patriot writing of the homeland that he loved and that she loved too. Why had she never heard it before? She rushed to her backpack and got out a sheet of paper to scribble down the main theme of the finale. Realising that she must rest she got into bed with the grand, astonishing tune that she had just heard resounding through her head.

After a hurried breakfast she caught the train to Vienna. As the train left Innsbruck, she got out her scribbled piece of paper and as she travelled she struggled with the tune and the words she was trying to fit to it in Moltravian Russian. The beauties of the Enns and Danube valleys passed unnoticed and she only stirred herself as the train crept into a damp, grey Vienna in the afternoon.

She wanted to press on north but decided to pause long enough to ring the *Musikverein Bibliotek*. The woman sounded distant and slightly frosty but yes they did have a copy of Waldhuter's Hansa. She went round straight away. An equally frosty woman, perhaps the same one, eyed her scruffy student appearance up and down. After this chilling inspection, she said dubiously that perhaps Frau von Ritter would be able to consult the Waldhuter. She would, however, have to give a letter of introduction from a recognised academic or musical authority before

358

she could be allowed access. Detty thought desperately until, with inspiration, she said that Professor Doktor Meisl at Bayreuth would certainly provide her with the required reference if only it were possible to telephone or email him. The frosty woman suddenly looked more helpful and said, 'Are you then connected with the *Bayreuther Festspiele*, Frau von Ritter?'

'Yes,' said Detty sensing she was on firmer ground. 'I am singing at the next Festival.'

'Chorus or principal?'

'Principal,' said Detty thinking very ungenerous thoughts about her interlocutor which wisely she kept to herself.

'In that case I think I could accept authorisation from the telephone. Do you have the direct number?'

By good fortune Detty had written it in her diary and found it after searching clumsily in her thick winter clothes.

Still doubtful the librarian went into an inner office to telephone. After a very short call, which was obviously satisfactory, she emerged all smiles and suddenly the difficulties melted away. Of course there would be no problem in Frau von Ritter consulting Waldhuter's score and of course she could photocopy any sections that she needed for her research. She should have said, at the outset, that she was a soloist at Bayreuth and they would have just looked up the casting for next year. How did she find the Japanese designs for the new *Ring*?'

Detty had other preoccupations at that particular moment than design styles for the *Ring* but she managed to stutter out something that she hoped sounded interested and intelligent. Finally, she was left alone with her score. It was all there as she had hoped and she made some notes and photocopied the relevant pages. Thanking her librarian profusely, she then set out for the station to catch her train north. She had several more changes as she crept north through Moravia and via Brno into Poland. All the time she worked on the text for the tune of the final passage of Hansa. First, she wrote them in Moltravian Russian, which she had mastered during her two enforced stays. Finally fairly satisfied, she translated them roughly into German and English.

She sat back looking out, as the hills receded, at the flat grey landscape racing towards an ill-defined horizon with the dark sodden sky. Occasionally a dripping mixed broad leaf and conifer forest, stretching for some kilometres, broke the monotony. Between the busy roads the houses were few and only the occasional narrow, ill-kempt road or axle-bogging forest mud track was evidence of human presence. This plain, which stretched from the Urals to the Elbe was in one sense a cradle of civilisation. It was also a terrible land, in tune with the horrors of its past and unconcerned by the political labels that its transient overlords attached to it. Why then were its people so generous and stoical, and why did she love it so much that she was prepared to sacrifice her very real happiness, perhaps even her life itself, to return to it again?

She couldn't give herself an answer, only recognise the strength of the compulsion. It wasn't Mara for, much as she loved her, she was a symptom not the cause of the attraction. Had she had any other husband but Marc she had no doubt that he would have made her choose between Livonia and her marriage. Marc, perhaps because his military training bred both understanding and fatalism, however, seemed to know and accept the way she felt. Although she knew he had suffered agonies when she went, after the outburst at Oberdorf he never objected and she half thought he shared her obsession. After all he had gone to Moltravia voluntarily in the first place and, unlike her, on her first visit he knew full-well what the country was like. She must be mad to be sitting on this damp draughty train going to, she knew not where, when she should have been at home learning *Woglinde* and the other bigger roles that she had been studying with Bernhard Meisl. After all, most young singers would have given their right arm for the opportunity that she was treating so casually.

It was a reasonable service and with a couple of changes she was able to reach a country station about fifty kilometres from the border by nightfall. Her few words of Polish succeeded in finding her a bed for the night with the station master's family. Over stewed dumplings, bacon and vegetables, Detty tried to find out news of the uprising. The Poles, kind and sympathetic as they were, showed a great weariness when the subject was raised and were unable to provide any accurate information.

They thought that the bridge at Bialovsk was still in insurgent hands. The husband spoke some Russian and German and with Detty's stuttering Polish they managed to communicate fairly well. Her hosts clearly imagined that she was following her man into the uprising and she thought it was wise not to disillusion them.

She retired early to a spotless fresh bed in the room normally occupied by her hosts' merchant seaman son. She slept soundly waking with a start at seven thirty to find it fully light. She dressed quickly in thermal leggings and her replacement leather jacket and went downstairs. In reply to her question the station master told her that she could get a train at nine fifteen to a station only nine kilometres from Bialovsk but that no trains now crossed the Bial river into Moltravia. From the station she would have to hitch a lift or walk.

She tried to pay the kind couple but, endlessly generous and probably imagining from her clothes and back pack that she was a penniless student, they refused to take as much as a zloty. Detty felt awful as she was, after all, an extremely wealthy young woman married into a banking family with a castle and a great estate. She could so easily have repaid the kindness of these generous people with a sum that meant nothing to her but might have kept them comfortable for some time. She knew, however, that she must respect their dignity and accept their kindness.

She said only, 'When I return from Moltravia, may I come back and thank you properly?'

This was agreed and Peter, the husband, who was off duty that morning accompanied her to the station and waved as the train drew out. Finding a hard slatted seat on the train, for a moment Detty thought about the generosity and kindness of her hosts before contemplating the possibilities of the day before her.

11
DER WALSTATT

Auf der Walstatt allein erschein' ich Edlen:[35]

WAGNER : DIE WALKÜRE ACT II

A fine cold drizzle, near sleet, was falling as she trudged up the flat road. There was mud everywhere, mud on the road with frozen puddles in between, mud over the bare fields which had been churned up by heavy trucks and track vehicles trying to pass each other. From time to time lorries ploughed past through the mud-splattering Detty as she went. Finally, a heavily laden truck drew up and the fair-haired young driver signalled to her to get in. Mud caked she thanked him, edging herself onto the bench seat.

'Where can I drop you?' he said in heavily accented Polish.

She smiled before answering him, 'I'm afraid I don't speak Polish very well. Could we speak German?' He nodded and she went on in Moltravian German. 'It rather depends on where you are going.'

The driver looked startled and puzzled at her Moltravian accent and said, 'You're Moltravian then?'

---

35 Only on the battlefield I appear to heroes

'No,' said Detty, 'I'm Irish."

'Irish! Where on earth did you learn to speak *Königshofer Mundart* then?'

'Oh, I spent some time in Moltravia,' replied Detty truthfully.

The driver looked anxious. He thought that he had picked up a striking Polish village girl who would ease the gloom of his journey for a few kilometres but he was now worried. The strange female claimed to be Irish and yet spoke Königshof German like a native. He smelt a rat. It would be entirely in character for the NAS to try and smuggle a spy into the insurgent ranks from Poland. He wondered if he should just drop her or shoot her but he wasn't sure and decided that if, as he expected, she wanted to cross the river it would be far safer to hand her over to the revolutionary authorities and tell them of his suspicions about her. After a pause he said, 'I'm going to the bridge at *Bialovsk.'*

'Over it?' enquired Detty.

'As a matter of fact – yes,' was the reply.

'Well I want to get over it too.'

'OK,' he answered suspiciously, 'but why?'

'Because I know about the revolt and want to help.'

It sounded lame and Detty knew it. In this game of verbal poker she had considered saying that she was trying to find her boyfriend. She realised, however, that the insurgent force was relatively small. Her suspicious driver might enquire what unit the boyfriend was in and would be even more suspicious if there were any more inconsistencies.

They settled into silence as the bridge approached. The Polish army, smart in spite of the mud, in their square caps, had a considerable presence on their side of the bridge but did nothing to interfere. Detty assumed that, while remaining strictly neutral, they did nothing to impede the passage of materials across the river into the insurgent zone. Travsky's government had persistently protested to Warsaw about the lack of restraint of the Polish government. The latter, however, had a natural sympathy with the rebels. They knew well the concern of their frustrated and largely impotent colleagues in Europe. Travsky and his henchmen therefore received a diplomatically deaf ear. The real problem was obtaining adequate supplies, not that they could not get through.

Organisation of the Moltravian expatriates was, however, slowly improving finance and supplies.

In spite of the mud and the cold, Detty felt a shiver of excitement down her spine at her first public sight of the green and white flag emblazoned with the falcon of Königshof and the sacred chalice of Zablovsk. It was flying over the guard post on the Moltravian – no – she corrected herself with another tingle – Livonian – side of the bridge. The bridge itself had been destroyed several times by enemy raids and showed signs of the frantic temporary repairs made by the insurgents to this essential lifeline. Indeed, at this moment the centre span had been replaced by a mobile military unit and there were considerable delays on either side. Livonian engineers were working frantically to reopen the more permanent structure.

As soon as they had crossed, reality returned as she got down with the driver to report at the control post. The driver presented his papers and then made some lame excuse to talk to the guards in the back office. Detty was virtually sure he was expressing doubts about the *bona fides* of his passenger. Her suspicions were confirmed when a thickset sergeant major appeared from the back office and started to question her about the reason for her journey.

She stuck to the simple truth. She had been contacted by Frau Tamara Oblova, who was a close friend of hers, and she had offered her help. Frau Oblova had said that unfortunately no flight could be arranged and anyway it was safer to travel overland through Poland. The kind driver who had brought her here had given her a lift and could they please contact Frau Oblova to say that she had arrived.

The sergeant major eyed her scruffy appearance up and down and looked extremely dubious, 'It's hard to believe that you're here at the express request of the *Chef's* daughter.'

'Yes, I am,' said Detty looking him straight in the eye.

'Tell her that you have a woman here who is seeking the *Weltesche* and she will confirm it.'

'Young lady, you are quite an attractive *Dirne*,' he used the vulgar Moltravian dialect word, which was not actually obscene but was still fairly insulting, 'but I don't think that you are exactly in the class to know the *Chef* or the Frau Tamara.'

Detty noticed almost with amusement that he spoke her young friend's name with almost religious reverence.

'Would they let a friend of theirs arrive here unheralded – hitching a lift through the mud? I am going to have you taken to the cells until we know a little more about you and your suspicious little escapade.'

The day passed in frustration. She was provided with coffee, a plate of steaming pork stew and plenty of enquiries as to whether she was OK. She realised that this was a very different reception to the one that she had been accorded by the Moltravian authorities. In this respect at least the new Livonia was impressive. There was, however, no progress towards her release except that a senior intelligence officer would arrive to interview her sometime that evening.

She couldn't understand why Mara had not let the frontier post know of her possible arrival. It was true that she had arrived several days earlier than the seven allowed but surely Mara would have realised that this was always possible. She cursed herself for not carrying a photograph of Mara on her, showing them together as bridesmaid and bride, which might have convinced the sergeant major. Then she thought with grim humour that the last time one of her wedding photographs had been produced it was on Konradin's desk and hadn't done her much good. At a certain level she could understand that they couldn't let strangers into their small and vulnerable enclave unannounced but it was still maddening to be detained by the very people that she had come to try and help.

Eventually the evening came and the sergeant major re-appeared and signalled for her to follow. It was already dark and they crossed the space in front of the improvised cell and into the main hut. At the back was a door and the sergeant major knocked. Detty immediately thought that she would be faced with some pompous senior officer barking questions at her. She didn't believe her own ears when she recognised the female voice inviting them to enter. The sergeant major motioned Detty through the door and saluted.

The events of the next moments were ones that he would never forget. He announced his charge saying, 'Oberleutnant Zahnsdorf, this is the young woman that we detained crossing the frontier this morning.'

His voice trailed away as he realised that the interrogating officer and the detainee were each in each others' arms. All that he heard was a whispered, 'Detty!' and in reply, 'Liese!' as they hugged for several minutes.

The sergeant major had never approved of women in the army but this confounded even his expectations. Besides Liese Zahnsdorf had established herself as a courageous and extremely competent officer over the last few weeks and until this evening the sergeant major would have been inclined to make an exception in her case.

Finally, Liese remembered that there was a third party present, straightened her green and white cockade of the FWL, the Livonian Liberation Army, in her cap and addressed the astonished NCO, 'Sergeant Major, you may be interested to know that your detainee is Bernadette O'Neill, a heroine of the Livonian freedom movement and, like me, a former inmate of the Farm concentration camp. She is the woman who, single-handed, dispatched the Farm armourer, the torturer Gregor Tushkin. On a subsequent visit to this country she shot dead the notorious Dr Kovacs, the then the commandant general of the NAS. You have before you a living legend and the woman whose achievements President Oblov said last week that we must all strive to follow if we are to win this terrible war. She has returned to us and I pray that she will help us do it.'

'Oh, my God!' said the sergeant major. 'I am truly sorry, ma'am – what can I say?'

'Nothing,' replied Detty, holding out her hand to the sergeant major. 'Nothing needed. You did your duty as a soldier perfectly correctly. You strived your upmost to protect the cause that we all hold dear. What is more you treated me extremely decently although I was a legitimate suspect. I don't have to tell you that this is not the kind of treatment that I have previously received in this country and I am impressed and grateful to you.'

She shook his hand firmly. He still looked shaken so she continued, 'If the free Republik is defended by men like you we have little to fear and I hope that I have the chance to serve with you.'

'But I called you a *Dirne*,' he said even more miserably.

Detty laughed, 'I've been called worse things than that, Sergeant Major. I don't suppose that you are the first soldier who used that term for an odd girl who turned up like a beggar on the doorstep. Forget it!'

'You are very generous, Frau O'Neill, I just hope that I can make it up to you one day.'

He relaxed a little and smiled wanly at her.

Liese broke in briskly, 'The first thing that you can do, Sergeant Major, is to find out what happened to Frau Tamara's dispatch that she mailed down three days ago saying that Frau O'Neill was to be expected and taken to headquarters as soon as she arrived.'

Jawohl, Frau Oberleutnant, at once,' said the still dazed sergeant major.

'Oh and by the way here is a warrant for identity papers and A+ security clearance for Frau O'Neill perhaps you would get the necessary pass made out for her at once. I have used "O'Neill" and given your status as personal adviser to the supreme commander. Is that OK?'

'Fine on both counts,' nodded Detty.

The sergeant major was relieved to bustle about his jobs and happy to leave the two women alone. For a few moments after he left they just looked at each other in silence. Detty broke it, 'Tell me everything. How you got here? How's it going? Where are Mara and Nicklaus? What can I do now I'm here?'

'I'll try and do all that but first I must make a phone call. This line is scrambled but we are still not completely sure it is effective so I will use my cipher and you will have to leave talk until later.'

She picked the field telephone up and continued, *Ich bin FL 1S 67 am apparat. Darf ich mit Ännchen sprechen?*

Detty drew in her breath sharply – it would be typical for Mara to choose as her code name the character that Detty had said belonged to her at that far-off Oberdorf Easter party. There was a pause. Then Liese said, *'Wie gehst du?* I have found the consignment of green potatoes but the invoice from here never arrived.'

There was some more talk with Liese interjecting, 'OK,' from time to time until finally she put the phone down.

'She sends her love and says that it is better for the news to wait until you see her tonight. Meanwhile I am to have your papers made out as an Oberleutnant Liaison Observer. That's the *Chef's* instruction. I will get you fitted with uniform fatigues, fill you in on the general situation and get you transport. Our unit camp is only five kilometres from here. We had better go back there – it's more comfortable and I can get your papers and kit sorted out.'

They made their way out to the battered jeep, wishing the sheepishly saluting sergeant major farewell as they went. Liese drove over the ruts at a breakneck speed bred of familiarity. The camp turned out to be in a small village with the officers' mess in the only substantial farmhouse and the rest of the troops billeted in the Church, the school, a few cottages and some farm buildings. The sexes seemed equally represented with young women and men going about their duties with Armalites and Kolashnikovs never far from their side.

Liese gave some instructions to a girl wearing corporal's stripes, 'Daneeka, can you fix Oberleutnant O'Neill up with combat clothes and get her papers from the office?'

She turned to Detty, 'Have you got up-to-date photographs?'

'Sorry, I haven't got any at all.'

Detty thought inconsequentially that she could hardly put a wedding photograph on an ID card even if she had had one.

'No problem,' said Liese, 'I've got a camera in my room. We will take some now.'

The three of them climbed two flights of stairs into a small shabby room with two chairs, a wardrobe and a bed. Liese attempted to find her camera rummaging in a rucksack whileDetty tried to push her long hair into some sort of order. Eventually the photos were taken and the corporal dispatched to have them printed and to collect the other gear. It all reminded Detty a little of her arrival at *Neubrandenwald*. That was only two years ago but it seemed like a lifetime. The difference was that that morning there was all joy; here there was tension, anxiety and even some fear as well.

The arrangements made, they sat down over coffee and Liese began to talk, 'After you left the Farm and the raid to rescue Mara took place, it got very horrible. For several months they got up to every foul trick they could think of. The old slightly school atmosphere of the "keep them alive to be useful" days, unpleasant as it was, that we had experienced had gone and was replaced by full time naked brutality. They hanged another three of us for no very good reason – just as a warning to the rest. They treated us all pretty badly. I was very lucky not to be one of the ones to be hanged as they knew I was friendly with you and Mara. They were beginning to be afraid though and I think what saved me was that my father was, is, an air force commandant then living in exile in Russia. I think that they thought that if they hanged me he would be bound to throw his influence behind the next revolt which they were beginning to fear more than the previous ones.

'After about a year they began to be less brutal and even quite civilised particularly to those of us who were deemed to be strategically influential. One night the governor sent for me and offered me a glass of vodka and a cigarette and in general was revoltingly ingratiating. At this time he had already become vice president of the Republik but for some reason had decided not to give up his post at the Farm. You and I could guess his motives for that decision. In fact I thought that he was wanting some home comforts when he sent for me. In those later days he appeared less often but was always there for major events, although he delegated the day-to-day running of the place to the deputies.'

'Anyway, on that particular evening he was oily charm itself. As I said I first thought that he wanted to have me and was going to subject me to the candlelit dinner routine, which I knew he had used with some of the others prior to raping them. Not a bit of it, however. When he finally stopped beating about the bush, it appeared that he wanted me to go to Russia to persuade my father to come back bringing some newer MiGs with him and take up his old post again running the air force. They made all sorts of offers of the rewards that we would both get and there were some veiled threats of what would happen to my friends still in the country if it didn't work out properly. I thought about it hard and came to the difficult conclusion that, like you before me, right had to be done regardless of the threat of reprisals.'

'So I played along with them. I got some money out of them, some civvy clothes, a passport and a chauffeur driven car and was dumped across the Russian border at Litovsk. The joke was that my father wasn't

369

even there, Travsky's men didn't know it but he was already in Bratislava joining the FWL and negotiating with the Russians for our aircraft and other supplies. It was fairly simple for me to get on the next train and go and join him. One part of the governor's plan was correct, my father did have the capacity to find some MiGs from a Russian arms dealer and the three squadrons of these constitute the Frei Luftwaffe Livonias now under his command.'

'For a short time we thought that the opposition might be about to fold up. Particularly when old Travsky had a stroke last year, it seemed that we only had to wait and the regime would collapse. Unfortunately, the stroke meant that Stefan Travsky, the son, was able to seize power. This was a case of the father chastising with whips, the son with scorpions! Stefan immediately increased the size and power of the NAS and introduced a fighting arm, which swore loyalty to him personally – just like the Waffen SS. There was a huge new purge with mass arrests and many executions.

'*So nimmt meine Eigen Nibelungen Sohn,*'[36] interpolated Detty to herself seriously.

Liese looked at her, puzzled, and then continued, 'Anyway the country seethed and was cowed at the same time. Nicklaus Oblov, who was waiting in Bratislava, decided that at last he had to act. He had dissociated himself with the previous revolts which he thought were hopeless and just a waste of good lives. This time, however, it was essential to act and there was just a chance that we might succeed.'

'At first things went very well, we were prepared enough to put a force of 50,000 across the Bialovsk bridge before they had time to defend it in strength or blow it. We occupied the *Interfluss* between the Bial and the Fojn rivers in a few days and there was talk of Königshof in a week. Initially we were pleased to have a large waterway to protect us while we regrouped but it has now turned into a major snag. The problem is that the bridges are all blown, Travsky's men did that, and we don't have the engineering equipment or the armour to cross the Fojn. It has turned into a war of attrition and a war of attrition which, unless a miracle happens, we are going to lose.'

---

36 So now take my blessing son of the Nibelung

'There are several factors all going against us. We have better aircraft than the government but nothing like as many. We can only loose one of ours to every three of theirs. Then we have no tanks. Originally they were coming from Russia as part of the same deal as the aircraft but the authorities shut the dealer down. He had delivered the aircraft but the tanks couldn't get out in time and the bastards have now, possibly, sold them to Travsky. The most important factor, however, is that, although we know that we have massive support across the Fojn, with every day that passes our supporters are being put in concentratiion camps where they are tortured and massacred. Travsky has no popular support but he has still enormous power through fear.'

'There is a domino effect because the more that we are bogged down here the more worries our people have about their families and friends the other side – and they are right to be fearful.'

Liese paused and Detty's brow furrowed in thought until she broke the silence, 'When do I leave for headquarters and how far is it?'

'Tonight and about sixty kilometres.'

'Liese, I just might be able to find a way of helping. I came here to be with my friends, try to help the morale and the wounded and, if possible, shoot a few NAS but I think I may have a more urgent job to do. I must talk to the Oblovs.'

Liese couldn't leave the frontier and found Detty a driver but it was still the same dilapidated jeep. The mud and ice were continuous as they travelled, mostly in open subsistence farmland with the occasional cow, and even more occasional horse ploughing, notwithstanding the war going on around. Sometimes they passed through deep conifer woods. There was never a slope or a hill in the land that was completely flat between the rivers which, given the ice and the driving sleet, was probably just as well. As they passed through the villages Detty was aware of the green and white flag with its falcon and golden chalice hanging from every public building and many private ones along the road. Free Livonia certainly didn't lack support but that was never the danger. Detty gloomily pondered the tragic likelihood of it all failing with the slaughter and the horror that would result.

It was midnight before they reached headquarters at the Schloss Klouberov. Their papers were carefully checked and they drove through the outer courtyard into the inner private quarters. Mara rushed out before they had stopped moving and threw her arms round Detty. She thanked the driver and they climbed the two sided outside staircase to the private apartments. Mara was as warm as ever but looked tense and drawn. She had lost a lot of weight again as she showed Detty to her room and then guided her back to their private drawing room.

Almost immediately her father joined them, kissed Detty and thanked her for coming and supporting them. He said she must be hungry and asked for supper to be served.

It was a family meal in front of a large fire and Detty found it hard to realise that she was in the middle of a war to the death being conducted from this very building. The arrival of General Malinov for coffee emphasised the latter. Clearly, though, this was not the moment for business and after Nicklaus had introduced him to Detty, they just chatted about the war and how it had affected all their lives. Detty was dog-tired and aching to get some sleep but as the chat died down she spotted a piano at the end of the room. Almost zombie like she drifted towards it – the first she had seen since leaving Henley. She started to play Waldhuter's tune and then to sing her Livonian words. Had she been alert and in her right mind she would never have dared do it. She had not mentioned the song to anybody since she had arrived in Livonia. Gradually her excitement at the stirring music took over. She hadn't been able to practise for over a fortnight and some of the sounds weren't as she would have wished but the fire was there. As she finished Mara and her father were silent. Miserably Detty thought she had been wrong and it was all inappropriate and a dreadful failure. She had inflicted her romantic fantasies on people struggling for life.

At last Nicklaus whispered, 'That spoke the essence of our fight.'

Malinov broke in, 'Forgive me, *Chef*, but I think it was more than that. I believe that with that song in the souls of our men, we can and will win this war. Look what the Marseillaise did for a beleaguered France.'

He turned to Detty, 'How did you find it?'

She laughed with relief and pleasure, 'The tune comes from the tone poem Hansa by Gustav Waldhuter. I wrote the words in the train coming here. It's wonderful that you like it.'

'Like it!' chorused the others.

'I wonder why it took an Irish girl to capture the spirit of our cause,' said Mara reflectively.

'Perhaps because we know a bit about fighting oppression.' Detty said simply suddenly feeling drained.

Mara, sensing the exhaustion, got up suggesting bed. Before they left Nicklaus told them that there was a staff meeting tomorrow which both of them were welcome to attend.

12

LAUSCH KIND

Lausch', Kind, das ist ein Meisterlied[37]

WAGNER: DIE MEISTERSINGER ACT III

Colonel Kramm's voice was clear over the scrambled line. She had explained the need for the call by saying she must contact her husband.

'It's feasible, Frau Bernadette, but formidably dangerous and political dynamite. We could probably cover our involvement but we could do nothing to protect you.'

There was a pause. 'If you really want to go ahead, come to Stuttgart and discuss it.'

The atmosphere in the old drawing room of Schloss Klouberov had been tense. As well as Mara and Nicklaus, General Malinov, the commander-in-chief of the FWL, and General Zahnsdorf, Liese's father, the head of the airforce, were all present. Each had with them two aides. The state of grim stagnation of the campaign was outlined by Malinov. They could not cross the Fojn because of lack of armour and equipment. In the meanwhile the reign of terror was crushing the morale of their

---

37 Listen, child, that is a mastersong

374

supporters on the other side. Unless they could break out, the war would be lost and there appeared to be no way of breaking out. Morale in the FWL itself was falling and many were justly appalled by the fate of their relatives over the river.

'To stand any chance of success,' said Malinov, 'we need three near-miracles at once. The first is to obtain some serviceable tanks, as without these we cannot oppose the government armour. The second, which seems impossible, is to strike a blow at the vitals of the enemy high command, disrupting it and the terror campaign. The third is to achieve a successful crossing of the river. They are all important but if we could achieve the second, the gain towards the others would be immense. We have irregulars on the other bank but they are being reduced in numbers day by day and they would never be allowed to penetrate to anyone of importance.'

'Who really is of importance?' Detty had asked quietly.

'Ultimately Konradin who I believe you may remember as the governor of the Farm Detention Camp. He commands the army and the NAS now and has become more powerful than Stefan Travsky who is just mindlessly brutal and orchestrates some of the gratuitous horrors. But the country is under Konradin's thumb and he uses torture and death with vicious intelligence to maintain and advance his power. As you know he was always a sadist but he is far more logically cruel and ruthless now than he was before. He has one or two henchmen but ultimately he has much more power than anyone, even than Stefan.'

Detty had noted that Malinov seemed fully familiar with her personal history which presumably had been told to him by Tamara. She nodded and said nothing but the germ of an idea had entered her head to be quickly followed by a mental picture of Marc screwing up his face in agony. Malinov might know what had happened to her in the farm but she doubted if he knew about the extreme efforts Konradin had made to get her out of the Winterburg to be his mistress the year before.

As the meeting broke up, the younger of Malinov's two adjutants, a fair young man, approached Detty rather diffidently. She noticed he spoke excellent high German.

'Entschuldigung Sie, Frau O'Neill,' he started looking embarrassed

'but we are holding an entertainment for the troops on Friday in the Market Hall at Fojnheim and Frau Tamara has told me that you are a very fine singer. I am sorry for the very short notice but could you possibly perform something? You understand that at this critical time morale is very important.'

'I should be honoured, Herr Major,' she said without hesitation. 'Had you anything particular in mind? What else has been arranged?'

'Please sing anything that you wish. We have been able to form an orchestra and chorus and there will be a dance display.'

'Then if it fits with the programme I would like to sing five – no – six songs at the end of the evening. The last one has a chorus and would be better with an orchestral accompaniment. Can that be done? Who is conducting?'

'I'm sure it can be done. Hauptman von Grunstrand from the Third Brigade has formed the orchestra and will conduct. He is young but had good experience in Dresden as a repetiteur at the Semper Oper before he joined us. Would you like to meet him? Perhaps we could go to the mess now,' he smiled. 'He promised me that he would be there just in case you said yes.'

The captain was standing at the makeshift bar playing with a glass of beer. He shook hands with Detty and they quickly got down to work. She felt elated to be planning something positive after all the travel and waiting. Also, at the back of her mind was the thought that an increase in her profile would help the plan that she was working out secretly.

Helge von Grunstrand was a real enthusiast. 'The theme is light-hearted but patriotic of course,' he said. 'We start with a military march sequence by the orchestra. Then there is a choral medley from operetta interspersed with national dances and a couple of popular songs by one of the sergeants who has a good baritone. We still need something stirring for the finale. We hoped that you might be able to help.'

'How good are you at orchestrating, Herr Hauptman?' she could barely control her excitement. 'Because, if you are, I think we might be in business.'

Without pausing for an answer she went on to explain how she had heard Waldhuter's Hansa by chance on her journey and had been startled to learn that it was written by a yearning exile from Königshof.

Von Grunstrand was nodding. 'I have heard of Waldhuter. I once heard his string quartet played. I think this also uses your theme. He is hardly ever played now apart from some of the chamber pieces. I came across a score of Hansa in Dresden and read it. It was marvellous, particularly that haunting melody from the finale. I imagine that is your tune. I have longed to hear the whole thing played.'

'I stopped in Vienna on the way here and unearthed a score so I was able to copy the melody accurately. Then I wrote words to it on the train coming up here, I have them here. I want to sing it as the climax of the concert but it needs the chorus and an orchestral accompaniment. The concert hall version won't do.'

'It's going to have one! Can we work on it today? Then we will have two days to rehearse.'

He fetched some music paper from his room and together they worked out the scoring and the soloist and four choral parts. By mid-afternoon they had a full orchestra score and the choral part lines. Then they copied parts for the orchestra as if their lives depended on it. By supper they had them finished and triumphantly photocopied them.

'This calls for champagne,' said Helge, 'only one problem – no champagne so it will have to be beer or plum brandy as usual. What will you have?'

'Beer please, I'm parched.' said Detty clutching her score 'Do you really think it will work?'

'Not only will it work but I think you may have found today a key to the morale question.'

'What have you been doing?' said a voice behind them.

'Oh Boris' said Helge 'I'm sorry we were so preoccupied that I didn't see you come in. May I introduce Frau Oberleutnant O'Neill. Frau O'Neill, this is Hauptmann Boris Vorachek who is in charge of broadcasting across the river. In answer to your question, Frau Bernadette has just produced a majestic Hymn to Freedom and we have been working on a score so that she can sing it with full chorus and orchestra at the end of the concert on Friday.'

'I was going to mention that to you anyway.' said Vorachek 'You know that we have started transmitting TV across the river now. Well, would you mind if we televised your concert? It might be good for morale and God knows they need it over there. It's my job you see, Frau O'Neill, to try and encourage and inform our supporters in government-held territory.'

Detty couldn't believe her luck. This would really make sure that her presence was known.

Still bleary-eyed, Detty crawled out of bed the following morning. She wished she could have heard from Marc but knew that her hurried cryptic message to Stuttgart might have reached him without his being able to find any means of getting a reply to her. Meanwhile, she could only tackle the job in hand. Fortunately the piano, though badly out of tune, was there in the drawing room.

The choice was difficult. She had no music and had to rely on the things she knew. A balance had to be struck between light entertainment and high seriousness. The message and the morale were vital but they were, after all, soldiers with soldiers' tastes and they had to be entertained. She needed four songs before the finale that would be the full *Freiheitslied*, as they had decided it should be called, with fanfare, chorus and full orchestra. She was just agonising over the last song in the gloomy half-light of morning when there was a discrete knock at the door. It was Vorachek. 'I just thought that you would like to know that we've fixed everything for the broadcast.'

On the night the orchestral pieces went with great verve and, given the circumstances, considerable skill. She admired the sergeant baritone's really excellent voice and enjoyed his Baltic fisherman's songs immensely. After a short interval, performers and audience alike threw themselves into the spirit of the national dances. She realised with some surprise that she was hearing Mazurkas and Polonaises as they had originated.

Then it was her turn. She wore a simple trimmed black full knee-length skirt with a white blouse suggesting but not imitating Livonian traditional costume. Mara had scoured the country for materials and then used her considerable charm to persuade the owners to 'lend them'. She had also found an excellent dressmaker amongst the service staff who translated the ideas into reality and the result was professional.

She started with *Kalinka,* the gypsy song of the guelder rose familiar to everyone, allowing the flat vowels to drift mesmerically over the audience as she wickedly caressed it. She followed it with Danny Boy, sincere and emotional, which she explained was a folk song of her birth place. She then led the very popular baritone back onto the platform and together they sang *La ci darem la mano* with him every inch the wicked Don and Detty a very coquettish Zerlina. It took several minutes for the applause and cheers to die down and enable her to complete her solo programme with beautiful local *Zogen einst funf wilde Schwane.*She then called again upon her native land and sang the rousing *Irish Soldier Laddie* of 98. She realised none of them had any idea of the whereabouts of Wexford or Enniscorthy but it did talk about 'marching with O'Neill' and the situation somehow seemed appropriate. She prayed silently though for a better outcome than in 1798. The audience loved the rousing martial tune even if they didn't understand a word.

After her bows she left the stage with her accompanist who now had to resume his role as conductor. While the chorus and orchestra reassembled she made a lightening change with Mara's help into her dress for the finale reappearing into the single spot light in a long green skirt, white silk blouse and gold shoes. It was very simple but stunning with her tall figure and long auburn hair. It was also unmistakably the Livonian insurgent colours. The cheers redoubled to be hushed only by the long trumpet fanfare of freedom followed by the drum rolls and the orchestra swelling into Waldhuter's majestic hymn. Somehow she was disembodied both from her voice and the words that she had written. She remembered nothing afterwards such was the emotion and only came to with her arms spread wide as the orchestra thundered its close. She must have controlled herself somehow because she was assured afterwards on all sides that it was a very beautiful and thoroughly professional performance. The illicit television screens of the nation carried her image into the homes and hearts of the land. At the end it was as if, one old farmer told her later, her wide-spread arms were embracing and consoling the whole people. And who, he said, would not fight on after that whatever the fearful dangers that they all knew that she had shared?

The summons to go to Nicklaus's office came at mid morning. She had been feeling rather let down after the excitement of the night before. Her excitement had been rather dampened anyway when, on her way from Fojnheim to Kluberov, she had run her jeep off the road and had to wait several cold hours for the FWL Sappers to pull her out. She had sat there staring at a half-destroyed sign reading *Vierkirche zum Interfluss* and wondering, irrelevantly, how a hamlet could have four churches. She was very cold, worried at making more work for the hard pressed engineers and also frightened as she had time to think things through. It was quite one thing to think of her mad-cap scheme in theory but she had now done the preparations and she either had to go ahead or back out. She knew she would never back out but was somehow glad when the summons to the *Chef*'s office forced her hand.

By good fortune Malinov was with him. They both thanked her for the night before with Nicklaus adding, 'I suppose you realise that as well as raising morale at a moment when we desperately needed it, you have given new Livonia a national anthem. Every soldier in the camp is whistling your song this morning. What do you call it by the way?'

'It hasn't really got a name. As you know the melody is in the finale of the tone poem Hansa and I believe Waldhuter also uses it in one of his string quartets but I have never heard that. Up to now we have just referred to it as *Freiheitslied*. Perhaps you should choose a name.'

Malinov broke in, 'What's wrong with *Freiheitslied, Chef*? Surely that's why we are all here anyway?'

He agreed and *Freiheitslied* it was to remain. Nicklaus then looked serious. 'We have also heard from the other side. Apparently most of the population watched last night in spite of the ban and the authorities have already said that anyone heard singing or whistling your tune will be shot. That response shows just how effective you have been over there as well.'

Detty took a deep breath. This was her cue. 'I'm glad,' she said. 'There was something else I wanted to mention to you. Do you mount any raids across the river?'

'Yes, of course.' It was Malinov who replied. 'We have to because we need to supply the partisan groups and also show them we care for

380

them. It is usually done by helicopter but whatever way we choose it is extremely dangerous. We have had many casualties and worse, many captured and interrogated. I don't need to tell you how they do that. We always ask for volunteers and so far we have always got them. We try to pick single youngsters without families but it isn't always possible. Why do you ask?'

She took a deep breath. 'Because I wondered if you would let me join one of them.'

There was silence for a moment as Nicklaus stared first at her and then at Malinov speechless. Finally he stuttered, 'Of course you are making a bad joke, Detti, you know how valuable you are to us, particularly after last night. You might well be captured – many are – and then think of the propaganda coup and also… well you actually know what they would do to you. You have seen it. I am sure you were not asking seriously but no, of course you can't go.'

Malinov spluttered agreement and then Detty spoke very quietly, 'No, I am serious and have been planning it ever since I arrived here. To a large extent I saw last night as a preparation for this plan. If I go I would plan to be captured.'

She paused, troubled, and looked out of the window. It was snowing heavily and the old garden of the castle looked beautiful and clean.

'You see I think I could lead you to Konradin. I know he is very cunning and resourceful. His meticulous security and keeping constantly on the move have kept him safe. He is utterly ruthless and almost without weakness – all this I know. He does, however, have one chink in his armour – me. I think he is infatuated with me even to the extent of taking risks that he wouldn't otherwise consider, and we might, just might, be able to use that. I do have some evidence. If you will agree I will go to Stuttgart to get some help and advice from Marc's unit. I have phoned Oberst Kramm and he will see me as soon as I can get there.'

She then told them about her weird visit to Konradin in the Winterburg the year before and she detailed her plan. When she had finished there was a long silence. Nicklaus looked the colour of the rutted snow in the castle courtyard when he finally spoke.

'Bernadette,' he said and Detty realised that she had never heard him use her full name before.

'I think that you know that you are a second daughter to me and a sister to Tamara. I wish deeply that you had never come here and put me in this position but you have and I must answer. The risk to you of the plan that you have given us is enormous. You probably have a ten to twenty per cent chance of getting out alive – possibly less. You also know that if you are captured, as you wish, you may be summarily executed during the rescue raid but, worse, if there are any hitches with the raid or your psychology is less than pin-point accurate, you may be taken away and tortured hideously. I know that I don't need to tell you about the habits of the NAS.'

As he was speaking Detty realised that she had got her way. He wouldn't have gone to these lengths if he was going to say no. He continued, 'Nonetheless, I am here leading a revolution to get rid of an odious and cruel regime. Brave people are being tortured to death every day and the future of an army is in my hands. Your plan is well thought out and does give us a reasonable chance of neutralising Konradin in one way or the other and this would be of immense value to us. In the final analysis I said to myself that if it was Tamara and not you who had been able to offer to do this, would I have let her? My answer was yes and my answer is yes to you too. Go to Stuttgart and God go with you! I will arrange your flight out to Vienna as soon as we can manage it. Meanwhile General Malinov will arrange for you to contact Marc.'

Malinov had not been consulted but he nodded agreement as he spoke. Detty was more conscious of the awesome responsibility she had put on the little man than her own predicament. She left to prepare for her flight.

*

She was woken in her hotel by the telephone ringing. She had so schooled herself that she answered in Moltravian dialect, as always using her maiden name. A polite *hoch Deutsch* voice said, *Wie bitte?* and she remembered where she was, apologised and changed her pronunciation.

'I am to tell you that a car will be calling in an hour.' Came the voice.

'Very well, *danke schön*' said Detty with an effort throwing her still tired young body out of bed.

Back in Germany she was even more conscious of the interruption of her preparation for Bayreuth to say nothing of her university degree which, truth to tell, worried her less. She had tried to keep up daily practice although it hadn't been easy. This morning she sang her vocalises and a small section of the part, hoping that the hotel room walls were reasonably thick, then had her shower. She had a brief panic wondering what she should wear from her extremely limited wardrobe and finally settled on a sweater and a smart pair of ski pants. She finished her face and hair looking intently and not entirely approvingly at the result, made a few adjustments, splashed on Marc's favourite *Source d'Ete'* and rushed to the lift. The chauffeur was already waiting.

'Frau O'Neill?' he enquired.

She nodded adding, *'Guten Tag,'* and in a few minutes they were immersed in the freezing cold of the Stuttgart winter rush hour. To her surprise the destination was not an office in the town but a small and rather charming country house near Esslingen just off the autobahn to Augsburg and Munich.

She was ushered into an elegant dining room laid out for a small meeting. The garden looked over the park to the frost-sparkling meadows covered with a light dusting of new snow. The men were already there. She kissed Marc and shook hands with Oberst Kramm. The third member she had never seen before, and he was introduced, unusually without rank or title, as Stanislaus Schedrin. He had a weather-beaten face and swept-back steel-grey hair and a faint Slavonic accent. The colonel gave no explanation as to who he was but merely invited everybody to sit down and poured coffee himself. He then asked Detty if she would be so kind as to outline her plan.

She nodded and began, 'I am sure that you all already know that Moltravia is in the throes of a brutal civil war. I suggest that, placed as it is between Russia and the West, it is essential for political as well as humanitarian reasons that the FWL win the struggle. You would know more about that than I do. Russia is increasingly unstable and I also suggest that, if given time, the present Moltravian regime may seek a totalitarian alliance with the Russian right which could bring a hostile force to the borders of Germany again. This could well be even more dangerous to the peace of the world than the cold war of fifty years ago.

'Internally the Travsky regime is highly unpopular and only maintains power by savagely brutal repression carried out by the secret police, the NAS. Wholesale executions and widespread torture are daily occurrences. Travsky senior, the first fascist leader, had a stroke last year and is now incapable of leading the government. Power passed to his son Stefan Travsky who is cruel and violent but not a great organiser. In the ordinary way this might have led to the collapse of the regime but, unfortunately, he was supported by two ruthless henchmen, Frederick Kovacs and Leon Konradin.

Konradin now has overall control of the country and to all intents and purposes is the dictator. Kovacs originally shared power and was appointed head of the NAS but he met with an accident and was killed last year.'

Detty deliberately kept a level tone and avoided looking at Marc. Not a muscle moved in the other men's faces. Somehow, however, she was fairly sure that they knew of the nature of the 'accident', which had taken Kovacs out of circulation. She went on, 'There is now a considerable gap in the command structure below Konradin but this has made little difference because Konradin is so ruthless and has such energy that he does without subordinates. The revolt is deadlocked. The insurgent army is established in the *Interfluss,* but to advance their campaign they need three things. The first is the ability to cross the Fojn very quickly in force. Currently they do not have the engineering hardware to achieve this and if they attempt to cross with less than a hammer strike, the crossing will fail. The river has marshes on both sides and the terrain is treacherous. The second need is connected with the first. They must have tanks. Originally there was an undercover agreement with Russian arms dealers to acquire both tanks and aircraft. The aircraft duly flew in and although they are not the latest neither are the government's and Zahnsdorf, the insurgent air force commander, has trained good crews and high-quality maintenance staff so although we have fewer machines in combat strength, we are roughly equal in effectiveness.'

She had slipped into the possessive and cursed herself. It had come naturally, however, nobody seemed to notice. Her allegiance was, by now in any case, quite plain.

'The tanks, however, never came. The reason, apparently, was that there was some sort of clampdown on arms trading by the Russian authorities, before the tanks could be trans-shipped, and now they are no longer available from that source. They may in fact have gone to the enemy – possibly we didn't get the bribes to the right place.'

'The third requirement is the main reason why I am here. There is little doubt that the removal of one man, Konradin, would help enormously in neutralising the driving force behind the Moltravian army. It would also probably save many lives by stopping much of the terror. Unfortunately he realises this and protects himself very thoroughly. He has a fanatical body guard who are personally loyal to him and he is continually on the move. Even if we discover where he is, he has left before any operation can be mounted. To date, our attempts have always ended in failure, usually with the loss of brave people. However I believe that I can get into his presence and that might help.'

'Can you clarify that?' asked Schedrin in a precise clipped accent that Detty still could not fully identify.

'Of course, I have three reasons,' Detty turned to him. 'I am a young woman and would not be seen to represent a general threat,' she hesitated and added, 'at least up to a point.'

This produced an unexpected reaction. The colonel laughed loudly and even Marc smiled wanly. Schedrin looked puzzled and the colonel, still smiling turned to him, 'You may not know of Frau von Ritter's previous activities but suffice it to say that if I had to organise a defence against her threat I would indent for the whole Special Forces Unit and even then would be uncertain of the outcome.'

Marc, ashen, said nothing but the tension was broken and even he struggled to smile wanly again. Detty made a rude face half directed at her husband's CO, instantly regretted it, and continued, 'Second, by my TV concert and appearances in insurgent leaflets I am fairly well known and have some publicity value. If I were captured and offered to trade support for the government for my life I don't think that I would be believed but I think that they would want to check it out with Konradin. The third reason is more personal.'

In spite of herself she reddened but she knew that she had to go on. 'I have some reason to believe from my previous captivities in Moltravia that Konradin has an... er... personal fascination with me, verging on an obsession. I am not stupid enough to think that that would stop him killing me but I believe that he would... er... want to play with me first.'

She blurted out the last words heartily wishing Marc had been somewhere else.

Schedrin, incredulous, stepped in. 'And you are saying that you would be prepared to let that happen?'

'Not exactly. I first thought that I would carry the means to kill Konradin before anything could happen. This is clearly impractical as first, I would certainly be body searched probably upon capture and certainly before I was taken to Konradin as he, at least, is aware of my previous activities in the country. Also, if by any miraculous chance I was successful I would have no chance of escape. I would like you to know, Gentlemen, that I am not made for martyrdom and I have a great life in front of me to enjoy. Although I would do a great deal to stop the carnage and misery in Moltravia, I want very much to come out of this alive.'

She stopped and there was silence for several minutes until the colonel broke it. 'What do you propose then?' he asked.

'Two things would help. First, if it was possible for me to carry a transmitter and tracker device, which would be undetectable on body search. Second, if a highly skilled and high-speed intervention force was available to attack instantly the moment it was summoned. I believe, under these conditions, that I would stand a reasonable chance of achieving my goal and escaping alive. This would only be possible with your help and I need to know if the project is technically feasible and politically possible. That is my proposition. There is no reason why you should help except that once before I remember you explaining how important a stable and friendly Moltr... Livonia was to Germany and Nato. This gave me the courage to approach you.'

Kramm turned to Marc. 'I don't want to meddle in your matrimonial affairs, Hauptmann, but may I ask how much of this you knew in advance and how you react to it?'

Marc was white as a sheet and paused for some time before replying. 'Do you know the prologue to *Götterdämmerung*, Sir?' he asked finally and apparently inconsequentially.

The colonel replied, 'A little.'

'Well, you may remember that Siegfried and Brünnhilde are deeply in love but she still realises that he must leave her, go away and fulfil his destiny. I think our situation is the same only the genders are reversed. I pray for a different outcome from *Götterdämmerung*. I have come to realise that Bernadette will only be fully mine when the Moltravian conflict is resolved. I wish it were not so but I know that I cannot alter it. Furthermore, I recognise that she feels a compelling personal responsibility to help those suffering people that she has come to know and love. I am horrified by what I have just heard but I cannot say that I am surprised. She is headstrong and independent and is devoted to justice. For these qualities I admire and love her and like her I trust in God and the Mother of God to help her. I cannot prevent her going.'

Detty listened gravely to the evidence of the suffering she knew that she was inflicting. The image that rose before her eyes was not *Götterdämmerung* but *Wotan*, in misery, with the broken spear standing aside to clear Siegfried's path.

Marc went on, 'If the scheme goes ahead and we provide a disguised intervention force, may I volunteer to be part of it?'

Kramm looked at both of them in turn. 'Frau von Ritter spoke to me before this meeting so I knew in advance something of her proposal. I have talked to the technical bureau and her proposal is feasible operationally but that does not alter the fact that it is very highly dangerous. In fact, I would not think it justified to allow my men, even volunteers, to go on such a mission. There is no defensive weapon, with one particular exception, with which you could be equipped which would be undetectable on a thorough body search. Even if your reasoning is correct, you are sure, and I think that you are right, that you will be subjected to such a search before being allowed to meet Konradin. That would probably be true whoever you were but in view of the fact that you have killed two of his senior colleagues, it is a certainty. The same problems are, however, not true of tracking devices and transmitters. We are now capable of fitting a combined transmitter and tracking device under the filling of a tooth in such a way that it can transmit over long distances and be completely undetectable. With this it would be possible with variable tongue pressure to signal exactly where you are and the moment an attack should take place. To stand any chance of success the equipment and location of the intervention team would need meticulous planning.

'The problems, however, do not end there. In spite of our interest in the stability of Livonia and our sympathy with the cause of the FWL, there can be no question of any identifiable involvement of Germany. All individuals would have to be anonymous volunteers working on their own. Furthermore, although it may be possible to use men from Hauptmann von Ritter's unit, I am going to ask him to temporarily transfer the command of these men to Stanislaus Schedrin so that they will cease, temporarily, to be members of the federal armed forces.'

Detty noticed that Schedrin was still given no rank or title.

'Herr Schedrin has enormous experience in organising special operations and suffice it to say that he is not a member of our armed forces and is not in fact German.'

Marc momentarily looked sullen and resentful but remorselessly the colonel continued, 'I also think, Marc,' humanity at last broke through protocol with the use of first names, 'that it would be unfair on the splendid men you lead, unfair on Bernadette and unfair on you, to give you command of a project in which you are so personally emotionally involved.'

'I did manage it before, Sir,' said Marc.

Detty was astonished to hear this near-insubordination from her normally disciplined husband. Kramm was aware of the stress he was under and replied calmly, 'I am aware of that but that operation was not subject to the same split second timing and Frau Bernadette was not then your wife.'

Marc gave a submissive but despairing gesture and Kramm went on. 'However, I think it entirely appropriate that you are involved in the overall operation. I therefore intend to give you the task of providing the armour that the Livonian operation will require. I think that you have already done some research. Would you tell us about it?'

Marc outlined the problems with the Russian supplier who had defaulted after the supply of the aircraft.

'The FWL have requested assistance in obtaining replacements. At the moment I have nothing definite to report but as soon as this meeting is over I intend to pursue further confidential enquiries. Fortunately money is not a great problem as we now have access to substantial overseas assets and generous support by Livonians in exile. The main problem is access if we don't use a Russian supplier.'

Kramm nodded agreement, 'I am happy to leave it to you. If you need further contacts just let the office know.'

'Thank you, Sir, I will.'

His composure seemed to have recovered. The colonel in his turn looked distressed and hesitated before saying, 'There is one final thing. I mentioned a defensive weapon to Frau von Ritter and I think that I should explain what I meant. A similar dental drilling to that required for the transmitter can be made to contain a lethal capsule. We have advanced since these were last in the news and they can now procure a comfortable and painless death. If you wish we can equip you with one at the same time as the tracking device.'

Kramm looked earnestly at Detty who appeared to be struggling inwardly for some time. At last she roused herself from her reverie and looked at Marc and then Kramm.

'Herr Oberst,' she said, 'I am deeply grateful for your concern and I know that you are doing everything that you possibly can to help me. I shall however decline your offer and perhaps you will allow me to explain why. I am – we are – devout Roman Catholics and therefore I have two problems. The first is that I would have difficulty in taking my own life, whatever the circumstances, although I have contemplated it before. The second is more complex and you may find it ridiculous. During my visits to Moltravia I have prayed to the Virgin for help and succour on several different occasions. I have felt that that support has always been forthcoming in the moment of my deepest distress and need. Now if I accepted your offer I would feel that it showed a lack of faith in the Mother of God who has come with me thus far. So thank you, but no.'

Kramm had nodded several times as she spoke. 'Frau Bernadette, you are facing an ordeal calling for extraordinary courage. You must use the resources that you have. I wish I could pray for you but I know that Marc will.'

The meeting broke up. Marc left immediately looking anxious but determined. They kissed in the moment that they had to themselves. Marc said quietly to her, 'I have come to think that you have only been lent to me. Something so strange and wonderful cannot be permanent. One day I will wake up and find it all a dream although I pray that I may not.' He forced a smile. 'To think that I might have married a legal secretary from Frankfurt and have three kids under five.'

'I'll promise you one thing,' she said, 'Livonian freedom is the only thing that moves me and if it comes and prospers it will see the end of my self-destructive urges. I will survive and then we will see about the three kids under five.'

*

As Marc reread the notes that he had made during the meeting, he realised to his dismay that the situation required, indeed shrieked out, for Lawri. He picked up the phone and dialled 0451 for Lübeck and the number. There followed a quick cryptic conversation. He put the phone down, dialled another number and booked himself on the next flight to Hamburg. He looked anxiously at his watch, grabbed his overnight bag, cursed the lack of time and phoned for a taxi to the airport.

The more he pondered the problem on his journey the more he thought that he was correct to invoke the bizarre alternative world which Lawri could unlock. Officially, Lawri was president of a loose, knit organisation called in various languages the *Confrerie des Bijoux Gastronomiques Regionnaux* or CBGR. His own business was run from a smokehouse/gastätte at the roadside north of Lübeck. The casual passer-by might have thought that it was a rather disorganised village garage or scrap depot. The building appeared to be halfway between a shed and a barn. Closer inspection, however, would have revealed blackboards announcing the current fish delicacies. Behind was a door leading to a shop displaying smoked fish of every imaginable type which led in turn to a comprehensively stocked bar with the local *Hefeweizen* well to the fore. Beyond the bar were the ranges and grills where the fresh fish were cooked. These were presided over by Birgit who, for thirty years, had been delighting the customers with perfect Ostsee herrings and immaculate soles. Hidden from the doorway and on the left of the ranges and bar, a large oak-beamed room opened, furnished with refectory tables and benches in front of a huge wood burning stove.

Although it was late on a bitterly cold late winter evening when Marc arrived, several parties of discerning Holsteiners were still doing full justice to the *Lachssuppe, Geräucherter Forelle* and other delicacies. Lawri moved quickly between the tables missing nothing that his customers might need. He greeted Marc with a warm smile as he came in and indicated a seat near the stove. A moment later he returned unasked with a *Hefeweizen* and a plate of the finest smoked eel in Europe. He then returned to his other customers and Marc, urgent as his visit was, knew that he must wait his turn, comforted by the food that Poseidon himself would have relished.

Marc had first met Lawri under very different circumstances. The genial rustic landlord had then been under arrest and Marc, representing the security services had been sent to interview him at Hamburg Police Headquarters. He had been briefed by Colonel Kramm before he left Stuttgart and told that his quarry was president of an innocent sounding organisation devoted to fine food. Lawri and his colleagues in the *Confrerie* included producers of hand-marinated herrings in Copenhagen, the owners of the last family distillery in Delft, the producers of exquisite bourride in Brittany and sublime jambon persille in Dijon. There was a Sliwowitz producer in Ljubliana, a tartuffiere in the Appenines, a caviar merchant in St Petersburg, a wild salmon smoker on the Tay and a specialist in tinned laverbread in Swansea. They were too many and too widespread to be listed and stretched all over Europe and even included a wild date stuffer from Tunisia. They produced a newsletter, arranged tours for well-heeled gastronomes and held several meetings a year in prominent hotels whose owners felt honoured at being asked to host them.

All of this, however, although taken extremely seriously, was a front to cover a second business – for Lawri and many of his *Confrerie* were gun runners. Their activities had become known to NATO some years before but it had been exceedingly difficult to obtain proof for convictions. Besides, as the dossier grew, a strange pattern began to emerge. Lawri and his friends appeared not to act indiscriminately and even seemed to examine the motives of their customers before supplying the goods. Revolutionary activities in a country with an appalling human rights record would, for example, find supplies forthcoming quickly and at reasonable rates but terrorist movements with dubious aims would meet prohibitive prices and unaccountable supply problems. Nobody was ever directly refused but somehow there were unexpected difficulties.

Marc and his boss had set out with the straightforward intention of suppressing the organisation and indeed Lawri had spent some time behind bars as a result of their counter measures. Gradually, however, the military intelligence of the Bundeswehr, the AKA and ERRF began to appreciate the benign nature of this strange organisation. In time they even came to realise that it could be extremely useful in circumstances where official government action was impossible. Lawri was not a man to hold a grudge against Marc. They had developed a mutual respect, which amounted almost to friendship.

Eventually the Holsteiners had eaten their fill and the last customers filed out into the frozen, misty night. Lawri filled a monstrous briar pipe and, while his minions finished the last of the clearing up, he flung himself onto a bench near the fire opposite Marc.

'*Wie geht es*, Herr Hauptmann?' he enquired and Marc replied, 'Personally well enough but there are problems.'

'In what way can I help?'

'Tanks,' said Marc.

'Tanks!' echoed Lawri, a smile flitting over his face. 'Well now that is surprising – I knew the economy was strapped and perhaps equipment for the Bundeswehr wasn't perhaps as easy as it used to be, but I really didn't think that you would be coming to me for tanks.'

'They are not for us,' said Marc, smiling at the banter of his strange friend.

'Oh, I see,' said Lawri, feigning surprise and taking a long draw at his pipe. He knew that this was a game but realised it was leading to a serious question. 'Might I ask who they are for then?'

Marc decided to get his own back. 'My wife wants them.

'Now that does surprise me!' twinkled Lawrie. 'I have never had the pleasure of meeting the beautiful Frau Gräfin. From the accounts, however, that I have read in the press about her activities before your wedding, I would have thought that she was capable of holding her own on the domestic front without the help of a Panzer division!'

Marc smiled and allowed the badinage to subside before he continued onto the serious heart of the discussion, which they both knew was coming. There was a few minutes silence while they both thought and Lawri puffed his enormous pipe. Marc opened his mouth to speak but Lawri pre-empted him. 'This is Moltravia, of course?'

Marc nodded.

'Tell me more. How many do you need?'

Marc outlined the military details and then came to the crunch. 'About thirty-forty would be better – the government has about sixty but they are dreadfully maintained and thirty would give us – them – parity. I have just come from Detti in Stuttgart and she is very close to the insurgent high command. The need is desperate but besides getting them at all, how do we get them to the war theatre? You know as well as I do the problem of any overt German help or intervention in that part of the world. That territory has been partly Polish and partly Russian and was once German. Need I say more?'

Lawri puffed his pipe and thought. Then he said suddenly, 'You need men as well as tanks. They must understand the machines and they would have to come from the sea. That would mean a diversionary landing and air cover.'

'Air cover might be possible. Zahnsdorf, the air chief, has done a fantastic job with the small insurgent air force and they have air superiority, not command unfortunately, and the range might be a problem covering the landings.'

'You land to the east of Königshof and cross the dunes and head straight south following the frontier. You might have to nip into Russia at times but they claim not to like Travsky, at least up till now, and if informed first, they would be unlikely to stop you. Even if they tried you could plough through anything they could muster quickly. You could deal with the political flack later.'

'You've echoed my thoughts almost exactly and you're now going to say that we have to have Ukrainian tanks and mercenaries.'

'What other possibility is there?'

'I hate the idea of Ukrainians after what they did in 39 – 45. I know that sounds funny coming from a German officer but they really were worse than the SS, if that was possible, and people have long – and inherited – memories. Can they be trusted now?'

'If you threaten their goolies with a sheath knife.'

'I can't help being anxious but I suppose we will have to do it. Only one Ukrainian per unit and I will try to get one experienced Livonian and one "volunteer" who might just have had some experience in armour before joining our special services. The *Chef* has given us a lot of support but he has made it clear that one hint of German involvement before we are in Königshof and we are disowned and all in the unemployment queue.'

'Forgive me mentioning it, but just one more thing. Have you – they got the money?'

'I know your terms,' said Marc sharply. 'The money's OK certainly up to forty units. Now I am thirsty. Will the house stretch to another *Hefeweizen*?'

'*Natürlich*, I'll put it on the *Rechnung* with the tanks.'

13
IN WILDEM GRIMME

Was hast du vor in wildem Grimme?[38]

Fidelio, Act 1

Detty bowed her head displaying a despair which was largely real and pressed the dental transmitter in her tooth with her tongue firmly three times. Satisfied that she had done the best she could with her all-too-fragile lifeline, she looked up at Konradin.

'I don't have much choice, do I? I believed I could always get away on these short raids and escape in time. I lived on the thrill of the moment. I now see that I was stupid and wrong. I didn't listen to the warnings. I never really understood how efficient a modern intelligence force could be and now you've got me. I think that that lot over the river were quite prepared to sacrifice me – they told me it was easy – they didn't care – after all I'm not one of them…'

She tried to sound really bitter, '…I want to live so I will come with you and do what you want. I can't withstand torture or your prisons any longer – I am finished. I have seen that the revolt is failing. Oblov and

---

38 What are you planning in your wild fury?

the leaders now realise themselves that they will never have the strength to cross the river. I heard them talking about it and I know – whatever they tried to make me say in public. I did my best for them and they have done nothing to save me now. You are still in command and now I know that you will remain the masters. I will do as you wish, as there is nothing else, and, as I have said, I would like to live for a little longer but please don't make me suffer – I just couldn't take it any more.'

It didn't sound convincing but she hoped to put a tiny seed of doubt in his mind. She hoped that he would want to believe it and that that would bias his normally cool judgement. She turned her face again to the floor in a hopelessness that was not feigned and gave her transmitter three more pushes before raising her head again.

Konradin remained silent for a long time, as if grappling with an inward struggle, looking at her hungrily all the while. 'How can I believe you after your previous activities?' he spoke at last almost to himself. 'But I would hazard many things for that photo that I always carry to become a reality. It seems so mad to destroy my dream at the moment it might become true. I will have you transferred to a safe house under my personal guard. They will not touch you, as long as you have not played me false in word or deed. If you have deceived me then the sufferings that you have seen already will be nothing…"

Detty felt some relief that at least she had been right about his feelings towards her. For a moment she almost felt sorry for this lovelorn monster. Then she remembered the shrieks from electric batons, the mutilations, the floggings, the tears of loved ones, the gallows and her own immediate peril.

Suddenly the telephone on Konradin's desk rang. He picked it up and talked anxiously for a few seconds in a fast low voice that she couldn't hear. He snapped the phone back on its stand looking quite changed and turned to Oleg saying sharply, 'They may have discovered the plans for the crossing. There is a lot of activity this evening on the other side. Intelligence think that there's trouble and some sort of counter attack may be on the way. It may not just be opposition to our attack. They think that there may be a raid directed towards here judging from the aircraft movements. We haven't got much time – there are enemy aircraft heading towards here. They may be paratroop carriers. I must get out at once. I suspect that she…' He pointed at Detty, '…may have something to do with this and we don't want them to find her. It is very odd that since I have been moving around they have never found me and yet tonight when I am with her they home in on me unerringly. Best get rid of her rapidly and not allow her to play any more little games. Take her out of here, see what you can find on her then dispose of her, don't let them ever find her body – you know what to do. I must get away.'

Detty was terrified that Konradin had divined the truth so quickly. Above all else at this moment she wished to remain near to the vice president where rescue was still possible. She had always realised that at the moment a raid was apparent, she might be summarily murdered. This was the risk that she had had to take. Oleg grabbed hold of her in a neck lock. She disengaged herself and threw him off with the skills she had learnt back at Stuttgart. He grabbed at her again and tried to pull her towards the back door of the office. She struggled and fought him but two NAS appeared and held her while Oleg beat her round the face. She heard Konradin saying, 'Don't waste time now beating her up. Just get her out of here, search her for a signalling device and get rid of her!'

Then all went black. She must only have been out for a few minutes but she had a sense of complete confusion as she recovered consciousness. Gradually she realised that she was being carried through a dark narrow space, like a tunnel, head first by two men. Her hands had been handcuffed behind her neck. Her head and neck throbbed dreadfully. Her feet were tied together. There was blood running in her mouth making her choke. The worst horror, however, was to come. She ran her tongue round her bruised mouth and realised that the tooth holding the precious transmitter had been broken off in her beating. She felt the jagged edge of the empty tooth with her tongue again to make sure.

They emerged into the grey half-light the other side of the tunnel. The two men dragged her backwards by the shoulders for a short distance and then picked her up and threw her roughly into the back of a parked van. Her handcuffed body hit the floor painfully and slid uncontrollably across the bare metal crashing into the bulkhead behind the cab head first. There was a short conversation outside which she couldn't hear because of the ringing in her bruised ears. Somebody got into the front of the van, she couldn't see who it was. The gears crashed and the van moved off. Seemingly endlessly the van bumped and jolted. Clearly they were going over very rough roads. She was thrown about helplessly like a meat carcass. After about an hour the jolting suddenly got much worse for a few minutes then the van stopped.

She just had time to murmur a prayer to the Virgin to receive her. She knew she was to be killed. This time there could be no clever tricks, no escape. She just hoped that one of the others, not Oleg, had been sent to search her and dispatch her and would do it quickly but she didn't have much hope. Sure enough there was a scratching as the back of the van was unlocked and there framed in the open door was Oleg triumphant. He didn't seem too concerned about his boss's order for speed and he seemed prepared to take his time. First he pawed her all over ostensibly to try and find evidence but really he was just enjoying himself. Behind him it was now pitch-black but Detty could just make out the darker shape of tall trees against the night. A very distant owl hooted. She had no idea where she was. After all she had survived until now she would disappear without trace in this nameless, featureless place. She remembered that it must be somewhere near that the mass graves of the thousands murdered sixty years ago which were still being uncovered even now. What was one more amongst the carnage? What chance had her body of being discovered in this vast gloomy forest? She tried to identify some feature. They seemed to be in a small clearing deep in one of the conifer woods. That didn't tell her much. Hopelessly she realised that Oleg had contrived to take her far from the headquarters and be left alone with her for his revenge.

He dragged her feet first out of the van, through the icy muddy slush and pine needles of the forest floor to a nearby tree. There he pulled her up on her bound feet and, taking another thick length of rope from his belt he tied her handcuffed hands behind her head to a fork in the tree. He then pulled a huge knife out of its sheath on his belt and stood looking at her like a butcher about to joint a carcass. It was icy cold but the helpless terror prevented her from feeling it.

'You were going to see that there was not enough left of me to ever abuse or humiliate another woman, I remember.'

He quoted the words that she had used to him two years before exactly. They had obviously burnt into his stupid cruel soul. 'Well, it seems that you got it wrong. I am going to delight in abusing and humiliating you, my proud lady, in every way I can devise. When I finally get bored I shall slit your throat with this.'

He brandished the sheath knife under her chin and then muttering, 'We need to look again for a transmitter first.'

He slashed her cotton prisoner's shift from top to bottom. Detty realised that his boss's instructions could be used to justify any invasion of her before he killed her. Anyway, in that deserted forest clearing he would hardly need ever to justify his actions. He stood back looking at her gloatingly. She closed her eyes waiting for his next assault and prayed for strength. Nothing happened and after some seconds, which seemed like hours, she began to feel the dreadful cold piercing her. She lifted her lids a fraction. Oleg, obviously savouring the situation, was still standing there grinning and working out his programme of horror. Suddenly behind him she thought she saw a movement in the darkness. It was so stealthy that at first Detty thought she must be wrong or hallucinating in her terror. Then it came again with the faintest gleam of metal reflected from the sidelights of the truck, which were still lit but very dim with mud. Oblivious in his moment of triumph Oleg was still smirking at her. Suddenly, there was a unmistakable disturbance – a whirling gleam in the darkness followed by a loud crunch like a woodman's axe striking a log. It was, however, no log which had been struck. Without a gasp or a cry, Oleg crumpled on his knees, his skull split wide open. He lay still in a pool of blood and brains.

The woodman came over to the body and took his victim's knife from the dead hand. Then, still silent, he walked over to Detty and cut the rope from her ankles and freed her handcuffs from the tree with the knife. He smiled at her and stripped off his great coat slipping it round her shoulders.

'It is very cold, *dyevooshka*,' he said gently in the Russian dialect. 'This will keep you warm. We will go back to the cottage and I will free your hands. But be quiet because there may be other vermin around.'

Back at the cottage, the woodman sawed carefully through the handcuffs taking great care not to scratch Detty's wrists, while his wife fed her hot coffee and thick cabbage soup. After the food they left her to wash the blood from her face and chest in a deep bowl filled from the caldron over the winter fire. The wife fetched her some clean darned clothes for her to wear and a countrywoman's scarf for her head. Detty thought that she had stepped back two centuries but time did not matter and, as her body came alive, so hope returned.

'We will hide you in the false loft to sleep, *dyevooshka,* while we go and get rid of the pig-corpse. They won't find you tonight. Tomorrow we will decide how to help you.'

Detty stammered her thanks. If it isn't help they've given me already, she thought, I wonder what they think help is. She followed the forester's wife up an open ladder to the attic and through a hidden door. Moments later she was curled up in straw asleep.

She woke before the winter dawn that she had never expected to see. At first she didn't know where she was then she slowly remembered everything. She looked out of the loft through a crack in the trap door. The grey clouds scudded obliquely across the sky. Each cloud line sank below the horizon to be followed by a darker, deeper purple, stripe. The weather, bad already, was deteriorating and storms were coming but at least she was alive to see them. She was pleased at first that there had been no disturbance during the night. She was pretty sure that she would have heard if anyone had come to the door, particularly if they had been soldiers or NAS. She shook the straw out of her clothes and wondered if she should go down. The matter was decided as there was a discrete knock and the woodman's wife appeared at the door signalling her to descend.

The coffee was steaming on the hob and the forester was busy blowing the embers of last night's fire into life. It was still bitterly cold in the draughty cottage kitchen. The wife found Detty an old wool sweater and a balaclava helmet to go with her thick coat and she prepared to leave.

'Where do you journey to, *dyevooshka?*' said the man using the archaic present.

'Back to the forces of freedom,' she replied, using the old words in the same dialect.

'How are you to go? The roads are full of soldiers and worse. You would not get to the bridge and I hear that it is no more.'

'The bridge is no more? How do you say that and how long will it need?' She loved the old sing-song Russian dialect and revelled in speaking it even under these circumstances.

'It has been said that the bridge has gone but rumour may kill truth. More than two days on foot – say sixty kilometres – and it is not easy underfoot – besides the soldiers and the vermin.'

'I shall go back the way that I came.'

'The van? That might succeed but it is very dangerous.'

'Everything is dangerous now. I think that I can do it and besides it is safer for you who have done so much for me if I take the van away from here. I know that there are blood marks but perhaps you can bury them.'

'Do not care about the blood. That will not matter – there.'

He emphasised the 'there' and Detty cocked a quizzical eye at him.

'How is that so?'

'You don't understand, *dyevooshka*. There is much blood in that clearing besides his. Three days ago the vermin brought five men from the village including my brother and cousin. They took my axe to cut their heads off. They said it was to save bullets to kill rebels and laughed – laughed as they killed my kin! When I heard the van go past last night I thought that they were going to kill more men. I was determined that it should not be with my axe so I took it out to hide it. A woodman's axe is sacred, *dyevooshka*, for centuries it has been our right arm. Now we have motor-saws and tractor splitters but the axe is still in our soul. Mine was defiled by murder, foul slaughter of my kin. When as I passed the clearing last night I realised that there were only two people there – one guard and one prisoner – forgive me but you are tall and I thought you were a man – so I saw my chance. The rest you saw. My axe is now pure, it has cleansed itself in righteous blood. It has been lifted against oppression and in defence of the innocent. I am grateful to you, *spaseeba, dyevooshka*.'

'Grateful to me!'

'All roads, you know now, why there is plenty of blood on that ground.'

'I am so sorry for your grief,' said Detty inadequately, feeling the tears running down her cheeks at the end of this sad stoical story. 'There is nothing that I can say except my thanks.'

'There is no need for more. God attend you!'

He walked back with her to the clearing and directed her towards the main road to the bridge. The diesel engine coughed in the bitter cold but to their great relief eventually it stuttered into life. It had snowed heavily overnight and large drifts covered parts of the forest floor interspersed by frozen muddy puddles but Detty was able to avoid the worst of them and skid across those she couldn't. With much wheel spinning she reached the track. Fortunately it was covered in coarse stones, which, in spite of shuddering bumps, gave the truck some grip through the snow.

It was on the main road that the risk of being caught increased. She realised that she had no papers of any kind and that once stopped she would be arrested immediately and, given the state of emergency, probably summarily shot, even if she was not recognised. Fortunately the driving snow from the storm that she had predicted that morning had now arrived in earnest. Also in her favour was the fact that she was driving a vehicle with the black star in a red circle of the Moltravian army on its side. Her balaclava and bulky coat left no hint of her gender and soon the driving mud and sleet covered the windscreen except for a small part cleared by the one functional wiper. The traffic was all heading in the direction of the destroyed bridge. She gathered that some sort of offensive had been launched presumably to cross the river and retake the insurgent positions. Fear gripped her that everything, including her miraculous escape, was in vain. She was, however, able to blend into the heavy traffic and keeping in convoy covered about fifty kilometres. As she neared the site of the bridge, many of the trucks had been stopped at the roadside. The drivers were talking to officers from a farm building with the black star on red of Moltravia fluttering in the wind over it.

Detty thought quickly to herself. If she went on in the van she might get near the bridge but that still gave her no way to cross the river and the chance of being stopped was considerable. A side turning would be better and she slowed right down looking for a suitable one. Eventually she found a narrow road that appeared to lead to an abandoned warehouse with a quay onto the wide Fojn. One end of the building had been destroyed either by bombs or artillery but the other appeared intact. The only disturbance to the calm was the stutter of machine gun fire, which came from the end of a jetty stretching out into the river beyond the main quay. Otherwise there was nobody to be seen. From a distance, the artillery fire was increasing all the time. Up and down the river the mist and snow swirled reducing visibility sometimes down to a few metres. At other times the mist rolled away and a temporary bridge full of vehicles crossing south could be seen down river. Detty parked the van in a corner of the warehouse and studied the scene gloomily. It seemed that the government assault had gone ahead in spite of her efforts and had gone ahead pretty well. She felt a cold impotent fear for her friends gripping her belly. The Moltravian army was surging over the bridge and would soon overwhelm the insurgents' fragile defences. The frozen mist closed in again blotting out the scene.

She wrapped herself in some old sacks and sat in a corner of the warehouse. A starving looking rat ran over her feet then disappeared down a crack in the boards in its fruitless quest for food. She noticed that there were several cases of ammunition together with explosives and detonators stored in the dry at the other side of the warehouse. Presumably they belonged to the unit manning the machine-gun emplacement. This was typical of the slovenly behaviour of the Moltravian army to leave such equipment unguarded and it certainly made her situation more hazardous. Sadly, however, all the artillery appeared to be directed across the river towards the insurgent side and anyway she didn't give much for her chances. To be blown up with an ammunition dump might be as quick a way out as any. She was too tired to care and despairing and exhausted she fell asleep.

She slept soundly and it was nearly dawn when she was awakened by a crescendo of new sound, still quite distant coming from the road on the up-river side. Shaking herself, she moved cautiously over to the shoreside loading bay. Far over to the east a column of tanks was heading towards the Moltravian camp. As she watched, a motor cyclist in NAS uniform joined the main road from a side turning and hurtled past in advance of the tank column which was going much more slowly and still a good kilometre behind. More armoured reinforcements to dash her hopes and slaughter her friends, she thought. Suddenly she was filled with energy and hatred. She must do something to stop them and the explosives and detonators stored in the warehouse seemed the God-given answer. Crossing the floor she dragged the nearest explosive case to the outside emergency stairway. It was far too heavy for her to carry and heart in mouth she bumped it from step to metal step. She had read a bit about explosives in a manual at Schloss Kluoberov and had seen somewhere that explosives without a detonator could be moved safely. They seemed to be an old-fashioned type. She just hoped that the information was correct.

She dragged the case near to the road and with the last heave rolled it alongside the ditch next to the road. To make it less conspicuous she covered it with old cardboard boxes, trying to make it look like a pile of the abandoned rubbish similar to the rest of the military garbage that lay around on all sides. She hoped that nobody from the machine-gun post on the pier head would hear but they seemed too fully occupied firing across the river. She attached the detonator to the simple plunger mechanism, rolled the cable back so that she was out of sight behind the corner of the warehouse and sat and waited.

The first tank rolled into sight trundling slowly up the road out of the fog into a small patch of sunlight. Her hand tightened on the plunger. Suddenly the dawn sun struck the side of the tank and, after she had begun to ease the plunger down, she froze. Instead of the black and red medallion on the armoured side was the golden falcon and chalice of Zablovsk on a green and white background. By the time she had recovered, the first tank was past. She tore the leads from the plunger and scrambled down the slight slope towards the road. Then bemused she stopped. No Livonian soldier would recognise her and anyway the tanks were probably manned by Ukrainian mercenaries and she was well aware of their reputation. For all that, the tanks were her best and perhaps her only chance of regaining her own side in the middle of confusion. She felt she had to chance it. She struggled through the ditch and, mud bespattered, pulled off her Balaclava allowing her long hair to stream down her back thinking of *Leonore*. In spite of the obvious risks she calculated that declared and obvious femininity was her best bet.

The next tank slowed to walking pace and the hatch opened. Her heart was in her mouth as a head appeared. Instead of a gun pointing at her there was a familiar but startled face.

'Frau Leutnant, what on earth are you doing here?' said the astonished rubicund face of Rudi the Navigator wearing the nondescript forage cap and green and white cockade of a Livonian irregular.

'I might ask you the same, Herr Rudi.'

'We are just leading the assault.'

'What assault?' asked Detty increasingly dazed and confused.

'We have come down from the coast over the last three days and now we are here to provide the armour to cover the flank of the assault across the bridge.

'How can you lead an assault across the bridge? The Moltravians have been crossing the bridge in numbers for days. I have seen them massing – I actually drove down in a convoy with re-enforcement's of the government army.'

It was Rudi's turn to look surprised, 'How on earth did you get mixed up with that, Frau Gräfin?' he had remembered her title and felt that perhaps it was more correct than the former military rank. Detty bruised, battered and caked with mud from head to foot didn't feel much like a countess but smiled at the Teutonic correctness.

'They are not having it all their own way,' he continued. 'When the fog clears look further up the river and you will see the real crossing. And another thing, they are rudderless now with no dictator to put the fear of hell into them. He, that Konradin, was captured two days ago by one of our undercover operations. There is a rumour going round that it was all due to the bravery of one woman. Forgive me, Frau Gräfin, but I sort of guess that I just might be talking to that woman.'

'So it worked!' yelled Detty punching the air like a footballer who has scored a goal and not listening to the end of Rudi's sentence. Then suddenly she said, 'Where's Marc? Where's my husband?'

'Up front in the first tank.'

Detty saw the detonator plunger in her mind and shuddered with the realisation of how close she had been to blowing up the person she cared about most in the whole world. Meanwhile Rudi helped her up onto the tank and through the hatch.

It must have taken an hour or so but from the crowded turret of Rudi's tank it seemed like an instant. There was radio silence and the signal was from the front tank of one rocket shot echoing through the early light. Rudi muttered, 'That's the *Chef's* signal. Let's go!'

So saying he started to turn the tank round and Detty, through the armoured turret, was able to see in front and behind the entire column wheeling like clockwork in perfect precision to turn to face the Moltravian camp making a defensive arrowhead of armour. After a few minutes the infantry trucks and the machine-gun carriers of the insurgent army began to flow through the guardian rampart of tanks. Even the inexperienced Detty was aware that she was witnessing something special. Later, she heard the manoeuvre referred to as a near perfect armoured combined operation, which was the more remarkable as much of the equipment was obsolete and out of condition. Then she heard the singing. As the infantry trucks passed by them sweeping forward into the bridgehead the young men and women confident of their shield, Marc's shield, were singing the *Freiheitslied*. They swept forward with her song surging into the cold morning air. With tears streaming down her face, she watched the sight that she had dreamed of so often but never thought that she would see. Almost unable to bear to go on looking she glanced round the tanks on each side and was enormously impressed to note that the crews with their volunteer commanders never relaxed their vigilance for a moment. They watched ceaselessly for a threat, for a counter attack while the main FWL streamed across the Fojn. It took several hours to complete the crossing of the pontoon bridge and then in an elaborate manoeuvre the tanks leap-frogged along the side of the advancing army, returning spasmodic enemy fire and still keeping amazing precision.

The speed of the advance was spectacular and even by the first nightfall several villages and a great tract of land was in insurgent hands. Each village produced its group of volunteers with green and white flags appearing as if from nowhere.

They grouped into full defensive positions for the night but it hardly seemed necessary as the opposition was so little. Rudi explained that they were afraid of mines and could do the necessary reconnaissance better in daylight. Leaving the crew on guard, Rudi suggested that they should find the *Chef* and he accompanied her to the Schloss Krenek, a grand abandoned manor house, which was the temporary HQ. Marc was bending over a VDU in the outer hall. Unconscious of the soldiers milling around, she hugged him from behind and whispered, 'Oh, my darling, I nearly blew you up! I was going to do my bit by detonating enemy reinforcements. It really wasn't as stupid as it sounds as I had been travelling all day surrounded by enemy troops as they poured towards the bridge.'

'So that was what you were up to back at the warehouse. I somehow thought that you wouldn't be wasting your time when I got Rudi's message to say he'd found you alive. Do you know, young lady, that you are being hailed as the warrior St Joan of reborn Livonia. We all thought that you were dead until this morning but I would much rather have a live wife than a dead saint.'

'It's far too wicked a temper that I've got, ever to be a saint.'

They both laughed and he hugged her again.

'There is another thing. They are all singing your song – the *Freiheitsleid* of Hansa. They drive and march with it calling them forward. Mara says it really will be the new national anthem. But how did you find Rudi? I am worried about him.'

'Perhaps a little subdued but kind and thoughtful like before.'

'I am not surprised he is subdued,' said Marc. 'He must be worried sick. You know the pretty dark young woman called Mariya Sostenova who is a captain in the intelligence section? – very cool and enormously brave -full of fun and always raising a laugh even in a crisis. Rudi helped to train her in Bratislava about six months ago when a few of us were giving the FWL under-the-counter advisory help. To cut it short they fell head over heels in love. Rudi simply adores her and she him. They were talking about getting married and working in broadcasting here when the war is over. Well, as you know, she was with you on the last morale and supplies sortie across the river – when your capture was stage managed. Her's wasn't stage managed but she was captured all the same. It was an unlucky fluke. She and her partner disappeared making a final search of the castle looking for you. We have no idea how they – or you – disappeared.'

'There is a very well-hidden tunnel to the woods on the lake shore' said Detty. 'I was carried through it earlier. They must have been surprised by the NAS, dragged into it and kept there until our people had taken off again.'

'I thought as much!' said Marc. 'That had to be the explanation – it was the only possibility. We don't know where they are now but we suspect they have been taken to the new interrogation centre that they have built behind the Farm and the Farm Barracks. From what we have learnt about it from our own agents it sounds pretty nasty.'

'Poor Rudi!' said Detty. 'He must have been dying to ask me whether I'd seen or heard anything of her. I haven't I'm afraid. I was nowhere near the Farm, though, which suggests unfortunately that you may be right. A FWL intelligence officer must be a pretty useful catch for them.'

'I just hope that she will be valuable enough to keep her alive. As for their interrogation methods, we both know that it doesn't bear thinking about. I was trying to work out a way of doing a rescue attempt like the one we did for Mara but there are a lot of snags. This new centre has the highest security NAS guarding. There would be no surprise – in fact they probably expect it and would make absolutely sure she was dead by the time we got to her. It would also mean taking key trained men away from the strike force and we couldn't in conscience do that as we have few enough of them anyway. We can't hazard the whole war even for Masha. It has been very easy so far but it won't stay like that. The best course is probably to overrun the place in the normal way hopefully in about three days time and hope that she can stay alive while we do it.'

He paused thoughtfully and sighed and then changed the subject. 'The Oblovs should be here soon. It is a bit safer for them to come up as we have total air superiority with the capture of Lovets with fifteen enemy aircraft earlier today. They just changed sides and ran up the Livonian flag. It's great as we have the pilots too. Ulrich Zahsdorf is over the moon. I signalled to the chief after consulting General Malinov who agreed it still wasn't safe 1 but he insisted on coming anyway. It was tricky to arrange as we didn't know how much ground we would make -in fact we didn't know if we would make any. The chief signalled back about an hour ago and they are on their way. I'll get one of NCOs to show you your room and we can meet in the main hall later. I even believe there is some hot water which should please you.'

'Worker of miracles!' she laughed.

The shower and hair wash were wonderful and, adorned in a new set of fatigues, she went down to the main hall. Marc was deep in some calculations on a clip-board which he put down as she entered. He stood up and clicked his heels. 'Beauty restored to its flowing grace,' he said in English.

'Whenever you click your heels it reminds me of the first time we met.'

'We can go back for a reunion soon,' he said and, as he was reminded of the enduring horrors of that accursed place, a shadow of a frown crossed his brow.

'Can we talk now?' Detty asked. 'I want to know everything. This morning I thought that we had lost and would all be killed and now… I still can't believe it's true.'

'It has been a near thing.' started Marc. 'We have known for some days that Konradin was massing all his forces for a major effort to cross back into the salient. He had the bridging gear and the armour. There was some disaffection but he terrified them into loyalty – while he was still there and had the personal loyalty of the NAS – that is. I took delivery of the tanks in the north from the sea only five days ago. The plan was to drive south through the forests and not be too particular about the Russian and Polish borders. In fact we were tipped the wink that as long as we didn't make a nuisance of ourselves the Ivan command would turn a blind eye as long as the top brass didn't find out. We knew in fine detail where the tracks through the trees were and the frontier there is, surprisingly, not closely manned as Moltravia is supposed to be a subservient ally. Where there was a post, we nipped back into Moltravia proper. The going was very slow but we only had a few skirmishes with government forces, which served as target practice. We had to train as we came. It was a tough five days but the FWL volunteers were very keen and even the residual Ukrainians got quite enthusiastic once we controlled the vodka. We kept in contact with General Malinov who signalled that he had got the bridging gear at last and it was agreed that he would try to throw a pontoon bridge across the Fojn as we arrived. It was touch and go whether we got to the north or the government troops crossed south first. When I left he hadn't got the bridging gear but it had eventually arrived in order.

'In fact we wouldn't have made it without the capture of Konradin. As you know he kept things very much in his own hands and it was a very personal command. Once you engineered his abduction there was a delay of twenty-four hours, which saved our bacon. Also the morale and terror factor took a dive and the junior commanders argued amongst themselves. A few days earlier they would have had the fire power to knock us halfway to Warsaw but when they in fact crossed it was half-hearted and a simple matter to seal off the northern side of the bridge and cut off their retreat. By that time many units were surrendering and joining us anyway.'

'Your operation was incredible. Not only your own part but the assault helicopters had to land under heavy fire on the roofs and courtyards of the island castle. Konradin couldn't get to his helicopter and was already in a boat but they picked him up from the water. They were sure they would find you dead or alive inside the castle but there was no sign and then Masha and Sergeant Petrov disappeared which put gloom on an excellent operation. Without it we couldn't have been here tonight. Oh and by the way – congratulations Frau Hauptman – Malinov promoted you as soon as he knew you were safe and somehow I have a hunch that Livonian gratitude won't end at that.

'Once we held Konradin the government command began to fall apart. Most of the other capable senior officers were dead, in prison or with us. Konradin never encouraged initiative and most of his second-in-commands were weak non-entities. Although the attack was thrown across the river at dawn, much as planned apart from being a vital day late, our defence fought like tigers and the line held easily. In the event it was almost no contest. Then units began to surrender and by that time we had arrived with the armour that effectively sealed off their retreat. The rest is history and as you saw by nightfall last night the *Chalice of Zablovsk* was flying over the former government headquarters.

'It is not over yet though. Once the NAS had shot a number of young soldiers for desertion they made good their escape. They have joined their colleagues and the rest of the army – about half – around Königshof where they are organising the defence using their usual terror methods. There are nearly ninety thousand of them in all and they will defend to the last man as they have nowhere to go. They know that to say they have no place in the new Republik is to put it mildly. They must fight and they will fight to the end.'

There was a stir in the vestibule and one of the soldiers came to the door into the hall, which had been left ajar while Detty and Marc had been talking. She flung it wide open as she did so, announcing, 'The *Chef*' and in came Nicklaus Oblov followed by Malinov and Zahnsdorf, a group of high ranking officers and finally Mara and Liese. Nicklaus seemed to have grown twenty centimetres since his tearful arrival on the tarmac at Munich. He was clearly delighted with the day but it showed against a background of gravity that announced that here was a man of stature dedicated to the safe piloting of his fledgling, half-formed democracy.

Marc stepped forward and saluted Nicklaus and the other officers. 'On behalf of the Armoured division of the FWL, I would like to welcome you, Sir, and the other ladies and gentleman here,' he said continuing, 'And may I give a special welcome to The First Lady of the Hanseatic Republik of Livonia.'

Mara looked startled as he went over to tower over her, clicked his heels and bent low to kiss her hand. There was general applause from the other officers followed by handshakes and congratulations all round. Everyone qualified their enthusiasm by agreeing that there was still much to do. Detty had not met some of the staff officers who were now introduced in a flurry of compliments and hand-kissing which she shamefully admitted to herself that she rather enjoyed. Eventually Mara, doing the rounds, reached her. Detty, taking her cue from Marc, whispered to her, 'Is it a breach of protocol to hug the First Lady of the Hanseatic Republik of Livonia?'

Mara's quick wit and easy phrase hadn't deserted her, as with tears running over the smiles, she retorted, 'If new titles are in order tonight then I would say that to be hugged by the Heroine Saviour of the Hanseatic Republik is the highest privilege any true blooded Livonian patriot, let alone one with dual nationality, can be granted.'

They stayed in each others' arms for a long time, their bodies saying the words that their speech couldn't form until the woman officer appeared again at the door and announced that dinner was served in the dining room. Nicklaus took Detty's arm to lead her through followed by The commander-in-chief escorting Tamara. Detty found the touches of ninteenth-century middle-European chivalry in an egalitarian twenty-first century army an intriguing contrast. She really felt out of place in battle fatigues, the occasion called for gorgeous silk evening dresses.

Given the circumstances and the short notice the dinner was a miracle of invention. Trout in dill sauce materialised as if from nowhere and was followed by roast wild goose from the lake behind the Schloss and preserved cherries, excellent goat's cheese and a classic French apple tart. The conversation was general and cheerful. It appeared that the quality of the food was a tribute not so much to the overstretched catering division of the FWL but rather to the fact that one of Marc's tank corps gun layers was a former sous-chef from *Le Grand Vefour* in Paris. He had shot the geese and returned to his former trade for the evening and when congratulated after the meal by the company he smiled modestly. He said that at *Le Grand Vefour* he had frequently been told of the feats of Napoleon's chef after the victory of Marengo. He would like to think that he had contributed to the same kind of celebration of the great Livonian victory that day.

At the end of the evening over the inevitable plum vodka, Detty was asked to sing. There was no accompaniment of any sort but she was quite pleased with her rendering of Schubert's Forelle after many weeks of irregular scanty practice. Asked for another song, she announced that she would sing the *Freiheitslied*, which met with a murmur of approval. There was general surprise, however, when she began, not her arrangement of Waldhuter's grand tune which had already been accepted as the new national anthem, but Mozart's setting of Blumauer's cynical poem about the worthlessness of princes, gold and women compared with contentment by the fireside.

Nicklaus reflected quietly that perhaps the sentiments of this song also were apposite but asked if to close the evening she would also sing her own song. This time she had an accompaniment with Pepov, the sous-chef on a mouth organ, one of the women intelligence NCOs on a penny whistle and Malinov's adjutant on a balalaika. Everyone else stood singing the chorus reverently as Detty swept through the stirring song that she had written on a draughty train a seeming age ago. At the end of the evening the captain in the intelligence section and the acting colonel in command of tanks managed to get off to bed together for a night, which short as it was, gave them back something that they had pined for for so long. She felt Marc slip out of bed and leave a couple of hours before dawn to rejoin his unit and relieve his second in command. She felt desperately lonely as he left and couldn't get back to sleep although her limbs ached and she still felt tired. She started the long walk to the bathroom down a damp leaking corridor pausing to look out of the window to the just-lightening landscape with the dark tracery of the trees and bushes etched against the snow which had fallen in the night. What would the next few days bring? She knew that, with all their success, the most difficult part was to come. The NAS guards were dug into carefully prepared positions around Königshof. They were well trained and equipped and would fight to the last, thinking that capture would mean a noose or a firing squad for many of them. The only comfort was that at least their nuclear potential had been neutralised by the bravery of two partisan units aided by Zahnsdorf's tiny but highly efficient *Frei Luftwaffe Livonias* from the air. Sadly only two partisans had escaped, the others had been tortured in the Winterburg before being publicly hanged outside its walls.

She joined Mara for coffee and bread and reported to the field headquarters where she was issued with an Armalite AR-10 .308 LW. These weapons were invaluable particularly for the women as they weighed so much less than the Kolashnikov in routine issue. It gave her a strange frisson to be handling one of the weapons which had played such a role in the IRA war of the 80s and 90s. The latest mark was much more advanced but it was unmistakably the same weapon. She was detailed to the Forward Reception Unit, which had the job of receiving enemy casualties, looking after their wounds and other needs and if possible interrogating them and sifting the information obtained. Potentially it was a busy and responsible job but that day there were no enemy casualties. The tanks and infantry carriers rolled on over the eerily empty countryside. The only activity for the FRU was interviewing government deserters and a few farmers who were only too happy to share the meagre information that they possessed.

It all seemed too good to be true. There was, however, a feeling that this was the calm before the storm. There were also some practical problems. The huge number of deserters and volunteers coming to join up was undoubtedly a psychological fillip but it had a downside. Few of the men had military skills, some might well be enemy agents and it was too late in the campaign to train them. In addition the sheer numbers strained the quartermasters' equipment and victualing and there was only limited additional food to be obtained in the middle of winter. Although the service colonel was a farmer from south Moltravia himself, he was finding it difficult to persuade his former colleagues to part with treasured grain and lovingly prepared Krakowska sausages. He did not want to forfeit the FWLs jealously guarded reputation for fair dealing. Somewhat perplexed he came into the FRU's trailer and said, 'Anybody got a clue how I can persuade these mean bastards to part with some food?' There was no immediate answer and he glanced round the trailer until his gaze fell on Detty. Suddenly he broke into a broad smile. 'Got it!' he said. 'At least assuming that the Frau Hauptmann will come on a short trip with me.'

Rapidly he explained that Bernadette, with her reputation from insurgent TV, would persuade the farmers to part with some food. The rest of the day was spent in an exhausting but not unfruitful tour of the countryside. There was a much simpler, but still convivial meal that night and exhausted, Detty went to bed early.

She slept alone as Marc had returned to duty with his tanks preparing for the morning push towards Königshof. She woke with a start wondering what she had heard. At first she thought that it was the beads of the antiquated sash cord rattling in the draught from the ill-fitting windows. Then the staccato rattle was repeated and she knew it was far too precise and loud for any window noise. It had to be machine-gun fire and getting closer. To confirm her worst fears the boom of heavier guns started to add the dreadful base stave to the machine-gun noise. The chaotic clamour now sounded very close. She leapt out of bed, dragged on her fatigues, grabbed her Armalite and went down into the hall. It was dark and empty. There was no sign of life except the embers of the fire gleaming in the great fireplace through the open drawing room door and a faint glow from the conservatory near the front of the house. The signals operators were still at their VDUs. The nearest operator looked up, 'Guten Tag, Frau Hauptmann,' she said quietly and correctly then returned to her screen.

'What's happening?' Detty asked the next time she paused.

'Counter attack by a NAS Strike Column – apparently they had formed one in reserve. They set it against this Schloss. They must have known it contained important people if not the *Chef* and Frau Tamara themselves. Our armour has turned their flank but there was a fierce tank battle and we still think that there might be a commando attack on the Schloss so all the HQ staff that could be spared have deployed to encircle the house. They are a bit thinly stretched but they have every point of access under observation.'

'I'll join them. Can you tell them that I am coming? At least that will make one more.'

'Ja, naturlich, Frau Hauptmann.'

'Who's commanding and where do I find him or her?'

'Frau Hauptmann Zahnsdorf at the summerhouse. The commander-in-chief has returned to field headquarters and of course Oberst von Ritter has gone to lead the armour.'

'Of course,' said Detty with mixed emotions and set off, Armalite in hand, towards the garden door and the summerhouse.

She skirted through the remains of the formal garden keeping close to the overgrown rose hedges. It reminded her of the night that she had raided the governor's office at the Farm creeping round the buildings of the quadrangle. As she was fighting her way along one overgrown path she was startled by a familiar clatter in the sky overhead getting ever nearer. She froze gripping her Armalite tightly as the great black shadow wheeled deafeningly overhead. Helicopter – probably a gunship she thought, but is it ours or theirs?

There was no machine-gun fire, however, and the shadow disappeared behind the hedge. The noise stuttered to a stop. It had landed. She peered anxiously through the thinnest part of the hedge. Sure enough the chopper was now sitting quietly on an old tennis court or croquet lawn. The falcon and golden chalice on its green and white shield was clearly visible on the side. There were sentries on each corner and the pilots were talking quietly beside the still rotor. Detty recognised the pilot as Leo Storen who she had met in the mess before the crossing. She gave the counter sign of the day and walked up to them.

'You gave me a real shock,' she said reproachfully. 'What the hell's going on?'

'You have heard about the counter attack?' Leo answered. 'Well we – or rather your man seems to have got that licked and is sealing them off in the salient. There was still worry about undercover activity and we were ordered here to fly off the *Chef* and Frau Tamara if there is any real problem.'

As if to confirm his fears there was a burst of small-arms fire from the direction of the summerhouse and the lake.

Detty resumed her journey as quickly as she could, keeping under cover. About three hundred metres from the helicopter she came to a clearing. In front of her was the dark against dark of the reed-choked lake. Presumably in days gone by the owner of the Schloss and his guests had shot wild fowl there on winter mornings. That was long since past and the scene now, as far as she could make it out in the fitful moonlight, was one of desolation reminding her of Keat's poem *La Belle Dame Sans*

Merci. There was a frozen mist over the lake, which patchily reduced visibility. Near the reeds on the side of the lake closest to her she could make out a small island, presumably part of a bird sanctuary, which formerly had been connected to a lawn by a wooden drawbridge. The wrecked remains of the bridge were sticking out of the shallow water between the rushes. Behind this was the summerhouse with its brick lower walls still standing but the wooden upper part and roof fallen in. She could see figures moving silently under cover of the brick walls on her side. She gave the counter sign and, moving up, whispered her name and rank. Liese's voice came back sounding oddly soft and feminine given the military precision of the message. 'Detti, Are you armed?'

'Yes, AR-10 LW.'

'Right black up.'

The blacking was passed down the line to her and she proceeded to smear it over her face checking with her neighbour that it was adequate.

'OK, ten metres to your left you will find a shallow trench, its part of an unfinished drainage scheme. Crawl up that and it will bring you to the back of that willow you can see silhouetted. Stay in the cover of that and watch the right side of the lake. We know that they are on the other side. They may come round in force or just send snipers. Return fire if you can spot a target. There are only about twenty or thirty of them. We have stopped them for the moment but they are quite determined and we have had some brisk exchanges. The problem is that we don't know if they have ground to air missiles so to be on the safe side we have kept the chopper grounded. They didn't interfere with it coming in but then, if their intelligence is correct, they would be waiting for it to take off. Anyway be careful and keep your head down. Some of them are not bad shots.'

She did as she was ordered crawling through the freezing damp late winter grass until she was soaked. In spite of the cold and the danger, strangely, she realised that she was enjoying herself. She wondered why and then realised that for the first time she was actually fighting with the FWL. Even at the crossing of the Fojn she had really only been a spectator albeit a front-line one. After all the prisons and undercover activity her heart was singing to have an enemy in front of her and a rifle in her hands. She reached her assigned position wondering whether Liese, her CO of the moment, would know that she had arrived. She had been impressed with her friend's cool matter-of-fact command and the way she had deployed her contingent of miscellaneous HQ staff to best advantage.

Suddenly there was a burst of machine gun fire from the other side of the lake at this point only seventy-five metres away. The line of bullets threw up a shower of mud ten metres in front of her. She took aim at the origin of the points of flame and fired twice. Liese's machine gun to her left crackled after Detty had fired. Silence – no idea if they had hit anything. More waiting – the night was now windless and bitterly cold. The time passed slowly but she kept scanning the darkness attentively.

At first she thought her mind was playing her tricks and then she was sure it was a movement in the gloom up the bank to her right. She froze still and watched attentively. The rushes moved again in the still air. It had to be somebody crawling through the reeds along the shore of the lake. She raised herself slightly to take aim through the telescope of her rifle. The movement must have attracted the other for as she fired she heard the crack of another shot doubling her own. A sharp kick of pain shot through her right thigh. Still not daring to try and move she watched intently the target area searching for further movement. There was none. He might be just waiting to pick her off. She felt a warm throbbing pain in her thigh and very slowly put her hand down. Her army trousers and thermal long johns were soaked with blood which was warm and sticky as she withdrew her fingers. She wondered how much she was losing and the throbbing pain was certainly getting worse.

Suddenly there was another furious exchange of fire, this time all from the other side of the lake, then silence again. She heard a movement behind her, and turned rifle at the ready to see the grinning blackened face of the sous-chef, this time without his improvised toque.

'Captain Zahnsdorf said to tell you that she thinks that we have got them all captured or killed this time. She is going to sweep right round the lake with her contingent just to check for survivors and booby traps. She would like you to please keep look out here but be careful not to shoot at her party coming towards you. They will identify themselves by giving an owl call every thirty seconds as they approach.'

More waiting, then to her relief the owl calls coming out of the first dawn light. They met up with quiet satisfaction. There were no other FWL casualties and there were fifteen NAS prisoners herded together and ten dead including Detty's opponent who had an Armalite bullet through his neck. Liese grimly congratulated her on her marksmanship while Detty calculated that had his shot been fifty centimetres further to his right she would not have been around to receive the congratulations. She shuddered. As she looked down at her own bloody thigh she muttered in English to herself. 'As a fellow countryman of mine once said "It has been a damned nice thing."'

Liese, whose English was school standard, overheard but didn't understand the allusion to the Duke of Wellington's famous saying. She turned looking puzzled in the half-light and saw Detty's blood covered leg for the first time.

'You had better get that seen to. Field hospital – behind Marc's tanks or rather where they were yesterday. Corporal, take Captain O'Neill down in the jeep. It really was a good thing you were a better shot than him.'

The wound was deep but miraculously had missed the bone. It had to be laid open, cleaned and packed. In spite of pain killers and a local anaesthetic it was very sore and throbbed unmercifully when she put it to the ground. The jeep took her back to the Schloss. Sergei Malinov had returned and was talking with Nicklaus Oblov in the great hall. There was no sign of Marc. Detty had refused a wheel chair but found that she had to use a stick to support the injured leg, which now felt very weak.

'Detti, what have you been doing?' said Oblov. 'You've done enough for us already without risking your life again and getting wounded?'

She turned to Malinov with a mock serious look. 'Excuse me, Herr General, but will I be shot at dawn for high treason if I contradict the chef?'

Malinov smiled. 'It seems to me that you have been shot at dawn already, Frau Hauptmann. We couldn't do it twice in one day. How's the leg?'

She used the soldiers' vernacular, *'Wi'borsig schmerzlich!'* Bloody sore!

They both smiled sympathetically. As she went up to her room to change into her own fatigues from the ones she had been lent at the casualty dressing station, she heard Oblov say, 'I don't think I shall ever understand that girl. She was not even born one of us.'

'She seems to have forgotten that and is certainly one of us now. We wouldn't be standing here at present if it wasn't for her.'

'Don't I know it,' said the Chief, 'but I hope she doesn't go and get herself killed. She really doesn't seem to care. Apart from the fact that I adore her as a second daughter, the damage to morale would be staggering. She's become a national icon.'

Detty, climbing the stairs with difficulty, swore at her leg again under her breath and thought to herself that the chief was being absurd. But it still pleased her, particularly the second daughter bit.

She pushed open the door of her room. Staring at her on the marble mantle shelf was a vase with a dozen red roses. Under it was a message saying, 'What the hell have you been up to again? I can't let you out of my sight! It's going OK. All my love, Hunding.

'Where on earth did he get those on a battle field in mid winter?' thought Detty, looking at the roses, and the warm feeling inside her fought with the throbbing leg.

14
THE NIGHTINGALE

Once more, and once more seem to make resound
With love and hate, triumph and agony

MATHESW ARNOLD: PHILOMELA

For three days Marc tightened his ring of armour, squeezing the encircled salient containing the enemy break-through group. It was far from easy going. The best NAS fighting troops, copied from Hitler's Waffen SS with their oath of personal loyalty to the dictator, had been chosen for the assault and they fought skilfully and desperately. He lost three tanks from missile fire and the casualties mounted.

Detty worried ceaselessly about Marc and scanned the casualty lists anxiously. On the second morning she read that Rudi had been seriously wounded. She immediately made enquiries and found out that he had been working away from his tank trying to defuse a booby trap under a canal bridge. The device had gone off badly injuring his chest and shattering his right leg. He had been taken to the base hospital back over the Fojn where he had had a high amputation of the leg. For several days he hovered on the brink of death. As soon as she could arrange it, Detty hitched a lift in a helicopter over the river to visit him. She had difficulty finding transport from the airfield and her own wound made walking difficult but eventually she got a lift in an ambulance transferring other wounded. She found the ward, long and old fashioned but the FWL charge nurse was warm and concerned. He told her that Rudi was still on a respirator and gravely ill but she could certainly see him. He added that he thought morale was a problem and, with his unit still in action, he had had few visitors.

Detty sat with him for half an hour talking to him about the campaign and old times. He seemed to respond a bit but couldn't speak. When she had been there for some time he indicated that he wanted the clipboard and looking agonised wrote 'Masha?' with much effort on the paper.

'No news as yet but we will find her,' replied Detty with a show of confidence that she found difficult to make convincing.

By now feeling very inadequate, she was about to leave when the charge nurse rushed in exultantly with his cool professionalism awry.

'I am sure that you would both want to know that the enemy break away force in the salient have surrendered to Brigadier von Ritter.'

Detty squeezed Rudi's hand and he broke into a smile, which was a ghostly reminder of his old cheerful confident self.

'Now Marc can really start looking for Masha,' she said, and left after another squeeze of his hand.

She was mightily pleased and relieved at the news of Marc's victory and promotion to a higher, although still of course acting, rank but still felt very sad as she limped back to the airfield trying to strengthen her wounded leg by exercising it. What had Masha and Rudi done that their happiness and even their lives should be stolen from them like this?

After waiting a couple of hours she got a lift back to the Schloss in a returning ambulance helicopter. Marc was standing in front of the fire teasing his CO about the defects of Baltic sausages and nobody would have guessed he was the victorious commander fresh from a famous victory. There was, however, something special in the hug he gave Detty before enquiring anxiously about her leg. 'You're not fit to be allowed out alone.'

'You've left it a bit late to include that in our marriage contract,' his wife laughed back.

Over dinner they planned the advance towards Königshof and it was agreed that Detty should go with Marc as intelligence liaison officer because, as Malinov said wryly, they seemed to work well together in spite of their relationship.

The following morning the column rolled out across the rutted tracks under an icy blue sky stretching as far as the eye could see, between the patches of forest. There was little opposition but the advance was still not as fast as they would have liked, being slowed by the sporadic dense trees and the constant presence of booby traps and mines. The counter attack had bought time which the enemy had used to lay more mines. Fortunately the FWL had now acquired better detection gear via a certain Lübeck fish smoker but the operation still needed immense care.

The weather remained unusually good for mid-winter although still piercingly cold. There were a series of remarkable sunsets with the sun sinking in a misty glowing ball behind the western flatlands and forests. On one afternoon in particular the light was so striking that Detty realised, for the first time, that her adopted country could be beautiful as well as ferocious. She felt yet again that she was being given a sign that they would succeed. It took them two full days to reach Ziatov and the Farm that they both knew so well. For so many reasons Detty's heart was thumping and her stomach churning, as she knew the complex of buildings making up the labour camps and the barracks were coming nearer and nearer. As the tanks pushed up the long straight road from the south, the actual buildings were still hidden from sight by the conifers but she knew that they must be getting very close. Suddenly the trees stopped and there they were, less than 800 metres away, clear in the afternoon sunshine. The terrifying but majestic old hall stood surrounded by ugly concrete just as she remembered. Some of the new buildings were familiar but some were new to them both.

The electronic gates of the labour camps had been abandoned half open and both the camps and the barracks seemed deserted. They checked carefully for mines and booby traps but found nothing in the main buildings except the signs of hasty departure. There were abandoned clothes and evidence of fairly recently eaten food in both the staff and the detainees' quarters. It appeared that the inmates had either been transported elsewhere in a hurry or turned loose to fend for themselves. For the moment it was impossible to tell which. As soon as they had checked the main buildings Marc took a party of men round the back to the new central NAS interrogation centre. Detty, still limping from her thigh wound, followed with her heart in her mouth for Masha. She was deeply despondent. The buildings had clearly been abandoned and surely nobody could have survived in the interrogation centre.

A four-metre-high wall circled the centre. From a ladder on top of the tank Marc was able to see over. The inner quadrangle surrounded by the iron barred cells seemed deserted. The cells were arranged like dog kennels round the walls open to the elements via their steel grid doors. Marc came down looking grim.

'It looks as if the prisoners have all been shot through the bars,' he said. 'I can't see any signs of life through the binoculars and it looks very messy. We had better get inside.'

This time the gates were locked and crudely booby-trapped. The Engineer NCO decided to blow the gate open rather than try to defuse the device. He checked the far side of the gate but there was nothing important in the way. The explosive erupted in a flash of black and orange flame.

'Typical – poor quality explosive,' said the sapper disparagingly. They made their way inside cautiously.

Detty was able to see for herself for the first time. The wall was double with offices and services round the outside of the inner wall facing towards the plane concrete outer wall. They passed through a second locked gate, this time not booby-trapped, into the inner courtyard. Round the wall were about one hundred and fifty concrete hutches each closed off by a steel grill door, which gave no privacy or protection from the elements to its inmates. In the centre of the courtyard was another structure like a roofed barn but supported only by beams and uprights with no sides. Under the roof were a number of tables and benches and some miscellaneous electrical equipment. It suggested that the NAS had followed their usual practice of torturing prisoners in front of the others. Ominous as this was they ignored it for the moment and turned their attention to the cells.

Marc's observations with his binoculars proved devastatingly accurate as they began their inspection. They started with the cells nearest the gate and made their way gradually round the perimeter. Each cell contained a prisoner and each had been shot. Clearly the NAS had taken no chances with their sensitive political detainees. Detty felt any hope for Masha and Piotr that she might have had finally trickle away. Again there was evidence that the NAS had left in a hurry. The blood on each corpse had congealed but the bodies were still warm as they touched them through the bars. They found Piotr dead but, unlike the others, he was stone cold and seemed to have been dead for some time. As they stood silently looking through the bars at Piotr's body, there was a groan from the next door cell. With a wild surge of hope Detty thought for an instant that it might have come from Masha. That hope was dashed but the cell, like all the others that they had looked at so far, contained a man who had been shot in the chest. He was alive – just.

Marc snapped, 'Helicopter ambulance – send most urgent. Land behind the farm in the courtyard. Give them the reference and set a beacon.'

'Yes, Sir,' said the signalman already transmitting.

Marc shot the lock of the door carefully avoiding the wounded man.

'Signal for Sergeant Karl Minden. Get him wherever he is. We need him urgently.'

Detty remembered the huge ex-forester ministering to Mara and knew why Marc wanted him urgently. Meanwhile they were looking into the next batch of hutches with increased urgency. Sadly it wasn't rewarded, some of the next twenty cells indeed contained the first women but all were dead like their male counterparts. Hope ebbed away again as they came to the last side and, at last, another man who was breathing – again only just. Marc added him to the first aid and heli-ambulance roster. Three cells down they found Masha – pale sickly grey and still. Clearly the panic stricken NAS man hadn't checked to see that she was dead. She wasn't. She had lost a lot of blood and had almost succumbed to the dreadful cold but she was breathing. It appeared that her would-be murderer had become more panicky and even less accurate as he came to these last cells and the bullet intended to kill Masha had struck her at an angle, glancing off her ribs and passing out, tearing a hole in her left chest and shoulder. As they found her the heliambulance clattered down and in a moment the paramedics were loading on board the only three left alive out of one hundred and fifty detainees.

'Do we get them to tell Rudi now?' asked Marc, quietly suddenly deferring to Detty and abandoning the command he had exercised previously.

'No – wait until we know if she will live.'

He nodded.

Subdued, they resumed the advance leaving the service units to clean up, record evidence and bury the dead. The prolonged stop at the Farm had held them up and only a few more kilometres were possible before night increased the hazards and they halted.

Marc stabbed a finger at the map. 'Just over that wood is the village of Zablinsk where our lorry came from.'

'And where I sheltered after the Winterburg,' added Detty. 'May I borrow a driver and a jeep? I have a debt to pay.'

'To the farmer for your coat? I thought you might. Of course you can. You know the road?'

'Sure – I learnt it the hard way.'

'Take three men. There won't be any enemy in force but be careful about mines and snipers although the flank unit should have cleared that bit but you can't be too careful.'

The farm was as she remembered it. Ulev, the farmer, and his wife, Mara, sat in the big kitchen huddled over the stove with their remaining daughter, Katrna, who had lent Detty her clothes.

'God greet you. You have returned at last,' said Ulev. He retrieved his flag which was still under the floorboards.

'You and only you must hoist it,' he said.

'Through God I have kept my promise,' said Detty slipping into the Old Russian vernacular.

They went into the centre of the village together and joined the other villagers and neighbours grouped round the flagstaff. It was as it had been once before on that awful day when Detty had first seen evil come amongst the innocent. This time it was still sombre and emotional but there were no NAS. She remembered her first visit and muttered Telramund's bleak *'So zieht das Unheil in dies Haus,'*[39] to herself.

In silence Ulev handed her his flag and helped her attach the toggles. She began to hoist. The ensign of freedom – the Falcon and Chalice on the green and white – fluttered in the freezing morning breeze. The dreams of the bystanders had come true. There were smiles and tears but no cheers.

Detty fixed the halyard to the cleat and faced the audience.

'I would like to offer you a prayer,' she said in her best attempt at the old Russian of the country people. She knelt down on the frosty ground.

'Our supplications go out for the souls of the lost and those that grieve for them. Our thanks go to Almighty God who has allowed us to live to see this moment. May the love of God and faith in hope and justice rest with you from now on all the days of your life.'

'Amen,' came from the villagers responding to the old language, and the provisional form, of the prayer.

'God prosper you and go with you,' they muttered.

There were tears in the eyes of the soldiers and the villagers as the jeep drove slowly out of the village to join the road to the capital.

The almost unnatural calm of short cold days was spent searching for mines, but with no active evidence of the enemy. It produced in Detty a sense of false security and a feeling that it was all over bar the shouting. It wasn't. As the columns approached the wide *Wilhelms Schiffkanal* which encircled the city on the land side, a murderous artillery and ground-to-ground missile fire started that necessitated a temporary withdrawal to positions further inland.

Zahnsdorf's aircraft, which were not equipped as bombers, did their best to reduce the enemy strength over the next few days. They flew sortie after sortie into murderous ground to air rocket and gunfire with considerable losses but little apparent effect. The FWL was bogged down again frustratingly within sight of its final objective. Oblov, Malinov, Zahnsdorf and Marc spent long hours in conference

---

39 So evil enters this house. Lohengrin: Act 2

often emerging looking anxious. It was difficult to see how they were going to break the deadlock. The NAS seemed to have recovered some command structure and were being led by a Colonel Ziehert who was responsible for multiple atrocities and was the leading brain behind the interrogation centre where they had found Masha. As well as being an expert in sophisticated torture, he was utterly ruthless in his treatment of the citizens of Königshof, sparing them nothing in his search for food and supplies. Armaments were still coming in from the sea and a general warning was issued by the FWL that any ship entering the port of Königshof would be regarded as hostile and sunk. Here Zahnsdorf did have some success with his aircraft sinking several inward-bound freighters of dubious nationality which seemed to deter most of the others. Weapons, however, had been stockpiled in considerable quantities and for the moment at least these successes seemed to have no effect on enemy firepower.

Frustrated and feeling helpless Detty did a couple of concerts for the troops. Thinking that for the moment she could do nothing more, she asked Marc if she could return over the Fojn to visit Rudi and Masha. It was easy to get a lift in one of the many planes flying back, and with some trepidation she walked up to the hospital. Her own wound was now virtually healed after careful dressing and she was pleased to note how much less she was limping than on her previous journey.

At first the news at the hospital seemed good, Rudi's morale had improved enormously once he knew Masha was alive. Detty met him proudly practising his first few steps on his newly fitted artificial leg. He told her that Masha was getting better fast but Detty noticed the charge nurse pulling a dubious face behind his back. After spending an hour chatting with Rudi, she went back to the unit office to find out how to get to Masha. The charge nurse said Masha was in a nearby suite but said rather seriously that he would like to talk to Detty before she went in. Clearly there was a problem.

Detty was shown into the office and given a cup of coffee. The charge nurse started to explain the problem. Masha, he said, had been near to death when she arrived. They had worked hard on her hypothermia, her blood loss and her wound and she began to improve remarkably quickly.

428

She was a strong young woman and at first showed remarkable powers of physical recovery. After a week or so though things began to go wrong, she progressively lost interest in food and exercise and had begun to lie curled up all day staring into space. Occasionally she would be overcome by terror shrieking incoherently. Once or twice she could be understood yelling out, 'Not the belt, not the belt. No! No! Kill me please kill me.'

She seemed to have no recollection of this afterwards but was emotionally flat and withdrawn. Her nights were rent with blood curdling nightmares but, again, at no time did she seem able to talk about or even remember her dreams afterwards. The nurses and a psychologist from Bratislava had talked with her and agreed she was suffering severely from post trauma but so far had got no further. The charge nurse wondered if Detty, with her first hand knowledge of NAS methods, could help particularly about the belt, which seemed to be at the centre of her terrors.

Detty thought for a few minutes. 'It does seem odd. I was in the Farm and then in the Winterburg and I witnessed all sorts of horrors but I can't explain the belt. NAS staff were not above beating prisoners with anything that came to hand. Compared with some of their weapons, however, a belt would be pretty innocuous and unlikely to provoke terror in a courageous young soldier. No, I will think about it, but for the present I am as puzzled as you are.'

'Thank you. For the moment we have been able to keep these developments from Rudi by saying that she was tired or had just had treatment when he visited but he is not stupid and must realise soon.'

Gloomily she returned to Königshof. Everything had gone wrong. The frozen mist was swirling over the *Kanal*. The happy triumphant times of a few days ago were forgotten and even the fine weather had gone. The FWL lay back from the *Kanal* impotent and frustrated. For the first time there were whisperings in the ranks about the war, the command and the future. The enemy, in immense numbers, were dug in on the other side of the *Kanal*. Their broadcasts were booming forth their confidence with ghastly mindless militaristic songs and propaganda, saying in effect that from the citadel of Königshof they would break forth to win a victory through fear.

Detty was anxious and furious as she drove back to the FWL transmitting station and begged air time. She had no need to beg, it was gratefully granted.

'Never shall we surrender the cause of freedom and justice to the rabid mouthings of the murderers and torturers. In the country of my birth nearly a century ago, we had our darkest hour when our patriots were captured, tortured and murdered. It seemed that all was lost. Within ten years we had freed our country. Here we will not see darkness again over the land, we will not see terror prevail. We shall open the doors of the Winterburg, we shall restore the right.'

She finished by singing, not this time the Freiheitsleid, but the haunting *'Zogen einst funf wilde Schwane'* a *Volksleid* from Livonia itself, which although a song against war had a special meaning against the brutal opposition. A group of young soldiers sung the soaring chorus. She knew it was gentle but effective and hoped it would provide a much-needed boost of morale. Inwardly, however, she felt empty and hopeless and thought of those other Irish swans, the four tragic Children of Lir, adrift and tossed by storms and fate for nine hundred years.

Exhausted she flung herself into bed in the half-ruined house that they were using as a billet and felt all the remaining energy drain from her. She sobbed herself to sleep wreathed in a feeling of desperate helplessness dreaming of the storms of her western ocean. In the middle of the night she woke and stirred as she felt Marc slide in beside her. She turned and hugged him, 'God, I am so miserable!' she murmured and was suddenly wide awake.

'I may have found your wild swans,' said Marc sounding quietly excited, 'but they will have to swim under water. Come to the staff meeting tomorrow and I'll tell you.'

The morning meeting was tense but more expectant than of late. All the senior staff were there plus Detty and Liese who had both been asked to help with intelligence details. Marc started briskly with a map on a flip chart, 'I will start with what we know from Jan and our FWL people inside the city.'

'You know the lay out. In front of us is the *Wilhelm's Kanal,* which is two hundred metres wide from sea to sea round the city. Behind the canal lies the causeway of the *Zehnheiligenweg*, with the old medieval pilgrims' way on its top. This took pilgrims dry shod from the sea round the city to the eastern road leading to the Shrine of Zablovsk. This was where the Sacred Chalice was kept until it disappeared at the time of the Russian invasion in 1943. The causeway is twenty metres high up to fifty metres wide and made of piles covered with stone and then earth over the top making a considerable depth. The NAS have riddled it with missile emplacements and other weaponry. That wouldn't matter as we could knock it to pieces with our missiles and artillery easily enough. The problem is that they keep many thousands of civilian prisoners in the old storage chambers let into the wall under the city side of the causeway to use as a human shield and forced labour. These are our people from the city and the NAS know that we could never bury them alive.

'The causeway does not reach the sea as on the east as it tapers down to become the ordinary road to Zablosk but from there to the sea is marshland honeycombed by the river delta which makes it impossible for tanks and armour. I have come to the conclusion that there is only one way to get in. That is to get the engineers to tunnel under the canal and join up with the medieval *Abwasserringkanal*, the great medieval sewer that rings the city. It is nearly dry now and there are wide paths on either side of the sewer tunnel. We should be able to gradually stock-pile arms there safe and dry. Then if we can arrange a small task force to join with Jan and his FWL men inside the walls, arm them and seize a sector of the bank while we throw the bridges over and breach the *Zehnheiligenweg*. Liasing with Jan won't be easy. Obviously we can't signal so we need a messenger to reach him. It must be somebody completely secure who knows the city and can disguise himself if he has to travel over ground. If the faintest hint of this got through to the enemy we would be massacred underground as they were in the Warsaw uprising. Any ideas who would be suitable – and willing to volunteer?

'Let me go,' said Detty firmly.

Oh my God, thought Marc, looking despairingly at his colleagues, not again – please – not again! I should have realised that she would volunteer.'

Detty was continuing. 'It seems a reasonable job for a reliable intelligence officer. A woman would have advantages. Liese and Masha are out of the question, which leaves me!'

Much as he wanted to, Marc felt that he had no military reason to object to the cool logic of the suggestion. It was decided.

*

Detty peered desperately at the crumpled damp paper map. She shielded her dim torch between her body and the shining, malodorous wet brickwork of the sewer wall. She tried to stop the drips from the roof falling on the map. It wasn't easy but she knew that a glint of light seen from any grating above – if there was one – might mean the end of her. She had travelled about four kilometres through the Styx-like world of the city's medieval sewers. She should have reached her destination by now but she had missed the correct branch at one of the complex junctions. Now she was lost, condemned, she thought, to wander the subterranean world like an infernal Flying Dutchman. Her hand compass gyrated wildly and was as good as useless. Something had clearly corrupted it. She would have to surface somewhere but how? If she had been able to reach the *Maienplatz* School, the local FWL would have raised the heavy grating and lowered a ladder at the pre-arranged signal. Now she couldn't reach the roof of the wide passage that she had strayed into, let alone lift the heavy inspection plates unaided. She realised that she must look for one of the smaller side conduits to find any possible accessible exit. This would mean leaving the dry side path of the main sewer and trudging through the variable depths of indeterminate slush that still lay on the bottom of the smaller branches. It would be unpleasant but that was now unimportant, the main thing was to find a side conduit and then a grating that she could reach and might be able to lift.

After about a further fifty metres she came on a side conduit, it was still wide but substantially narrower than the main sewer. She could reach the roof with her hands. Suddenly there was splashing all around her. She had disturbed a colony of rats, which milled all around her splashing past her boots as she disturbed them. One jumped onto her trousers and began gnawing at the cloth. She was just able to knock it off with the butt of her beloved 92FS before it drew blood. She reflected that a few years ago this experience would have reduced her to a gibbering wreck. After the things that she had experienced and witnessed in Moltravia, it only induced a feeling of anger tinged with nausea. She looked up and there ahead was the faint glimmer of light through a grating up a short chimney. She had to climb the rest of the way between the wet walls trying not to think about being bitten on the face by another rat on its way down. Presumably the rats congregated near the grill because food might come down with the waste from whatever lay above. She was able to reach the grill with the flat of her hands at full stretch but she could exert no force and was unable to move let alone lift the heavy metal.

She was now really frightened and moved slowly back towards the main channel thinking hard. If she couldn't lift one grating there was no reason to believe that, without help from outside, she could lift any of the others. If that proved to be correct she was not only immured in this foul-smelling hell but had completely failed the people who had trusted her. Absentmindedly she noticed that, in the near total blackness one part of the wall high up seemed even blacker. She lit her precious torch for a minute and sure enough leading out of the high part of the wall to her right was a very small side channel measuring barely fifty centimetres across. Trickling out of the opening was a thin stream of fluid which, even in this foul smelling place, had a noticeably more pungent malodorous sweetness.

Detty thought for a minute. The channel was just reachable and big enough for her to crawl through. She didn't fancy crawling along it with her face almost in the liquid and she had no idea how long it was or whether it terminated in a grating or just an impenetrable down pipe. However, it represented the only possible chance of reaching somewhere where she could exert enough leverage with her body to be able to lift a grating. She decided that she must take the chance. With determination she hoisted herself up the rough slippery brickwork and eventually succeeded in getting her body into the hole. Very slowly she began to crawl along it. Again she feared she might meet large sewer rats head on but miraculously there were none. She progressed a few centimetres at a time with the foul sweet smell close to her nostrils almost overpowering. She realised that it would be extremely difficult to reverse back if she found nothing. She had almost resigned herself to failure when suddenly the conduit took a sharp left turn, widened slightly and there above her, miraculously, was light.

So far so good. The light came through a few bars of a grating which her fingers told her was much more extensive but must be blocked in part by leaves or rubbish. The foul smelling fluid dripped through it sluggishly. She could reach the grating all right but would it move? She arched her back and to her relief the open side of the grating moved slightly. She tried harder and the slight movement was repeated but no more. The depressing truth now dawned on her that the dark side of the grating was blocked, not by leaves or rubbish but by a heavy weight. Her only hope was that it might be a sack or something similar that could be made to roll out of the way. She moved her body as far as she could to the open side to get the best leverage where she could try with all her might knowing that her life depended upon it. She was physically strong but even so it was touch and go. She sought and found a grip with her feet on the rough side, gradually she arched her back and then with a desperate effort pushed for all she was worth with her hands and feet. Slowly the grating rose, hesitated and then gave way. Something rolled off the side with a dull thud and the metal swung back aslant in the opening catching her a painful blow on her exposed right shoulder. No matter, the dim light of the winter sky was above her. She levered the grating out of the way, stood up shakily and looked around her. Her triumph in her freedom evaporated as quickly as it had come.

The object that had darkened one side of the grating, held her in and produced the foul-smelling fluid was now obvious. It was a decomposing human corpse. That was not all as all around were heaps of other corpses, some quite fresh, some in advanced state of decomposition contributing to the foetid fluid. The yard, for that was what it was, was surrounded by smooth walls between two and two and a half metres high and surmounted by barbed wire. At one end of the yard was a double steel entrance gate. She walked over and pushed it. It was firmly locked on the outside. Clearly whoever ran this charnel house was keen that it remained secure. Detty wondered for a moment why. Surely nobody would want to get in and clearly apart from herself none of the other occupants were able to leave.

She was recovering from the shock, fighting back nausea from the smell and trying to decide what to do next, when she heard the sound of a heavy diesel engine nearing the other side of the gate. She held her breath, waiting for it to pass by. It didn't. The gate rattled as it was unlocked. She flung herself face down over the open grating beside her dead companion thinking that she could well be crushed by whatever vehicle was entering the compound. She heard shouts and the rumble of the wheels as it entered. She peeped out of the corner of her eye. There it was, a large tractor with a great mechanical shovel on the front. It was loaded with fresh corpses which were poised above her head. Around it were three men in NAS uniform arguing about where to dump the new consignment like workers on a building site considering where best to stack the bricks. One man argued particularly fiercely that it was OK where it was and kicked Detty hard on the side to demonstrate his point that there were bodies already there. His kick hit her on her pocketed automatic. Again she held her breath wondering if he would explore the hard object he had inadvertently found and find her warm and alive. Fortunately his attention was distracted by the arrival of a NCO who started demanding anew that the bucket should be dumped at once. Detty expected at any moment to be buried under a heap of fresh corpses. At last the NCO ordered otherwise and the tractor turned away to discharge its gruesome cargo the other side of the yard.

The filth had obscured all evidence of her uniform and this had probably saved her, as lying in the yard she looked essentially no different from the corpses on either side. It was still a relief when she heard the tractor start up, move off and the gate clang shut with the bolts being shot and locked behind it. She was, however, left with the original problem. How could she get out? Appalling as her surroundings were, she had to work on the problem. She calculated that she needed a platform at least one and a half metres high and then if she could find some material to throw over the barbed wire she might be able to vault the wall. She had a stroke of luck immediately. It was not obvious how all the earlier corpses had been killed but most of them wore the standard Moltravian prison trousers, shirts and shifts. The new consignment had all been shot in the back of the neck, presumably in some haste, as they were still wearing normal civilian clothes. One man was lying in a thick leather coat, which would be ideal to throw over the wire. So far so good but there was no obvious means of finding a platform. The yard contained nothing but dead bodies and the products of their putrefaction.

She was beyond finer feelings and could see no alternative but trying to build a platform from the corpses. She selected a part of the wall that was adjacent to the gate. She thought that this must run alongside the road and began to drag the freshest, most intact, bodies one by one alongside it. She manage to get them one on top of each other two deep and with the greatest effort pulled a third body up to begin the third tier. It was a hateful business and she soon realised that it was useless. With enormous effort she might complete the third layer but certainly could go no further. This would leave her platform at less than a metre and well short of the minimum take-off height required.

As she stood pondering over the problem, she heard a sudden noise behind her. Turning with her hand on her pistol she found that she stood face to face with a gaunt tall man. Her first thought was that this was a vengeful ghost protesting at the rough disturbance of his dead companions. Further inspection revealed that he had some congealed blood on his neck but was definitely in the first life and about, she reckoned sixty years old. As she fingered her 92FS, he said calmly, 'I don't think you will need that and I take it, meine Frau, that you are not one of them.'

'No, I am not,' replied Detty not needing to enquire who 'they' were.

'In that case we should help each other,' he said with quiet firmness, "I am Virgilio Poliziano and am – was – professor of romance languages and literature at the University of Königshof.'

'Bernadette O'Neill, Captain Intelligence Corps, FWL,' said Detty completing this bizarrely formal introduction, 'but, forgive me, how do you come to be here alive?'

'I might ask you the same thing and in addition what an Irish lady, if I have identified your name correctly, is doing as an officer in the FWL,' said the newcomer.

'In my case it is simple, they missed and I played dead. But surely planning our next move is more important than reminiscing?'

Detty realised the force of her new companion and felt properly chastened for wasting time on inessentials. 'Yes, I agree.'

'What were you trying to do?'

'Build a platform of bodies so I could throw that leather coat over the barbed wire and vault to the other side.'

'Isn't it rather far to drop?'

She smiled at him through her filth. 'Yes, but I can't think of a better idea. Can you, Professor?'

Poliziano in turn felt reproved and began to have new respect for this young woman who, although filthy, was undeniably sharp.

'I can certainly help you to reach the required height. If you get onto my shoulders while I am standing on your "platform" you should be able to reach the top of the wall fairly easily.'

'Right, I will get the leather coat. One thing more, if I succeed without breaking too many bones, how do I get to the *Maienplatz* School.'

'I think that we are in part of the old coal yard complex in which case you are very near. Walk left along the road outside the gate and you should see the *Katherinenkirche* over the houses to your right. Turn right when you get level with the *Kirche* and the *Maienplatz* opens out five hundred metres down on the left. The school is on the far side.'

'As soon as I get there I will try to get a party to come back and get you. Meanwhile lie low.'

'*Jawohl*, Frau Hauptmann.'

Detty had the distinct feeling that she was being gently teased by her companion who was after all nearly old enough to be her grandfather.

Getting onto his shoulders proved more difficult than she had anticipated as her right thigh was still weak from the newly healed wound. Eventually she made it and clung onto the smooth wall. He passed the leather coat to her and with it she was able to smother the wire. 'Now for it,' she muttered. 'See you soon,' she said and launched herself with a rolling movement onto the wall. The thick coat did its job admirably and by gripping it over the wire she was even able to control to some degree her fall on the far side. Landing jarred the injured leg and for a moment she gasped in pain. Then she took a quick look round. The road was empty.

'Thanks – that was fine.' she called back over the wall.

'Good luck. *In bocca al lupo!*' came the answer back from her unseen companion. Wondering what wolves had to do with it and thinking that, at present, they were the least of her problems, she set off to follow his directions.

The streets were eerily empty. If there was anybody about they were behind closed doors. Once or twice Detty felt that she was being watched from the houses but the only vehicle she saw was an NAS armoured car that turned away from her coming out of a side turning into the main road. Apparently none of the occupants noticed the urchin with a filthy cap over the eyes slouching along the street behind them.

At first the school seemed deserted too but when she hesitated outside an old woman who was apparently the caretaker appeared and told her to go away.

'Can't I stay here?'

'No there are too many rats,' came the reply.

'I could bring a tabby cat to keep them away.'

'Very well then, but only until dusk.'

'Let me wait until the rising of the moon.'

In a moment she was with Jan in the school cellar. He was tense and angry.

'You took your time,' he snapped at her.

'I got lost,' she said half apologetically, and then felt angry in turn. 'Anyway, I followed your map exactly – here it is and it doesn't lead to here.'

He snatched the map abruptly from her and spent some moments looking at it.

'I'm sorry, Hauptmann,' he said after studying it. 'They've left out a junction. I'll crucify them. I'm sorry – I'm not surprised you got lost. How did you get here in the end?'

'Via a charnel yard in the *Esche Strasse* with the NAS all around me piling up bodies. I came up through a grating in the middle of it. It wasn't great.'

'My God, you've been there! They are murdering the detainees from the bunkers under the *Zehnheiligenweg* – but how did you get out of it? The place is locked and barred and guarded day and night to prevent anyone getting in and identifying their relatives.'

'There were no guards when I was there but it was locked and barred. Fortunately there was somebody alive inside who helped me. He's still there. Can you get him out?'

'We'll try but tell me later. I need to hear the orders from HQ first. What do we have to do and when do we have to do it?'

She explained the site and the split second timing needed. The partisans inside the city had to seize a mile of the inner bank of the *Kanal* for three hours to enable the FWL sappers to bridge the *Kanal*. There would be some support from the main FWL commandos who had crossed the river to the *Abwasseringkanal* with enough small arms and an artillery barrage but air support would be difficult because of the lethal ring of NAS ground to air missiles. She finished the details of the orders. Jan seemed to understand and sent off messengers to link up with the comandos from the other side at the mouth of the *Abwasserringkanal* to prepare for the rising.

Detty was taken up to the school showers where in the dark she washed the filth from herself in ice cold water and put on fresh but ill-fitting army clothes. She cursed her long filthy hair which she had decided not to cut because of her engagement to sing *Woglinde* on another planet. She could do with a bath in the Rhine just at present, she thought. She was given some black bread, sausage and coffee. Then she passed out on a bunk in the side cellar that passed for a barracks dormitory. She woke feeling better but found her wounded thigh was very sore after its exertions. Everybody was busy making frantic preparations for the rising. She did a few odd jobs but felt her task was over and for once was contented that it should be so. She found herself a new green and white cockade to wear on the morrow, had supper with Jan and his lieutenants and went back to her bunk to be ready for the morning.

The main partisan force augmented by the commandos from the other bank had been in position overnight. The operation so far had been carried out with immense care so nothing on the city bank was visible above ground. Detty was woken at the school in the intense cold of a dark winter morning. It was 4:30am. Her detail with reinforcements, logistic support and medical aid, marshalled under the school and entered the newly dug passage into the medieval sewer. There was no difficulty in finding the way this time. The tunnel was lit with all the gratings carefully blacked out and men, women and supplies crowded up and down. The medical officer for the partisans, called Boris, walked with Detty. When they had gone about two thirds of the way back to the *Kanal* Detty felt the earth shake and roar. They paused under a grating to listen. She had never heard a full scale artillery barrage before and this was a big one. Every gun and ground-to-ground rocket in the FWL had been prepared for this moment and now they were giving it full measure.

Boris turned to her and said above the noise, 'We've been able to tell them that the prison bunkers have been emptied in order to station NAS there – they've shot most of the prisoners – but the bastards now have massed their men along the *Zehnheiligenweg* and the *Kanal*. The evacuation makes it easier for the ordinance. It's horrible to think of the slaughter but at least they can blast away at the *Weg* without worrying about the prisoners now.'

Detty felt ashamed of herself for relishing violence but couldn't help the excitement and feeling proud at the same time. This was Marc's army, her army, freedom's army, giving the bastards who had slaughtered her friends and reduced this gentle people to abject fear and misery, a bit of their own back. She was too Irish not to thrill at the idea of a good scrap after all the cloak and dagger stuff. In the darkness of the sewer the word came through that the first objectives had been achieved and the partisans had the city bank for five kilometres. They went up to survey the scene. The great mobile bridges were swing into place unhampered while the artillery and rockets still pounded the NAS positions. All around was the crackle of small arms and clearly the partisans and their support were having to fight fiercely and desperately to maintain the bridgehead against superior numbers of NAS. Suddenly in mid-afternoon the right flank of the FWL on the *Zehnheiligenweg* broke and the reserve units near Detty's position moved out rapidly to seal it off. There was always the fear that if one sector of the front went badly the entire FWL force might be encircled and cut off before or even after the bridges were in place. The crossing of the Fojn had been a triumphant walkover but this was a serious battle with both sides fighting for survival. This time there was no singing. After an agonising wait the first of the two bridges was operational and the tanks, Marc's tanks, began crossing followed by the armoured cars and their infantry. Detty at once felt the anxious lump in her throat relax slightly. She feared for her husband whose tanks were soon fighting fiercely but once they had crossed she knew in her heart that the great enterprise should not now fail.

All day the insurgents crept forward metre by metre against fierce house to house resistance aided by mines, booby traps and sniper fire. By evening the huge NAS force of about fifty thousand men on the right flank suddenly surrendered finally removing the threat of encirclement. The main remaining body of opposition was fighting fiercely while falling back towards the city centre and the Winterburg fortress which Detty knew so well. It was only seven kilometres in distance but the urban fighting was difficult and dangerous. It was not until the morning of the third day that Marc's armour stood in a menacing circle round the Winterburg. There was another loaded pause as Marc prepared to assault the fortress. Suddenly there was a series of three massive explosions and tongues of flame leapt from the inside. The defenders had blown up their headquarters and presumably themselves. Air reconnaissance confirmed that the inside of the building was being gutted by a ferocious fire. They could do nothing except let it burn itself out. Fortunately the whole Winterburg was surrounded for strategic reasons by an open space which extended on one side onto the *Rathauseplatz* so that there was no danger of the fire spreading. The heat was intense but apart from sporadic sniper fire, mainly in the suburbs, opposition was at an end. The FWL were the masters of Königshof.

Too tired to move further, Detty stood in the middle of the *Rathausplatz* gazing at the blazing inferno that had been her prison and wondering how many unfortunate prisoners had perished in the fire with liberty almost within their grasp. At this moment of triumph she felt drained and sad, but then suddenly the full joy of their achievement struck her. Yes, it had been terrible but the terror had not been inflicted by her or her friends and now at least they could begin to build and mourn the dead with dignity. Suddenly she was aware of people around her rejoicing.

Marc watched her standing in her battle fatigues towards the middle of the square. Her long hair at last released from its forage cap was silhouetted out behind her in the dark against the flickering light of the still burning Winterburg. Men and women crowded round her and came right up from time to time to shake her hand or kiss her on both cheeks. Marc's military training told him uneasily that even now she was still far from safe. He winced each time there was a rattle of sniper fire from the streets north of the square. He knew that she was now a celebrity, a symbol and that to shoot her would be a dreadful solace to the dying dictatorship. His martial training told him that war was risky and his marital training also told him that there was no way that he could restrain his wife in the moment that she had gradually come to live for. Apart from his concern about her safety, he felt amused and only slightly jealous at being cuckolded by the fledgling republic of Livonia.

While he stood pondering he suddenly felt his hand being squeezed, startled he looked down to see Tamara standing beside him. Thinking aloud, he said, 'You shouldn't be out here either – the First Lady and future president's daughter. It's not safe.'

Mara shrugged. 'It would be a good time to die. An Englishman said it in a poem once – Keats – I remember reading it but it was at school in Russian, it made an impression but it probably sounds a lot better in English.'

Marc spoke softly:

'Now more than ever seems it rich to die,
To cease upon the midnight with no pain,
While thou art pouring out thy soul abroad
in such an ecstasy!'

'Yes, that's it,' said Mara excited. 'I recognise it, even with my English.' She suddenly smiled, 'Anyway, I'm not going to die because I want to hear *Fidelio* at the old Hoftheatre. I don't know how we shall manage because it hasn't been used as an opera house for years and it has been quite badly damaged during the war but Detty is determined. We all know what happens when Detty is determined. She said she was going to organise it straight after Bayreuth and I guess she will. I think that at this moment the Könighofers would walk on water, if your wife asked them to.'

*

Nicklaus Oblov, in his hastily organised office in the only undamaged bit of the Hansehaus, was struggling with a stream of visitors and an even larger mass of papers which now threatened to engulf him after his three-day tenure of his nascent republic's capital.

There were requests for food, enquiries about missing persons, denunciations of fascists and messages of congratulation from all over the world. The security officer knocked tentatively at the door, fearing the frustrated anger of his normally good-humoured Chief.

'*Chef*, there is a man outside who says that he needs to speak to you. He looks harmless enough but I am not sure.'

'What is his name and what does he want?' asked Nicklaus somewhat wearily – keeping open house to all was a good principle, which it was sometimes hard to achieve.

'He says his name is Gunther and that he's a violinist.'

'A violinist – I will always speak to violinists – particularly those called Gunther.'

Nicklaus' eyes suddenly developed a distant look. 'You had better let him in and make him welcome.'

The officer turned and left the room. He re-entered followed by a little bent old man who shuffled behind him into the room.

'Nicklaus Alexandrovitch, it is so good to see you again, but perhaps I shouldn't be so familiar. You are a very important man now.'

'Gunther, my friend, don't talk nonsense. It is a pleasure to see you again. How are things? Yourself and Sarah?'

'They took her to the Winterburg eighteen months ago and I haven't seen her since.'

'I am so sorry. What dreadful times we have lived through.'

'I have heard about Gisela – I am sorry too – more than I can say – and Tamara?'

'Is well and in love with this country and her new one.'

'That is good – now the reason for my visit. With three of my friends I will play in the Dom tonight. We would esteem it a great honour if you and Fräulein Tamara could be present. Times have been hard but we feel that we should not delay in welcoming liberation with music – will you be able to come?'

'Old friend, Konradin and the whole of the NAS could not keep me away. What will you play?'

'Waldhuter's second quartet and the Beethoven Opus 132.'

Oblov nodded approval at the choice but then for a moment was lost in thought. 'Thank you. I couldn't think of anything more appropriate. We will certainly be there but would you be able to add to the programme?'

'Of course, if it is your wish and if we know the piece – what do you want?'

'The Haydn opus 76 no 3,' said Oblov looking hard at his friend.

Gunther looked startled – then smiled and said, 'Yes, of course, I understand. We will play it.'

They had managed to make one wing of the Hansehaus reasonably waterproof and habitable although there were still great shell holes in the other end that had faced the righteous onslaught of Malinov's artillary in the final bombardment. Detty, abandoned by Marc who was back with his men and beloved tanks, had had a quiet supper with Mara and Nicklaus before walking across the *Rathausplatz* to the old cathedral. They entered under the great west door with its supplication to the Mother of God and sat quietly in the crossing. The bodyguard of FWL men drew back to a respectful distance. There had not been wide publicity for the recital but the choir and transepts gradually filled.

Gunther Nadal brought his elderly companions into the crossing, where the stools and music stands had been set out. The Waldhuter starts with a repeated soft D minor theme taken from the old Baltic volksleid of the 'Flight of the Five Wild Swans', which Detty had sung at her last concert. This tune on the cello gradually broadens to sweep up to the higher instruments then goes through repeated key changes to a quiet close. The second movement is a minuet followed by a short scherzo based on a Livonian folkdance. This climax leads directly into the finale with the Hansa theme and variations as a *largo cantabile*. The church stirred at the introduction of the noble melody which everybody now recognised and which had come to symbolise the hopes and now the salvation of those fortunate enough to survive.

The cadence faded gradually through the ravaged stonework and ancient peace of the great building. While applauding, Detty stole a glance at her neighbours. Oblov, Mark, Sergei Malinov, his son Andrei and Ulrich Zahnsdorf were inconspicuously dressed in dark civilian suits. The two civilian girls, Mara and Natalia Malinova, wore dark trouser suits. It had been agreed that this was a civilian occasion of reconciliation. Liese Zahnsdorf and Detty, however, had faced a dilemma. They had been in the field so long that they had lost trace of civilian clothes. Detty had only brought with her rough winter clothes which would hardly do and the remains of Liese's sketchy civilian wardrobe was still in Bratislava. They had searched the war-torn streets in vain for something even remotely suitable for young women to wear formally. They had even tried the second hand shop where Detty had bought her coat after escaping from the Klinik. She found the old woman who had been shocked that evening by her NAS uniform. Now she eyed Detty's green and white cockade saying, 'I knew that you weren't really one of them from the moment I saw you, *dyeevoschka*. You have a kind face and brave eyes. Their eyes are always dead – particularly the women.'

She couldn't help, however. Her shed at the back where she kept stock had been burnt down by an incendiary and the rest she had given to the cold and homeless children during the siege.

As they left Liese had said: 'There is nothing for it we must ask to go in uniform after all. It's better than showing disrespect. In our days in Bratislava we had some French grey dress uniforms made by a local tailor. They were simple but formal and well cut. They enabled us to go to diplomatic receptions there and in Vienna. We tried to persuade foreigners that we were a serious army worthy of support and not just a rabble. I think that they will have been sent up with the rest of the supplies and will still be at Bialovsk in the stores.'

She had phoned the quartermaster there to find out if the uniforms were available and then sure enough they arrived by plane with a load of medical supplies that evening. Detty was a bit apprehensive but was impressed once she saw them. They were well cut in fine serge with tailored skirts and jackets. They were completely new and packed in good-quality boxes and tissue paper. The quartermaster, who Detty suspected was one of Liese's admirers, had even had the correct gold wired captain's crossed swords and falcon badge sewn on the shoulders before dispatching them.

'I must give Ernst a big kiss when I see him,' she said smiling with an absentminded flirtatiousness. Detty had to remind herself that this coquettish young woman had coolly and efficiently commanded a successful and important commando operation at the lake at Schloss Krenek only a week or so before. She looked very young and beautiful this evening. They had both managed to get their hair done and Liese shone in blond highlighted glory as she sat applauding bare headed with her beret with its immaculate FWL cockade on her lap. Detty hoped that she looked as good.

The quartet began the spirited allegro of the Haydn. She felt her tension rise as they paused before the slow movement. She knew that Marc beside her was as immobile and expressionless as a rock as the old men began the theme of his national anthem. She knew Oblov had asked for it as an oblique but very certain expression of thanks for the help that they had received when it was so badly needed. She also knew him well enough to be certain that in his heart he was just as pleased by the gesture as he had been on that joyous morning when she had sung the same tune on the banks of the spring river. Because so few people ever say thank you to Germany, he had said later, it means that it is so much more valued when it happens. At the end of the quartet he allowed himself to turn and smile at Nicklaus before whispering to Detty, 'I've never seen two more beautiful soldiers. I really must think about joining the army.'

'The blond one's a lot too beautiful for my liking. To say nothing of a certain small but important young blond civilian,' she replied, 'Eyes front!'

The musicians tuned again and began the dark yearning sostenuto of the A minor Beethoven which was to be the climax of the evening. With each movement Detty became more cocooned in a web of emotion. With the miraculous struggles and tensions of the *Heilige Dankgesang*, she felt an emotional casket tear open inside her. She wept long and silently as the music swept her upwards to an empyrean where the world seemed very small below her and her experiences of the last weeks suddenly transfigured into a meaning. It was a meaning that she still did not completely understand.

15
AWAKEN!

Was du sein wirst,
sei es mir heut[40]

WAGNER: SIEGFRIED ACT III Sc3

It was a leisurely lunch. Several festival goers cast amused glances at the three young women, occasionally recognised as *Rheintöchter*, quaffing beer and sausages, deep in conversation. The jealousies and tensions of working together sometimes result in strained relationships even between young singers. These three, however, had become firm friends cemented by the physical contortions that they had had to undergo to fulfil the half-geisha, half-sea nymph fantasy of the Japanese designer and the Irish producer. All three had admitted that their dancing careers had been severely restricted by having two left feet apiece. Maddy had, at least, had a formal Juilliard stage training but it seemed to have made little impression. Ilse said wickedly that she had survived dancing classes during the early years before her gymnasium but only because she was taught by a Prussian Oberst's daughter who she swore sported

---

40 What you will be, be that today

jackboots and a whip. Detty had endured, rather than enjoyed, ballet taught earnestly but not very inspirationally during her early days at the convent but she had thrown herself into Irish dancing later with, as she was the first to admit, more enthusiasm than skill.

The movement coach was a conscientious elegant young man imported by Gerry Flynn. His last endeavour had been at an Asiatic gay nightclub which had been set up to entertain Japanese visitors coming to the offices of *La Defense* in Paris. Presented with three well-grown, attractive, aggressively heterosexual and undeniably clumsy young women who had been selected originally for their ability to sing, it was all nearly too much for him. After the first rehearsal he retired with a migraine and the girls began to have serious doubts about his adequacy for the job and the wisdom of Gerry's choice. They were impressed, however, when Tiam Si, which they rapidly and predictably modified to Tamsy, reappeared with renewed vigour for the next bout with his three occidental Amazons. As they began to make progress with the willowy chiaroscuro movements, they realised that the director might have been right after all, as the coach undoubtedly had great feeling for the strange hybrid that Gerry was trying to create. So hard did they work at the movement, they almost neglected the vocal side. They need not have worried however as rumours were already spreading round Bayreuth that these were some of the most talented *Rheintöchter* for years. Ilse had caused a minor sensation earlier that year with her Octavian for the Deutsch Oper am Rhein at Duisberg and had immediately been booked to sing the same role in London, Dresden and Prague. Maddy had conquered the anglophone world with her French vocal line in a stunning Delilah at Dallas and had been booked to sing Carmen at the Metropolitan in two years time. All this was common knowledge to the Bayreuth regulars but the whisper before the new *Ring* began was, 'Yes, but have you heard the Irish soprano?'

'I know what they say, a voice like the young Leider, but she's done nothing and I think it's all hype. I'll wait to give my verdict after *Rheingold*.'

Das Rheingold had been four days before. A rich vibrant young voice had broken the unrelenting chord of E flat to initiate the new

Ring. Bayreuth and all Europe now knew that the Irish soprano was no press man's fantasy. By the time she had sent shivers down their spines, greeting the gold, and her two immensely talented colleagues had contributed to a magnificent trio, it was widely agreed that this was indeed probably the finest set of *Rheintöchter* heard in many years.

They had become fairly well known and were often recognised about the town. They loved the old traditions of the place and often lunched in the Eule, which was now largely abandoned by artists because of the glare of publicity. The faithful visitors in the old inn imagined that the serious conversation between the young singers concerned musical values and nuances of interpretation. In fact, it covered the price of shoes in Germany, the superior quality of the Canadian hamburger and the tortures of Irish convent meals. Maddy and Ilse then became engaged in a furious argument about the relative merits of Canadian and German skiing, finally referring to Detty as a referee. Her natural inclination was to support Ilse but she felt that would not be fair as she had never actually visited Canada and wasn't a skier. She refused to arbitrate, remarking only that she was glad that the argument didn't concern beer. That immediately started an argument about beer and the rival merits of Labatt, EKU and Beamish.

They finally collapsed in gales of laughter and got to discussing the progress of the current *Ring* cycle. Against the assumed bored professionalism of the other two, Detty maintained that she wanted to be in the theatre for *Siegfried*. After all it was the first cycle and it was artistically important to witness the whole work.

'Gee, just listen to her,' said Maddy, exaggerating her Canadian accent. 'Come on, Ilse, let's go and buy up *Nürnberg*.'

This was initially agreed but slowly the two hard-bitten young professionals decided that for various reasons after all they needed to be in Bayreuth for the afternoon and if they were in Bayreuth they might just as well be in the Festspielhaus – what a bore! In fact they were both intrigued to hear Anneliese Seiling's awakening – the tour de force of the greatest dramatic soprano of the current generation.

'Anyway,' said Detty, 'I'm going to hear it – you can buy up *Nürnberg* if you want to.'

They finally both reluctantly agreed that they would grace the theatre with their presence in the wings. Everything decided, they were getting up to leave when, suddenly, Kaspar, the general director's PA burst through the door into the dining room.

'*Ach*, Frau O'Neill, I am so glad that I have found you. Frau Wagner would like to see you at once. I have a car at the door – if you don't mind!'

Detty looked amazed and muttering, '*Ja, naturlich*,' she got up to leave saying, on the way, to the equally astounded Ilse and Maddy, 'See you tonight in the theatre.'

'Fine,' they replied as she got into the Mercedes, illegally parked nearby.

As they drove up the Green Hill, she wondered what on earth Christa Wagner could possibly want her for at short notice. The obvious thought occurred to her, which she dismissed as sheer fantasy. They couldn't need her to sing. After all there was only one soprano part in *Siegfried* apart, of course, from Brünnhilde. She had seen the current Woodbird, Liv Olfsen, that morning looking aggressively healthy – impossible – forget it – the *Waldvogel* part didn't lie right for her voice anyway.

She was ushered up to the general director's office and Christa Wagner was sitting at her desk, her brow furrowed. She smiled, 'Ah, Frau O'Neill, I'm so glad that they were able to find you. I will come straight to the point. Dr Bernhard tells me that you know and can sing, and sing well, the Brünnhilde in *Siegfried*. Is that correct?'

Detty felt the colour drain from her cheeks but pulled herself together and replied, 'Yes, that is correct, Frau Wagner, I have studied it during the last year with Dr Bernhard, as an exercise you understand.'

'But you have never sung it on the stage?'

'No, Frau Wagner.'

'We have a great problem. Poor Frau Seiling fell in the bathroom of the hotel an hour ago and has severely bruised three ribs – she is having an X-ray as there are probable fractures. At all events she cannot possibly sing tonight. Her cover, Frau Stevens, has allergic laryngitis. She walked amongst the pines in the *Frankenwald* and came back voiceless. She knew she was sensitive. I am not pleased. Frau Muller was to take the

451

second cycle Brunhilde anyway and she has faxed to say that she will do the *Götterdämmerung*. There is a space of three days, however, and as she does not come back from New York until this evening so she cannot possibly do the *Siegfried* tonight. I asked about Frau Beltringe and Frau Davies but they are engaged already. There is nobody else that I can get in time for this performance. Ironically there appears to be no established Brünnhilde left free and near enough in Europe and it's far too late to get one from outside. I must cancel the performance in the middle of a *Ring* cycle-unheard of in over 130 years – unless…?'

'Unless I sing it?' said Detty, suddenly calm and determined.

Christa Wagner nodded.

'Frau Wagner, two years ago when I had just returned from an experience so terrible that I still have horrible nightmares about it, I dreamt of this moment. Of course, I will do it – I have waited two years for the chance and would have gladly waited a lifetime. How could I refuse an opportunity like this?'

As she finished she remembered Anneliese Seiling's long dialogue with Wotan on destiny and the will that she had heard two nights before. Somehow it had all come true and here was Christa Wagner asking, *'Wollen Sie?'*

There was a pause while the two women thought about the oddities of fate and then Christa said quietly, 'Thank you. That was a courageous decision. I know that, potentially, you have the voice, your Woglinde has proved that but without experience and at short notice… and it's the most difficult one. I must make a curtain announcement about Frau Seiling. Do you mind if I say it is your debut in the part?'

'Please say anything that you think appropriate.'

'Go and talk to Herr Flynn about the blocking – and then to Dr Meilin. I am sure he will talk you through the orchestration although you won't be able to rehearse with the orchestra. Herr Schleissen is about and I will try and find him for you – so that you can have a word together. Do you feel able to do it on stage as you already know the sets or do you want to do it from the wings – do you know the part well enough – up to you?'

'I know the part well. Dr Bernhard is very thorough, so on stage – please.'

'OK, about the costumes – the tights are fairly standard and there should be no great trouble in getting the kimono to fit. After that rest and once again – thank you – our thoughts will be with you.'

Detty stood there for a moment as Christa looked at her with great warmth and understanding. After a few moments she realised that she had left her Handy at her hotel and she felt emboldened to ask, 'Frau Wagner, may I please use your phone?'

'Of course.'

She quickly dialled the Oberdorf number and recognised Hildegard's voice, '*Detti am apparat, Hildegard, ist Marc da?*'

Some discussion followed and apparently he had gone to the village to get a few items but wouldn't be long, 'Please tell him to come to Bayreuth as soon as he gets back. Tell him I am going to sleep on a mountain with a chunky American.'

Christa Wagner had suddenly abandoned her general director's formality and dignity and was killing herself with laughter and relief. She thought that she had made the right decision if her cover-elect had the confidence to joke about it. Hildegard, however, was not amused and it took Detty several minutes to explain the plot of the last act of *Siegfried* and the current Bayreuth casting in order to assure her that she was not about to besmirch the honour of the von Ritters. It was only that she wanted Marc to be there for the greatest – no perhaps the second greatest – challenge of her life so far. Eventually the message got through.

As she was finishing the conversation Christa Wagner whispered, 'Tell her to get Graf Marc to ask for me when he gets here. I will tell the stage door staff. I hope he will join me in the *Mittelloge*.'

This casual reference to the box where Richard Wagner and Ludwig II had watched the first ever complete *Ring* produced a shiver down Detty's spine. Christa saw Detty's face and, misunderstanding, said, 'Don't worry I will look after him.'

Detty thanked her and was about to leave when there was a knock at the door and Gerry Flynn, the ebullient Irish director came in.

'She'll be doing it then – in costume?' he enquired a touch anxiously in English. Christa nodded. He turned to Detty, 'I knew you wouldn't let old Ireland down. Didn't our ancestors fight together at Vinegar Hill. Sure you'll have no fault with the blocking. Just sit up, stand up and sing but I'll show you anyway. They went to the first rehearsal stage, which they were hurriedly setting for Act III Scene 3 in Detty's honour. The beautiful Japanese set lost some of its magic close to but none the less she was familiar enough with it to be able to take up her position high stage left with the misty oriental gorge of the Rhine underneath her without prompting.

Gerry got her to sit up and open her eyes as he wanted and then went over her positioning in relation to Siegfried. At the end he said, 'Don't worry – you know the work backwards and you have real talent – play it naturally and it will be fine.'

As they were finishing she heard a rich American drawl behind her say, 'Of course, it will but can I help?'

'Good to see you, Hank, meet your leading lady for tonight.'

Henry Schliessen, the Henry Schliessen of Detty's adolescent fantasies and the signed photograph, looked down from his great height at Detty with unfeigned male admiration and said, 'Gee, I sure don't think that will be any problem. But please remember, young lady, that you are young and fit and I am old and raddled and I've sung two and a bit acts before we get going together – so be a bit kind, won't you? But I have to say, that you may not be the greatest Brünnhilde that I have ever partnered but you're sure damn well one of the best looking.'

'Thank you, Herr Schliessen, and I'll try to remember, but you have sung more Siegfrieds than I have had hot dinners and two nights ago my highest ambition here was to sing Woglinde. So I guess I will be trying not to make an ass of myself.'

Hank grinned and said, 'Fair answer – but if we are about to fall in love, Bernadette, you had better call me Hank.'

Used as she was to German formality, she warmed to this frank open hearted mid-Western who she had known up to now only from the autographed photograph, record covers and the rehearsals of *Götterdämmerung*. Joining in the flirting, she said, 'If you call me Bernadette you will remind me of my father being cross with me – call me Detty – everybody else does.'

'OK, but, by the way, aren't you some kind of German countess?'

'As a matter of fact, I am, but that's a long story, just think of me as a poor Irish girl who you've got to help out in a tight corner.'

'That will be a real pleasure.'

He was serious for a moment and smiled at her. 'Somehow, Detty, I think that we are going to get on just fine. You sing it and I'll fit in where I can.'

Detty thought that that was a remarkably human comment from the world's leading *heldentenor* and her already considerable admiration for Henry Schliessen was increasing. Suddenly she was aware that Anton Meilin was standing behind her.

'Congratulations, Frau O'Neill, I somehow had a feeling that one day we would collaborate in a major work. I knew it when I heard you sing Elisabeth for Herr Doktor Bernhard two years ago. Your Woglinde was splendid but I am not sure that I realised that it would be the Siegfried Brünnhilde quite so soon, however. Are you ready to go through the scene?'

Detty sang her part with full voice and convinced any remaining doubters that she was a serious performer. Gerry and Hank exchanged meaningful glances and surreptitious thumbs up signs. Dr Meilin allowed her to flow through the scene, just marking her cues, as she wished realising that it would be pointless to try and change her interpretation at this stage. At the end he said, '*Wirklich gut*, Frau O'Neill, you have a wonderful, young natural voice. Just sing it like that this evening and we will all be very happy. Remember to take your beat from the prompt box – the orchestra will make you too far behind, but of course you know that from singing Woglinde.'

Costumes were simple. Silver-green, filmy kimono over grey-green tights with Gerry and Tori Moronu, the designer, saying that she should wear her own red-gold hair loose behind a figured clasp high on her head. Once all was settled she left the theatre gripping her vocal score of *Siegfried*, like some sort of lucky totem, to return to the *Goldener Anker*. She did not quite know why she preferred the old traditional hotel in the centre of the town to the modern smart *Bayerischhof*, where many of the singers stayed. She liked the current members of the family who owned the *Anker* and somehow it seemed more in tune with her mood. It was now half past three and the performance started at four o'clock. The first two acts and the hour-long intervals meant that she had at least four hours before she needed to be back in the theatre.

On impulse, she changed into a tracksuit and training shoes. She slipped out of the hotel and walked quickly across the *Ludwigstrasse* and into the *Hofgarten* behind the Neues Schloss. Once in the park she started to run rapidly skirting the perimeter. There were a number of locals and a few visitors enjoying the Friday afternoon sunshine or watching the ducks on the lakes. Nobody seemed surprised at the sight of a tall, athletic girl running fast round the park between them. Had they realised that this same young woman would be in the Festspielhaus singing *Brünnhildes Erwachen* in a couple of hours time they might have been more interested. Perhaps, it would not have completely surprised them, however, as there had been a long tradition at Bayreuth of the singers mixing with the citizens and public. Although, sadly, media attention meant that you could no longer see a Siegfried in swimming trunks or a Gutrune playing tennis in the quiet roads below the Green Hill, there was still a greater closeness between artists and public than would be usual at other festivals. After her second circuit, she stopped behind Wahnfried, looked at the tomb where Richard Wagner lay beside Cosima and said solemnly and quietly, 'Give me the courage and I'll not let you down.'

She turned quickly and walked out of the *Hofgarten* to wait for her car back at the hotel. She thumbed unseeing through the vocal score, learning nothing.

The second act was in progress so there were few people around as she was driven up the Green Hill to the theatre. Klaus Burman, her repetiteur, was waiting for her. They went to work immediately. She sang the opening and the *Friedenmelodie* in full voice. Satisfied he quietly wished her, '*Hals und Bienbruch* – broken leg and broken neck,'

She just restrained herself from thanking him. She said that, in view of the reason that she was taking the part, the traditional wish was a bit near the knuckle. He smiled.

456

She went to Brünnhilde's dressing room trying not to tremble. On arrival she found two emails both of which touched her greatly, one was from Dublin, from Adele O'Mara, who had presumably heard from Oberdorf. It congratulated her and said how much she would give to be there. The other was from the *Bayerischerhof* just down the road sending her all good wishes from Anneliese Seiling whose injury had led to her good fortune. Detty was touched by the generosity of the great soprano and made a mental note to visit her and thank her in person afterwards.

She was hardly aware of what she was doing as she went through the routine of make up and costume. Ready in good time she shocked her conventional dresser by slipping out into the wings in her dressing gown to hear Manfred Erfult consult Almeida Tulla on the future of the world. She had always loved this scene and wondered yet again as so often before how the young Manfred had learned his huge part so quickly. He had got the Bayreuth contract before he had ever sung a complete Wotan – in fact his first had been at Hamburg less than a year before. Then she pinched herself realising that she was about to sing her first *ever* Brünnhilde in this Olympian place and at an age when most singers were not yet out of college.

Almeida was a high profile personality who Detty had long admired from afar. As well as being one of the great contraltos of the day, she was a black South African whose forebears had suffered in the murky history of that formerly benighted country. Conscious of her ancestry, she had led a world campaign against oppression and the abuse of human rights. She had sought out Detty, as a fellow warrior for freedom, and they had become friendly. Almeida's political activities had caught the imagination of the public and far beyond Bayreuth, she was known as the jet-black earth goddess who made tyrants shrink. Years before Grace Bumbry had had something of the same effect as the first black Venus in *Tannhäuser*. She, however, was an elegant coffee coloured American whereas Almeida was all African and showed the fire and passion of the sorely-tried native people of her country.

She had reached her spine tingling lines:

'Ein Wunschmadchen
gebar ich Wotan:
der Helden Wal
hiess fur sich er sie kuren.'[41]

Detty envied the contralto this passage – it reminded her of her conversation with Marc in Munich the day they ordered her engagement ring. Detty pinched herself again – in a few minutes she would be portraying the *Wunschmadchen* at the centre of the discussion. She thought how much she needed the next lines:

Kühn ist sie
und weise auch:

As the first ascending theme of Wotan's resignation rang out from the orchestra, Detty returned to her dressing room. She knew she had fifteen minutes before she was on. She relaxed her shoulders and did her breathing exercises and warmed up. She then sang a scale, which was forced and sharp, 'Do that in a few minutes time, Bernadette,' she said muttering severely, 'and your career will be short and remarkably undistinguished. 'Don't be so stupid,' she added to herself, 'you will love every moment of it – it's fun – it isn't the Farm quad.'

She completed her warm up and sang the scale again – somewhat better and decided to leave it at that. She looked at herself in costume under the unflattering dressing-room lights and laughed aloud at the mirror. A moment later came the final PAS announcement:

'Bitte, Frau O'Neill zur Bühne.'

---

41 A wish-maiden I gave to Wotan
     From the battlefield
     She selects heroes for him
     …
     She is brave and clever as well

'Ja, ich bin fertig!' she answered to herself and feeling slightly unreal, she went back into the wings. As she took up position Manfred and Hank brushed past her, the first with a smile and the traditional *'Toi,toi,toi'* and the latter with a thumbs up. As the stage darkened and the orchestra swelled into the music of Siegfried's ascent of the rock, her assistant stage manager led her out behind the gauze to her rock niche above the cavernous gorge in which she had floated in and out as Woglinde.

She lay and relaxed her shoulders and confirmed her position. The growing green gold light picked up the mists in the gorge and the colours of her kimono as she had seen it light up Anneliese Seiling's in the *Hauptprobe*. Finally she checked the sight line to Elfriede Hann, Anton Meilin's right hand and the all-important prompter. All was well and the gentle music introduced Hank's reassuring musing. The huge American's voice showed no sign of wear and tear after his gruelling evening. She followed the text line by line. Never had the beginning of the scene seemed so long. Eventually he removed her veil with the famous exclamation of:

'Das ist kein Mann'

which he sang with wonder rather than shouted and somehow or other made sound convincing.

At last the brass chords followed the arpeggios as he kissed her and she began to sit up with the lift bearing her forward. It was a complicated effect but she dismissed it from her mind and concentrated on sitting up slowly. She waited with a cue-eye sideways on the prompt box. The next thing she knew was that her voice on cue, apparently independent of her body was swelling rich and secure:

'Heil dir Sonne !
Heil dir, Licht !
Heil dir, leuchtende Tag!
Lang war mein Schlaf;
Ich bin erwacht:

wer ist der Held,
der mich erwecht?[42]

All nervousness had gone and she savoured the moment as she waited for Hank's answer. She cautioned herself not to be overconfident. She felt the voice was all right but the cues were tricky. Eyes cast down, she slid into abject misery in her ex-goddess's sexual angst. Then her eyes stared in tune with her terrified gestures as she begged Siegfried not to touch her. She found it easy to sing with Hank – whether this was because he was consciously helping her from his great experience or not, she did not know. Finally, she calmed down and reached the *Friedensmelodie* of the Siegfried idyll – magical and tranquilly beautiful then leading on to the final high climax as she begs Siegfried to leave her alone – while the music telling the world that his love battle is already won.

Then she admits it too with the:

'*Oh Siegfried! Dein*
war ich von je!'

Which had been the answer that Detty herself had given to Marc when he had asked her to marry him in the garden at Oberdorf. Somehow this scene had been the centre point of her life since she first tried to learn it at her convent in Ireland. They swept into the final duet, passionate, vigorous leaving the foothills behind to reach the summit with its ringing climbing phrases culminating in the glorious triumphant second high C. She threw herself into Hanks huge arms feeling unusually tiny. She was full of relief, gratitude and affection and for a second the emotion was not entirely theatrical. For a very great tenor he was an amazingly sensitive and generous man. She whispered, 'Thanks, thanks, thanks – you made it so easy.'

---

42 Greetings sun!
    Greetings light!
    Greetings radiant day
    My sleep was long but now I awake
    Who is the hero who has woken me?

'Nothing to do with me – you were just wonderful, baby!' he whispered back in his native mid-western accent contrasting with the perfect German dialogue he had been singing so naturally a moment before. They stopped whispering as the final chord rang out and the curtain fell.

All opera houses express their corporate personalities at this moment. Covent Garden with an un-British impetuousness often applauds over the orchestra. La Scala murmurs, at Vienna the claque follows its appointed line and Paris considers. Bayreuth pauses for only a split second and then the verdict – good or bad – is emphatically stated. This audience had an unusual situation to judg – a substitute singer, very young, tall, and beautiful who was yet another of the exotic foreigners who had made the festival such a truly international occasion for singers in the last half-century. In Bayreuth the audience is also cosmopolitan but its heart is Bavarian. Proud Bavarian chauvinism is never far below the surface and sometimes breaks through. Tonight, however, was unusual in this respect also, in that the substitute exotic foreigner was also a Gräfin of one of Bavaria's oldest families. All of this might have been enough to see almost any performance through to a measure of success. There was, however, more, the ringing dramatic singing and the passionately intense commitment of the performance had been added. In all it was bound to be one of those evenings with an electric sense of occasion which those present would never forget.

A tiny pause after the triumphant last chord sounded, the silence was broken with a crescendo of cheers that echoed round the extraordinary acoustic of the unique theatre. Then the cheering came again with the thunder of Bayreuth stamping on the hollow floor as the curtain went up to reveal Bernadette still enfolded in Hank's arms. Their position was as it had been when the curtain fell with her tall figure dwarfed by the huge American *heldentenor* – both of them silhouetted against the misty golden brightness of the illuminated oriental rock. They hadn't even had time to consider curtain calls – possibly their present position was as had been decided by Gerry, Hank and Anneliese at rehearsals, Detty had no idea but it seemed right and the audience loved it. Finally after three or four more calls, they separated, bowed and went off, allowing Almeida, Manfred, Liv and Horst Stiegen, the popular Mime, to take their turn. Then they were back all together as the cheering and stamping continued to thunder.

Detty was proud that she did remember that etiquette demanded that she should lead Anton Meilin onto the stage. As he joined them, Detty said breathlessly, 'I hope that there weren't too many mistakes, Herr Doktor.'

Her looked at her sidelong – very serious and scholarly in his steel rimmed glasses and said in his clipped voice, 'We must have a rehearsal immediately to correct the defects.'

As her face fell, he burst into a broad grin and she realised that he was teasing her.

'You were wonderful – it was as it must be – all emotion, love and enchantment. I have never heard a more convincing performance.' and he kissed her hand.

It was Detty's turn to tease, 'You need to be careful, Herr Doktor, teasing me like that. You forget that I have just being portraying a wild mountain woman and in real life I am a wild Irish girl. The Siegfried Brünnhilde murdering the Herr Music Direktor at Bayreuth before the start of *Götterdämmerung* really would give the tabloids something to talk about.'

They all laughed and went back on together. As Detty took her final curtain she looked down behind the *Klangblende* into the cavernous *Orchestersraum* and noticed a knot of orchestral players gathered round the podium still applauding her. This she realised was a rare privilege from that hidden orchestra of street-wise professionals taken from all over Germany.

When she arrived back at her dressing room Marc was waiting for her. Flushed and for once speechless, he just clasped her in his arms and hugged her. She became aware that behind him was a tiny familiar figure in a black silk dress with her long blond ringlets streaming behind her.

'Look who I have brought,' said Marc, and Detty transferred her hug to Tamara casting a quizzical glance at Marc.

Breathless and flushed Mara explained,

'Marc rang me at my digs as soon as he got your message. I was coming anyway to here you sing Woglinde in the second *Rheingold.*

I thought he was joking at first and then I realised that he wouldn't joke about something like this. Fortunately, I was in and hurtled to the Hauptbahnhof, I changed out of my jeans in the loo on the train and Marc met me at the station during the second interval. Frau Wagner organised the rest – I had to keep pinching myself – hearing Siegfried at Bayreuth sitting in the *Mittelloge* with my dearest friend singing Brünnhilde. Things like that only happen in fairy stories... but as I listened I knew your voice – even here you were still Detty – the same voice as those mornings at Oberdorf – the same as even...'

Her voice tailed off not wanting to spoil this magical evening with unpleasant memories. Detty, however, knew that she was referring to the terrible evening in the farm when she had whispered the words of the *Abscheulicher* in her pain and humiliation. They embraced again with the silent thoughts of their ghastly shared experience passing between them.

The sombre moment was broken by a broad mid-Western accent saying cheerfully, 'Are you all coming to *Abendbrot*? I've laid it on at the *Bayerischehof* for everybody.'

Detty looked at Marc saying demurely, 'Meet Hank, the man who has just been making passionate love to me in front of two thousand people. Hank, this is my husband Marc.'

Marc grinned at Hank and said, 'I guess we will fight the dual later. I'm a baritone although not in your league, so I suppose it fits – but if you don't mind leave *Nothung* behind... and sure, we would love to join you for supper.'

Detty's dresser who had been removing her make-up coughed tactfully, '*Entschuldigung Sie*, is the *Frau Gräfin* dining? If so what is she wanting to wear?'

'Oh I'm so sorry,' said Detty. 'I've nothing here except the cotton sun dress that I came up in. Yes, we will all be joining Herr Schliessen for supper at the *Bayerischehof* – oh dear – it's a bit awkward – what shall I do?'

'The Frau Gräfin has something suitable at the hotel?'

'Yes I have a green silk sheath at the *Anker* which would do fine.'

'Accessories?'

'Yes – those too.'

Detty was pleading to maintain her standing in the eyes of her formidable dresser.

'If you will permit, Frau Gräfin, I will take a car to the *Anker* and find what you need. Perhaps you could call them and say that I may have the key to your room?'

'Yes, of course,' said Detty, and thoroughly chastened that she hadn't thought about life after The Awakening, made the required call. Still embarrassed as she put the phone down she added, 'Thank you very much – I'm sorry that I am so disorganised – but I was thinking of the music and it was such short notice.'

'Of course, *Frau Gräfin*, very natural,' and with an expression that implied that Birgitt Nilson or Waltraud Meier would never have behaved like that, the Teutonic female Geeves disappeared to find a Festspielhaus car. As she swept out, Detty thought that she looked every inch like a Valkyrie riding into battle to protect the honour of the festival against the Celtic whims of its latest parvenu leading lady.

They were at last relaxing over the champagne when there was a knock at the door and Christa Wagner appeared. She added her thanks and congratulations and then said, 'This is going to be very big news indeed – here and all over the world. Now we must arrange the press conference.'

Yes – thought Detty, imagining to herself the headlines of the British tabloids: 'From whore to diva' or something of the sort and various references to moments in her past that she would rather forget. Christa was talking again.

'Do you want it here or in your hotel?'

'What is customary?'

'Either, but the rooms at the *Goldner Anker* are quite small and not as used to that sort of thing as the *Bayerischerhof*.'

'They might enjoy it at the *Goldner Anker*,' said Detty, thinking of the couple who had run it so well for the last three years bringing the famous old inn back to life, 'but perhaps it had better be here.'

There was further applause and a florist's shop of flowers as they entered the dining room of the hotel. The audience correctly assumed that Marc was Bernadette's husband but the gossip declared that Tamara must be Hank's new mistress. 'He has a terrible roving eye for the girls, you know.'

In the early morning they returned to the old hotel. Detty felt exhausted but content and very relaxed in a dreamy sort of way. The music of the *Friedensmelodie* flooded through her head as she went off to sleep. The tranquillity didn't last and she was woken by Marc whispering reassurance to her as she screamed in a nightmare. Brünnhilde's rock on stage had turned into a trolley at the Klinik and the horror of that place flooded through her. After Marc had woken her he held her tight for some minutes until she calmed down. The flashbacks and the nightmares were less frequent now but when they came they were still as bad.

She felt weak, exhausted and all the elation of the previous night had drained away. She thought with horror about the press conference and how she would be questioned about aspects of her past that she least wanted to discuss. The Brünnhilde parallels kept coming back to her but now it was the dispirited goddess of the second act of *Die Walküre* with her care-laden eyes and onerous weapons not the radiant girl won over by love that she had portrayed the night before.

She adopted her usual remedy and took a long bath while Marc slept on peacefully. She thought about what to wear and decided that it must be the elegant green silk trouser suit that she had bought as an impulse in an expensive boutique in the *Bahnhofstrasse* two days before.

*

The third and final *Götterdämmerung* swept majestically to its apocalypse. Henry Schliessen had moved the polyglot audience with his death scene and the cogniscenti were heard to remark in the previous interval, 'Probably the greatest voice since Melchior and a far better actor.' A solitary cynic mixing with the throng in front of the theatre made a quick calculation that even the most precocious Wagnerite would need to be nearly ninety now to have seen Melchior and thought that the judgement on his acting was based on tradition rather than fact. The final fanfares were played and Anneliese Seiling, mercifully recovered, sang one of her grandly moving Immolation's and after tumultuous cheers and many curtain calls the audience trooped out to their hotels, *Sekt*, beer and the warm summer night.

As they were dispersing, a *Rheintochter* still in her dressing gown was seen knocking urgently at Siegfried's dressing-room door.

'Detty, honey, great to see you out of the river,' boomed the inexhaustible, good-natured twang of the American tenor.'

'Hank, you were wonderful and forgive me but I know that you are off early tomorrow and I want to ask you a great favour before the others come.'

He nodded, 'Sure. Go ahead.'

'You know you said after *Siegfried* that you would like me to sing a lead with you again. Well, I'm going to take you at your word.'

Detty thought that cheeky effrontery was the way to the heart of great Heldentenor who, although pursued by managements from Vienna to San Francisco with ever more fabulous offers, never lacked a sense of humour and adventure. She was also beginning to know her Hank and did not underestimate her attractions or his good nature.

'Be great, honey, if we can wedge it in. What's up?'

The recent revolution and Civil War in Livonia were common knowledge and Hank was vaguely aware that the tall young Irish soprano who had conjured that amazing awakening out of thin air had been involved in it. Detty breathlessly filled in the details, finishing by telling him, 'Livonian freedom is something wonderful and very special to me. I was imprisoned there twice and twice escaped with the help of the ordinary people, wonderful people. I fought with them to free their country and against all the odds they made it. Tamara, the daughter of the President-elect Oblov, who you met after *Siegfried,* is my closest friend and was my bridesmaid when I married Marc. She was badly tortured by Travsky's NAS.'

Hank winced.

'To cut a long story short I am trying to arrange that we perform *Fidelio* in the *Hoftheatre* in Königshof on the evening after the new democratic republic is officially declared on September 30th. Could you sing Florestan to my Leonore? I know it's an enormous thing to ask and incredibly short notice but I just thought you might be still on holiday. I need hardly tell you what it would mean to the Livonians, the greatest living interpreter of the role and a citizen of the world's leading democracy.'

'How many performances?'

'Well, one would be superb but if you could do three…?'

'Flattery and beauty are a very powerful combination as you and I learnt on the rock together.' teased Hank as he reached for his diary. 'Let's see. I'm supposed to be singing a recital in Sioux City, Iowa, prior to starting rehearsals for *Tristan* at the Met. It's my home town – but you're on, I can reschedule the recital.'

He was rewarded by a hug and a slapping kiss from Detty.

'Hey,' he laughed, 'I had to work for four hours for the last one.'

They both burst out laughing and, as the well-wishers began to arrive they realised that they had added to the inexhaustible supply of Bayreuth gossip, but, for different reasons, neither really cared. Detty prepared to leave, 'See you in Königshof – the hotels aren't wonderful but Tamara and I will see that you get the best there is.'

'I'll be there – the 26th for the *Sitzprobe*.'

*

Detty drove Marc to Nuremberg for him to go back to his duties with the British Army at Bulford. Returning to Oberdorf she packed everything that she could think of and telephoned Haydn Roberts in Oxford. She knew that he had been a renowned Pizarro and hoped against hope that he would come to Königshof.

'Nothing that I can't cancel for that.' came the reply to her question. 'I'll email you when I have worked out flights. I suppose it's best via Berlin.'

'Probably,' said Detty.

'There are more flights but Warsaw and Vienna are also possible. It just depends.'

Feeling warm and satisfied she headed towards Berlin. As she drove through the late summer sunlight on the woods and fields the thought suddenly occurred to her that she might need a visa to get into Livonia. She called up the president's office on her mobile and spoke to Nicklaus' private secretary. The man sounded incredulous, 'Excuse me but *who* did you say it was?'

'Bernadette von Ritter – you see I want to come to Königshof to rehearse for the *Fidelio* performances and wondered if I would need any documents.'

'Just one minute, Frau von Ritter, the president is here and would like to speak to you.'

A familiar voice broke in, 'Detti, the day that you are not welcome within the borders of this land, I'll turn it back to Travsky. I'll call the frontier to tell them to welcome you. Come to the Hansehaus as soon as you get here. Mara will be thrilled that you are coming at last. She's missed you even for a few days and still wants you to talk more about Bayreuth.'

Smiling she rang off and headed for the once-dreaded Livonian frontier. When she reached the crossing point she saw for a moment a NAS woman pointing a gun at her and handcuffing her. Then the nightmare fantasy faded and there was only the FWL officer on duty insisting on providing her with an armed escort in the form of a young soldier who shyly slid into her Z4 beside her. As she chatted to him, she learnt that he had fought in the tanks and he told her how much he admired Marc.

'Do you realise, meine Frau, that as soon as he took over I just knew we would make it. Before we all worked like beavers but we didn't know where we were going and often it all seemed to be slipping away. Then the Herr General arrived and he was so calm and had time for everybody and everything and, all of a sudden, we knew it would work. He gave us all such confidence.'

Detty broke in musingly,
'*Der blickt so still, so friedlich nieder,*
der spiegelt alte Zeiten wieder,
und neu besänftigt wallt mein blut'[43]
The young soldier muttered. 'Exactly,'

---

43 It looks down in tranquil peace
Reflecting times past
And my blood flows serenely once more

But he still looked puzzled and Detty added simply, 'It's a phrase from Beethoven's *Fidelio* that I am singing in Königshof.'

Detty couldn't get used to her husband, who had only just become a major in his own army, being referred to as 'Herr General' but then realised he had had the temporary rank of Brigadier in the FWL which she supposed made him 'Herr General' to the men. She smiled. 'I have felt that too – not just as my husband – when he rescued me from here the first time and afterwards when I once fought under his command. We raided the Farm Detention Camp to release Frau Tamara. He was amazing. Nothing was left to chance. Nothing panicked him.'

'But I believe,' the soldier said shyly, 'that you saved Frau Tamara's life.'

'I was only a small part in it. What you probably don't know is that she saved mine. Your first lady is the bravest person that I have ever met and I have seen some real bravery often since I first came to this country.'

The sun was hot as they passed through villages and small towns. It became rather like a royal progress with Livonian irregulars guarding key installations still compensating in enthusiasm for what they lacked in uniform, standing back and making a passable attempt at saluting as she navigated between them. For some weeks now her photograph, as the heroine of the nation, had been plastered over every newspaper and in any case her smart BMW was hardly likely to be overlooked in the poor countryside. Wounded the country might be but on every side the thin faces were smiling and waving and she waved back with enthusiasm.

She needed a few things from a chemist and stopped once before reaching the capital. The chemist was at the side of a school in a medium-sized market town called Sovils. She tried to keep the car out of sight and, in spite of his protests, left her body guard behind as she got out. She went to the chemist and walked back to the front fence of the school. All the children were in the playground and she watched them through the wire. The younger ones were playing but the teenagers were in groups talking with some of the teachers. It so much reminded her of the school that she had visited from the Sacred Heart when she first arrived in the country a million years before. Then it was the depth of winter but now the sun was warm and somehow symbolic of the changed land.

She was wearing the tee shirt and jeans, which was standard Livonian summer wear and she hoped that she looked like some of the mothers of the younger children who were standing around presumably waiting to collect their offspring. In this way she was able to watch the scene for a time without being noticed. After some minutes, however, she noticed a stir in one of the teenage groups and realised they were looking at her surreptitiously. Finally a fair young man of about seventeen walked over to the fence and bowed. She had another flashback of a tall young man bowing and clicking his heels to her under very different circumstances.

'Excuse me, meine Frau, for the impertinence but my companions and I would like to know if you really are Frau Bernadette O'Neill.'

Detty smiled at him, 'Yes, I am.'

'In that case, Frau Gräfin,' he said very formally in correct but slightly laboured high German, 'the School of St Paul would be greatly honoured if you could spend a few minutes to visit us.'

'I would like that very much,' replied Detty.

She spent about half an hour touring the school buildings with the headmaster, the head girl and the young man who proved to be the head boy. The school was shabby but very clean and well run. There was a science laboratory suite and a small library with old but meticulously cared-for books. When the tour was over the head asked Detty if she would mind saying a few words to the school assembly. She agreed readily but felt oddly nervous as the head introduced her as the great heroine who had suffered for them and was one of the principle figures in obtaining the new freedom that they now enjoyed.

As she stood up to speak she was trembling. She was furious with herself – the woman who had sung Brünnhilde at Bayreuth, nervous at addressing a school. She explained that she felt nervous and was greeted with incredulous smiles. She told them a little of what she had done that summer and what she would be doing when she got to Königshof. She explained about *Fidelio* and what it meant to her as the spirit of freedom and hoped some of them would be able to hear it at least by broadcast. She avoided platitudes about youth being the future as she had always hated them when she heard them from the pompous old visitors at her own school. At the end she said that she would like to do what she did best and that was to sing to them a song from her country, Ireland, a song from her adopted country, Germany and finally a song from their country that she loved, Livonia.

She crossed to the polished but battered upright and softly sang Danny Boy. After the shy applause she started the old Rhenish volksleid, *Muss i dem* in the rich accent that she had learnt from Marc – lively but still mezza-voce. The applause was louder and she felt they were less shy and beginning to enjoy themselves. She started to play again and heard the gasp and the scrape of chairs as they all stood up to the first bars of Waldhuter's majestic tune. She gave the *Freiheitslied* full measure allowing her voice its flowing powerful head. The entire school joined in the chorus at first diffidently then with increasing vigour.

They had all heard it before, sung it and indeed seen her sing it on snowy television screens in a hundred homes but the effect of her voice live and vibrant in the school hall was different. At the end she was cheered to the echo and the cheers were mixed with tears of rejoicing and relief. The head declared that this was the school's proudest moment and one that they would never forget. Finally, amongst waves she was allowed to leave and rejoin her anxious bodyguard to drive to Königshof.

Mara met her and showed her to the official visitors flat at the Hansehaus, which was now fully equipped as the president's residence. Kurt Hansen, the local producer who was in charge of the *Fidelio* arrangements, was there to greet her. She showered and met them again for drinks before dinner. She was too tired for serious planning and they just talked gossip. Suddenly she asked them whether there could be three more tickets for the Gala First Night.

'We can hardly deny you, Detty,' said Mara dubiously, 'but they are very tight. Who are they for?'

'Dr Nicolai Arensky, Natalia Luberova and Stefan Leanov,' replied Detty without further explanation. Mara raised one eyebrow in a quizzical look.

'OK, you'd better know. They are the principal, head girl and head boy of St Paul's School, Sovils.'

She then told the story of her afternoon and Mara, with a sigh, told her that she would fix the tickets although heaven knows what dignitary's nose would be put out of joint. They said their goodnights and exhausted Detty went to her room to dream of the pupils of St Paul's singing the *Götterdämmerung* vassals' chorus to the tune of Danny Boy.

16
RETTERIN

"O donna, in cui la mia speranza vige
e che soffristi per la mia salute
in inferno lasciar le tue vestige;[44]

DANTE: PARADISO XXXI

Detty sat up in bed to the knock at the door. She had slept deeply after the concert the night before. The newly reformed Königshofer Philharmonica conducted by Helge von Grunstrand had played Mendelssohn's Rhenish Symphony and Waldhuter's Hansa in the courtyard of the Grosse Schloss. The grand impression had, for the moment, driven even Leonore out of her head. She had been delighted to hear her friend find time to conduct the concert in between the *Fidelio* rehearsals, which had now been in full flight for some time.

Coffee and rolls arrived on a tray, far fresher but still of the same brown thick rye bread that recalled the Sacred Heart and The Farm.

---

44 Trs Mark Musa
Oh lady in whom all my hope takes strength
And who for my salvation did endure
to leave her footprints on the floor of Hell

There were also emails, which the Hansehaus maid brought, printed, with the breakfast. The first was from Hank confirming that he would be in Königshof a week before the performance for the *Sitzprobe*, the second from Marc saying that he would arrive from Norway at the weekend and there was also a letter postmarked Dublin. It was from Adele and read:

'I don't know how well your press-cutting agency is doing but I thought you might like to see the enclosed. *Toi, toi, toi,* for *Fidelio*. Can you get me a ticket for the third night? I think that I can get to you by then. Love Adele.'

Attached was a copy of a page from the London Times. Half was occupied by an advertisement for a well-known building society but the other half was headed ARTS – *Bayreuth 20* – by Henry Knight who she knew as Sir Henry Knight – the irascible doyen of British music critics. The first part of the article was true to form consisting of a petulant criticism of the filmy, evanescent Japanese sets and 'the mannered production'. Detty felt her blood boil in defence of her friends and colleagues and almost threw the paper away wondering why Adele had sent it to her.

Snake-fascinated, her eyes moved on until she reached the part devoted to the singing. There was grudging acknowledgement of Henry Schliessen and Anneliese Seiling's position as the supreme exponents of their parts accompanied by some nit-picking criticism of phrasing and minutiae of characterisation.

'But,' and this was where the words leapt from the page in front of Detty's eyes, 'the one truly exciting feature to be found in this year's festival was the performance of the very young Irish soprano, Bernadette O'Neill who covered for the injured Frau Seiling at the last moment as Brunnhilde in the first cycle *Siegfried*. There may have been more accurate "Awakenings".'

'Here we go,' thought Detty as she read on.

'But total accuracy hardly mattered. I have never experienced this very difficult passage sung with more warmth and beauty. In addition, there was a rare commitment to the spirit of the scene which made it come alive like the summer's morning that it is supposed to represent but so seldom does. It is hard to believe that all this was achieved by a twenty-three-year-old soprano with virtually no stage experience beyond singing a stunning Woglinde at this year's festival. Miss O'Neill seemed to inspire Mr Schliessen to be back to his youthful best and sing with the fine abandon of his early career. Indeed, after this one glorious evening the rest of the *Ring*, and indeed the festival, seemed completely anticlimactic. We understand that Miss O'Neill has been impeded in her singing career by the active part that she has taken in the recent Livonian Civil War and indeed will be singing Leonore in the celebrations of the newly formed Livonian Republic in Königshof in September. If the Bayreuth experience is anything to go by, the government and diplomatic audience in Königshof will be in for a rare treat, which they may not deserve. I would greatly like to be there but, for some extraordinary reason, no press or public tickets have been made available for the three performances.'

Detty leapt out of bed with a thrill of guilty pleasure which she savoured all through her long shower. It was partly the pleasure that the old ogre's praise had given her and partly the thought that he couldn't get a ticket but that Stefan and Natalia from Sovils would be there. It was really remarkable that she had even succeeded in captivating that old bastard but, she remembered, perhaps she was good at captivating old bastards. Her track record suggested that she might be. Finishing the almost cold coffee she scribbled a quick reply to be sent by email to Adele:

'Ticket waiting – thanks for cutting, love, Detty.'

Mara and Kurt, the producer, were already waiting in the breakfast room. Mara could hardly contain herself, 'It's all fixed,' she said, 'the provisional parliament meets on the 30th and my father will be installed as acting president pending the elections. We heard today that we have an immediate grant in aid of 500 million Euros from the EU, which will make a tremendous difference to sorting things out. I also heard that a certain Graf Max von Ritter had been fairly eloquent in putting our case to the European Central Bank. Detti, what can I do to thank you?'

'Nothing to do with me,' said Detty briskly. 'I don't control my father-in-law. All I am doing is trying to help mount a production of *Fidelio*. By the way, I've fixed Hank.'

'You haven't really, have you?'

'Yes, I told him I would never sing with him again if he didn't come.'

'Stop teasing.'

'OK. He's an amazingly generous guy and like all the best Americans has a bit of a hang up about freedom. Now let's have a look at your disaster of a theatre.'

'It used to be an excellent theatre,' said Mara, a touch haughtily asserting her local pride.

'Sure,' said Detty grinning, 'but what's it like now? We are going to try and use the old Berlin *Unter den Linden* sets that they are sending over. From the measurements you sent of the arch and the old cyclo position they should be about right but of course they won't fit exactly. What's the stage carpenter situation?'

'No specialists but three useful general craftsmen.'

'They won't be offended then if I ask Gerry if he can pursuade Gerd Muller, the *Buhnenobermeister*, and his *Schreinermeister* to come over from Bayreuth. They are on holiday and did half offer but I think they are waiting for a formal invitation. They should be able to fix the set up if anyone can. Meanwhile, I've got to make sure that I know the part – you can't get away with just the *Abscheulicher*. Fortunately Haydn's coming over from Oxford to sort me out.'

She was bubbling on a high and her old friend knew her too well not to realise it.

'Detti, before you get too carried away. Don't arrange to be too busy on the 30th itself. It's a National Day of Remembrance and rededication and we would like you and Marc to be our personal guests of honour at the session of parliament, the Cathedral Mass and the reception.'

Detty looked suddenly pale and embarrassed, 'What a stupendous honour, Mara, to be the guests of honour of the president.'

'Elect,' Mara corrected her.

'OK, then "Elect" but we all know that that's a formality.'

Mara, who knew what was in her father's mind, smiled to herself realising that her friend still had no idea just how great an honour was really planned for her. Detty was continuing, 'You know how I feel for

476

this country and, next to Marc, nothing could mean more to me, but country GPs' daughters somehow aren't usually guests of honour on high state occasions. I will email Marc at once.'

From then on it was the theatre every day. Haydn arrived relaxed and cheerful and was installed in the Hansehof Hotel, which had reverted to its old name from the somewhat dysphonic Neues Volks Stern. On the first morning, puffing slightly and swearing in Welsh under his breath, he followed Detty up the creaking, carpetless stairway to the dust covered gallery bar. This had been the only place that she could find to install the battered but fairly tuneful upright Bechstein that she had found abandoned amongst other refugees' property. She did not know how it had got there in the turmoil of the last few months. Nobody could see any objection to using it, at least until the owners could be traced, if they were still alive. Anxiously she found a tuner and was relieved when his efforts confirmed her first impressions that it wasn't a bad instrument.

Two long abandoned wine glasses stood opaque and stained on the bar. Haydn sat down heavily on the stool,, beamed at her and said, 'Well now then, you can do the difficult bit so we shouldn't have too many problems with the rest.'

She laughed at this casual dismissal of one of opera's great parts. He went quickly through the whole role pointing out some problem points and getting Detty to sing a phrase here and there.

In the following days they met early every morning as the golden autumn sunlight of the continuing late heatwave slanted in from the eastern sky. Detty hoped that the fine weather would hold and not test further the soundness of the old theatre that they were trying to nurse back to life. In the sessions that followed Haydn profoundly broadened her insight into this work that she already knew and loved so well. As she felt more confident Haydn slid tactfully and unofficially into the role of head of music staff guiding the two young and inexperienced *repetiteurs* in their work with the other singers.

Hank could only arrive five days before the performances but Kevin Scott, the Don Fernando, who was a friend of Adele, had already arrived from Dublin. Max Hieren the young bass baritone who had agreed to sing Don Pizarro came two days later. He was a rapidly rising star from Freiburg. He was being groomed at Bayreuth for the Dutchman and Telramund and thought to be a probable future Wotan. Bernhard Meisl had found that he could make the dates and had suggested him for the part to Detty. Lev Forjela, the Jacquino and Martina Schlerova, the Marzelline were both local as was Dieter Tinsel a veteran Königsberger who was singing Rocco. Haydn began to do a lot of work with Martina and Lev later in the day, after his sessions with Detty. Eventually the four of them under his guidance were working together on the tricky balance of the 'Mir ist so wunderbar' quartet.

There was a huge amount to do. The orchestra was largely new as there had been no orchestral music in Königshof for several years. There was no chorus in existence except the FWL choral group, which fortunately formed the core of the choir aided by sundry other choristers of the required quality collected from every corner of the war torn city and country. To Detty's joy Bernhard Meisl, as the Festival at Bayreuth was over, as well as finding them an international quality Pizarro, had agreed to come himself to audition and direct the chorus. This took an immense load off Detty's mind and allowed Helge to devote his whole attention to welding together his patchwork orchestra. Fortunately in years gone by, the Königshofer Philharmonica had had a considerable reputation and some of the older players remained. After years of silence, however, there were many gaps due to sickness and death from torture, war and disease.

The lovely old theatre charmed them but was in a terrible state of repair both through neglect and recent war damage. They just had to do some very makeshift repairs or else they would have had no chance of mounting the performance. Fortunately the stage was large and the Berlin sets fitted pretty well and only a few of the dungeon and castle flats had to be modified. The Bayreuth party with some very capable local help made the adjustments quickly. Much of the machinery was derelict and they had to work out how to make do with the minimum of shifting during the performance. The unique enthusiasm of the enterprise had grabbed them and finally they got it as good as they possibly could manage. Then some of the most highly skilled and expensive theatre engineers in the world were to be seen stripped to the waist acting as plasterers repairing the coffered ceiling with unexpected skill. The chorus, when not rehearsing, had a rota to operate concrete mixers for the local bricklayers filling shell holes at breakneck speed. There was a lot of laughter particularly when Detty announced that she wanted to join in and try her hand at plastering. To the consternation, mixed with laughter, of both Königshofers and foreigners alike, after about ten minutes one of the best known faces and head of hair in Livonia was liberally laced with white wall plaster and looked '*wirklich schrecklich*'.

A newspaper reporter revelling in his new freedom asked cautiously whether Frau O'Neill could possibly permit him to put her photograph thus adorned in his morning edition. Both onlookers and the reporter looked tense until Detty said, 'I think that in future I'll stick to singing. I don't think that I'm cut out to be a plasterer's mate – but of course you can print it – it's fun. That's what a free press is all about and anyway at least it shows that I'm trying to help.'

The picture filled a quarter of the front page of the following morning's *Königshofer Tageblatt* with the simple caption:

'Frau Bernadette O'Neill takes time off to help the repairs between rehearsals for *Fidelio* at the Hoftheatre.'

The picture became one of Detty's favourites and later always made the family laugh.

*

The medieval hall had a grandeur and dignity in spite of the water from the heavy rain seeping round the tarpaulin inadequately covering the huge missile hole at one end. Detty in the visitors' gallery was able to hear the drip drip drip in the silence after the Herald's Proclamation. It was probably inaudible, however, to the ranks of representatives hushed as the acting president arose to speak, 'Fellow members of the provisional Consiglium and Livonians everywhere. This is a joyous occasion but one which must, however, be tinged with great sadness. So many have died and so many suffered over the long dark years to make this day possible. I would like to ask you everywhere to pay tribute to them by observing two minutes silence before we continue with the business of the day – please all stand.'

It wasn't hard for Detty to let her thoughts and prayers roam for the two minutes over the death and the suffering that she had seen in this brave but tortured country which always tugged at her heart strings. Beside her on one hand Mara was weeping silently. Detty squeezed her hand before stealing a glance at Marc, grave and handsome in his formal uniform, as a visiting Major of the *Bundeswehr,* on the other side.

Nicklaus Oblov cleared his throat and continued, 'The dead and injured, however, sacrificed themselves for freedom and we owe it to them to celebrate and build on the liberty that they have bought for us at such a terrible price.'

There were murmurs of assent.

'You will by now know the programme for these days to celebrate the rededication of Livonian freedom. The signing of the Oath of Allegiance to the Republic will be followed by the vote on the Provisional Constitution – all the elements of this will of course be fully debated and amended if necessary later in the session. After the business here is finished the whole Consiglium will cross to the *Frauenkirche* for an ecumenical combined Requiem Mass and Te Deum to commemorate our dead and give thanks for our freedom. This afternoon there will be a carnival procession put on by the citizens and children. This is emphatically not a parade – this town has seen far too many parades. It will pass through the *Rathausplatz* to the *Hofgarten*. I sincerely hope that my first act as your provisional president will be to get the weather to relent and remain fair.'

Cries of hear, hear, and laughter echoed for a moment in the hall.

'This evening we will have a reception at the Hansehaus and the celebrations will culminate in the first performance of Beethoven's *Fidelio* at the Hoftheatre tomorrow. Again we must pray for a dry evening as the performance is being broadcast publicly in the *Rathausplatz* as well, of course, as on television. In case there seems a degree of privilege for those of us who are lucky enough to have seats inside, I should point out that even after the superhuman efforts of the last few weeks the weather proofing of both stage and auditorium cannot be guaranteed.

You are advised to wear raincoats or at least have them with you. (More laughter.) It should, however, be a truly momentous and memorable evening. I would like this House to acknowledge the generosity of the great Henry Schliessen. He has not only come here to sing Florestan for the three performances but has donated his fee and a magnificent additional contribution to start a trust fund for the refounding of the conservatoire for the education of our young musicians. I move that we send him an Address of Thanks from the Consiglium.'

Detty had known nothing beforehand of this gesture and muttered, 'Oh, Hank,' with tears in her eyes as she joined in the applause. She had half-feared that Nicklaus Oblov would mention her role and was relieved that he hadn't. She was overwhelmed by the generosity of her great colleague and this was the best surprise she could have.

Oblov was speaking again, 'We must acknowledge that for us this is a second start on the road to peace and democracy. We still have many problems – today we are impoverished as never before because, to the enduring long-standing poverty of this country, has been added war, famine, extortion, mismanagement and savage oppression.

'Why is it different this time and where do we start? It is different because we have gained in national pride and confidence in a revolution the justice of which has impressed the whole world. We have triumphed against the odds in defeating a fearsome oppressor. We now live in a world where stable frontiers and peace towards neighbours are at last being valued if not always achieved. Last, but by no means least, we have substantial material support from the European Union, that great united enterprise which we hope to join and which follows in the traditions of our own noble Hansa. At this point I must pay tribute to the sensitive support we have received from the Federal Republic of Germany – our powerful,' he paused, 'and generous neighbour. The historians will recall that our capital was a prominent city in the German Hansa and that some of our territory was formerly in Prussia. The nightmares of the twentieth century destroyed all that and much of the country suffered grievously at German hands. We grew to hate and fear our neighbours but today I record that without the humanitarian assistance of the new Germany our enterprise could not have succeeded.'

Detty wondered wickedly if the activities of a clandestine commando unit could really be classified as 'humanitarian assistance' but knew the reason for the diplomatic paraphrase which she suspected anyway was inserted at the direct request of the German Government. He was continuing, 'We must start by working and learning, as Livonians are renowned for working and learning. It won't be easy but it will be a life without fear and torture and this time it must and will work!

'Before I finish I have a one important but, I think uncontroversial, matter to raise. The provisional Consiglium and indeed this house will be aware that our revolution and our country owe more than it can ever repay to one person particularly amongst so many. That brave person, a foreigner from another tiny land, which has had to fight for its own freedom, has suffered with us, fought with us and finally engineered and inspired our victory. I acknowledge that my family and I also owe an enormous personal debt to her, but it is as the provisional Head of the State that I now speak. It is most poignantly fitting that with her beauty and talent she has arranged tomorrow's performance of the work that is the apotheosis of freedom in which she will sing the leading role with Mr Schliessen. She will portray on stage the very virtues that, in a highly practical way, she herself has displayed in her outstanding part in our struggle.'

Detty felt faint. She had thought that she had got away with it but this was far worse than she had feared.

'The provisional *Kabinett* have discussed how we could acknowledge our debt to her. They decided that there was no adequate way but I now call on General Malinov to propose our thanks in the manner that was finally decided. General Malinov.'

Sergei Malinov stood. 'I can add little to the provisional president's words except to say that without the extraordinary bravery, strength and resource of the person he has mentioned, we would still be enslaved and not be meeting in this Consiglium in Königshof today. I ask the Consilgium to approve by acclamation as its first legislative act the award of the rank, degree and honour of *Komturin* of the Hanseatic Order of St Nicklaus to Bernadette Niamh O'Neill, Gräfin von Ritter .'

Everything was misty and the floor was waving in front of her chair she was just aware of the cries of '*Gesagt*' ringing through the hall in acclamation. Detty was aware that Malinov was saying something about the medieval order being specially re-established in order to honour her adding that, with her permission, the investiture would be at the end of the performance at the Hoftheatre the following evening.

Marc whispered in her ear, 'He even got your second name nearly right,' and she suddenly giggled.

She did not remember crossing the road to the ancient cathedral, only passing through the great grey stone arch with its apostles and '*Mater Dei Ora pro Nobis*' carved into the stonework. Passing underneath she muttered her 'Amen'.

As Marc guided her gently to her seat she was aware of a double shaft of light striking down from the high east window and crossing just above them. It reminded her of that other shaft of light comforting her while Mara was being tortured and she looked across at her companion, now amazingly healthy and the acknowledged, if unofficial, first lady of Livonia.

The massed choirs and the children of Königshof sang the requiem. The cardinal archbishop led the congregation in prayers for the dead, the bereaved and the injured followed by a public two minutes silence of remembrance. Dramatically, without further announcement the choirs, orchestra and organ surged into the Te Deum pealing thanks for the rebirth of the nation in liberty – after mourning comes renewal and rejoicing. As they left the cathedral, every bell in Königshof rang as they had not rung for seventy years – this time there was confidence.

Luncheon in the Hansehaus was a joyous and light-hearted affair – smoked eel, Baltic herring and long sausages with local beer and a copious supply of Franconian wine which had appeared as if by magic decorated with the green and white shield of Livonia surmounted by the chalice and falcon. Detty had recovered sufficiently to join in some broad jokes about dill cucumbers, which were also served, but still found the congratulations of all and sundry on the extraordinary honour that had just been announced overwhelmed her normally cheerful garrulous self.

*

The heat wave had broken only three days before and ushered in the rains of autumn. Hastily erected FWL military shelters keep some of the outside audience reasonably dry. Rain was falling unrelentingly as Mara steered the long black taffeta evening gown that she had bought in Berlin, away from the puddles as she was helped out of the official car. The portico of the old opera house had been regilded and repainted and was decked with flowers. At the back of the foyer, however, the rain still dripped through a shell hole incompletely sealed in the high roof. In a sense Mara felt this symbolised her reborn country. It struggled bravely to show its joy in freedom but still clearly sported the scars of its recent travail. The evening was one of mystery and excitement. She had been too busy supporting her father in his many duties to go to the theatre during the preparations as often as she would have liked. She had heard the odd rehearsal but still felt that she knew all too little of this opera, which symbolised freedom and meant everything to Detty. The FWL guard of honour presented arms and sounded a fanfare. She looked at the slightly tense faces of the eager young men and smiled. This was a new experience for them too.

She allowed herself to be escorted to the old royal box and enjoyed a moment's relaxation. The house lights were still up, however, and she was aware of many curious looks being cast up from the stalls. It was amazing how Königshof had decked itself out for the occasion. Beautiful if slightly outmoded evening gowns mixed with uniforms and tailcoats.

Mara spotted Marc alongside General Malinov in the stalls. She had asked him to join them but he had replied that although he was greatly honoured he felt it would be better to remain a private citizen for the evening. Mara had sensed that he wanted to watch his wife achieve her ambition untrammelled by official protocol. For Mara knew that this was a sacred evening. No church was involved but this was an occasion dedicated to the triumph of humanity. Detty had always said that this opera reflected the Livonian struggle and now it was to be performed as the final celebration of their freedom.

After a seeming age the lights went down and Mara impulsively gripped her father's hand. Helge von Grunstrand looking incredibly young edged through the Philharmonica players onto the rostrum. The staccato of the opening chords of the overture contrasted with the noble but delicate theme weaving through the wind and strings leading onto quiet reflection and the triumphal brass tutti of the finale of the overture. Mara found the beginning stirring but thought, at first, that the domestic squabbles of Jacquino and Marzelline, although beautifully sung by the two local youngsters, were a bit of an anticlimax. The singing eventually took over and Martina Schlerova as Marzelline in particular sounded so fresh and beautiful in 'O war ich schon mit dir vereint', which was greeted with such rapturous applause that Mara even feared that she might steal the thunder from her friend.

Suddenly Detty was there, tall and passably masculine in her doublet and breeches with her hair up under a cap, but unmistakably Detty for all that. Her first words were spoken and Mara realised that every phrase of the strange fragmented text was fraught with double meanings in the context of Livonia. At last she sang, her voice mixing with the three others in the canon 'Mir ist so wunderbar' and Mara realised that she had nothing to fear as the full richness of Detty's voice as yet subdued and gentle blended with Martina's lighter-weight freshness. The largely bankrupt audience enjoyed the irony of being reminded of the virtues of gold by Dieter Einsel. Then as Detty spoke the line: 'Warum denn nicht? Ich habe Mut – und Kraft,'[45] applause and cheers broke out in the auditorium. Helge, in the orchestra pit, able to rest for a moment during the spoken passage, reflected that he had never previously heard a piece of spoken dialogue in an opera, get such a reception. The house settled down and Mara felt her spine tingle when Detty sang out for the first time in the trio declaring for God and right. Her friend's glorious soprano blended with Martina and Dieter and rang into the depths of the old theatre, stunning the audience who had never thought that they would hear the like again in their stricken capital.

The soldiers marched in, not as NAS, which would have been too obvious for the subtle mind of Kurt Hansen but as sunken-eyed faceless masks stripped of all individuality. Pizarro also bore the facelessness of cruelty. Max Hieren delivered the 'Ha! Welch ein Augenblick' with just

---

45 Why not? I have courage and strength

a touch of the bureaucratic monster, the monster who has orders and regulations. He discussed the murder of Florestan as everyday business – more important than most, but still business, like ordering new furnaces for Auschwitz or electric batons for the KGB. Supplies and arrangements were important they had to get through and the arrangements for murder must be finalised correctly.

Leonore was now alone with the lights fading around her. The poring of passion on the head of the monster and the reflection which Detty phrased ever so softly on the rainbow of peace bringing calm. Mara felt her whole body and the whole theatre around her tingle with electricity as Detty reached the prayer of *'Komm, Hoffnung'*. Suddenly she was back sustaining the pain – wracked body of the girl who was now drawing magic from the very air as she sang. She realised that she had never heard Detty sing the great song before at full voice under 'normal' conditions. She remembered vividly the moment when, through her own agony, she heard those words in her friend's loved voice just as she felt she was about to die. The pulse of a nation prayed with Leonore and as she sang *'Ja, Ja sie wird's erreichen.'*[46] The theatre and the country held its breath until at *'O du, für den nun ich alles trug'*[47] the fusion between Livonia and Florestan was complete. She soared on to her crescendo until the final held high B of *Gattenliebe* and turned away rapidly while the theatre, the city and the country with over a million television sets thundered about her. Mara, weeping and unable to applaud, was seized by a vision of all the oppressed, all the tortured of centuries who had echoed the sentiments of that prayer and how she herself was amongst the few blessed who had come through her own ordeal to witness the prayer's fulfilment.

It took a long time and Detty said afterwards that her most testing professional moment was when she turned to Rocco to request the release of the prisoners, controlling her speaking voice from cracking. Mara heard it cool and well pitched and also wondered how her friend could manage it. The prisoners in Kurt Hansen's conception represented all the colours of the world entrapped and confined. The only direct reference

---

46 Yes, love will find it

47 Oh you, for whom I have born everything

to the local oppression was that Sergei Leoni, the first prisoner, had indeed been in the Winterburg until the liberation and had miraculously escaped from the blaze. Pizarro repeated his regulation rage, the prisoners returned and the act flowed on to its quiet conclusion.

Mara had never heard the long sombre introduction to the second act before and even after the first act, the tension of Hank's voice swelling from the gloom and pain of the dungeon to his vision of salvation stirred her with resonance of her own torture and fear.

'*Gott – welch dunkel hier…*'

How dark indeed! Many in that theatre had experienced just how dark, the darkness of hopelessness could be.

Somehow she realised that this was a very special Hank performance. Like many supreme singers, facing heavy demands, there were nights when the routine took over, but not tonight. This was vintage Hank and she knew it was for Detty and for Livonia. '*Ein Engel Leonore*' had a special quality about it. She wondered… just wondered about how Hank really felt about Detty – he was kind and generous to everybody but… She then cast it from her mind to get on with watching the melodrama of the grave digging. Suddenly Hank, Detty and Dieter Einsel were in '*Euch werde lohn*' together with the tenor and soprano at last united. Detty was sounding amazingly controlled and masculine. Pizarro appeared with murder in his voice and eyes – a regrettable bureaucratic necessity of course.

With the cry of '*Tot erst sein Weib!*'[48]

Detty released her own long auburn hair from its cap with one hand and let it stream down her back while drawing her pistol with the other. Strength and femininity combined – her own enduring hallmark.

The trumpet call, sounded on stage by a veteran of the FWL, also sounded through every village in the land from the loudspeakers and the bonfires were lit. Freedom had really arrived.

'*Oh namenlose Freude,*' they sang with Detty's voice soaring effortlessly over the stave, blending thrillingly with Hank's. Mara was no musician but knew that Hank was right. They were perfect partners as they had been in *Siegfried*.

---

48 First kill his wife

Breathlessly Helge launched his orchestra, inspired if not note perfect, into the last scene. The whole theatre and for all they knew the whole of Livonia was singing with them. First, the hymn to freedom *'Heil sei dem Tag, Heil sei der Stunde'*[49] sung with a conviction that shone through the music. Mara hardly noticed when Kevin changed *'ihm'* to *'uns'* as he requested Leonore to strike off Florestan's shackles but there was a subdued murmur from her father and the audience. The country also recognised it for the symbolic gesture it was. The chorus thundered out the repeated *'Retterin, Retterin'*, turning towards Leonore as drama melted into reality on the stage. Leonore and Bernadette merged and the curtains swung down with the roars in the theatre echoing round the country.

Mara had forgotten that there was one final act to the drama until she realised that, silently during the cheering, her father had slipped from his seat. The curtain calls gave the audience a chance to release their pent up feelings – roars for the Livonian chorus and leads, a huge cheer for Hank, which recognised both his performance and his gesture in coming. As it died away he walked slowly into the wings and emerged leading Detty, convulsed in laughter, by the hand. Nobody knew that he had just whispered to her, 'Gee I guess I've done most things in my time but that's the first time I've played a nation. I've never seen a chorus go like that. Jeez' they sure meant all that. They weren't just waiting to hit the bar.'

She was still in her leather jerkin and breeches, which she had worn throughout the opera. Her own red gold hair glinted luxuriantly in the lights. Hank stood back leaving his partner front stage alone. The stamping and cheers built layer upon layer until Mara feared for the fabric of the old building. After an age, Kurt Hansen and the stage staff did their best to submerge Detty in flowers. She kissed Hank and Kurt and as he arrived later from the pit, Helge von Grunstand. She applauded the chorus, the orchestra and her other soloist colleagues. Then suddenly everybody stood back leaving Detty alone in the subdued light. The small figure of Nicklaus Oblov in his white tuxedo

49 Hail the day, hail the hour

appeared from the wings. Detty realised afterwards that the security risk to them both at that moment must have been immense but at the time nobody seemed to care. His voice, sounding small after the tremendous choruses, he announced, 'By virtue of the Will and Command of the Consiglium of the Hanseatic Republik of Livonia, I, as acting president of the Republik invest you, Bernadette Niamh O'Neill, Gräfin von Ritter with the rank, dignity and honours of *Komturin* of the Order of Sankt Nicklaus in recognition of your outstanding valour in the achievement of our liberties.'

Detty, in truth ill-rehearsed for this great moment in her life instinctively sank onto one knee as Oblov took the medal from the cushion carried by his attendant and passed the green and white woven silk sash over her head. She rose with the gold image of St Nicklaus surrounded by the exhortation to the Mother of God to pray for us glinting at her waist. Mara heard the voice of her friend, as it had always been, but uncharacteristically small and very young, in that great theatre which she had filled with music. '*Herr Präsident, Frau Tamara, Meine Damen und Herren*, I will give you thanks for this great honour and show my gratitude to free Livonia in the way that I know best. I dedicate my-our-song to our brave and fallen.'

Whether by instinct or pre-arrangement Mara never knew, but Helge had already silently returned to his waiting orchestra. With a drum roll and fanfare they struck up the introduction to the *Freiheitslied.* The house leapt to its feet as Detty, the green and white sash round her shoulders shimmering in the spotlight as she took two steps towards the footlights. The great gold medallion flashed at her waist as she began to sing the national anthem – her song – to Waldhuter's tune. First the chorus and then the audience joined her. As long as she lived Mara would never forget Detty's unmistakable voice soaring over two thousand others at that moment. The nation was celebrating its deliverance and the student teacher from County Kildare was rejoicing that she had been allowed her to fulfil her impossible pledge.

AUTHOR'S NOTE

Moltravia/Livonia will not be found on any map although its whereabouts are described in fair detail. The name should not cause confusion with the historical Livonia to which it is culturally, but not geographically, similar. Our Livonia has a Baltic coastline and a Baltic port, with a long Hanseatic history, as capital. It lies on that great plain which stretches uninterrupted from the Urals to the Elbe. It has land frontiers with Germany, Russia and Poland and takes its languages from the first two and its culture from all three. Perhaps it is best imagined as an adventitious landmass which has arisen on the northern border of Germany and Poland.

The geography was chosen because this is an area which has given so much to Europe over the centuries and yet has suffered so terribly from changing regimes and mind-stretching inhumanity. As ever in the twenty-first century, Moltravia with its brutality, suffering and upheavals is everywhere, even if it is also nowhere.

The opera Fidelio, the last influence, was the reason the book was written at all. This flawed masterpiece is a paean to liberty which has inspired many people, as well as this author, in a way which is hard to explain. The music is, of course, glorious and is part of the reason but storyline is crude, fragmented and rather improbable. The message of the story, however, is unfailingly moving. Perhaps it is Beethoven's own suffering and obsession with liberty that shines through the various re-writes and inconsistencies. We know that it was enormously important to him, which is why he worked so hard to try and perfect it.

Finally, our heroine and hero. Neither is based on historical figures although some facets were suggested by real people. The choice of Ireland and Germany as their countries of origin was an attempt to show how two countries with widely different, but very clouded, histories can produce modern people with hope and ideals.

Acknowledgement I am very grateful to Fern Bushnell and Hayley Russell of Troubador for their patient assistance.

For exclusive discounts on Matador titles,
sign up to our occasional newsletter at
troubador.co.uk/bookshop